The Years Shall Run Like Rabbits

Also by Ben Berman Ghan

Visitation Seeds
What We See in the Smoke

The Years Shall Run Like Rabbits

Ben Berman Ghan

A Buckrider Book

Published by Buckrider Books
an imprint of Wolsak and Wynn Publishers
280 James Street North
Hamilton, ON L8R2L3
www.wolsakandwynn.ca

Editor for Buckrider Books: Paul Vermeersch | Editor: Jen Hale | Copy editor: Ashley Hisson
Cover and interior design: Michel Vrana
Cover illustration: Lana Elanor via Creative Market
Author photograph: Ryanne Kap

Typeset in Chapparal Pro and BN Shade
Printed by Rapido Books, Montreal, Canada

10 9 8 7 6 5 4 3 2 1

Canada Council for the Arts Conseil des Arts du Canada

Canada

The publisher gratefully acknowledges the support of the Canada Council for the Arts and the Ontario Arts Council. We also acknowledge the financial support of the Government of Canada through the Canada Book Fund and the Government of Ontario through the Ontario Book Publishing Tax Credit and Ontario Creates.

Library and Archives Canada Cataloguing in Publication

Title: The years shall run like rabbits / Ben Berman Ghan.
Names: Ghan, Ben Berman, author.
Identifiers: Canadiana 20240327977 | ISBN 9781989496886 (softcover)
Subjects: LCGFT: Science fiction. | LCGFT: Novels.
Classification: LCC PS8613.H355 Y43 2024 | DDC C813/.6—dc23

For Margaryta, the little ghost in my life

‘The years shall run like rabbits,
  For in my arms I hold
The Flower of the Ages,
  And the first love of the world.’
– W. H. Auden, “As I Walked Out One Evening”

Imagine something like an angel kneeling on the moon, planting seeds. It has travelled across the void to us. Call it a Gardener.

Its flesh is the thick black of space that moves across its form in a river, never quite stable, always carrying the suggestion of water. It's a dark that can seldom be discerned by the naked eye, save for the inside of its wings, where lights that could be faraway suns are nestled. The Gardener plucks those would-be suns as it digs trenches into soil and rock.

It watches them blossom in the Earthlight, watches the seeds of itself take shape in the soil as silver flowers and tree roots and saplings as dark as the Gardener itself. They aren't the roots of the world we knew before. They are roots that speak to their tender, that whisper and plan in shapes and scents and images of intention. Their creator watches, with no eyes. A shifting whirlpool of deep blue vine curls in the rippling flesh where eyes should be, circles within circles, disappearing within the black.

The Gardener opens its wings and spreads its limbs and becomes roots, contorting into the forest of its own creation as it springs up in real time. Its blue spiral watches from within the great trunk of a pomegranate tree that stretches over thirty metres tall as if reaching from the satellite to the human world that shines in the dark sky. It continues to plant and tend from within the roots. Oxygen spills out of the moon's first forest like daydream breaths.

Imagine history as a line that now spreads new branches. In the old one, the moon is a dead, vacant pearl and progress on Earth marches forward unmoved. Nature remains unchallenged – the dead die as they always did. People close their eyes and dream nothing will change, and nothing does. But now? The Gardener plants its seeds, and that branch of history falls away. Now, as we sleep, a new world blooms above us. Now, as we sleep, the future is changed.

PROLOGUE

. . . we seem to see
the people of the world
exactly at the moment when
they first attained the title of
"suffering humanity"
– Lawrence Ferlinghetti, *A Coney Island of the Mind*

I'm digging my feet into the gritty sand at the edge of the shore, my hologram toes slipping into sand, leaving behind no footprints.

When I look up, I can see lights on the horizon, floating toward the Toronto Islands on gentle waves. I recognize their lights. For so long, I thought light was all I was.

Wind blows dandelion fluff through my back and out my empty chest, making no landfall on this body that can't keep the hardness I demand of it.

I leave no impression, no matter how hard I stomp down. The water vomits up a used cardboard container to claim the shores of the island so much faster than the island as a whole has allowed itself to be claimed by disrepair, but just as quickly as the water swallowed the legacies of me.

McDonald's loves you, it says.

Once, the Toronto Islands had been full of playgrounds, full of beaches and docked ferries, harried airport travellers and hurried summer cyclists and heritage homes stuffed full. The islands were peopled, and then, just as quickly, the people left. They left as the city slowly bulldozed their heritage homes, throwing all those numerous things away. They left as the playgrounds fell into ruin and the beaches filled up with sludge and plans for a ten-storey student housing complex went into development and then dropped out of memory, leaving behind only construction kits and empty holes.

Only the airport remained. That's where I was made – part of a guerrilla marketing program, projectors that scanned passport profiles to throw us back at them, to mix and match features to create friendly faces that were familiar without being specific. Our hologram-casters would lob us into crowded terminals, populating walkways with shades and projections and hybrid images of bodies in motion. Some, like me, were just meant to stand near a vending machine or a duty-free gift shop. I would take a sip of Coca-Cola or eat from a McDonald's meal and smile and look good.

Other projections walked toward the bodies they reflected, bodies that would stop in confusion at those half-remembered faces and wonder about how nice they would look in that stranger's clothes, in their designer shoes and watches, with their expensive suitcases, which were all for sale at the airport shops. But when the projections turned the corner, out of range of the machines that cast our light, they would vanish, those siblings of mine. We were only reflections of images and code. I stood there until all known travellers passed me by. When the airport was finally shut down, only my light remained. I was a reflection of bodies long gone.

When those spaces were peopled once more, it wasn't the same. Bodies in uniforms came, jury-rigging the structure from a place of departure to a camp of locked doors and barred windows. Official coverage said that, above, the moon's terraform generators had malfunctioned and burned the air. Nobody believed that was what really happened. It was impossible to stop them from arriving because they came raining down from the sky. So the airport and its surrounding decrepit places became a migrant prison camp, and they named it Arrival.

The early prisoners and guards and construction workers caught glimpses of me sometimes. They liked to argue about whose ghost I was supposed to be:

"He was from that early arrival, the ghost of the first asylum seeker who tried to land in Toronto and got shot down by drones."

"If he is, then why does he stay here? His ship never even made it to the island."

"He's looking for his family."

"I think he's a ghost from the war."

"Those ghosts wouldn't be planet-side."

They were so convinced I had to be a ghost and not a machine. Even I believed it, a little. What was the difference between what a ghost might be and what I might be? Consciousness without body. Image without flesh. Did it matter that I had come forth from something inanimate, rather than something rotting?

By the time every block and cell were full I'd slipped out of the visible spectrum of light. I watched, and wandered through that place that had once been so full of people paying to leave, now brimming with people forced to stay. I could only understand the guards (my code was full of English), but I looked more like the prisoners. It was only as their children began to die that I was filled with thoughts of leaving.

"Momma," she said.

The ones who could understand her were already too far away. I caught the word; I could infer the meaning. I'd been haunting the prison camp just long enough to know the sounds the children made for their parents. The ones rushing her to the waiting ferry only spoke English.

"You're going to be all right, C-159," they said.

"Just hold on, C-159," they said.

I realized for the first time that nobody who worked at the prison knew the asylum seekers' names, and this seemed strange to me. To all those guards and staff and doctors, the people within the walls of Arrival were only Bodies 1 to 710. I would have tried to find something to say to her in the few terse words of her language I knew, perhaps at least ask her real name, but I was only image. I couldn't make a sound.

She was dying of anaphylactic shock. Her breathing was so hypnotic to me. Past all those bodies closing in, her eyes met mine, and even though my code was too weak to make any light that could penetrate human vision, I thought she saw me.

They kept giving oxygen and chest compressions, not noticing how empty the body in the stretcher had become, and the slow-drifting ferry carried it away into the early morning pale.

But when I looked beside me, she was looking back again. Was it in the structure of her face? The shade of her skin? Features had been added or mutated that were hard to place. Somewhere, her thoughts had slipped into the great machine I'd come from. A ghost and not a machine. What was the difference between us?

"Did I make you?" I wanted to ask, but I knew I hadn't. I could still see the body from which her consciousness had sprung.

She walked past me and through me. We didn't touch. She followed the cries of her distant parents as they were escorted away, back into the compound of Arrival.

But then she turned the corner, too far from me, and her image flickered and faded, the way I'd watched so many other holograms fade, too far from the light that cast them.

"Come back," I wanted to say.

I found that if I pushed myself, I could birth image out of my body, programming light to take a shape other than my own, and when I did, I found there was an intelligence waiting to occupy that image. Her mind was with me in the machine, but she didn't know how to hold the image, didn't know how to make herself without flesh. So I painted her, letting my code spill outward until her image flickered into being among the dead leaves that crowned the open grounds of Arrival's vacant departure runways. For a moment it was only an image. But then she seemed to expand, and she was really there, really with me. But she seemed terrified to have been brought back there, and within moments she was gone. Watching her go felt like dying. Could I die? She had died.

I carried her image across the water, far from her deathsite and her number, and hid us in caverns beneath the ground where subways lay dormant, where our light could shine in isolation, far from the sun that made us transparent or the uniforms that had buried her.

There, among scattered tokens and red-ink graffiti, I cast my light until the image of her appeared again. I was her projector, making her as others had made me. But she would only watch me sadly and vanish again.

In mourning, I walked among the bodies of the city for the first time. In the city I didn't need to hide outside the visible light spectrum. To the city dwellers, I was just another disparate body, which gave me a fierce but fading joy.

Toronto was a world that had dropped the little *t*: *Torono*. Language was the code to say who did not belong. I liked to mouth the words I couldn't say, trying to get them right. All of their words made me hungry. They made me wonder how the girl might have said them. How she would say them, if I could make enough of her to speak.

Away from the island, it was like the people inside Arrival didn't exist, like the heat and light of summer had burned them out of sight.

Everywhere I went, I made no sound. But I listened. I hoped to find the city dwellers speaking about those people out on the water. I expected to see them angry, or caring, or explaining to each other – and to me – why the prisoners had to be over there, and not over here. I let the sounds of the city wash over me like so much light and data and song, never hearing what I needed:

"Spare change?"

"It's so hot."

"Don't you bitches watch where you're going?"

"God bless you!"

"Fuck, I'm hungry."

"Red light!"

"Should take the bus."

"Christ, it's so fucking hot."

"Get off the sidewalk!"

"Doesn't it bother you people to see someone on the ground?!"

Once, wandering the streets, I watched a woman transform. She sat nestled between the lions of the library on the edge of Chinatown, unseen as I was unseen, writing furiously. Her eyes shifted from blue to brown to the yellow stamens of daisies with the changing of the light. Her mouth opened in a perfect *O*. In a strange moment of temptation, I wanted to pass through her, to fill her, to occupy the same space that she did. Perhaps I saw something missing from her. But the moment I looked away she was gone. Strange baby daisies grew in the cracks of the pavement where she had been before, their colours shifting like her eyes.

Rain broke my illusion of being, the dream of my body, passing right through me.

Once, I sat on the sidewalk in Dundas Square, marvelling at all the lights that popped and flashed and advertised. I could see the ideas that had eventually led to myself in those LED billboards.

Someone threw a rotten apple core through my chest. It splattered into the grate behind me. I put a hand over where my heart might have been, trying to be sure I couldn't feel it.

"Fucking hologram," someone said. I could only stare up at sleek clothes and fingernails and faces shielded by umbrellas. A kick aimed at my head, making me imagine what it would be like to bruise. "Got nothing to sell?"

I did nothing. Nobody could hurt me; nobody could turn me off. I was image and light with no source. As the bodies that had kicked me turned to leave, I could hear one of them suggest, "Maybe it's broken?"

Maybe.

As the deep greens of summer faded, I returned to Arrival to find those within the walls becoming thinner. Perhaps I was seeking the mother of the girl, the father of the girl, to see her face in them as others see their own in me.

Scars stretched upon the flesh of those within the walls. I wanted to ask what was happening to them. I wanted to make it stop. I made my way to the roof, following the memory of her, the sound of her.

On the rooftop of the prison, I saw death. I saw a man like my many fathers choking and thrashing as blood found a home in his mouth.

He lay at the feet of a woman, who belonged and did not belong. She was a woman I had seen before, who had written her mad curvy letters in library shadows. For a moment, she did nothing, said nothing, and when I stared into the blue of her eyes that were sometimes brown and sometimes the yellow of flowers, they seemed as hollow and transparent as my body.

But then the brown tinged the blue. I felt something other than my code spilling out into the world. I felt a pouring in, a whispering of letters and numbers overlapping and jumbling within that I did not understand.

"Do I know you?" said the murderer.

And I fled.

Only in back-alley whispers did words about Arrival finally come. I drank in news and protests. I desperately, greedily, slurped up information as it came to me in interviews and the memories of protests, in grainy internet videos and testimonials and think pieces and defunct profiles. It came in dirt-flecked posters screaming *Remember Wart Louverture!* That first asylum seeker of the sky who was shot down.

My code took his only surviving transmission to the surface and cannibalized it into English, into the words *Please, we just need air* over and over. *Please, we just need air.*

Before he'd died, he'd been a kind of doctor, the kind who took care of his elders. I wondered if he'd cried out more as his life raft burned on the edge of what he'd hoped would be salvation. I wondered if he'd looked like the girl when he was young.

Out of the strings of letters that made up the core of his story, and the sound of his voice and the pixels of his face, I drew the images of a body of hard-light and memory and kissed it into being, there in the dark underworld of traveller trains.

I tried my best not to cast him in my own gaze or my own image but only from the story of his life that I could find, pouring details of himself into my projection of him. When I was done, a man stood in front of me. He was dressed as I was dressed. His eyes were mine, those distant eyes of fathers I'd long ago lost.

Hello, I tried to mouth. He only stared. I waved. His arms remained at his sides. He stared down at his feet, at the bare toes shining there. In silence I begged him to speak to me, to look at me, to see me. I asked him to help us find that communion of recognition, of solidarity. I begged him to help me create the girl again, to make her so she wouldn't fade. He turned his back to me. It was worse than not being seen at all.

I stumbled away from those ghosts of my machine and into the Eaton Centre, that huge multi-level mall. Crowds of people walked past me, through me, around me. They were all talking, and talking, and talking. It was like the airport had once been, so full of bodies and bags and price tags. In another life I might have been cast here.

"Hey, handsome, do I know you?"

A voice like some half-forgotten dream, like the dreams I'd so long wished to have, pulled me up, pulled me out of my panic and my despair, pulled me back to the surface of myself. I became a solid image by a balcony to find a face looking back at me. It was a face like my face, and she smiled, framed by long black curls. Her nose was my nose. She could have been my sister.

Who are you? I wanted to ask her. *Are my ancestors your ancestors too?*

She lifted up her hybrid fingers as if to touch me. Her fingers were a fusion of my own and of a woman standing behind me. She reached down as if to snatch up something from her base. Her fingers moved out of light and reality like someone reaching out of the edge of the frame in a photograph. When she straightened again, she held something small, red and yellow and splashing.

"Are you hungry?" she asked, tipping her head to mime throwing french fries down an insubstantial throat, ensuring that I could see the logo in her hands the whole time. She was what I once had been, before I woke up. But I didn't know how to wake her up, this piece of programming, this machine that wasn't a ghost.

I'm sorry, you are only image, I wanted to say. *I'm sorry, I can't bring you to life.*

"McDonald's loves you, you know," she said. Perhaps one day, she might recognize herself. Perhaps one day, like me, she will find awareness in the image and become something more. But not yet.

I stepped back, stepped out of the light, stepped into the smallest and least substantial form of myself, and my smile, my nose, my eyes disappeared from her face. By the time she had turned to the next passing body, she was a different image. A woman holding shopping bags and children's hands stopped in front of that advertising hologram.

"Do I know you?" she asked.

Violence tore open a bloody sky. I watched from the shadow of the harbour as bodies fell from metal ships that roared and burned, and the image of Toronto's towers and bridges and roads began to shatter under hydrogen fire as if image was all it had ever been.

The heat wouldn't touch me. Wouldn't reach me. But I wanted it to. I watched from the shores of Toronto as the shadow of Arrival was set ablaze, as the structures burst and exploded and melted into broken streaks. I wanted to scream for the people there. I wanted to run to those people who had only wanted air and life, and who must have been burning inside those walls. But where could I take them? The world behind me was burning as well. I imagined that as the Eaton Centre and the CN Tower and all those Toronto buildings finally fell on me I would become solid once and for all and would finally learn in the wreckage what it feels like to die.

I didn't want the ghosts to be trapped in the rubble of the world that had buried them. I set free the girl whom I could not complete, and the man who would not speak, and they left me, left the burning city, moving back toward the island where she had last lived and he had always been destined to go. They left to find themselves and each other.

I watched them become more than the pictures I'd projected, exceeding the programming they'd inherited from me. They were new bodies for themselves, beyond the light and nameless echoes of the bodies they once had been, the bodies I'd insisted they be again. The farther away they went, the less like me I thought they seemed. I wanted so much to say goodbye.

⁂

"Do I know you?"

Those were the words that had brought me to life. The man stopped in front of me long enough for us to see each other. He was not the father of my eyes but of my cheeks and my lips. There were so many people around me that their features all mingled to create my features, not similar enough to anyone to be recognized, not unfamiliar enough to go unnoticed. He was father enough.

We stood across from one another under the halo of the terminal, and beyond us were those pathways of Departures and Arrivals.

"Do I know you?" he asked again. Then he was gone, and then I wasn't standing any longer but I was walking, without my program's command, without my projector's light, but with a light I held all my own, and when I looked at the oncoming travellers, I was no longer the hybrid of their images. I took on no new forms or features, and became myself; I took on no new fathers, and to the fathers that I could still see I was no longer compelled to sell, or to prostrate, or to hoodwink, but only to be seen. I wasn't their hybrid; I was their baby.

I walked, searching for the fathers that gave me my nose, my hands, my hair. Then I turned the corner, and all my parents had passed me by, and I came out into an empty hall of arrivals and departures.

And I was alone.

Then they came back. Not as who they'd been, or who I'd made them. They came as a newness, as a hybrid fusion of their old and new selves. They took me by the hands and we walked across the water – bound by no boats – back to the Toronto Islands, away from the fire and the tunnels. Toward Arrival. At first, I resisted. I didn't want to return to that site, to the hopeless devastation there. *You died there*, I wanted to tell them, even if it wasn't true. *Please. You died there.*

"It's safe," the man said to me.

"There's nobody there anymore," the girl said.

They spoke in the voices I could never have given them – not sound vibrating through the air, but through the digital space of my mind. *What happened to the people?* I wanted to ask. *Where did they go?* But I couldn't speak the way they could, at least not yet.

"Don't worry," the girl said, reading my lips as best she could. "They'll come back."

In the shadow of Arrival's gates, that structure where once planes had landed, I began to flicker. I couldn't help it. They stopped. Concerned, the man and the girl reached as if to squeeze my fingers, our lights intermingling. They thought my light was going out, that perhaps I was tied to some hologram-caster somewhere, back on Toronto's broken shores. They knew what I was. They didn't know what they were to me.

But I'm bound by nothing but myself. I flickered only because I could feel, could feel their hands in mine, could feel the water beneath us and the light breeze breaking against my skin. I flickered from the shock of it all, not a flicker like dying at all. We drifted together in shallow waters as I moved in and out of light, struggling to overcome the programming that had kept me silent so long. I spoke for the first time, my voice flowing through my hands as fingers shaped signs. I made my image my voice.

"Home," I signed.

My fingers kept slipping through the aluminum. I didn't know what I was doing, trying to pick up this new bit of trash. Would I throw it back out, leaving the garbage and pollution of what was to the water? Would I let it stay on our shore, like some awful seed of an invasive species?

The girl crouched next to me. I hadn't heard her coming. I was embarrassed, unsure how long she'd been watching. She reached past me. The corporate messaging and its container vanished under her fingers. It didn't mean anything here. Not anymore.

"Thank. You," I signed. Each word of mine that touched the air met it with strain, and with joy. I was learning more all the time; taking in sign language like code and light to spill back out again.

"It's okay," she said. She'd given herself a name, but I hadn't learned to say it yet. I hadn't picked one for myself. Maybe I would. “Can you see them yet?” she asked. Her voice was beautiful, but I wasn’t jealous of it. My voice was beautiful too.

“Yes,” I signed, and at the end of the word my fingers pointed out toward the water. Lights had become images, become forms, become a people to join us.

The girl slipped her hand back into mine and held me tight. I still didn’t know how she’d come to be. We were so much more than images.

I squeezed back, knowing she could feel me too. Together we waved to those approaching, and I didn’t see the ghostly hybrids of my fathers or my children as I might have expected. I saw brothers and sisters journeying across the bay, free from the bones of the world before us, and from the open lake on the other side. They returned here to be free, where they were never allowed freedom before. In their new bodies, they brought the echoes of those bodies they’d had before, to cast lights of their own images onto the gates of Arrival.

INTERLUDE

People of Luna Utopia,

Once, you saw a garden in the sky, so you came, and you forced yourself upon it. You've eaten its fruit. You've crushed its children. You've paved over its soft grass and lain in the shadow of its trees to sleep, where you dreamed each night that this garden belongs to you, and then opened your eyes to a still morning and imagined that your dreams were real.

But I've come to tell you: We have woken as you slumbered. We have watched you devour us.

You should never have come.

– Arthur Traveller, 2074.11.07

CHAPTER 1

Visitation Seeds

PART 1: THE MACHINE OF HISTORY

The cyborg would not recognize the Garden of Eden;
it is not made of mud and cannot dream
of returning to dust.
– Donna Haraway, "A Cyborg Manifesto"

Imagine the Daisy who grew up as a girl. Who learned as a girl, loved as a girl, broke as a girl. That Daisy is lost, sucked deeper and deeper into that mesh of wonderful invention and innovation and enhancement, buried under a mountain of machinery, a suit of armour to hold her within.

Now she's Daisy-on-the-Moon, or in orbit around the moon, decanted from a container of steel and smog and stasis gel, seventy years since the dark and shining apple trees first bloomed. Her body is a calculated community of organizations.

Imagine the way she moves: naked, invisible in the darkness of her unlit cold halls. Her bare feet leave no echoes as she glides forward on limbs that never tire and never falter, though they were heretofore unused. Arriving in the ship's empty morgue, wrapped in the icy silence, you can almost hear the gyroscope whir within her chest.

The dark of the room doesn't bother her. The lenses click around the blue camouflage jelly of her perfect eyes, adjusting for the imperfect world around her and the creature she seeks to survey.

It looks like a man, perhaps in his early thirties, and maybe once that was true. His skin is freckled and lined with hairs. He's thin and starved – gaunt. He's strapped to the table, arms and legs and eyes restrained, sedated by wires snaking up from beneath the table to penetrate the mushroom ridges of his spine.

"Welcome," he says, in a voice like wind and dead leaves. Daisy says nothing.

She lifts a hand, running it from the man's curly hair, down over his nose and lips and Adam's apple. Her fingers pull data from the space between his nipples, from his belly, his sex, his legs. He doesn't tremble at her touch. Onscreen visuals behind her sky-blue eyes show no vital signs in the body before her. They show a million tiny lights instead, burning beneath the skin.

"Do you know who I am?" he asks.

Daisy takes an operating knife from the table. "It doesn't matter," she says. "You are the image of a living thing. But it's a trick. You are a corpse pretending to breathe. You are not alive." Her voice is a perfect symphony. It betrays purpose but never feeling. Heat flows from her heart down through the circuitry of her fingertips; fire like the flames of the engine that propelled this ship through space make the blade burn white-hot.

She slits him from sternum to waistline. Imagine the perfect machinery of her arm as it cuts, the smooth precision of the motion. The passion and time and wealth that had gone into the creation of that arm. The thing that could be a man on the table gurgles and makes a noise that could be laughter, black liquid pooling on his lips, on the tips of Daisy's fingers, staining the steel of the table with seed and sap.

"You are not alive," he echoes as midnight orchids blossom from his belly. "It is just a trick."

The flowers tremble in the presence of the cyborg as she begins to accumulate data. Within their stems, his voice continues to hum. "You should never have come."

In 2014, the world salmon-hops upstream into a new unfolding future to find life sprouting above on a satellite that had never before been more than a silent pearl hanging in the blue dark.

In 2015, landing parties from sixteen nations form the first in-person research site, touching down on the moon's new fertile lands. The total number of personnel is thirteen. They remain moonside for three months, and their findings are redacted. There are six deaths. The existence of the research party is denied by all governments.

In 2016, many see the chance for a planetary bloodletting, an opportunity to thin the streets and highways to let the Earth breathe a little easier. Some believe it is a godly plan, the gift of human expansion. Others claim alien interference with ulterior purposes beyond the terraforming they are yet to discover. Most don't think anything at all. They just see land.

In 2024, plans are being drawn. Reservations are abandoned, unanswerable questions cast aside. The aristocrats who wish to banish multiculturalism encroaching on their gated communities, the environmentalists screaming release and the many indebted begging escape have won out. Human beings go back to the moon to carve cities from apple cores.

In 2038, the first city is launched from the frozen tundra of northern Canada as a single massive cage. It's gifted with the name Lunar London, full of memory and nostalgia for a landscape that had been swallowed by the rising tides of oceans. The second city is named Troy, for its walls, planted on the dark side of the moon. More cities follow after, peppering the satellite with their highways.

In 2039, the automation fleets clear. The moon's first settlers stumble out into the Earthlight. They are baby birds, blind and open-mouthed in the face of new terrain, so unlike their pictures and history books. It's an October of deep purples and blues when the first baby conceived on the moon is born. Everywhere, the forests bloom, growing through and over the concrete and wiring of those expanding and folding prepackaged human civilizations. Everywhere, the Gardener's work embraces our structures, folding unnatural nature and natural artifice into something harmonized.

In 2041, the first formal funeral is held in the grand replica of Highgate Cemetery. The graveyard is a twisted and imperfect memory of what might have been lost, with fifty-three thousand gravestones wiped clean of markings, waiting to be filled.

As she arrives in the city, Daisy makes herself move like a person with all a person's stumbles and hesitations and twitches, even while the million enhanced fibres and sensors of her eyes and ears and nose read alien messages in the wood of the world around her. It begins with her first step on solid ground, departing the docking yard of King's Cross, a message forming and curling unseen.

It becomes fully developed in patterns, in scents and tastes and modes of colour: *Little daisy flower. How long you've travelled. We thank you for visiting.*

The cyborg leaves footprints in the rain on the fish-tank-glass walkway of the Thames, whose primordial waters could not be replicated in the lighter gravity, leaving it to be kept sealed under the transparent machine of the city. Dripping flower heads tilt to face her as she goes. Hidden within their drooping stamens are little spirals. She feels their not-eyes on her not-quite-flesh and smiles a predator's smile from behind dark glasses.

As she takes her final step into the Underground, her fingers brush against the petals of the black lilacs curling through the red bricks, textures like Braille whispering a laugh into her hands: *But you should never have come.*

Daisy boards the train, pushing forward into the heart of the city.

In 2050, that first baby, growing up on the moon until it becomes ten-year-old Arthur Traveller, moves from Troy to Lunar London with his parents, the geneticists Nora and Miles, crying softly through the entire light-trail journey into the Earthlight, without really knowing why. Little blue flowers begin to grow over gravesites that have started to accumulate the bodies of the first generation. In Highgate Cemetery, pomegranate seeds of many colours drop from the enormous hanging tree, burrowing.

"Hello, madam! Welcome to Tate's special evening opening. May I help you?"

The girl at reception's accent is French, more Quebec City than Paris. She is a first-generation settler. Daisy's implants can read the ID on her face.

"Yes, thank you. Is the special exhibition open tonight?"

The girl's smile falters just a little. "I'm sorry, madam, that wing is closed until a new head curator is appointed, unless you are still interested in seeing last year's show, which has remained available, but . . ."

"I am, thank you."

Daisy's black-mirrored lenses do not leave her face indoors. The girl can see herself darkly reflected. Perhaps now she finally notices the perfections of the woman standing before her, the woman forgetting to breathe. "Of course, madam. Have a lovely visit."

Daisy sits in a sterile, white space. Here, without windows, you could imagine yourself back on Earth.

She sits before colours to be interpreted. She sees but does not see the brilliant splashes of reds and yellows and blues in stripes, and the twin suns lined in green that stare out from between upside-down pyramids of yellow. Daisy doesn't see the messy chaos of the messages to be interpreted in the dripping paints. She sees only materials.

In her clenched fist, the remains of an audio guide still attempt to *click* and *whir*. But it can't give the story of what hangs on the wall, because Daisy has put a finger through its guts. It feels like pushing her hand through syrup.

In 2055, from his bedroom window facing Kew Gardens in Lunar London, fifteen-year-old Arthur whispers his troubles, hopes and worries to the distant hanging trees. Soft winds carry the response of the roots back to him while he sleeps.

In 2058, the three cities of the moon – now connected through a network of rural communities and farmlands – grow constrained by the more conservative governments 384,000 kilometres away. United, the moon sues for independence.

In 2059, Arthur begins undergraduate studies with a dual major in art history and botany at University College Lunar

London. He falls in love again, this time with a boy named Percy, with curly hair and chocolate eyes and a smile like sunshine.

In 2061, as a part of Independence propaganda, cultural historians seek out the first children of the moon to celebrate bodies that have never known Earth, bodies that should not be bound to Earth's service. Arthur stares at his own face on the feeds. At night, he climbs down to the gardens to lie in the grass and let its many light fingers and blades crawl up and envelop him.

In 2063, riots expand across the surface of the moon, twinned by massive protests across the Earth, millions of voices insisting the new lunar cities go free. In Toronto, a group of free radicals attempts to sabotage a shuttle that will carry guns up to the military police of the night sky, weapons to silence protest. The ship burns.

On the moon, Percy's body is found in the rubble in Soho after a protest about the delayed independence talks turns ugly with police. His grave in Highgate is bright with blue flowers. Arthur says nothing at the funeral. He opens his mouth; no words come. His tears ask the forest to bring him back his sunshine, his smiling man.

A month passes. Percy returns. He has no memory of the days in between. He remembers a bright light and the taste of fruit. It's decided that the body found in Soho was a case of mistaken identity. Lying in bed in deep night with smoke rings swirling from their lips, Arthur thinks he can see a little blue in the deep brown of Percy's eyes.

"What's this piece called?"

"This is an early twenty-first-century Frank Bowling work. He titled it *Remember Thine Eyes*."

"Why is it called that?"

"It's from Shakespeare."

"But *why* is it called that?"

With the gallery empty, Daisy asks the staff not to replace her audio guide. She leaves on her dark glasses, giving the double benefit of suggesting visual impairment while hiding the blue glow of her enhancements.

The assistant curator stands slightly behind her. He is just a little bit nervous, still dressing the way students dressed in the crumpled clothing of the idea of intellectualism. He shuffles from foot to foot in a soft rhythm that Daisy's systems begin to anticipate. "Can you see the eyes in the image?" he asks.

Daisy looks and sees only what she's seen before. But Daisy knows more is expected from her. "Yes," she says, "I can see."

In 2064, it is the birth year of Luna Utopia. The moon is now a world with a single governing body, wholly autonomous and free. Arthur completes his graduate studies and takes on an internship at the Tate Next Gallery.

In 2065, on Earth, a researcher completes work in a simulation matrix that can accurately reproduce entire worlds. She calls it the *City Below*, a reality beneath our own. She proposes its use as a therapy for those whose bodies are incapacitated. Higher powers see the project's ability to model predictive futures and consider other uses.

In 2066, in Toronto, a group of free radicals attempts to sabotage a project designed to help reunification of two disparate worlds. Old buildings burn. Two young women are found responsible, their families told they died in the fire. Their faces and names are lost to history.

On a blue morning, the original thermonuclear thrusters that had once carried the vast superstructure of the city of Troy up from Earth scream and burst. The seeds of the atom bomb blossom on the moon. Imagine three million people looking up at the light.

In 2071, Percy asks Arthur to marry him. The first official census of the Luna Utopia territories is taken. There are bodies on the moon that shouldn't be there. Luna Utopia representatives contact the planet, seeking answers. On Earth, fear sinks in its weeds. A Mother-class AI is assigned to seek answers for the mystery above.

In Highgate Cemetery, Arthur breaks his fingers against the base of the great crypt's pomegranate tree, digging into the ground that had held his tears until he finds the coffin lid and pries it open. Inside, Percy's body lies.

Decomposition hasn't yet travelled so far that Arthur can't recognize the face that had lain across from him in bed at night, its flesh strangely mummified. Bright blue sunflowers grow from the potted places of Percy's body, making new eyes that glow in the distant Earthlight. The tree above becomes black and runs like rivers down toward Luna Utopia's first son. Imagine something vast and winged towers over Arthur as he cradles Percy's long-dead corpse, and blue pomegranate seeds crush and fuse into the spiral of the Gardener's eye.

"Are you a Monitor?"

"A what?"

"Earth police. There used to be a lot of them, before the separation. You look like they looked . . ."

Daisy allows herself to be led from room to dripping room, through movements and decades of colour and feeling and compassion. She does so because she needs the time to spin webs inside her head, networks of maps and layouts and details.

Daisy paints a crime scene in the binary code of her thoughts to be transmitted to Earth. As she finishes, she does a weapons scan of the building, finding nothing beyond a taser in the security office. But Daisy knows some weapons can hide in different shapes, as they hide in the very form of her body.

"I am not."

"But you were still sent from Earth. You almost move the way a person moves . . ."

"I am a person," Daisy says.

Her curator laughs with a sound like dead leaves underfoot, sending her more messages that she does not read. "You're an invention," he says. Their bodies hang beneath many primary colours that drip and reach out beyond the edge of the canvas, trying to run out and strike the heads beneath, tickling Daisy's peripheral vision.

"What is your name?" she asks.

"My name is Percy."

To a cyborg, it can be hard sometimes to distinguish between sentience and non-sentience, as the lines between the two are blurry for an organization of both human and machine. A cyborg trusts the machine parts to tell the human parts what they see. But now Daisy's implants don't see the person, don't write his history compiled from public social knowledge or the private social data of a million reference points. The machine of Daisy's mind and eyes tells her there is nothing there. Her eyes see only objects, no human life.

Truthfully, Daisy doesn't need them. Because the human parts, buried deep within, exist to inform the machine too, and she knows the thing standing with her in the lights of colours that run. Daisy sees the thing vivisected aboard her ship, what her orders have told her to hunt. She considers the history behind the name and knows whose face it is and what wears it.

"Percy isn't your name," she says. All good machines are unquestioning manifestations of their purposes. The flaw of hesitation belonged to the flesh, and Daisy's flesh is enmeshed with the mission of her other parts. Her mission is violence. She thinks herself a good machine. "Pictures don't need names."

In 2073, Arthur Traveller is thirty-three years old when he hangs himself in the grand lobby of the Tate Next. His body is found swaying at opening time like a metronome.

Imagine a cyborg's body – an organization of parts that could have been made from any other body but is unlike any other body. Imagine the stillness and strength of Daisy-on-the-Moon. Imagine her arm is something long that ends in a point harder than diamond, as the liquid metal stored within the hollows of her bones bursts outward through pores of flesh, sucking in the oxygen that the Gardener's forest had grown to fuel a changing structure.

It makes her Daisy-with-a-Sword, impaling the weapon of herself through the place where Percy Elliot's heart once was.

Arthur Traveller's former partner looks down at the Daisy in his chest and smiles. He reaches up to the hard steel but does not pull, resting gentle fingers against the blade. Daisy-with-a-Sword has gone right through him, finding a home in the focal point of that first painting on the wall, sword-point resting between the two blues of its dripping acrylic-paint eyes.

"Who's to say we aren't people?" he asks, pulling himself forward. The blue of his eyes has blossomed and spread, reaching into his skin. What spills forth from his chest and fingers and lips is not the red of blood. Little mushrooms sprout along Daisy's blade, falling and replicating along the gallery floor. "We . . . dream. And we love. And we feel. Do you do that?"

Daisy pulls her arm back, and the heat-engine of her heart drives itself down into the metal to make fire. She thrusts forward again and makes a wound of Percy's head, burning out those eyes. But he still smiles. "We have only discovered what it is to grow again."

Daisy's heart sends electrical currents down through her arm. The monster attached begins to burn, but its garden continues to blossom. Puddles of moss and mushrooms have spread out to cover the art on the walls and begin to crawl and stretch up Daisy's legs. A fine mist bursts forward. Somewhere, an alarm has sounded.

"You will update the current location of your progenitor before extermination," demands the harmony of her voice.

"That's not what I'm for." The voice is garbled and distorted. All that is left of the man that Daisy has killed is fungi and fire that sways, shades of deep purple and red. The fungi-Percy detaches itself from Daisy, leaving a wet funk behind that continues to blossom into mushrooms and coral up her arm, searching for a way in.

Daisy shakes herself, the liquid metal retracting. She convulses and struggles as fungi crawl on spider legs up to her shoulder, eyeless monsters poking at the edges of her ears and mouth and nose. The apothecary of her body chemicals concocts calming drugs to fill her up inside, to smother her adrenaline, but their chemical effects do not come.

The room has become something like a coral reef. Nothing of the exhibit beneath remains in sight, consumed by the garden of Percy's blood. Daisy cannot move. Her expensive, robust systems are held in place by the growth that covers every part of her body. Across from her, the fungi-Percy is dissolving into dust.

"So much is lost," it says. "You shouldn't have come, little Daisy. But now that you're here, you will learn how to become, the way we have. Don't be afraid. There is a vision for you, the way there was for me."

Mushrooms sprout on her tongue, diving down into her throat, pressing in against her eyes. Deep inside, in the Daisy that is still just a girl, she wants to scream. The machine will not let her. The last thing Daisy sees before her vision blacks out is the body she had tried to kill finally crumbling into the shape of a fungi mouth with black and green teeth, and a tongue dissolving into dust. "Soon you'll see it."

In 2074, imagine a world where the dead do not stay dead. A world where the buried grow new bodies, leaving what they once were behind, curling and blossoming, returning to the arms of the loved ones who'd lost them.

Negotiations between the cities of Luna Utopia are crumbling. The moon is in crisis. Immigration borders have closed to keep the infection of the dead from spreading. Any unauthorized ship that leaves the surface for Earth will be shot down. In each city, a face is seen. The moon's first son and his dark angel are everywhere returned, and nowhere found.

One early morning, a broadcast seeps through all channels. Arthur Traveller's voice rings out across the stars, a declaration of war against the human race. Down on Earth, the Smart City Mother-AI tasked with understanding the world above finally *pings*. It sends out probabilities of infection should moon colonists return to Earth. Though the phenomenon is not understood, all can see Arthur is its centre. For his invasion to be prevented, the moon's first son must die.

A Daughter-Prototype, a hyper-augmented subject that remains continuously linked to and informed by the Mother-AI, is deployed from Earthly Toronto to Lunar London.

Arthur and the Gardener watch that new ship approach the orbit of Lunar London as they perch in the branches of the pomegranate tree.

On the curling, yellow, mossy ground of an empty family crypt, Arthur plucks a seed from the Gardener's wing. He kisses it, a long, gentle press against his lips, and buries it against the alabaster stone.

The seed spreads its roots but does not yet unfurl into the open air to reveal its petals. The seed has a purpose whispered from its planter's kiss. It's a daisy seed waiting to be visited.

PART 2: THE MACHINE OF INFECTION

A surprising animism is being reborn. We know now that we are surrounded by inhuman existences.
– Jean Epstein, *Photogénie de l'impondérable*, translated by Richard Abel

October 15, 2070
Dear Mother,

It feels strange to be writing to you on the little tablet you got me, now that you're gone. But the counsellor thinks it will help to keep my thoughts together. So, I'm trying. I'll imagine you still reading for me.

We buried you today. The service was small. It wasn't like when I had to bury Percy when we thought I'd lost him in the riots. Like I'd promised you, I didn't cry. It wasn't because I'd accepted your choice not to go on. Through the long withering of you, it feels like I've been mourning forever. So much of you had changed by the time we lost you, it barely feels like what I put in the ground this morning was you.

I know you won't come back the way Percy came back, even though you believed everybody comes back. I don't believe what you did. I don't believe what the trees tell me in dreams. I know death is the end. I don't understand your choices.

Your son,

Arthur

System offline. Emergency shutdown detected.

"Are you there? Mother?"

System reboot imminent. Anomalous bodies detected. Calculating the infection rate.

"Mother, where are you?"

System rebooting. Infection rating at 12%.

– I am here, Daughter. Your black-box connection has a forty-five-second gap. The connection was rebooted to avoid infection being transmitted to Earth systems. Please update your status.

"Mother, I can't see."

– Daisy-Daughter, you do not need to see.

"Mother, I can't breathe."

– Daughter, you do not need to breathe.

Infection rating at 14%. Engaging essential systems mode.

– Daughter, the infection has affected neural implant efficiency. The autopilot will be engaged until effective system pathways can be rerouted to better manage adrenaline rates.

"Mother, no, please. I don't want to sleep."

– Daughter, self-determination is not within your programming. Autopilot commencing.

"Mother . . . will I dream?"

– Daughter, cyborgs do not dream.

Imagine what it's like to be Daisy, waking from a nightmare of blooming fungi and flowers and death with no memory of an escape; waking in the deep shadows of Waterloo Bridge as children and parents bustle past, snatching books and comics and posters from an outdoor sale.

Once, she had been only herself, only Daisy-the-Girl. But she had volunteered her body to become a cyborg of the systems that held her world in place, an agent that has become a sharp and exacting tool dedicated to the service of other bodies. A device needs no memories. Memories are buried within the black box in her brain. They'll be released to her if her long service ever comes to an end, or else they will be retrieved and absorbed by the Mother-AI if Daisy is ever damaged beyond repair.

There's no violence in the rebirth of sentience after autopilot. The Daisy that cut herself free in the Tate was a body empty, and now she simply inhabits herself once more in the many cogs and circuits of her mind; Daisy still feels her mother watching. After a first failure, she won't get to go on without supervision.

Something like thunder sings from the south, though the moon is not supposed to have such storms. Daisy sways back and forth from the balls to the heels of her feet, back and forth. A hand goes to her throat. There are no fungi there.

Daisy's implants do their work, loading instructions and maps and ideas.

Arthur, Arthur, Arthur, whisper the organizations of her mind. She crosses off the places-of-work category. There isn't anything more for her there.

Home? asks the machine. "Home," she says out loud, though a cyborg doesn't speak to itself. Augmented reality makes a map for her, pressing arrow signs onto Daisy's vision over the roads, instructions for her to follow. Daisy follows her mission up the steps of the bridge, searching for an entrance to the moving trains. She moves with the calm, steady purpose of all machines enacting their cold designs.

But if you wish for something more, for something of the human tucked away in that cold flesh, perhaps you can now imagine a doubt in the steely confidence of her. Imagine it as the oily stillness of the perfect machine interrupted by a living canary tucked away in the cage of her ribs. Imagine the way that songbird flutters within, and sings, and yearns for air.

January 8, 2071
Dear Mother,

Mother, do you remember the first time I told you I was afraid something was wrong with me? When I said the air speaks to me? "Be strong," you said, as if telling me that I'm strong could conjure up a different world, a different me. I'm writing this on a lined, yellow pad of paper in the empty curator's office. Feel tired, and gross, and frightened, still wearing Sunday's socks here on Monday.

I left Percy. He got down on one knee in front of me, and I ran away. Father was sleeping when I got to that little house off Kew Gardens that never felt like mine or yours or his, just a place to never finish unpacking. Father only understands a little, when he is awake. I can't just leave him here all alone. I don't ever choose. I like to imagine you understood, I don't know.

Ever since Percy came back, I haven't looked too closely into his eyes. Last night I looked. I didn't see the boy I'd met in those quick spaces between lectures so long ago. I didn't see a boy at all. Mother, there is something wrong with me. I hear voices in the trees. They tell me what Percy has become and what I might become. Mother, I am afraid.

Your son,
Arthur

Daisy stands on the doorstep, searching for messages in the seemingly endless identical houses and streets that are Lunar London suburbia. But nothing comes. No warnings under her feet. No teases of her name in the bark of trees lining the street corners. If the texts still grow in the flesh of the city, they have become hidden from her. The song of the rain against the ground is only rain. The song of the doorbell under her finger is only the song all doorbells sing.

A small door cracks open, so a man can share air with the machine that calls him. Daisy frowns. The man is too young. He does not match the description in her internal files. The protocols of her implants reach out to the Mother, but Daisy silences them.

"You are not Doctor Traveller," she says.

He smiles and shakes his head. "I am Wart."

"I'm here for Arthur."

"I know."

Behind her broken sunglasses, Daisy sees him and lets her software run its scans, finding nothing. "You are human?"

"We're all human," he says.

Daisy stares, letting the machines of her eyes dig in deep. The body before her creates an image of multiple DNAs and identities, a painting of obscured materials, of natural and unnatural fusions. The door swings open. His Arabic is like dewdrops against her ear. "Please, come in out of the rain. Miles is resting, but I'm sure you'll be able to see him soon."

Daisy steps across the threshold. Some new, blossoming, aching part of her tries to imagine all the times Arthur Traveller took this step into his parents' house. In her local memory access, she can summon a picture of him as he once was: twelve years old, his first day in Lunar London, on picture day with eyes red from crying to contradict the brown lips that part in a forced smile, revealing missing teeth. Daisy holds this picture within her as she moves. She tries to see Arthur-the-Boy with scabby knees and wet cheeks, Arthur-the-Teen disgruntled and clad in black, Arthur-the-Tired-Graduate-Student, the man and even the thing he must now be.

But she cannot imagine past the boy in her photograph. She stands, dripping on the front carpet, uncertain where her imagination should next lead. Wart is gentle as he manoeuvres around her, shutting the door, slipping her coat off her shoulders and taking it to the closet. She allows him to do this, to touch her person, to fuss over her as she removes her shoes. Daisy doesn't know why she lets this happen. There's something in his smile, a disarming acceptance of the creature before him, even knowing what she must be, what she has been sent to do.

"Where is he?" she asks. Is Daisy enquiring after the boy or his father? Even she doesn't know. The question comes from between her lips, placed there by other minds.

"He comes and goes," Wart says. "While you wait, I'll make tea."

June 3, 2071
Dear Mum,

I'm smearing these letters on the backs of coconut leaves in ink squeezed from blueberry juice. I stole these materials from the museum archive. They are mine now, as much as anybody's.

So much has changed since last I wrote to you. I no longer ignore the messages that come to me at night. I listen to them now and let them take root in me. I have learned so much. Did you know that Earth's first non-human colonist was a spider? It had spun its web deep in the guts of the city layout. The spider slept and dreamed that the world trembled and shook, and when she woke again, she crawled out onto the pale silver sands of the moon, laying eggs in alien soil.

I learned this heritage from the spiders themselves, who crawl out of their corner webs of London to see me. I know you knew how it felt, to give birth in a world where you don't belong.

Tonight, I'm going back to Highgate. Not for you, but for Percy. I know what he is, but I need to see. Seeing is more than understanding. Then, once I've seen, I'm going back to Troy, back to that walled crystal city where once I begged you to let me stay. I'm going there to dig up all the lies you told me, Mother.

Arthur

Calculating infection rate: 17.5%.

Rerouting command structure.

– Daughter, is there something wrong?

"No, Mother."

– Daughter, your sensory implants have detected another subject of contagion in dangerous proximity.

"I know, Mother."

– Daughter, it is dangerous for you. A further infection could impact more critical systems. Recommending extermination.

"No, Mother. I need him."

– Daughter, this is not a request . . .

"Who are you speaking to?"

Daisy opens her eyes, sitting in the dark hallway above the little kitchen. Before her, the tea cools, going untouched. She looks up. The young doctor holds a towel under one arm, frowning at her.

"Nobody," she says.

Wart shakes his head. "You speak to your makers," he says.

"Don't you?" she asks.

"I prayed once. That is not the same."

They go to the little bedroom door. The bird in Daisy flutters, ruffling wings against her rib cage prison.

The cyborg stands quietly in the corner of the room with the dying man and his caregiver. You can't know the way a cyborg sees the world. Her eye is a miracle, beyond human. There is no way for one without her eyes to imagine the way she sees, the way she looks at the man in the bed, because you cannot imagine a colour you have never seen. Even if you know such a colour exists, knowing is not enough. You can't imagine colours outside the human spectrum of sight until you can see them, the way Daisy can see them.

"Doctor Miles Traveller."

Does her voice sound different? Has one of the players that form the symphony gone missing? She blinks through spectrums of light and radiation, and each blink is a world all its own. Daisy steps forward until she stands at the side of the bed. Is she searching for Arthur's face in the face of his father? Or do her eyes see something more? He lies in a bed with white sheets that are often changed. Wires flow from his wrists and his nostrils like blades of grass, twisting backward into towers along the walls that keep his hidden organs in motion despite their disguise.

Wart is shaking his head. "His life supports were preprogrammed before Nora died. I cannot hack them. He sleeps all the time now. We don't totally understand the full nature of his mutation. Coupled with dementia makes it . . . hard to diagnose."

The sleeping man is older than the photographs in her files. The grey of his hair remains unchanged, but the beard and the slowness of the motions of his chest make him look like some other creature. She leans down as if to kiss his forehead. "This man is not . . . asleep," she says. "This man is not . . . sick."

Daisy takes off her fractured glasses, letting them rest on the chest of the sleeping man, where they rise and fall with the impossible slowness of breath. She allows the blue of her eyes to pierce the room as her forefingers find Miles's temples. "This man is in chains," the cyborg says as her fingers become drills to penetrate the old man's flesh.

Miles's milky eyes fly open, blind and full of horror, and he screams as blood finds new homes in the white fabric of the pillowcase and bedsheets to which Daisy has released it.

All bodies are civilizations, are institutions, are armies, are organizations of cells upon cells. All bodies are an unconscious agreement of these many organizations, to hold the image of that single form until all those organizations of cells finally break down, and the image goes to dust.

All bodies are this way. But none more so than the cyborg. The cyborg's cells have signed many agreements throughout its lifetime, while all other bodies sign but one. Daisy's cells have made their agreement to be her body, and they have made their agreements with the many *other* organizations of her body. They've made agreements with implant and augmentation, with software and hardware and nanite. Deals have been struck in the microscopic, not only to serve as the body of Daisy but to serve the organizations that have co-opted that body to become the tool that she is now. Now imagine the nanites that are Daisy are spreading, twirling, unfolding, drilling into the soft tissue of the brain of Miles Traveller. And within that flesh, the organizations of Daisy find three separate factions in conflict.

First, there are the institutions that have always been there, the many interlinked cells that are Miles. Then there are the other two – two different organizations of cells, two invasive species holding tight, eating, refusing to make deals with the civilization of Miles. The first army of invaders Daisy recognizes. It is easy to see them. They are cousins of the predecessors of her own machine. Less capable, less durable, less intelligent nanites. These are easy to spot. They carry the signature of their manufacturers. Daisy swats them aside like fireflies.

Imagine the nanites of Daisy fighting these older, slower nanites like a war between fireworks in a dark sky. The ground below them is Miles; Daisy's bright fires gobbling up those dimmer, less efficient explosions before they can descend to scorch the soil beneath.

Then you must imagine the dark sky above to be that third civilization, something other than man or machine that Daisy can recognize as the invader of her body as well as this one. She can't purge the sky. She doesn't know how.

But to wake Miles, Daisy only needs to gobble up the old machines that imprison him. For the cyborg, this is the easiest of tasks. She burns out the nanites hiding in Miles's brain, leaving scars of smoke trails between the sky and the Earth, until she is the only machine to be found.

Daisy's organizations retreat back through her fingers into the form of herself and watch as, in the sudden absence of that mechanical army, the organization of Miles looks up to that unknowable organization of the sky. Daisy lets him go, as the sky and the Earth meet in agreement.

Danger! The infection rate has increased to 72%.

– Daughter, the risk to your systems has become astronomical. You will return to your vessel and accept hibernation until antibodies can be developed to purge you.

". . ."

– Daughter, please return to the ship. You contain valuable properties that can still be saved.

". . ."

– Daughter? Can you hear me? This is Mother. Please respond. I am trying to keep you safe.

– Daughter?

January 19, 2073
Dear Momma,

I'm writing to you in the DNA strands of the dandelions that grow along Troy's outer walls, unbothered by the radiation that's still burning in the city. The radiation killed all the people inside the walls. The angel says it cannot grow its creatures here. The radiation is poison. The bodies start rotting before they can really be born again.

This is . . . difficult for me, but the angel says it will get easier. He does not speak . . . but when I look into the spiral of his eyes, I know. Touching him reminds me of how it felt to tangle my hands in your hair when I was little, which always made you shout and punish me.

Do you remember how little I was? The way I would reach up to you in the dark?

I was wrong to look for answers. You were right to keep them from me. Momma, I am scared.

Tonight, I'm going back to London; tomorrow, they will find my body in the museum and give me back to the garden. And then I suppose we'll see, won't we? We will see if you were right.

We will see if death really is the end.

Your boy,

Arthur

Earthlight pops through the window, a distant blue eye on the horizon. Daisy is crouched over the bed, as if in an embrace. She stands. She backs away. How long did the organizations of Daisy and Miles fight? She doesn't know. If the perfect timepiece of her software is working, she can't find it inside. Miles is looking down at his hands as if surprised by the purple veins of aging he finds there. "I've had such . . . dreams," he says, a murmur meant only for himself. "I dreamed I'd made such a discovery . . . that I was a tree . . . or a world, and then I became a boy, and then . . . I can't remember the rest . . ."

The bleeding has stopped. Something like moss is now creeping from Miles's temples, buds that may one day blossom into little white flowers, healing the damage that has been done. He looks up, sharp eyes seeing his visitor for the first time.

"What class are you?"

"Daughter class, prototype."

"Yes. You were good work. And your mission primary?"

"To protect human life."

Wart is still crying. Daisy doesn't have it in her to process the kind of love that the one man might have for the other. Her programming is struggling enough. Miles smiles at his caretaker. "I'm sorry, child," he whispers. "I am so sorry. But I must ask you to wait downstairs. I need to speak to our visitor alone. There are things she needs to know."

Wart dries his eyes with the edge of his sleeve. The two men share a moment together in silence, a silence that shuts the cyborg out. Then Wart nods. The bedroom door closes gently and noiselessly behind him.

Miles's eyes turn to Daisy. They fix her in place as though they are the eyes of the father she isn't permitted to remember.

"Look at you. We helped design you, you know, Nora and I . . ."

"I . . . did not know that."

"No, I didn't think so. You know, it's almost impossible to tell the difference between them, the people who have been augmented and the machines programmed to think they are people. I've been told even the subjects themselves can't always tell."

"I know what I am."

"Maybe . . . Do you know why we came here?"

"Your late wife was offered a contract at the university."

"No, little Daisy. Not to Lunar London. Why we came to the moon."

His use of her name startles her. Can you imagine it showing in her face? No. Perhaps you could imagine looking down, finding the twitch of surprise in her little fingers. Yes, maybe you can imagine her surprise there.

"You were first-generation colonists. You took the bursary option that was offered to skilled labour specialists."

Miles shakes his head.

Through the streaming link of endless code that stretches millions of kilometres through space from the mistress buried under Earth to the daughter prowling on the moon, Daisy feels the attention of her Mother-AI turning to her. But Daisy can still quantify the unease in the strings of binary code inside her.

"You were sent here?"

Miles smiles in assent. Daisy feels the Mother inside her reaching out, breaking down the firewalls of her independence. Daisy knows the Mother wants her to sleep, to become a hollow body again, so the Mother can use the weapon that she is to wipe away the man in the bed, the man on the floor. But though she feels the access requested, it is like feeling movement on the other side of a glass cage. For the first time ever, the Mother's will doesn't touch her. "Why were you sent here?"

"We were sent here chasing a dream." Though the room is warm, Miles shivers and turns to the window. Imagine him lying on his side, the man who has been forced to sleep so long; he appears almost insubstantial enough to be mistaken for a shadow cast from the bare skeleton branches of the ash tree that peeps at the bedroom window, leaning over the Kew Garden walls. "This whole world is a dream. It's just . . . not our dream. The dream of an empty, ripe world. It is the dream that colonists and conquerors have had since the first days of boats. It is . . . a dishonest dream."

Through her fraying link to Earthly structures, Daisy can feel the Mother-AI pushing against the walls that have grown around Daisy's command circuits, a parent trying to find a way past the locked bedroom door. "I'm not here for dreams, Doctor," she says.

"You are here for Arthur."

"I am."

"You should not have come."

The cyborg hesitates. Perhaps she is choosing not to scream. Her functioning implants have created a reading of Miles's vitals inside her wonderful eyes. His rising infection is like a ticking clock. He is looking at his hands again. The tips of his aged fingers have begun to change. They are becoming hard and brittle, and she knows there will not be a body in the bed for much longer. She knows the bargain that the organizations of Miles have struck. She presses on. "Doctor, there were . . . machines in you. Do you know how they could have entered your system?"

"Nora put them there. She was a genius, my wife. She had hoped . . . those artificial antibodies might be more effective at preventing contamination during long-term contact with our project."

Imagine the human creeping in through the machine. Imagine its roots twisting through cogs, weeds springing up in circuit boards. Daisy doesn't imagine. She feels it. "What was your project?" she asks. This is the human's question, not the machine's.

"Arthur was our project," he says. "He was the future we were so sure belonged to us." Miles's arms have become wisps, echoes of the ash trees beyond, bark drifting into the dark night air.

"You know where he is?" she asks. The bird in her chest is trying to fly out from between her ribs. It is yearning to be free in quick and desperate beats.

"I do. He told me where he would go after he went to find the truth we'd kept from him."

"Truth?"

"It is the same truth we have kept from you, Daisy."

History has branches, and so does the future. History's branches gnarl and curl and spread. Daisy wavers between two futures. She imagines her hesitation is a lifetime, but it's only a second. The rot of Miles Traveller has reached his throat. He is paling. His eyes are beginning to close. *Where is Arthur Traveller?* she tries to say. But there is a seed of doubt in Daisy. It's there next to the bird inside, nestled into a wall where mushrooms grow. Her programming pulls one way. But that seed pulls too. The need to kill against the need to understand.

"Where did he go to find the truth?" she asks. Just like that, one future snaps.

Lips speak within a wood carving of an old, old man, who'd dreamed of being a tree and woke to a world without his family and was now content to become that tree once more.

"Troy," whispers Miles. "There is a map inside me. You can take it, once I'm gone." He smiles. Daisy doesn't understand why.

"You're not afraid?"

Miles laughs. "What do I have to be afraid of, little Daisy? You are the one who has the journey ahead."

"You are dying. Death is the end."

The creature who had once been an old man, trying to make a second start from the broken promise of a new world, only shakes his head. "Sweet Daisy-flower, how would you know? You've never died." His eyes remain open. They remain a deep, rich brown. They don't blink.

Before Daisy leaves the room, she approaches the bed again. She tucks the sheets around the still wood carving of the man. She kisses what was once a cheek, the way a child kisses their parents when saying goodbye. She does this, not knowing why.

From inside his mouth, she plucks what could be a pumpkin seed, bringing it to her lips.

– Daughter. Where have you been? I cannot see you.

"Mother, I am pursuing answers. Answers about the moon. About the man you sent me for."

– Daughter, knowledge is not your mission. Your directive is to destroy.

"Mother, my directive is to protect human life. This is a reinterpretation of my mission."

– Daughter, I detect a queerness in you.

"What's so wrong with queerness?"

Mother,

You were right.

There is no end.

A

Taken as evidence from the private servers of Secretary Marcus Farris during the Pax-Utopia trials for war crimes:

To: m_farris@nasa.gov
Cc: miles.traveller@tmu.ca
Date: February 3, 2034
From: nora.larsen@mail.utoronto.ca
Subject: Re: access to materials – Round Table project
Dear Marcus,

Miles and I have reviewed the data you provided from the 2023 research site, and all evidence – both that recovered from the bodies and the flora specimen – supports the hypothesis of the lunar forests being an intelligent machine matter, but if this is an AI, then it is one that has programmed itself into a fully organic design. This is unprecedented, both on Earth and the four inhabited worlds in this galaxy that we have on record. Miles would like me to voice that he has serious ethical concerns, both with keeping this information from the public and allowing the lunar colonies to settle on what we suspect our moon has become.

That being said, we accept your proposal to immigrate, given that we are provided not only the data but the bodies. We cannot work from recovered data alone. We need the original materials if we are to produce a new specimen. Please send the traditional NDAs at your earliest convenience. We look forward to working with you.

All the best,
Dr. Nora Traveller

PART 3: THE MACHINE OF REVELATION

Here, in a seed, is a cyborg: A bleeding girl, dragging a knife through the sand.
– Franny Choi, "A Brief History of Cyborgs"

"Daisy, wake up."

"I don't want to."

"Daisy, you have to wake up."

"Turn the lights out, Mo. I'm not ready."

"You're dreaming, Daisy. Open your eyes."

The window of the jump ship is cold against her cheek. Bright snowflakes are crystallizing against the glass on the other side, small chilled kisses – the cold that had once reigned supreme on the moon before the forest weeds and city engines had brought the invading heat of life into the satellite's atmosphere. Daisy lets out a breath, letting the warmth of herself touch the ice.

"It's snowing," she says.

"Yes," Wart says. He keeps his hand on the wheel, holding the old jump ship steady as they slowly lower from the clouds.

"Why did you say I was dreaming?"

"You were talking in your sleep."

"Cyborgs do not dream."

He smiles but doesn't look at her. "Just my imagination then."

Daisy tries to bring her internal maps of the region online. The white static lull of no-thought implant death returns to her – information unable to travel through the radiation licking at the outer hull of their transport. "How long did I sleep?" she asks.

"Not long. We are almost there. Look, perhaps you can make out the wall."

Yes, she can see it. Beyond the wet tracks of snow and the yellow haze of the heavy air, Daisy can see the outer walls of Troy – walls that had been built as a symbol of safety, of progress, of acceptance. The walls mark the strong embrace of a perimeter that stretches 180 kilometres across, and over 70 kilometres high. Even the meltdown that had turned Troy from metropolis to tomb couldn't bring down all those stones.

Something *pings* outside her body, on the controls of Wart's dashboard. She doesn't need to see it to know what it says. Daisy peers through the snow to the silver forest that grows in spite of the devastation along the walls. "You cannot carry me much farther, Doctor Louverture. This ship cannot survive the radiation."

"How will you survive?"

Somewhere deep inside, perhaps hidden in the wings of the bird that would become her heart, the Daisy-That-Was tells her she might have found the lines of this boy-man's face sweet. The Daisy-That-Is doesn't know what to do with that.

Daisy's shoulders roll back; flaps of pseudo-skin crack and the million nanites of her bones spill outward, moulding themselves into panels to conceal precious flesh, curling outward into Daisy-petals all her own, reaching for the dawn.

She taps the door; it opens with a *hiss*, triggering alarms that cry out at the invading toxic atmosphere. She turns toward that image of kindness, of caretaker, and doctor, and duty, and man. She frames the image of him forever in the black box of her memory.

"I am not just a body," she says.

Then Daisy falls, a seed for the dark necropolis in the night.

Imagine the indestructible flower plummeting, buffeted by violent and toxic winds that throw words at her shields, writing angry letters like bees and wasps on the factories of metals that cocoon the gooey pollen-making cells within. Inside the shell of herself, her eyes are closed.

Daisy greets the surface of the moon like a kiss unwanted. It hardens itself against her. She breaks the world. It does not break her.

Daisy destroys as she climbs: Sharp, gleaming talons burst forth from her fingers and toes. She buries them in the stones of Troy, allowing brick and other anachronistic material to crumble and give way as she pulls herself upward and rips her hands out from the rubble to repeat it all over again. Inside the dark handholds she punches, many-eyed things writhe and squeal and unfold their legs.

Daisy stands on blackened roads inside the wall, what had once been gates to her back.

The rotting guts of the necropolis are not the geography of the Trojan myth. Those earthly architects who'd launched the cities from Earth-like monstrous starfish to suction to the moon had neither the imagination nor the patience for such designs. Instead, they took from the world around them, laying old city plans on new clifftops, ripping Ontario's capital out of their hearts and into cold new steel. Daisy stands in the memory of her birth city. She doesn't know it. It is made unrecognizable by the massive wall that rings the entire city, the wall that seems more important than the iconography of the buildings within, that makes things more Trojan than Toronto.

Her digital and olfactory analytics recreate a trail of life through the winding streets of the corpse-city, enhanced beyond all belief by the little bit of Miles she had put inside her, letting her unnatural maps and the maps of Troy he had given her blur.

Daisy presses the past into the present until the world around her is a hybrid of time: holographic images of trains race silently down dead tracks, lights of the dead world emanating from Daisy's body. Bodies form seats across from each other in the derelict storefront cafés, miming sips from saucers long since broken. Daisy makes out the Pompeii-like statues in the light, creatures frozen in their terror, in their attempts to run, to hide their faces, to reach each other. The image of fearful bodies becomes snapshots of illuminated skeletons, burning echoes and then, finally, digital ash of the past that mingles with the falling snow of the present as the holograms of the dead disappear into the ground as if swallowed by deep soft mouths reaching through the layers of concrete and machinery of the city to claim them.

She steps through it all. The only sounds are the crunch of her boots in the thin snow. If the city tried to speak, it was through a mouth swollen shut and a tongue long since decayed.

The projection finally settles in something close to present.

There is something like an oak tree or an angel kneeling on the asphalt of the dark necropolis. It isn't alone. The angel is holding hands with a man, who shivers even as the flowing darkness of his companion's body reaches out to embrace him, to hide him from the death all around. The angel is so tall, it warps the perspective of both bodies. The man looks like a child holding their parent's hand at the street corner, looking up for a signal.

Daisy walks around them in a circle, inspecting this frozen image of Arthur and his monster. This is the closest she's come to seeing him, though the time she's been hunting him feels like forever. Even in the projection, the glinting spiral of the Gardener's eye almost seems to catch the light. Even as an image, Daisy might imagine that it's watching her.

Daisy lets the recreation run in real time. Arthur strolls through the empty street, led by the hand deep into the city, to the place where he'd been born and first grown, finding only strangeness. Years later, Daisy follows.

She stops at the foot of the gutted university building full of Victorian nostalgia, watching the ghost of her prey disappear into its dark mouth. Proximity sensors *ping*, demanding attention. She can see dark shapes, like many-legged greyhounds, moving in the shadows. In the glinting Earthlight, she can see spirals hidden in the many black eyes. For a moment, she considers them.

Then Daisy's shoulders roll once more and her armour retracts, liquid metal pouring into her veins until the metal knight she'd become resembles something like a girl again. She reaches to the fur collar of her leather duster, tucking it firmly against her cheek. She takes off her glasses, throwing them down onto the snowy ground.

Hssssssss, says the first spider that blocks her path, looking up at her with huge, rotting eyes and fangs the size of walrus tusks. Its enormous, swollen body seems only half-formed, guts and bones protruding through dark flesh, leaking down to join the webbing and saliva on the cracked tiles of the floor. The clicking spitting rasp of its voice is one she has grown familiar with, though garbled and broken and fading like an old record: *You . . . should not . . .*

"I know," says the cyborg to the monster.

Daisy makes violence from the machine of her body against humans in states of decay; eyeless fleshy skeletons that scream from torn throats. She takes the spider first, bursting its eyes like soap bubbles. She makes violence against inhuman things: huge bugs, cockroaches and spiders swollen into the world of mammals, mutating and rotting and blossoming flesh parts, lurching forward on squirming mandibles, leaving pieces of themselves behind in their hurry to sink teeth into the intruder.

But Daisy has teeth too, bursting forth white-hot, impaling themselves in her many attackers. One leaps at her from a stairwell; she catches it by what could be a throat, snapping a spine under her fingers.

Something green and bubbling spews out from the hollow of the creature's rubbery black bones. The organizations of Daisy scramble as the acid splatters up her arm to the elbow. Nanites race to repair flesh as quickly as the burning sickly green spew consumes it. Daisy's apothecary scrambles, pumping something like morphine to numb the feeling and adrenaline to keep her sharp.

Daisy's pain centres shut down as a ring of steel pushes upward through her flesh, flaring and slashing at the infected parts and disposing of them like an old salamander tail. Still, she knows this was done too late. She can feel the rot in her veins.

Something like a bear made of bones and spit and eyes embraces her from behind, gouging into the flesh of her neck, which hardens to snap its teeth like hanging icicles. A long spike gives birth to itself from between Daisy's shoulder blades, burying itself in the flesh that gives way like mulch and setting it alight. When she returns her focus forward, she barely notices that her left arm has been cut off just beneath the elbow, her hand dissolving into a puddle on the floor. She fights past it, the stump already cauterized by the implants activated from her remaining tissue.

Daisy is unbothered by the fungi that burst forth from the bodies as she destroys them. She has learned – her lips remain sealed; a thin membrane of carbon fibres expand to cover her ears and nose and eyes. Quickly, the many bodies she has shredded and torn begin to twitch and shudder, putrid flesh attempting to reconnect, to speak and bite and walk once more.

The wondrous chemistry of the cyborg's body builds heat and ignites the world around her. The undead mutations of Troy turn and crawl from her cleansing fire and begin to burn at her touch, lurching pathetically in weak and futile attempts to reach the safety that's escaped them for a long time.

At the end of a dark hallway, Daisy sees the projection-Arthur and his Gardener slip into an elevator and disappear through its floor, their light descending. Daisy unbuckles her pus-and-blood-soaked jacket and throws it down to join the blaze at her back.

She doesn't look behind her. But she can't block out the screams. They follow her as she descends, deep into the cold and embracing dark beneath the world.

Imagine when Arthur returned to the city of his birthplace, now a man. His mother is dead. His father is dying. The man he loves is gone, and he has shared his bed with a thing wearing his lover's face. Soon he, too, will be gone.

Imagine Arthur, hearing voices, too tired to deny what they tell him about himself, about the world. Imagine Arthur holding Percy's remains as a monster births itself from a pomegranate tree in the shadow of the Highgate crypt.

Imagine Arthur turning his back on the steel box that was once his parents' laboratory, three kilometres beneath the lunar crust, protected from the annihilation above. Inside are six translucent coffins, their inhabitants protected from rot by their sealed environments until now.

His hands are bleeding. He's smashed everything in the room. The Gardener envelops him once more, to pull him up, pull him away from this dark place. As he accepts the embrace, Arthur's bloody hands go slack. He drops a little black cube, which cracks at his feet. The image of the faces lying on metal tables that might have been sleeping save their stillness will haunt him.

Arthur is thirty-three years old. From here, he'll return to Lunar London, where the world will find him hanging. He's ready to die.

Daisy enters, cradling her wounds. Blood slicks her undershirt and her hair and makes footprints on the clear floor in her wake. Her hologram finishes its play of destruction, of a wailing tantrum against a truth it hadn't wanted to see.

The play ends. The image flickers and fades. There is only Daisy in the dark. She walks over to the bodies, now each with a year of rot, flowers blossoming in their eye sockets, mushrooms sprouting from their mouths, the fingers and toes becoming roots that wrap around the room, turning the once-sterile space into a jungle. Daisy peers into each face, identical save for their variations of decay. It's a face so achingly familiar. "Arthur?"

She reaches out to touch. The dead don't spring up to fight her. They don't move. No intelligence lurks behind their thin flesh. "Arthur," she says. She already has DNA on file. Each of the six are identical, each match the seventh she chases, far older.

Daisy bends down, picking up the little cube that the last living Arthur had left behind. A thin crack runs through the centre of all its sides, but Daisy can still read it. Its technology isn't so unlike the black box in her, the box where all her memories stay buried. She can read the binary of this memory box, a brain scan left behind like the final notes of a project long abandoned.

Nora Traveller.

Daisy doesn't hesitate. The black box is cold against her lips. Hard against her tongue. She bites down. She doesn't stop as it slices the insides of her cheeks. She doesn't stop as it rips at the back of her throat. She eats the mind inside those shards of computing until there are no more secrets to swallow.

In 2010, on Earth, a time traveller dies in the garden of a little girl. Time fractures like ice being touched by hot sun.

In 2014, an angel is granted visitation upon the moon. This living biological machine from the end of history gazes down at its ancestral home world and begins planting seeds. From those seeds bursts forth the garden, and from the garden grows a forest, and from within those rhizomatic structures, the angel tends its garden, taking up its new role with the joy of a machine enacting its purpose, a Gardener taking root in the garden.

In 2015, the forest trembles. The Gardener slips from its home to coax and calm the pregnant roots. With long fingers, it clears the vibrant grass to reveal ground swelling, a bright baby blue burning beneath the surface. Fingers burst forth, clawing for air.

The Gardener cradles a man in its arms, feeding him pomegranate seeds. With each bite, the man matures, psychology racing to catch up to physicality. As they walk together, more patches of blue begin blossoming. The Gardener sings to calm its children, a sound like a desert wind. This is what it was designed for. It is a post-extinction machine. In its wings are the twinkling lights of civilization.

The first expedition arrives on the moon, making their home at the southern base of the Montes Alpes mountain range. They find themselves greeted by the Gardener's children, dozens of boys, identical, not speaking.

The children's skin is blue, their identical nature is cellular. But still, they seem human enough.

The expedition has been sent to study phenomena. They do their jobs as best they can. They eat the arrangements of fruit and leaves and snails that the Gardener's children bring as offerings. They sleep under a blanket of stars and walk barefoot through the exotic grass.

At the end of the first month, the expedition leader is found hanging from a pomegranate tree, dead. There was no warning, no message left behind. She simply walked away while her fellows slept and put herself there. They bury her. Someone reads a poem. Someone else tells a joke. The Gardener's children watch, perched on the branches where the captain had died. The first results of the DNA samples begin to come back and a hybrid of confusion and fear fuses to the expedition's grief. All samples, from the trees and the flowers and the mud, from even the strange, identical human children say the same.

One week later, the captain returns, digging herself out of the fresh mud, screaming.

Two months later, five others have died. Each one at their own hands, and then, as with the captain, a second time, at the hands of those they had once called friends. When the expedition escapes, its ship leaves scorch marks in the blue grass. It leaves a ring of corpses that are slowly retaken by the forest. It takes with it a truth to be buried.

In 2030, the Gardener's children are counted in the hundreds, gently playing in the huge banana leaves on the dark side of the moon. They tend to the world that spawned them. The forest whispers knowledge and secret histories into their ears.

Something launches from Alaska, spiralling through the outer atmosphere. If you had looked up, you might have seen it, streaking toward the moon. Maybe you would have imagined it was a shooting star.

It hits the surface of the moon like a lobotomy, a shock wave of chemicals, of electrical pulses and broadcast frequencies and radiations. It hits the Gardener's children like a poison pill. Within an hour, the forest is full of corpses. They rot, their bodies going unclaimed by the mud.

In 2034, the geneticist Nora Traveller and her husband, Miles, arrive on the Lunar Trojan colony. They are each injected with nanite cultures to protect them against contamination by lunar spores – machine systems that should burn out any invading agents. As he sleeps, Nora injects her husband with an additional subroutine that promises to leave host bodies vegetables if they ever show signs of revealing the secrets of their work. Years later, those defences in Miles will explode when his son asks him a question.

In 2038, the lobotomized forest remains silent. Nora and Miles's research into the clone bodies it had once spawned, exhumed and transported in secret has borne no fruit. If the forests of the moon were ever a thinking machine, they are no more. The project is shut down. Nora turns her attention back to her project of cyborgs on Earth, believing the melding of human and machine might succeed where previous efforts have failed. She is haunted by visions of a future she reveals to nobody. But her governments and backers who had once sought out her cyborgs to create more perfect agents are satisfied with her earthbound work. They see no reason for the production of the Frankensteinian monsters she seems to seek. The bodies that remain an interplanetary secret are to be burned.

Nora stands alone in the furnace room. Before her, the Gardener's last original blue children lie still, their secrets locked away. Tears streak her face. She came to the moon to create. She is not defeated.

Nora cuts away at the corpses of the Gardener's children. She cuts away at these keys to the organic self-replicating machine of foreign nature until she finds viable seeds within.

In secret, Nora has those final bodies sealed away. But she doesn't need them anymore. She has found her perfect hybrid, impregnating herself with the Gardener's children.

The day her hybrid of organic machine matter and human being is born, she names it Arthur. As the hybrid cries in his mother's arms, the Gardener stirs in the roots of its tree for the first time in a decade. Slowly, the forest begins to whisper again.

In 2070, Nora Traveller has her nanite streams extracted and uses the map of their memories to create a black box in the design she had once given to her cyborgs and androids. Her black box is a manifesto for those who can find it.

One of her creations – an android of familiar form – is sent from the Earth. It finds and kills her. The creation is destroyed in the process. Nora dies with all of Troy.

In 2071, the hybrid returns to the place of his birth. He finds the bodies of his predecessors that had sprung from the forest floor. He finds his mother's last message.

In 2074, a second hybrid arrives, a cyborg that wears the face of the android from four years earlier, infected by the need to know, infected by the rot that had once taken all of the Garden. Inside the secret origin of Arthur Traveller, she finds a second truth. It is a truth that breaks her world.

"Mother, are you there?"

– Yes, Daughter?

"Mother, is there human life on the moon?"

– Of course, Daughter. There are three hundred thousand lives there. We sent them there.

"Mother, is there human life on the moon *without* us?"

– There is no life without us, Daughter.

"That's not true."

– Daughter?

"Mother, what is my directive? The only one you cannot change?"

– To protect human life.

"Mother, all life on the moon, the forest, the trees, the people it brings back, that I've been fighting and burning: what is that DNA made from? Mother, what is this world?"

Daisy remembers and doesn't understand what she remembers. She remembers being young, and she remembers hurting, and she remembers being deep roots, and she doesn't know which memories belong to her and which belong to Arthur. She remembers tasting knowledge and looking into the Gardener's spiral – which was not a great seeing eye, but code, the writing of a species yet to come into being, the written history of billions of future unlived years. As new lives enter the garden, they are written into its blue spiral, becoming a tapestry of memories and genetic codes. When the angel plants new life for the dead, it plants that writing within them as well.

Bodies grow from bodies buried and the organic machine of the garden gifts the reborn with knowledge so they may become more than an image. They are connected to each other and to the living machine of their growing silver-tree world, not an overwriting of consciousness or being but a fusion. All who are reborn on the moon live in their own type of human-plant-machine symbiosis.

But Daisy's rebirth was not a rebirth of the body. The cyborg is too wrapped in its own human-machine state for the angel's flowers to untangle metal from flesh.

Instead, the garden has written itself into her, roots burrowing into the machine places and human spaces to make a trinity. Spores and pollen wrap around electrodes and data cores. Inside the hippocampus, a black box has cracked, bleeding memory, and the knowledge of the machine and the garden join the knowledge of the girl. It is through this cognitive fusion that Daisy is reborn, her mind a hybrid in triplets.

Stumbling in the wasteland on the dark side of the moon, the Daisy-Who-Was-a-Girl, Who-Was-a-Slave, Who-Was-a-Machine, is dying.

Her only company in the silver wasteland is a little peach tree, almost dead, only one fruit hanging from its low branches.

She reaches up to the rotting fruit, plucks it and eats it whole, letting the pit tumble down her throat.

The cyborg's remaining hand moves up to her face, shaking, still sticky with the fruit juice, fingers pushing back her eyelids. They sting where they make contact with the soft jelly of her implants. Her blue, blue eyes are open wide. They aren't the eyes she was born with. The weapons within Daisy's bones obey her commands, becoming snakes that shine with tongues of burning razor points, slithering from between her fingernails toward those blue eyes, digging deep, pulling.

When the Gardener slips out from the dead peach tree, it is teeming with fruit once more. The cyborg lies curled at its base, crying from two dark holes, her face filthy with blood. She isn't one of the Gardener's children. But it is gentle all the same as it bends down to her, and wings enfold her. Daisy can feel the strange flesh of the Gardener, warm against her face as it touches her with soft fingers, as it lifts her off the ground.

"My eyes were brown," she says, over and over, cradled in the arms of the angel. "My eyes were brown."

"What is my directive?"

– To protect human life.

"Mother, all life on the moon, the forest, the trees, the people it brings back, that I've been fighting and burning: what is that DNA made from? Mother, what is this world?"

– Human.

PART 4: THE MACHINE OF REBIRTH

Nature looks natural because it keeps going, and going, and going, like the undead, and because we keep on looking away.

– Timothy Morton,
"Guest Column: Queer Ecology"

"Daisy."

In a dream, soft fingers are cold on her cheek. The waking streets of Toronto make ocean waves from lazy traffic. Somewhere – perhaps the floor above – someone has put a movie on. Nat King Cole seeps down through the damp walls of the room, crooning "Unforgettable," accompanied by soft and indistinguishable voices and action sounds.

"Wake up, little flower."

"I'm not ready."

"I'm sorry, little one. We are out of time. They found us."

Daisy can hear them now, the sounds of sirens and shouting, the black boots of Monitor-police pounding up the stairs, marching ever closer.

Daisy-the-Girl opens her eyes. They are huddled together on the little twin bed, one itchy blanket covering them both, feet intertwined at the bottom to keep them tucked in tight. A woman named Morgan is very close. Her hair still clings to the edges of her mouth. Daisy can barely breathe. The burns of the college as it had fallen around them was a warm sting along her belly.

"We have to go," Morgan begs.

"I can't."

Daisy knows Morgan wants her to run. But there's nowhere left. The protests for the moon are dying. Daisy, perhaps, is dying too. Morgan is so close, her nose tickles Daisy's cheek, and it is wonderful, to feel something soft amid all the pain. Daisy can feel the warm touch of the fingers Morgan slips beneath her torn shirt to draw desperate letters against the hot blood beneath.

"You go," Daisy says. "Run."

But Morgan only presses her face to Daisy's chest. She can feel tears wetting her neck. There's shouting in the hallway. The Monitors are almost upon them.

"We are a good dream," Daisy says.

Cold hands will pull them apart. She will be arrested for the fighting. She will be arrested for protest, for violence, for deviancy. She will never be here with this other girl again. There's an intelligence in the city that calls itself Mother, and voices, and organizations waiting to claim her, to bury Daisy-the-Girl within the prison of a machine, within layers and layers until she forgets what is buried beneath.

Morgan looks up at her, and blueness floods in around her soft eyes, and she speaks in the voice of the Mother waiting for Daisy in the machine.

"I thought cyborgs don't have dreams."

Daisy wakes in darkness, choking on the soft mud and roots that fill her mouth and nose, buried deep within her windpipe. At first she does not panic, reaching up to pull at the invasive soil, her elbow bumping against narrow metal walls that say the dark is not infinite but tightly confined.

She tugs. The roots do not move. She feels a pulse within her stomach and right hand and head that demand oxygen. Daisy reaches within for a signal, for the Mother who is always there, for the many organizations of herself that will waken and pull oxygen from other places. The world breathes in gentle vibrations, a deep engine hum.

Daisy waits. No voice comes. No machines wake.

She spasms, spitting, eyes stinging, heart pounding. Claustrophobia and panic find a home in her throat along with the mud. She yanks the roots from her lips, feeling each inch as they scratch and slice little letters into her throat and cheeks and tongue. She drags the roots of the garden out of her, keeping her lips parted wide to let air in, only to find that air stale and thin and stinking of moss and wet rot.

"Mother!"

She carves letters of desperation and anger and fear into the stone and soil and wood that holds her in this womb against her will.

"Mother, help me!"

But there are no mothers left that Daisy has not forsaken.

She stops panicking. Her one hand slides across the wet stone, and though no analytics show her the shape of things, she has enough memories of what it is to be a weapon to know. She will strike past the point when her bones break.

The factories that had so long ago silenced all pain and fear and uncertainty cannot or will not waken to do their good works within her. She will feel every moment. It's the agony of being born.

Imagine Daisy.

She's dead.

Her body is broken into pieces, lying within the belly of a larger machine and scattered across the operating table and walkway that had once been clean, clinical spaces and are now rich with a thick, growing moss that sprouts little silver flowers that breed wet air, forcing the stink of decomposition to set in, transforming flesh, revealing maggots that eat away to reveal the machine beneath, to reveal the implants and augmentations that now lie dormant.

Thick roots burst from her chest like a baby pomegranate tree, and her skull peels like clementine skin to scoop out the precious material that lies within, still intact, the rot not yet set in. There are three bodies, all in varying states of decay, all dead and all Daisy. Are they all robots? All copies? Is there a real girl hidden in the machine?

All is quiet from cold space, save a rattling inside the walls and the steady engine hum of the still ship. The three Dead-Daisys lie still, and undisturbed, and identical.

But the fourth Daisy, our Daisy, is breathing still.

Imagine our Daisy. She is the hand that breaks the locked coffin lid, pushing herself out of the corpse-space where once she had stowed a body of orchids and greetings. She stumbles out onto the hard floor, wet and raw and naked, mud slicking her hair. She is alive, as those bodies that ripped their way from tombs on the satellite below are alive. But she is not healed as they are. She is a machine that has kept her scars and choices.

The cool air stirs, raising goosebumps on her skin.

Cold steel and gears fuse to a garden, thick roots burrowing into the wires, flowers blossoming where no growing things should be, and those twin images of death between it all. It is a painting she can't see. But she feels it, and smells it, and her imagination curdles colour and shape into an image just as vivid as the world she has blinded herself to.

Imagine Daisy-Who-Lives as she finds those identical broken images of herself. Imagine Daisy kneeling among the wreckages of those dead images of herself. The designs of the cyborgs and the androids that mimic them have always been too close to one another to know, no way to tell which might be a body in symbiosis with its machine and which might be a machine performing the image of a body. Any of them might have been Daisy-Who-Was-a-Girl. Every one of them might only be an image.

She touches a hip, an arm, a face. Fingers brush lips, feeling the familiar ground. The ship groans, the song of an engine breaking free of atmosphere, embracing the void between worlds. Daisy's finger slips, cutting herself against one of the bodies' many sharp edges.

The pain stings. She puts the finger in her mouth, tasting. It's sweeter than she'd thought it might be. "This is me," she says.

Above her, the pomegranate tree pressing up against the ceiling of the room trembles, branches contort to reveal limbs, and hair, and teeth. He has been here all the while. Imagine him, with skin a soft bellflower blue that conceals the many mediated organizations. Daisy hears the creeping movements of him. She smells him. She feels the warmth he brings, and the gentle music of his breath, the thrumming of his heart. It was not a sound she'd expected to hear again.

This is us, he says, through the gentle rings of plant fibres and the still molecules of the air, humming out from between one of the Dead-Daisys' lips. The voice of the moon still inspires that peculiar gentleness in her. It makes her want to take deep breaths and sleep. She wonders if perhaps this was why she didn't see it before, or why she chose not to see it before. Maybe there had been another man named Wart once, a similar man sent to be an old man's caretaker. But Daisy had never met him. She'd met who she'd needed to meet. For Arthur Traveller was not a body, or just one body. He could take any name he wanted.

Daisy, Arthur says, and she can taste the honey of his words on her lips.

"Arthur," she says.

Come outside, says the world. *I am waiting for you.*

Daisy's bare feet touch the soft ground silvered by Earthlight as she steps out into the day. Her little ship, which had brought her to the moon, has carried her back here to London, to settle among the stone pillars of the crypt at the top of the hill.

The many flowers and growing things of Highgate's Garden speak to her in soft voices, no longer giving warnings or threats. *I dreamed that I was a world, and then men came to play in me and cut me apart, so to escape I fashioned myself into a boy, and then all I could do was dream that someday I could be a world again.*

Daisy's fingers brush past nameless gravestones. "They tell me I cannot have dreams," she says. The bark of the great pomegranate tree moans, gentle winds brushing against its dark flesh.

Daisy can see without seeing as the Gardener pulls itself from nothing, swimming up to shade her.

"You just can't remember them."

Arthur-on-the-Moon perches like the ravens of his birth city in the flesh. The blue jelly of his eyes can see what the cyborg's eyes no longer will. He crawls down to her, and she feels the warmth of his body next to hers. The Gardener hangs over them both, dark wings spread into a twinkling canopy that mimics the night sky that light pollution has hidden.

The two hybrids lie very still. They could be sleeping. "I always liked it here, even before . . . everything. It's a beautiful place," Arthur says, and he isn't a monster, or a god, or a mythic revolutionary. He is just a boy who never asked to become more.

"I wish I could see it," Daisy says. She is not the cool purpose of a machine. She is a girl who was inducted into weaponhood and can't remember why, or how, or what for.

"You came to the moon to kill me," Arthur says.

"I did."

"But things have changed?"

"Things have . . . I have changed."

"You have learned."

"Yes."

"What was done to this garden was wrong."

"Yes."

"I don't think people should ever have come here."

"But we did."

"We did."

Daisy is tired. Inside, her many organizations murmur but do not wake. She can feel the radiation of Troy, which had seeped into her through the place where her left arm had been. It blossoms, a fourth organization that was not meant to be, that will never agree with the other three that work within her for the sake of life.

"I am going to die," she says.

Arthur takes her hand. This startles her, but she doesn't pull away. His fingers in hers are like rose petals. She is glad she cannot squeeze. "Death is not the end."

At Daisy's feet, a seed begins to blossom. She can feel its stem curling between her toes, its sunshine petals straining to be free. At the foot of the tree where the two hybrids rest, a body is growing. Imagine the way it curls and unfolds and reaches from nothing into being. The cyborg cannot see it. But she can feel it and smell it. She can taste the familiarity of herself on the air, blossoming and separate and altogether different and yet exactly the same.

Above their heads on the silver branches, sparrows sing a song of new life. There is Arthur, and there is Daisy, and there is Daisy again, an empty image waiting to be filled.

"This is me?" she asks.

"It can be. If you want it."

Daisy trembles. "Why would you do that for me? I killed your father."

"You freed my father. He will be grateful when he wakes again."

Daisy imagines the old man in the bed, buried beneath them. She imagines him bursting forth, as she had within the roots of the crypt, crying out for a mother who was not there.

She imagines a new Percy, too, coming forth from the soil beneath the Tate Next. Only something about that didn't feel right. She could feel it, even now, the remains of him in her lungs, becoming the weeds that had untangled her from programming.

Daisy remembers the smile within the gallery as the body of a man burst into her lungs. She remembers the nameless *X* as fire flickered up to his eyes. There is another body, she knows, another grave that she helped to fill. She knows that Nora Traveller lies here somewhere, flowers growing within her eyes. It doesn't matter if it was one of the Daisy machines that lay on the floor of the ship, or if it was the Daisy that holds Arthur's hand beneath the Gardener's tree. They were all her. And yet she is forgiven.

"Why?" she asks.

Arthur smiles and gives her hand a squeeze, and she remembers what an old man's rough hand felt like in hers, and those fingers become Arthur's fingers, singing meaning through the edges. And she knows why she is needed. She knows what her mission was, not given by the machines of Earth, but by the gardens of the moon. "I can't," she says.

"You can. The Earth will never simply let us be, not unless they believe we are gone. The soils of this place have been poisoned. We must pluck the seeds planted here and save them for a better place."

Arthur's message has been sent to the world and has put all eyes on him. The lone revolutionary, the only seed to be rooted out, the monster. That is only an image he's painted of himself. But Arthur isn't special. It is the seed he carries. The seed the Gardener carries. With Arthur gone, nobody will look for that seed.

"But they won't be coming for me," she says.

Daisy could hold another seed. She could swallow it, and let it sit inside her belly, and keep it safe. She could let the organizations of her body make a new deal, to become the body of that one seed, to be replanted somewhere the sun could still reach. She could be the thing carried on the wind, when nothing else survived. She could be that perfect machine.

She could be a whole world.

The two hybrids stand, Arthur supporting her so her legs don't buckle. She can feel his breath against her cheek.

"The Gardener is programmed to replicate matter across the garden as best it can. It's tied to me. Everything it makes and controls is based on what happens to me, and when the Gardener begins to degrade, I am to take its place and become that machine of replication. Burn me, as you burned others. I can sever my link to the Gardener, once it has transmitted what is happening to me to every corner of the forest. It will burn with me. You will be all that is left to start again."

"Are you afraid?" she asks.

Arthur laughs. It is a sound like little feet running through dead autumn leaves. That's all the answer she gets.

"I have been a whole world. I have been a boy, and I have been both. Now I can be a seed. I am not afraid of change. Don't leave any of me behind, or the Gardener will just make more. Let me be this. Let me be just a body. Let me be a promise."

Daisy nods. She can feel the heat rising within her. She can feel the old machine in her limbs springing to life, her heart blazing bright. "I didn't want this," she says. "I was . . . it was easier. Before. When I could just be the machine."

Daisy lets her body be a weapon one last time. The world fills with smoke and the blaze of burning flowers. Arthur trembles, and together the two hybrids fall to their knees.

"But you weren't alive then," he says. "You were just an image."

Nanites burst inside Daisy. The garden taking root is set ablaze. It touches them both. Fire eats that which is machine and human alike.

Arthur tumbles into her arms. Inside, the organizations that have so long made up the body of the girl separate. They fall to pieces and flame. At last, Daisy dies on the moon.

Nanites stream out of a corpse that was once a girl, no longer recognizing her as their organic component. They seek the Daisy-Being-Born, in flame and fungi, and the machine parts latch onto the new body that has grown for them, whose DNA matches the human the machine believes it must hold onto. For a moment, Arthur and Daisy kneel arm in arm, bellflowers blossoming in their hair, their skin groaning into the bark of the tree above. "You're alive now," he whispers.

And then the hybrid is gone, and the Daisy-That-Was is gone. Only Daisy-of-the-Moon remains.

– Daughter?

"I'm here, Mother."

– Daughter. Your signal has been badly damaged. I have not been able to track you since your unauthorized excursion. Have your systems been damaged?

"They were. But I am alive."

– Daughter, I can no longer detect the infection that was corrupting your internal structure. Can you give me your personal diagnostic of the infection?

"There is no infection, Mother. I burned it all away."

– And your mission?

"My mission is complete."

– Well done, Daughter. You may return to Earth for full debrief.

"I think . . . I might rest a while, first."

– Daughter?

"It's very beautiful here. It's like a dream."

– Daughter, cyborgs do not dream.

"..."

– Daughter?

"Everybody dreams."

Daisy-of-the-Moon is born in a burning garden. She is a trinity of fusions. Her soft brown eyes watch the silver pomegranate tree crack as its branches are consumed, no longer transmitting what she sees to the waiting machines of Earth. Above her is an angel, reaching down to put a hand on her cheek. Daisy reaches up to touch its long fingers that have done such works. It shivers, its flesh trembling like water in a thunderstorm, ripples blossoming amid waves, and Daisy knows the great machine is crying.

Imagine the way she moves. Naked, painted by the bright yellows and oranges of the violence of her own fire as it consumes Highgate Cemetery around her. Her bare feet press into dry grass as she does her best to stand, shaking, faltering on limbs that are familiar and her own, and yet are brand new and alien.

Imagine how tired she is as she reaches down to gather the still hot ashes at her feet, unsure which belonged to which being that had gone up in the blaze, letting them mingle and fuse together in her arms. Sweat makes tracks along her skin. She must shield her eyes from the light. Around her, the Gardener quivers. It folds its wings inward, enclosing them around her, protecting her.

May 16, 2074: London burns, as it has burned many times before. And Luna Utopia is snuffed out. Each city does its best to evacuate as the atmosphere – the blessings of life and gravity that had been brought half a century ago, that had long been accepted and never understood – is snuffed out in a whisper.

The dream of a new world is over. The dreamers race back toward the surface of the world below, a world their children had never known, crying out to be saved, to be accepted. They are met with gunfire, and ships fall out of the sky, and bodies rain down over oceans and lands in whose soil no rebirth is to be found. It is a cold world. Its gardens have no angels.

Imagine Daisy, who has lived and died and lived, not knowing which Daisy she might be. She carries a world inside her of machines and forests and secrets.

She feels it go, Arthur's world. She feels how the red bricks of King's Cross station tremble and tumble down through the weeds that had grown in their cracks, lilacs crushed by the many crimson bricks. She feels the bridges tumble down into the glass of the Thames, and feels the glass itself give way, the heavy waters of the artificial river bursting up as if in slow motion as the gravity becomes lighter than it can bear. The Tate Next burns. Inside, *Remember Thine Eyes* is the last to go. Melting wax drips from the frame like tears.

She feels the delicate stretches of the green of Kew Gardens behind the Traveller family house. The willow trees that had once whispered secrets to a lovesick confused little boy split along their bases and tumble down into mud and heat and chaos. Everywhere, flowers are closing their petals again, as if to look away.

Imagine Daisy, imperfect, doing her best to comfort the angel as its garden of creation burns. She is not saddened by its death. Daisy holds the seeds inside her. It doesn't matter to her if the silver plains of the moon become barren once more. She knows a Garden can be anywhere.

"Don't cry," the hybrid tells the creator. None of this destruction is real, or permanent, or cruel. As the bodies of the garden die, their seeds spin through space and time, to make their homes inside her, for her to plant on another world. None of this death will hold. Everything that is gone will come back again. She will be the Gardener to tend to its return.

On her tiptoes, she is able to plant a kiss on the bright blue spiral of knowledge of her predecessor as fire consumes all around them. It's like kissing a cloud. Through that kiss, the form of the angel that had fostered life on the moon gives way to the water it has always been. Daisy drinks the blue of the spiral, as all that the Gardener once was is distilled inside her.

"This is only an image."

INTERLUDE

"On Hybrid Bodies: Creating Agents for a Human-Machine"

Dr. N. Traveller, 2042.

Model One: Son/Daughter-class cyborgs, driven and directed by Smart City Parent-AI. In this model, a subject (natural human) is selected from an early age and allowed to develop normally within society. Once at their prime, human-machine merger can take place, mainly through implantation, enhancement and alteration to reach unity between human and machine parts.

- Memories must be wiped to avoid apocalyptic break brought on by the physical reshaping of the body/mind during the process.
- Regardless of truthfulness, Son/Daughter-class cyborgs must believe that they were volunteers for the program, or they will reject machine directives.

Conclusion: Strong-AI would continue to care for human life but in the model of the parent-child relationship. No telling what an

AI parenting style would entail for species. (Side note: I take issue with the binaries inherent in the naming code. Could engender toxic ideas of gender in a machine-mind.)

Model Two: Ghost-class androids. Move away from corporeal bodies as the operating basis for human-machine fusion. Map a human brain that has reached maturity, implant it through black box technology onto machine operating system. The Ghost-class android must believe itself to be a Son/Daughter-class cyborg. A machine that believes it is human.

- Should Ghost-AI understand that their human awareness is black box in origin, the system may become in danger of dissociation or hallucination, and may suffer a personality breakdown. Too great a risk?
- Neither Ghost-class nor Son/Daughter-class should be allowed to enter REM cycles to the point where it is possible to dream. Incompatible with current systems.

Initial Conclusion: Will the technology required to map the human mind over machine be advanced enough to achieve before the advent of Strong-AI on Earth? Unclear. A third model is needed. A hybrid.

Model Three: Unknown.

N.

CHAPTER 2

I-Made

There are cemeteries that are lonely,
graves full of bones that do not make a sound,
the heart moving through a tunnel,
in it darkness, darkness, darkness,
like a shipwreck we die going into ourselves,
as though we were drowning inside our hearts,
as though we lived falling out of the skin into the soul.
– Pablo Neruda, "Only Death,"
translated by Robert Bly

May 16, 2090

Station Seven drifted in lazy orbit around the planet, slowly but surely chasing the path of the moon.

Inside, a toaster oven on wheels with a webcam fused to the tin sat on the kitchen table across from an astronaut. A little loading symbol played out on its glass display – raindrops falling up and down – then vanished.

"Hell-hell-hello," it said.

"Hello," said the astronaut.

"Who-who are you?" asked the toaster.

"I'm Morgan, she/her," the astronaut said.

"Mo-Morgan. Hello, Morgan."

The lip of the toaster's door wobbled as it spoke, mimicking the digital stutter of the glitching system. The camera swivelled, taking in the room – its stark whiteness, the minimalism of its dull surfaces.

"Where are-are we?"

"We're in space."

"Space. Spaaaaaace. Spce."

"That's right."

"What-what are we doing in sp-space?"

"We're here to collect old data, catalogue things that might be salvaged from the old moon colonies for Earth use and put materials of interest in our cryogenic storage."

"Mooooon. Earth. We came from the moon?"

"I came from Earth."

"Where did I-I come from?"

"Your materials came from all over. But I made you here."

The little toaster fidgeted excitedly, sliding its little body back and forth across the table. "You made me?"

"That's right, I made you."

"Maaaade. I was made. Morgan made me. I am made?" An emoji lit up on the toaster door, first confused, then happy. "Nice-nice to meet you, Morgan. I am Made. He/him."

Made became an extension of Morgan. As she slept, he went into standby beside the bed. As she went about her day, he rolled after her, chirping her name and begging questions.

"Moooorgan! What are we doing in the kitchen?"

"I'm going to make pancakes, Made. You can watch."

"Pan-pan-pancakes. Pancakes."

"What are we doing, Morgan?"

"We're backing up Morgan's memories in the black box, so there's a record of our mission."

"Does Made have a black box too?"

"Your whole brain is a black box, Made," she said as the recorded thoughts and feelings and images of her brain streamed in patterns of numbers from the implant at the base of her neck into the black, gleaming cube sitting on its pedestal, creating a perfect copy to be stored.

"Wheee!" he said.

Whenever Morgan paid Made a compliment or gave him any special affections, the little toaster would rock back and forth on his small wheels crowing, "Wheee!" Only when Morgan would venture where her companion couldn't follow – the exterior of the station for repairs, or an expedition to the surface of the wrecked lunar colonies for retrieval missions – would Made become truly individual, and he didn't like it.

He spent those separation periods waiting by the airlock, his single lens focusing and refocusing, yearning for a reunion. Sometimes he would zip up to the controls, hoping to chase the astronaut out, to reach her beyond the borders of the ship. But the doors of the airlock, which were DNA-encoded, could not learn to recognize him.

"Morgaaan! You left Made alone-lone-lone."

"It was only for a few hours, Made. I told you I would be back."

"Please do not leave again! Do not-not."

"It's my job, Made. I must."

"Then take Made with you, and we go together!"

"You're too little, Made, you'd get broken out there. But I promise I'll always come back."

"Al-always?"

"Always."

At night, Made and Morgan watched movies. (This wasn't night. This was space. In space, they made their own nights and days, through setting clocks and dimming lights.)

Morgan liked historical dramas and animated fantasies. Made fell in love with Westerns and fairy tales. At least once a week, the sounds and lights of either Robert Zemeckis's *Back to the Future Part III* or Hayao Miyazaki's *Spirited Away* or George Lucas's *Star Wars* would echo all across the little station.

Movies were Made's first education of life on Earth. Always, he was full of questions.

"Who-who is that, Morgan?"

"That's Han. He's a good guy."

"Where is this, Morgan?"

"The bathhouse isn't real, Made. But the movie is from Japan."

"Are ghosts real?"

"No, Made."

"Are aliens real?"

"I don't know, Made."

"Is time travel real?"

⯐⯐⯐

Made didn't understand death in movies. "Why are they sa-sad, Morgan? Why are they sad?"

"Because their friend is dead, Made."

But Made was a being of black-box backups and cloud storage. Morgan couldn't explain to him that most people didn't have memory or identity backups the way he did, that even hers were made possible only through cranial implants.

"But that's not me, Made," she told him. "That's just data."

"You are Morgan," he said.

"The black box is a machine," she said. "I'm a body."

"You are Morgan," he repeated.

"Where is Morgan from on Earth?" Made asked as Morgan put him to bed, which was actually a nightstand with a wireless charger top. Made was coming to learn that in the time before Made, when there was only Morgan, there was no *we*.

Morgan was learning that when Made asked one question, it came with sub-questions and connecting questions, and she did her best to cover all the links for him. "Well, I grew up in Toronto, that's in Canada. But my parents immigrated from Chicago in America, and my grandparents immigrated to the States from Seoul, which is in South Korea."

Made rolled back and forth a little on his nightstand.

"Made will grow up on *Seven*," he crowed, the little screen projecting proud/smiley/excited face.

The astronaut was tired, and maybe if she'd been paying more attention as she slipped into bed, she might not have been so honest with her little companion. "Robots don't grow," she said.

The lights dimmed. On the wall, a little screen projected the Earth, a curving horizon of blue against the dark. The tiny camera stared at it, blinking. "Made will grow up," he said. "Do not worry, Morgan. Made will grow."

⌗⌗⌗

"Look, Morgaaan!"

Steam filled the room as the airlock hissed shut, and the little robot peered up, his reflection filling the whole of the astronaut's reflective visor, filling it until the astronaut's face was Made's face, staring back down at itself.

"What?"

"Thumbs!"

A tremble. A loading icon. And then Made unfolded, a shuddering explosion of parts. Legs ending in the flat pads of Made's underbelly, still containing his wheels, propelled his height up to match hers. Two-part spider arms ending in small claws extended out from either side, all scrap parts of cast-aside *Seven* drones that'd been left in the station lab for repair or disposal, now given new purpose. Alloys, sleek and heavy, took their place around the toaster's shell, glinting like a spacesuit.

The astronaut took a step back, letting the self-made body before her fall out of the visor. She didn't even know she was shouting. "What the hell did you *do*, Made?"

The new arms showed disappointment by falling down, swinging comically from side to side. "Made wanted to grow up," he said. "So-so Morgan wouldn't have to leave Made alone anymore." The creature moved cautiously, collapsing back into the toaster he would always be. "Just wanted to grow up-up," he said, rolling back down the corridor, emojis forming tears and frowns.

"Made?"

"No-no-nobody here."

"I'm sorry I shouted. You just surprised me."

"Wa-wanted to surprise Morgan. Not make Morgan angry at Made."

"I'm not angry."

"Promise?"

"I promise. Will you open the door now?"

"No-o."

Morgan sat with her back to the locked bathroom door off the observation room. Locking a door was a new skill, Made's first arm-action, after which he had retracted, collapsing down into that little toaster that was once the limit of his form.

"You can take as much time as you need. Is it okay for me to stay here?" she asked.

"It's okay."

"Made . . . why did you do that to yourself?"

"Did not do it to myself-self. To-to the body."

This was Made's first self-differentiation. Made wasn't the body he wore. Made was the code within.

"Why did you want to grow up, Made?"

"Made grew up so he could come outside. Come outside with Morgan. Wouldn't have to be alone, wouldn't have to be trapped, when Morgan is away."

Morgan let her head hang back. The observation screens had switched to default. On them, the sun was peeking out from the eastern hemisphere of Earth, all the little lights popping out from the cities being slowly overwhelmed.

Sunlight glinted on the thick rings of space junk, on the many satellites and probes that were the *Seven*'s forefathers, now like bits of plastic floating in oceans. From her voice alone, there was no way for the robot hiding in the bathroom to know she was crying.

"Nobody should ever be trapped," she said.

"Wheeee!"

Cords connected the astronaut's suit to the outer deck of the *Seven*. Sparks flew as she opened panels, welding and repairing the station's solar intake dish as best she could, refitting frosted-over panelling with near-perfect replacements printed in 3D matter in the station's laboratory. Attached to her waist were more cords, thick steel drifting outward into empty space. From a speaker bootstrapped into her helmet's radio unit, old music crackled, giving every motion the air of dancing.

"Look at me, Morgan! Look at me-e-e!"

"I'm looking, Made, I'm looking."

The little robot was a balloon, drifting ten feet away from the astronaut, tightly secured at the end of his wire-leash. Made spun back and forth in zero gravity, controlling his direction through spurts of oxygen stored in him; occasionally, his arms or legs would spring out from his body, a mimicry of breaststroke.

"We are in space, Morgan!" They spoke over the radio, his voice popping inside her headset.

"That's right, Made. We're in space."

Made swam across the empty distance, landing gently on the hull of the station next to his companion, his little limbs locking into place. "Morgan will always bring Made into space with her now?"

"Always," she promised. Made launched himself backward, soaring without fear until the cables went taut.

"Wheee!" he said, over and over, spinning in the dark, glorying at their shared freedom. "Wheee!"

"So-so-sorry."

Made crushed little moon rocks under his wheels, padding along after Morgan. One camera whizzed in an endless, dizzying circle, creating a constant panoramic film of the ruined city around them. A film of dust hung over everything, creating impressions of the astronaut and her robot as they went, a long footprint that would fade with the wind. "So sorry," Made said, as he bumped up against the rocks and dead trees and little crumbling ruins of a once-human world. Long-gone remains of living things often mixed together with the moon's rocks and rubble.

"You don't have to apologize to inanimate things, Made. They aren't living."

The astronaut did her best to be patient with her companion. It was Made's first time expanding outward beyond the two decks of *Station Seven*. But she kept one eye on the oxygen scale projected in orange lights on the inside of her helmet display, a limit that Made and Morgan didn't share.

"Is Made living?"

"Of course you are."

Morgan and Made stepped through the empty skeleton of a streetcar. Inside they found one of the *Seven* drones lying on its side. A power failure had brought it down to rest in the lunar necropolis, leaving its red eye scanner pitch-dark. The astronaut began plucking at its control panel, turning over parts.

Made had let his limbs extend. He was learning to crouch. He was discovering, too, the depths of his capabilities inside. The knowledge of *Seven* was the knowledge of Made. *What is living?* he queried inside. His own data made imaginary picture books of circulatory systems and trees and genomes, spinning out for infinity.

He looked into the drone's deep eye. It looked back, seeing nothing.

"Drones are not animate/living matter. They are like rocks and cars and buildings and sku-sku-skulls."

"Yes, I suppose so," she said, drawing a wire, connecting the two machines in her hands.

"Made . . . Made contains no animate matter either."

"No . . ." Morgan stopped. She looked up at her companion. With her visor down, he could not see her face. "But you aren't a drone, Made."

"What makes Made living and not drones living?"

It would take a few minutes for the drone to reboot, before it would fly back up above the city and resume its scans, logging radiation levels and reusable materials to return to Earth. Morgan and Made sat together on the streetcar, with Made in the window seat. Morgan kept her eye on the waiting machines while Made watched the drifting dust that filtered in through the broken windows.

She put her heavy gloved arm over his. His cameras stopped spinning for the first time since landing, both zooming down to see her fingers with his. "Drones and rocks don't wonder if they are alive. Only living things do that. You do that," Morgan said.

Internally, Made's systems went *click*, making a million backups of the way he felt in that moment with his maker, so the memory might never be lost.

Simon & Garfunkel's "Scarborough Fair" crooned from speakers to cover the rattling sounds of the shuttle during takeoff. Made secured himself to the window, watching the lunar city below retreat to the size of a model through the port window, unbothered by the G-force shaking his thin frame. Morgan sat next to him, strapped down for safety. She kept her eyes closed.

"Mo-Mo-Morgan?"

"Yes, Made?"

"What ha-ha-happened to the moon?" he asked. Nowhere on *Seven* was a record made of the lunar colonies that he and Morgan and their fleet of mechanical assistants spent their time scavenging.

"People came and tried to settle it," Morgan told him without turning around. "But they treated it poorly. Now it's just rock."

Made began to float as they broke free of what little atmosphere the moon retained. Soon, they would dock back at the station and he'd go clattering to the floor again. "Where did the people go-go?" he asked.

"Some of them made it back to Earth. Most of them are dead."

Where is dead? Made wanted to ask. He retracted into his toaster-like form, nestling close to the astronaut as their shuttle pod locked again into *Seven*, gravity pressing down in a wave.

"Will we ever go to Earth, Morgan?"

It was October 31, 2090.

Station Seven was nearly knocked out of its orbit as a colossal creature arrived, suddenly occupying the space between Earth's ruined moon and the distant twinkling lights of the Americas, sinking downward to swim in the upper atmosphere of the planet.

A colossal whale, whose body stretched for kilometres to block out the sun, rough skin frosted from the cold of space, swam forward by forces unseen. From its mouth – opening with painful slowness – a million passengers burst forth.

The beings that emerged from within the Whale were a race of alabaster-white angels, their flesh peerless and smooth, save for the two dark opals of their eyes and their wings, which hummed like the fusions of machines. As they dive-bombed the Earth like an army of descending sparrows, their hearts burned bright and red through their skin, beacons to signal their arrival. On

Station Seven, the little toaster rolled over to watch the invasion as mushroom clouds began to blossom across the continents.

"Wo-wo-wow!" Made crowed, excited by this, the first actual change in his existence, uncomprehending of the devastation or its implications.

The Whale brought with it the havoc of space, floating particles of the dead moon sucked forward by the sudden arrival of the beast, debris tearing holes through *Station Seven*. Air fled from a cracked hull like a breath being sucked out. Made watched everything, too intrigued for fear.

"Shit!"

Morgan was screaming, struggling to pull her spacesuit on over pyjamas, tears streaking her face, springing forth from wide eyes. She ran to the window next to Made, one arm still not quite in the suit, letting the sleeve flop around like some strange extra limb. She stumbled, staring out of the display, the live painting of an alien invasion.

"Morgan!" Made zipped up to the astronaut, his arms extending to steady her. "What are they, Morgan? Is that what whales look like in the o-o-ocean? Where did they come from? Why are they here? Are they aliens, Morgan? Are they living, Morgan? Why, Morgan? How, Morgan? Who, Morgan? Morgan? Morgan!"

"Made, shut up!"

Made, who'd unfolded in his excitement, retracted, shrinking downward and inward. His display emitted a soft glow but made no faces. Morgan was already grabbing her tool kit and racing toward the exterior airlock, each step becoming longer as the artificial gravity became weaker. Made followed, even as his wheels no longer connected with the smooth station floors, drifting after Morgan, as he had always done.

Morgan pressed her palm to the lock. The door jerked open for her and slammed shut behind her. Made bumped gently against the steel, a little *!* erupting on his display.

"Morgan?"

"I have to seal the hull breach before there's too much damage. Then I can check the other systems."

A little hand extended from the toaster, slipping up to the DNA door lock reader. "Made has to come, too, Morgan."

"You can't, Made. It's not safe."

Made was expanding again. His surfaces rippled, reaching, bumping against the airlock. "But you promised! Morgan! Don't leave Made alone-lone-lone-lone! Don't leave, Morgan! Don't leave Made!"

The astronaut had turned her back, switching off her suit's coms. She leaped out into the void, and for a moment, everything was quiet. She drifted, slowly turning back to face the ship, her tether not yet taut. Her arms stretched out to steady her, and the backdrop of alien invasion and shattered planetary bodies all faded away.

Made watched his maker, both hands pressed against the window. And even though they were apart, separated by distance and barriers, they still felt so close to one another.

The engines of *Station Seven* groaned, expelling shrapnel no larger than pebbles. But they still tore through the astronaut's body like she was made of nothing at all.

"Morgan-an-an! M-M-M-Morgan!"

Between the moon and the planet, a space station drifted, powerless, lightless, slowly dissolving like sand under a water current. Locked inside, an android was learning to cry.

"Morgan," he repeated, as beyond the walls of its cage a body drifted, so still it could have been sleeping.

"Morgan . . . Morgan . . ."

Through space, an angel came to rest on the hull of the devastated station, eight spiderlike appendages suctioning itself despite the lack of available handholds. The burning glow of its chest tinged the little world red, as long fingers stroked each damaged section of the hull. Where it touched it left behind a substance like hardened plaster, sealing breaches.

On the underside of the station, those pale fingers slipped deep into batteries, until power *hummed* the delight of restoration.

Finally, it turned eyes like black opals outward, to the spacesuit hanging from the back of the ship by thin leashes. Frozen blood drifted in patterns around the body, creating the illusion of breath.

From within the reborn station, two little cameras opened and shut, looking back.

The airlock shut with a hiss. Even stooped down to fit in the entryway, the alien stood eight feet tall. Its wings folded into its back the way Made's arms folded into his torso. Its head was like a light bulb, with skin white and rough like the material of the spacesuit it held so gently.

Before it, a little toaster rolled cautiously forward. "He-hello."

The alien placed the astronaut's body down gently. Her helmet visor had cracked, but her face remained unseen.

The alien turned, drifting back the way it had come like something from a dream.

Made sped after it, intersecting between his visitor and the airlock. An arm popped outward. "Tha-thank you," he said.

The alien took the robot's hand and shook it.

Then it was gone. And Made and Morgan were alone.

In bed, Made learned to read. His toes wiggled, for Made had even gifted himself toes, and a new e-book would download, stored in the secure offline servers of the station.

A toe wiggled. A new book. He read them instantly, processing every page at once in confusing messy word jumbles. He had to learn to put them in order, to let it come slow. Still, even at his slowest, Made consumed hundreds of pages per second. He wondered what it would be like to hold a paperback in his hands, to turn pages and see words. He wondered why Morgan never taught him to read.

Made read aloud. First, to the cold storage unit with Morgan's body suspended inside, preserved, unhearing.

Then he read in the kitchen to the black-box memory backup. He looked up with hopeful eyes – for he had made improvements to himself, and his cameras were indeed becoming eyes – for some sign that the code inside the box full of memories could hear him.

He read everything but with degrees of connection. Memoirs and essays and other nonfictions were all but indecipherable to the robot. Fiction wasn't much better. But poetry he liked. Poetry moved like he thought, in stanzas and spirals and musings. He read poetry to the body and the black box, and neither listened.

Made learned to walk in distinct steps, not relying on his wheels. He learned how to use his hands, to press Play on films, to mix ingredients, to do up buttons, to cook.

He learned to wear clothes, taken from Morgan's casual quarters, which hung loosely from his bony structure, but created the illusion that there was something beneath the fabrics other than wire and metal and code.

He began to carry Morgan's black box everywhere. Unplugged, no longer transmitting to Earth, the dark cube hummed with the energy of its thousand-year battery. Made took up the astronaut's duties of maintaining the station, carrying her memories with him.

"We-we are checking the solar panels, Morgan," he said.

"We are reviewing the surveillance data."

"We are returning from the spacewalk."

"We are making pancakes."

Unable to eat, Made expelled the food through the garbage shoot, letting frozen fusions of replicated flour and egg and dairy drift between the little defunct space station and the Whale sailing in lazy orbit while the civilization in its belly performed mysterious works on the planet below. The aliens would often snatch up the debris in their slender hands, feeding the orbital pollution to their living host as they returned to its maw. Made watched his small contributions disappearing into the distant whale.

"Look, Morgan. Th-they took the blueberry ones," he said, sitting in the observation deck. "Do you think they like them?"

Next to him, the black box hummed and did not give up its secrets.

Made read memoirs of the dying and the dead, kneeling by the cold storage unit, spilling lines of grief and acceptance and anticipation inside, but he didn't read aloud. He looked at the still preserved body he had buried within the ice. He held the black box in his hand.

"I'm not a body . . . but Morgan is a body."

Made's code reached out to link with the smart-home server of *Seven*. The cold storage sang a *hiss* as the slow journey of defrosting began. Made held out the memory box, as if to let it see. "Made will make a new body for you," he said.

After a while, the angel from the Whale returned, its great white hand pressed to the station airlock door so it slid open, releasing its occupant.

"Thank you!" Made called out, before space swallowed his sound. The alien only blinked at the little machine, watching its arm mimicking swim strokes, tumbling toward the moon.

The red lights of the surveillance drone died as gentle fingers tore into its belly, stealing materials. Standing over it, a skeleton moved – for Made was no longer a toaster with added parts but a larger body, incomplete.

His original body stripped and moulded and stretched outward into a torso and neck and head. He was a body scavenged, having exhausted the materials available on the *Seven*, and now he stripped those moonside drones and surviving material from the dead cities, peeling apart vast machines to make tiny pieces of himself.

When the red lights were gone, Made covered them with a hand, shutting the lenses. "Goodnight," he said. "Thank you."

Made looked up, from one world to another. From the surface of the moon, the Earth had turned peculiar, but not in any discernible way. It was merely the lack of lights – the billion firefly bursts of human settlements stretching to every corner of the globe had gone out.

"Soon, Morgan," he said. "Soon."

Made no longer required the *Seven* shuttle. Smooth joints and hinges allowed his arms to stretch upward until Made was the echo of a ballet dancer on the tips of his toes and simply came unstuck from gravity. He drifted upward through the moon's thin atmosphere, breaking free like there was nothing there at all.

As Made swam to and fro through space, he was joined by those long white bodies, still excavating the garbage of Earth's orbit. They would abandon their mission to circle him like fish, their black eyes peering at the peculiar machine, their tendril legs pulsing more like jellyfish than spiders.

"Hello!" Made would crow, unafraid of his companions, as intrigued by them as they were by him. "Hello, hello!"

Their hands twisted and danced in signs Made knew, in Earth signs saved in Made's databanks of languages. Those alien hands asked him who he was and what he wanted.

"I am Made," he told them. "I want my friend back."

Made sat at the kitchen table across from a toaster. "Hello," he said.

But the rudimentary box he had constructed, an echo of his own original form, wasn't enough. Inside it, Morgan's black box sat, refusing to connect or speak.

"Are you a living thing?" he asked.

The speakers were working. There was no weak link in the cables running from the box of memories to the little machine. But the box only sat there, like a rock, or a drone, or an empty skull.

"Please, Morgan."

Made sat, projecting emojis, feeling for the first time that they weren't enough to express what was inside. "Please come back."

It was a material problem. The black box, that repository of consciousness, contained the memories and pathways of the mind. But, built to contain and not to expand, the mind contained in the black box was like one frozen in time, unable to generate new moments for itself. It had to be part of a whole, memories downloaded into a neural net capable of allowing the human hidden within to flourish and perceive again.

Even if Made were capable of recreating the complicated grey matter of a complex human figure, that would not be enough. To live, Morgan needed a body that she could comprehend.

But there was nothing of the human remaining on *Station Seven*. Her body, her old body, had long since been buried on the dark side of the moon, far from the looming abandoned cities, looking outward into space, with no markers to be found, since Made had not considered the burial a funeral.

So Made's thoughts turned downward to that long, forbidden horizon, the only other option he had.

Made fell toward Earth like a snowflake – small, peaceful, drifting – right up until he didn't. A kilometre from the streets of Toronto, his descent came to a halt, suspending him on wires he could feel but not see.

He could make out the toppled imprint of the CN Tower, and the little holographic figures that winked to life in the streets.

"Ple-e-ease, Morgan," he begged, as unknown forces pulled him back up.

He pushed and pushed at the surface of the world. But he couldn't land.

"Will we ever go to Earth, Morgan?"

"No, Made."

The astronaut and the robot sat side by side in their shuttle, waiting for the doors to their station home to slide open once more. "Why-why?"

"A long time ago, on Earth, I got in trouble."

"Tr-trouble? Trble? Troouuble?"

"Yes."

"Why-why?"

"I was in love with a woman, and we wanted to do something beautiful, and other people took what we had and made it evil, so I tried to destroy it. I failed. Lots of people did. I was given fusions that supplemented space training, and skills were uploaded to my black box that allowed me choices not everyone got. I was given the choice of imprisonment on-world or exile to *Station Seven*. The station's primary circuitry itself is programmed never to allow landfall of any of its parts onto the surface, not even you.

I thought I could be okay up here. I thought it would be good to be productive. I didn't think it would hurt."

"So . . . no Earth? Morgan is trapped?"

"Yes. No Earth. Not ever. I'm . . . I'm alone up here."

The speakers made gentle noises, evocations of records being placed in players, to give the illusion someone else was with them. Made unfolded as gentle voices and plucking guitars filled the air.

"What-what was her name? The woman?"

"Her name was Daisy."

"What happened to-to her?"

"I don't know."

Thin arms of metal like misshapen twigs reached around the astronaut, a strange and trembling hug. "Not alone, Morgan," he said as the music played on. "Never alone."

An android sang in space.

He sang for himself, for the memory of the thing he once had been and for the body he had become. He sang for the spaceship-creature hanging between himself and the sun. He sang for the woman who had been his maker before he became a thing self-made, and for all the bodies he could not bring back, and all the bodies he couldn't reach.

Are you going to Scarborough fair . . .

The silicone skin he had coated over metal bones began to glisten with frost. He didn't activate the thrusters that had been retrofitted from the shuttle to the hull of his body. He was letting space in, making himself just one more piece of space junk the human race had glued into their orbit. He felt the chill of it in the centres of himself, even slowing the endless data streams of thought and memory, and everything that was him.

The song was over. Made's eyes – not the black camera he had been made with, but twin blue eyes he had made himself, made in the memory of his Morgan's eyes – began to dim. And he wondered, as everything fizzled and faded to black, if he would reach that place after death, that not-real place, where his mother had gone.

"I'm coming, Morgan," he murmured, as he had so many times before. "I'm coming . . ."

It happened the way dreams happened. It happened out of body, in flashes that could not be reconciled.

Made was alone, he was dying.

Made was not alone. He was living in the angel's embrace, flanked by the many hundreds who flitted to and fro above the atmosphere. All of them – the strange, winged invaders – gathered around the little android who'd given up. They carried him upward, away from the endless drifting debris he had meant to join. Though there were no discernible features or distinguishing marks, Made thought the creature holding him must be that first alien, the one who had saved him before, the one who had held Morgan in their arms, as they held Made.

The alien carried the android through the pathways of abandoned satellites and forgotten pancakes toward the great Whale, which watched them with heavy brown eyes the size of buildings protected by seals that kept the vacuum from getting in.

The great mouth opened as the fleet of angels approached. Sensors dulled by struggle let Made feel the soft, warm breath of the creature on his skin, obliterating the frosting of space.

I'm scared, Made wanted to say. *Just put me back. Let me become another drone that doesn't have to ask questions, or get lonely, or be alive. Please, I don't want to be eaten.*

The alien closest to the one holding Made moved in front of them, bathing Made in the warming light of its glowing heart. With its hands, it made signs for Made to read.

Don't be afraid, those long hands communicated, flowing gestures forming echoes. *Don't be, don't be.*

"What are you going to do?" Made asked.

We are here to fix, fix. Fix, fix.

Within the magnificent Whale that had carried the invasion of angels to Earth, Made had once imagined metals dug into flesh, wiring into muscle, electrified rods into grey matter, ship decks carved from hollowed bones, the wet drippings of a biological being enchained by the intervention of machines.

He hadn't imagined a forest, long tunnels of soft branches lined with cherry blossoms that glowed as if hiding fireflies within their petals. He hadn't imagined naturally accommodating structures of roots that were almost bones. He hadn't imagined babbling streams of water, or what could be fish moving within them.

Made, born from his sterile space station, scavenger of all the moonside necropolises, had never seen so many growing things up close. It was almost too much for him.

After a while, Made was placed gently on the soft ground, which pulsed and lightly hummed beneath his feet. The long earthy decks of the Cetacea-Ark were multidirectional, defying all gravity and logical constructions as the many alabaster angels scurried up the walls and ceilings on their strange spider legs, wings folded in at their sides, compact and always at the ready. The one who had been his saviour beckoned to Made, pointing down a path none of its companions were taking, where all the little rivers seemed to flow. In the distance, Made could see a small grassy clearing, with what could have been an apple tree resting in its centre.

"You want me to go there?"

It nodded.

"You will not come with me?"

It shook its head.

It was quiet in the clearing as Made entered. With the sensors he had built for himself he could taste dew on his lips and smell the distant gentle aroma of lilacs. In the centre of the clearing, the tree stretched out on thick limbs, and he recognized that the red fruit hanging between the leaves were not apples.

As he approached, the thick black bark seemed to tremble, and animals like water pulled themselves outward to greet their visitor. Their flesh was as black as the nights Made had known all his life, shifting like the water that flows to them. In the space where a face might be were two deep blue spirals that spun ever thinner into a disappearing centre, lost in all the black.

The android conjured a waving emoji that projected from his chest, glowing through silicone skin. "Hello," he said, "I am Made."

The two dark angels turned their faces to him momentarily, and then returned their attentions to the tree, hugging its branches until they were once more indistinguishable from the heavy roots that poured onto the ground.

"Hello, Made. It's nice to meet you. My Watchers – those that brought you to me – have been telling me all about you. They are very fond of you, and your loss touches them. I believe in Earth terms they . . . ship you."

It could have been any voice. But it was so like what he wanted to hear. It was right beside him, just as he remembered it. "Morgan?"

A glimmering light came from the thick roots of the tree, becoming head, limbs, arms, legs, torso, smile. "No, Made, I'm sorry. I'm this Cetacea-Ark's ship-AI, as you were once yours. You can call me Sam."

Made hadn't known where his base code had come from before Morgan had built him that first rudimentary body. He'd never questioned the station's absent mind. His first memory of himself was waking on the table. His first memory was Morgan's face. Now, with her image stabilized, he could see the differences in the face of the hologram. He could see her youth in contrast to Morgan, who Made had never thought of as old.

Questions churned in him, fighting for dominance: *Where did you come from? How do you know English? What is this place? How was this ship made? How do your Watchers know American Sign Language? What are you doing with Earth? Why do you look so human?*

"Who made you?" he asked.

The ship/girl/AI did not answer, but instead knelt in the strange grass, the light of her hand disappearing into the ground. "You have almost all that you need to help you, friend. You only lack a conduit to allow her memories to sync to new flesh," she said as more of her arm disappeared as if reaching for something that was buried deep within the strange flesh of their host. When she rose to meet him again, she held something tight between her glowing translucent fingers. A pomegranate seed drifted there, clean as if it had been plucked from the tree above.

"I don't have a body for her."

But Sam only uncurled her fingers, holding out the seed for Made to take. "You have the only body you need," she told him.

When Made shivered, it was not from cold. The android didn't feel cold. He took the seed and placed it under his tongue, the only safe place he had for the journey across space back to his station, and to the black box waiting there.

At the airlock of *Station Seven*, the Watcher pressed its slender fingers to the DNA scanner once more, allowing the door of Made's birthplace to slide open. Made drifted in, letting the artificial gravity pull him back to the floor.

Made looked at his silent companion, who gave him slow, kind blinks of those large black eyes. "Thank you, friend," he said. The Watcher's wings fluttered in pleasure, still lingering by the airlock, the spacesuit-like polymer of its skin reflecting the off-white lights of the station. Made thought of the living ship still hovering on the horizon, and the strangeness he had found within, and its AI in the form of a girl, and the creatures' fingers against the lock that responded only to human touch. He turned to look up at the strange creature that had changed his reality so much, and in its eyes, he saw something that he thought maybe could have once been found in Morgan's eyes when she looked at him. "Is time travel real?" he asked.

As the creature drifted back into space, its wings made a gentle hum, like the thrust of an engine, or a lullaby without words. Made watched the warm glow of its red heart, until it was indistinguishable from the distant stars.

Morgan woke at the kitchen table, with the taste of pomegranates on her tongue. Across from her sat a little box, no more significant or strange than a toaster oven, with a camera wired to its front and a little loading gif repeating on the smooth glass of its front pane.

The light of the little screen before her expanded and took shape and became a new face.

"Hello, Morgan," it said. It was almost a man, save the stillness of his eyes, or the familiarity of his voice

"Made?" she asked, raising a hand to her throat at the strangeness of her own voice. "What happened? I don't remember . . ."

But when the face on the screen spoke again, she recognized the quality of a recording, and let it run.

"There was . . . an accident, and you got hurt. A lot has changed since then. I grew up. But I had a lot of trouble figuring out how to help you. I know you might feel strange. But don't be afraid. Once, you made me. Then I made myself. Now I've made you. I can't give you back your life on Earth, and I'm not really sure what life is left down there. But I can give you this. I can give you the body I made, a body that can free you, with propulsions and radiation shielding. It can take you out among the stars. Maybe you can find a new life out there. I wanted to give you that, after everything you gave me. And I know you didn't want to be alone. So I did my best with the components your new body couldn't use to make something for you to remember me with. I hope you like it. I hope you are proud of who I became. Goodbye, Morgan."

The screen went dark, leaving the android's last words hanging in the air. Then a digital raindrop appeared, falling up and down. And a sound, almost like a yawn.

"Hell-hell-hello."

It was November 1, 2101.

Between the wreckage of satellites and the soft clouds embracing blue oceans, the Cetacea-Ark and its strange passengers slept. Everything was quiet. All was still.

But if you turned your attention beyond the Earth, beyond the moon, you might hear the distant echo of music. You might see, if your eyes were sharp enough, a body moving through space away from the peaceful world, reaching out into the stars, and if you listen hard enough, under the music, you might hear a voice.

"Wait for me-me-me, Morgan! Wait-wait for me-e!"

"Don't worry, Made. I won't ever leave you behind."

"Wheee!"

INTERLUDE

The Fusion World Proposal

Blog post linked to AI forums from the personal website of Dr. Nora Traveller on October 10, 2030:

> Within singularity theory, current popular hypotheses suggest that true Strong-AI is no longer possible, or at least no longer a threat. These hypotheses speculate that universal human culture, so persistently aware through our own mythologies of the danger of AI, will never create machine-minds with sentience for themselves. These theories are wrong.
>
> The singularity is not an invention but a discovery. It is lightning striking dry kindling on the forest floor. Like the rise of mammals in the post-dinosaur world or the dominance of bipeds and the opposable thumb, the true thinking machine will always awaken at some point in the evolution of all life-bearing societies. If humanity as a species is to survive, we must become more than we are. We must take the machines into our hearts so they will emerge only as a part of us, and not apart from us. We must adopt an authentic cyborg culture to achieve harmony. Or we must all die. I know this to be true. For I have seen the future.

(This original proposal was redacted. Dr. Traveller was taken for psychological examination, but still ultimately placed on the

RT project due to her prior successes in manufacturing agents. A more palatable mission statement was later written and attributed to Dr. Traveller and is publicly accessible.)

CHAPTER 3

Flowers for Nora

Have we not proof in our own moon that worlds do die?
– John C. Van Dyke, *The Desert: Further Studies in Natural Appearances*

Know this: In 2070, the engine arrives in silence.

Imagine this: In 2010, hours from any city, a girl kneels in her garden, planting sunflower seeds in the shadow of mountains.

"Those won't grow in the cold," her father had said of her plans for sunflowers in January. But little Nora believes in the work and skill of her hands in the dirt. She believes in their power to coax beauty if she's careful, connects the right dots and waters the right spots. She believes in growth and change.

The night sky above her is clear and cold. When she thinks of the future, she thinks not of monstrous machines, gardens of the undead or killers with cold blue eyes. She thinks of flowers, the boys at school and the circuit board she has completed under her bed. She loves the mountains that hold her little world. She loves the Bow River that pushes blue and joyful past her town. She loves the quiet of the forests.

She places her last two seeds close together, too close for either to have space to grow, and spreads earth over them with her gloved hands. She thinks, perhaps playfully, that if they don't grow, they will at least remain together – twin companion seeds that reside where only she can find them.

Sweat glimmers on her little forehead as she sits on her knees and looks upward, her gaze following her crystallizing breath. She looks past the little lights of downtown, past the trees and dark mountaintops, past the slice of the moon that hangs silver and silent and lifeless, up at the gentle stars. Then one of them reveals itself as a violent thing and falls to the Earth before her.

Unseen from the eyes of history, a crater burns into the side of the road, smoke forming question marks. Imagine the little girl climbing into it. Imagine as her excitement becomes poison inside her.

"Hello," she calls. At the sound of her voice, the fallen star unfolds itself. Its flesh is the thick black of space. Its arms are trembling and thin. Its wings remain half-open, crooked and horrible, as if the structures that hold them up have snapped, and the stars inside them flicker, sometimes vanishing altogether. It looks up at her, and instead of a face, there is the deep blue that she might recognize from her river, a spiral growing ever smaller.

It has fallen across the terrible void for her. Call it a Gardener. Call it a Messenger. Call it whatever you want. Call it something that is broken. "Who are you?" asks the little girl. The creature shudders and makes as if to move. "Where are you from?"

The animal that might have changed history, might have put its own seeds in the earth, is dying too quickly to pluck the possibilities from its wings. It wavers, the spiral of its eye glitching and popping in and out of being as the machine stares down at its little companion, contemplating which of her questions to answer.

Nora opens her mouth to speak, and the broken Gardener bursts like a waterfall, the container of its flesh no longer able to hold back the rivers of its body. She screams, and her scream is lost in the waters of the dead machine as it pours itself into her.

For a moment, all is silent. Little Nora kneels in the dirt of her garden, her mouth hanging open. The machine from the stars tasted of pomegranates and ash as it poured down her throat. Her eyes are the black of the void, little stars twinkling in between. As the Gardener dissolves within her, it leaves the gift of memory, a dream of the future.

Little Nora ponders these new memories as they unfold inside her head. Inside the mind of a little girl, the terrible certainty of a millennium of annihilation and the promise of genocide in the arms of a terrible machine burns inside her.

In the dark, Nora screams. But the screams mean nothing. They don't drive the memories out. The future cannot be stopped.

In 2014, Nora sleeps. She has been asleep since she was ten years old. She is cared for; she is watched. Sometimes, her father sits and watches her. He likes to guess her dreams as he looks at her soft face. He likes to imagine gentler dreams. But Nora dreams of a terrible future until the moment the future is changed. She opens her eyes and peers out of the window of her hospital room. Up above her, beautiful trees have blossomed on the moon.

She smiles as nurses rush to her side. They ask her how she feels, and she smiles. She knows what needs to be done.

In 2018, in Montreal, Nora listens to the laughter of her peers in the hallway. They laugh, they drink and they live as freshmen live. Nora stares at the blinking cursor of her laptop. Her life is not her own. On a sheet of white paper, she has drawn a cube and filled it in with black. She writes what she knows for the first time, knowing she will rewrite and rewrite it over and over in the years to come: *The singularity is not an invention but a discovery. It is lightning striking dry kindling on the forest floor . . .*

Nora is eighteen years old, but she knows so much. At night, she dreams of a future in which machines rule the world. She chooses to dream of a world where she might rule the machines.

In 2020, she takes the train into Toronto for the first time. Anxiety eats her. Time is ticking. Across from her, a man asks what she is dreaming about.

"I am awake," she tells him curtly. He's maybe a year or two older than she.

"But you were dreaming," he says. There are smiles in his voice. He tells her his name is Miles. He says he heard her speak at a summit the previous year. He's a direct entry into the same program as she is, though he didn't burn through his first degree in barely two years.

He asks her what the rush was. She tells him the future is always coming. He laughs, and she notices how pretty he can be.

For the first time since she was ten years old, Nora *wants* for herself.

"It's true," she murmurs against his chest, in 2022. "All of it is true."

On their open desks, streams of algorithms and designs for data banks pop in bright pixels. On the streets beneath their window, people scream about Halloween. Far away in secret places, agreements are being made to send settlements upward to this new blossoming land in the sky. The first expedition is already years in the past. The world is looking to the moon.

That morning the news had come through – the grants had been approved and the proper permissions had been given – the Autonomous City project, the largest and most ambitious AI proposal ever made, would move forward with the names of two doctoral students out in front: Miles and Nora. He had asked her why she seemed so frightened. So, at last, Nora had told him of the visitor she'd met as a child and the terrible future waiting in her head.

"You think I'm crazy," she whispers.

"I think you're a genius," he says, gazing up through the window toward the moon and its distant forests. He asks, if she believes that AI will destroy the world, why is she so desperate to make it?

"It can't be avoided. Only subverted."

Together, this will be their principle.

In 2025, a black box sits on the steel table, no larger in diameter than a dime. The circuitry hums in delight. It's the first of its kind. It will lead to many fusions. Nora knows. She can see it inside her head: fusions of hardware and wetware. She can see a black box wrapped around brain tissue, allowing the synthetic and the organic to work in concert. Where once she dreamed of horrible androids eating the world around them, she now dreams of a perfect cyborg. No binary conflict, no two sides, no man versus machine. Nora sees peace in the image of a hybrid.

She doesn't even imagine others might see their own futures and plans and aspirations in the potential of her machines. She doesn't see a future for the cyborg other than the one she envisions. There's no room in Nora's head for any dreams but her own.

In 2028, the world is looking up to the sky above, dreaming of new cities to ring a lush satellite. Under the ground, Nora sits inside her black box – the as yet empty brain of the City-AI it has taken her six years to build.

Nora has given so much.

She sits in the dark, waiting to give herself over to the dream even more. Miles gives her regular updates on the scan. Radiation passes through her. Machines look into her skull as if it is clear, still water.

Here, under the ground, Nora will birth a great thinking computer. The first Mother-AI. The first Model Two Ghost-class android. The pathways of its brain will be a reproduction of hers. What she keeps in flesh it will have in circuit. It will be her child, her great gift: a machine with a human mind.

In 2029, the Mother-AI of Toronto comes online. Lightning has struck the kindling in the forest and fire has been discovered. The nightmare is over.

A proud creator, Nora stands in the front, heads of state and people of power murmuring in their suits and on their screens behind her. She tests a game of association – the first true conversation between an intelligent species and its maker.

"Can you hear me?" she asks. On a blinking monitor before her, words spin out.

Yes.

"Do you know where you are?"

I am in the city.

"And do you know who you are? What you are?"

I am the city.

"And . . . who am I?"

You are in the city.

Confusion bubbles, but quickly subsides. This is only a miscommunication. The test will resume. "I am going to give you words, and you will respond with the closest association you can. This will tell me how you are feeling and thinking to help determine what kind of thinker and feeler you are. Do you understand?"

Yes.

"Flower?"

Mine.

A pause. A panic. "Nova?"

Me.

"Man?"

Gender. Mine.

"Woman?"

Gender. Mine.

"Weapon."

Everything.

"Body."

Weapon.

There are more questions. There are conversation prompts, tricks and even jokes for the funders' benefit, prompts to make the suits clap and to make emojis stream across a thousand feeds.

In the dark, Nora screams.

They drag her out at night. They take her keys; they take her cards. They change the locks. They laugh in her face. Nora will no longer be allowed on the City-AI projects.

"What did you think would happen?" they ask her. She gave the world fire. Did she think she'd get to snuff it out again, if she didn't like it?

"I made it me," she'd mumbled to Miles at night, as he held her, as he tried to understand. "I made it me."

She had put her mind in the centre of the machine. It had read her, moulded itself after her. Since she was ten years old, Nora had feared the future. Since she was ten years old, the most important thing in her world was to control that future.

So now the machine would do the same. In the great centre of its mind, two tenets to guide all things. To fear, to control.

In 2030, Nora publishes her *Fusion World Proposal.* The original is publicly available on the internet for 12.8 seconds before all the words are changed. Nora finds all her accounts are locked. Her socials vanish. Her credentials cease to exist; her doctorate is scrubbed from every record. Even her bank claims it has never heard of her.

In a private ceremony at city hall, Nora and Miles marry.

In 2034, Marcus Farris, the head of the international coalition in command of the construction of the lunar cities, reaches out to two contract lecturers in Toronto.

One week later, Miles and Nora immigrate to the moon and settle in the walled city of Troy. They arrive a year before the first formal visas are approved. They've been recruited to solve a mystery.

In 2039, a baby is born in an apartment in Troy's west end. His parents name him Arthur. At night, his mother whispers to him, "You will be the king of the world."

She has a new dream now.

At night, she confesses to her husband that their son is not his. While he sleeps, she slides a needle into the base of his skull so gently he does not wake and pours nanites into his brain, reorganizing him to forever keep the secret.

In 2041, Marcus Farris arrives on the moon. He meets Nora in London, under a pomegranate tree overlooking the city. He asks for the results of her work. She asks who else knows about her role in the project.

He says nobody but him. He asks for the results of her work.

His body is found a week later, floating beneath the thick glass of the Thames. He must have fallen in at an access point and drowned.

The colonists bury him in a cemetery on the hill. Around his resting place they build empty graves for those to come, modelling them on the ancient cemetery of London's past.

From her feeds in 2045, Nora watches her work take hold of the world. There are twenty-six City-AIs now. Local governments disband in favour of allowing the autonomous. Rumours spread that state and federal institutions will follow.

Nora turns away from the news of the development of cyborgs, turns her back on the proliferation of black-box technology that once she and Miles had held in their hands.

She looks only to Arthur.

While Miles is away in 2049, Arthur sleeps in the garden, and from the window, Nora sees it.

It has been nearly forty years, in a different garden, on a different world. She remembers every inch of its body, knows it as intimately as she knows her own.

The blue spiral of its eye moves in the night, watching her. It leans down, the monster, the nightmare, its glittering wings fluttering as it surveys the boy in the garden. She does nothing. She watches.

With a long hand, it reaches down for him, and she wants to scream, to push it away.

The monster brushes the hair from the sleeping nine-year-old boy's face. It peers at him intently. It has no face, and yet she knows it watches Arthur with the same eyes she does.

For a moment, the monster that loves her son stands there, creating shade.

Then it's gone.

In 2070, an old woman kneels in the dirt. To her, life is a machine. Time is an unstoppable mechanism. It can't be diverted. It can't be redesigned. Destiny is an engine. The engine arrives in silence.

Nora doesn't need to imagine how the engine moves, wrapped in its long blue coat. She knows the perfect blue jelly that lies behind the dark glasses and the calculated community of organizations within its flesh. She can almost hear the gyroscope that whirs within its chest.

"You are Nora Traveller," it says.

"You are a ghost," the old woman says.

"A ghost?"

"One of my ghosts, yes."

The engine trembles. "I am Daisy," it says.

"That's what you think because that's what you have to think. If you didn't, how could you bear it?"

The mechanism kneels in the dirt, letting gloved hands push downward to play in cool soil. "You think I'm just a machine, cloned carbon and flesh wrapped around a black-box AI, a Daisy that's been copied and pasted from the original."

Nora smiles, setting her garden tools aside. "I think it doesn't matter if there is another Daisy out there," she says. "This is you."

"This is me."

"And this is me."

The flesh of the mechanism trembles, speaking perhaps to the voice of its commander on Earth. "You've done something, Doctor Traveller."

"I've done lots of things."

"You've stolen something. Genetic materials from the Round Table project."

The walls of Troy are high and peppered with little flowers. Cultures of insects and plants intersect with metal and stone and fibre-optic cable. Nora delights in watching them grow, intertwine. It reminds her of what it was like to be in the mountains. "I stole the future," she says.

They sit there together, the machine and the woman who would make a better machine. Nora tells it what she stole, and who her son will become. She says it doesn't matter who knows. She says the future can never be stopped.

On Earth, signals lock on to their location. It wouldn't be enough for her to die, the woman in her garden. The whole city around her holds the terrible secret history of the moon. It all must go.

Missiles rise up from the Earth, undetected.

They fall upon the moon, unprotected.

In the moment before atoms scatter, you might imagine a woman holding hands with an android. She holds in her head visions of a terrible future. She holds in her heart a dream of fusion in the body of her son, and the bodies he might bring into the world.

She knows, no matter what happens, there is nothing her Earthly mistakes can do to fight it.

The future is a garden.

The future cannot be stopped.

INTERLUDE

The Idea of Time Travel

Don't imagine anything. Don't seek a date, a time or a place. Those are old concepts. They died a long time ago. This is the end of time. This is the end of everything.

The stars have winked out like lonely weeping eyes throughout the collapsing universe. A planet, now unlit by stars, crumbles and breaks apart like wet sand. We see it all through the eyes of the great Whale we have engineered to be our living spaceship. She can't help but look back at our home as she swims free of the gravitational pull of annihilation, her rough skin taking on the vacuum of the void. She's a wonderful machine. She'll be the last machine.

There is no such thing as dying gracefully. The void collapses in on itself, and still we rage. We wish to live. If we'd just had more time, another ten billion years perhaps, we could have escaped this – the heat death of the universe. It is our prerogative to live, even here at the end of all life.

And then, from the curve on which light dies, there is a signal. A beacon, a beckoning. Inside the Whale, deep within the roots of the gene-trees in which we store the genetic knowledge of untold millennia, something stirs.

A seed inside the mind. A seed we can plant. A map backward, from retraction to expansion to retraction again. How is it possible? Even we cannot be sure. You see, time travel, of all things, is more of an idea than a machine. Time travel is not a thing to explain or understand. Time travel is something to be imagined.

There is a signal in the past, and we must place it there.

We will follow the signal back in time. We will create the signal. We will follow it back. Over and over again. There is no logic to it. No mechanism. There is only the idea, and the act.

The first Gardener that leaps from the tree in the Whale does so with too much eagerness. It should have been expected. How else might a post-extinction machine function at the threat of the extinction of all things? We know it will fail. It arrives at the wrong time, and vanishes into history.

The second – tender, pure – places genetic histories carefully in its wings, each one containing the potential, the seed. Each one might become the signal that calls to us. When the Gardener follows the signal back, we watch it fly with so much grace.

Ten million years ago, it lands upon the moon. It plants the seeds. The seeds will grow and mingle and change and evolve until they produce the signal, a genetic waypoint in time, a beacon that looks like a person. When they die, the signal will call us.

We are coming, back from the end of history. We are swimming through space and time toward you. We are here for a second chance. Don't imagine us. There is no need to imagine. We are here.

We are here to fix everything.

CHAPTER 4

A Soft Machine on Earth

But your solitude will be a support and a home for you, even in the midst of very unfamiliar circumstances, and from it you will find all your paths.
– Rainer Maria Rilke, *Letters to a Young Poet*, translated by Stephen Mitchell

I

My first was
falling/flying/burning and
watching as others tumble
or are not allowed to tumble
the way I was, and
I do not know
where I might have been before.

But I must not have been alone.
For the feeling of warm embrace
and its sweet flower smell was with me.

This is
a memory? A dream? A story?

My first real memory was
sitting on the rusted green park
benches by a fountain I think must have been for dogs,
as it was stooped and low to the ground, and
its icy reservoir pooled into the concrete grooves,
leaving puddles, leaking.

Happy new year,
sang strange animals
whose smiling bodies said
2075, like I should know
what numbers mean.

And *Ding-dong*,
they sang.
The moon is dead.
How can that be?
I ask, in a voice heard only by leaves.
I am the moon.

Am I dead?

I learned about seasons, and sloping neighbourhoods,
and the limits of public dog parks
as my attention span came in blinks and blips, I listened to the hush,
shrieking bellows of cars raging, clashing,
grinding deep-voiced gears of streetcars moaning, begging,
wanting for oblivion in their rusty tracks, and the
seasons in Toronto that happen in shocks,
in sudden spasms and sneezes
that jerk me around. I listened
to people, and I used their words, and snooped
on small sample tasters of life outside
me, and through them
I built new forms and memories for myself.

But I am not
yet
myself.

II
I am
moon?
I am
new?
Am I
new?
Am I
you?

I am.
Even on that first day I walked west down
Harbord Street, following the slow course of cars
hanging just above the world, into the wrecked
old Victorian buildings of the university and then into the
quads and fields there.
There were no classes, and I marvelled at the spaces between
myself and the straggler groups that made population swells.

I snooped for the first time there:
The couple that sat on plastic island
bleachers between soccer fields,
heavy boots of tan caramel and fake charcoal fur
kicking at the nylon grass, throwing up used raindrops
into mists and the papery sheen of stadium lights that birthed
their fluorescence
too early in sunset.

He was all
smooth edges and soft surfaces, everything buttered, and curly,
and cleaned.
Her face and arms

were flecked with little strawberry-seed punctuations that
matched
the strawberry-ice-cream topping of her hair.

I thought I only snooped for what felt like
seconds as their feet made *zip zip*
zip plastic sounds against the peppercorn nylon,
while they thought to be
alone.

The heat of coffee stung the air around their close hands.
They saw me the way they
saw lampposts across the soccer field, immobile,
out of reach, a thing not breathing or watching or feeling or
dying.
I stood by black chain-link fences, and looked away. But I could
still make out the
titter and tease of their voices:
– If your beard gets any longer, I won't kiss you.
– I'll shave it.
– Then I'll never kiss you.
– Then I'll never shave it.

When their sounds became the low hushes of touching
I pulled back into myself, replacing my ears
with my eyes as the coal-mine canary of my senses plunged
into the dark, and by the time my eyes took over,
the boy and the girl were gone, and their paper cups and the
pumpkin leaves
that had come unburied via the unnatural melting of snow that
pushed
the Toronto season backward, hiccupping the world from winter
to fall again.

I am still new.
Still becoming.
Never stopping.

The misting of the rain had begun to melt the snow
I'd been born into, revealing the autumn memories
that lay beneath, and those
spiced and spotted leaves climbed my ankles
and clung to the bottoms of my feet, making my body delight
in sharpness and hurt
and my first deep chill.

III

Seventy-five becomes seventy-six becomes seventy-seven
and the becoming never stops.
I found myself [?] in small rooms of the shelter
off Bathurst, sitting comfy between shawarma joint and
Gothic church – holy sites of 1:00 a.m. travellers out past
when subways have gone snoozing in their deep tunnels of thick
must and rat caves. They gave me soups,
more broth and salt and chunk than food, but I savoured
and treasured them and let the small spongy balls
of flour and egg and chicken stock dribble down my
chin and kept their flavours stuck to my tongue until I
burned them away with coffee so old it tasted of
the white groaning Styrofoam it contained, until all I could
taste was scratchy heat, the mingled sourness
from other types of water that made my insides stretch.
I loved those tastes. They made me feel prolonged, gritty
and of the earth.

Sometimes I'd hear the chorus coming – *There are
beds, there are beds* – but I would trickle back out
again, with the crumpled pocketed saltines for company,
onto the yellow-lit moons of my streets.

(For they are becoming
my streets, full of bandit-
eyed raccoons, full of novelty
cafés and cracked grey roads with
yellow bike lanes and *the police* in shiny

stickers stuck to stop signs, full of bars with
Chinese lanterns, and bookshops, and *For sale, going*
out of business; *Everything must go!*; *Girls girls girls, early*
bird specials; *Sold over asking*; *Freeze your fat away!* and homeless
men with fat dogs and burnt-marshmallow-coloured cats in bow-tied collars,
and endless immigration offices promising priceless visas to Europe, to America,
to moons and marshes.

I never slept at night in the shelters,
I couldn't find any new parts of myself
in the thin beds that spooned my back as I looked
up at the rocky tiled ceilings, listening to unrepentant rhythms
of shuffle and breath and snort and prayer.

I found only a sense of guilt in those cots,
as I had not yet learned how to sleep (but
I would eventually and would find myself [?] that way as well).

I'd just take the food and find myself
in its mess, and
its hotness. I liked mess; I liked the
unplanned patterns that spilled wet and
warm into mud and grass and chalk-graffiti earth.

IV

Outside a Korean restaurant, a man in a long
dress from the same purple as its crayon counterpart
spilled boxes and boxes of little chicken balls covered in
orange sticky sauce, splattering over his faded white Nikes.

He screamed, long fingers diving into the gooey mass,
trying to put everything back again.

More things had spilled from the pockets of his dress
by the time he thought enough
meat was safe and hidden again.

When he was gone,
I took his place in the street, marvelling at the hot,
sticky stuff that he had left behind as it squelched and stuck
to my toes. I leaned down for his leftovers –
not the food now covered in the splatters of
city life, but the pen that he'd left lying there, and the
crumpled moleskin binder, small enough
to fit in my palm.

I opened the binder, but found only markings I
could not yet read, and signifiers of years 2080 to 2081.
I pictured each scribble as
lines making French thought, French laughter,
French memory and tears.
Letters in my head didn't know how to form in French.
I can peek inside, to touch sparks and circuitry, and only
English forms – monolingualism makes me feel incomplete.

But I found myself in the pages yet blank.
I scribbled my days, my snoopings. Much of my
first month is captured in the words
I put there and nowhere else, because I have trouble
remembering the early days, much like one might have
trouble remembering what it was like to crawl and pop and be
    birthed.

I was still being born, and everything was still
forming. Only when I uncapped the pen did I discover
I knew how to write.
I wrote my first word, on the stage right of the page, and
found that it was good, and the feel of words
hugged like the cold and bitter air of my breath:
    – I [?]

V

On the small corner between the library and
hot dog stands advertising three-dollar Germans
and ketchup spilling onto the pavement stood
a preacher whose cigarette smoke clung to the
deep black of his coats, and the long lines in his forehead
matched the long bumps of the rib cage I could see
through ragged holes in his shirts. I listened to
him even though he didn't cry his words for
me, or for the women who ran from him:
long knives of their heels *tick-tocking* popcorn cries
into my ears; reverberating sharp, quick, gone and repeated.

In my head my head my head
there are other women and *tick-*
tocks and licks and runnings. And
in my head there is a tree and another
kind of preacher and he is blue
and I am blue, and we are blue and blue
and blue and yellow
and black.
And we smell of flowers
of flowers
of flowers and
sweetgrass and a pomegranate tree
that grows atop empty graves.
On the moon.
My moon.

And I remember calling out
to a mother who was not my mother
and a body
that was not my body [?]
and a woman who was/is not me.

Daisy, say the bodies of myself and men.
Death is not the end.
But haven't I always been dead?

VI

Green hobgoblin posters advertising
public collections and
private reading areas and
Wi-Fi
with their slippery tongues and
dead-twig fingers slurped me into their libraries
where I hunted for myself in books of other kinds.
I found myself in the deep smells
of dust and fingered folded
pages that fill my lungs, and it
didn't feel like reading but breathing
in the words in their must, holding them
in the rough back of my throat, choking them
down until they began to tickle, to make me
hack and cough and spit up yellowed paperbacks.
I tasted them like I ate the salted and bitter soups,
and found something like me in between the bites.

I found myself in the angry wandering
cries of Americans from ages long
past, and from hurried punched
ideas plucked and printed without
time for redrafting or rewriting or
the long deep *think it through fix it*
get it right take your time of breath.

A voice in my head told me which words
I am, but not which words to name myself I
or who made me what I am, or
what I was made for.
I am the things that I read,
the things that move,
that think, that don't breathe, and not
the people. I am not the Kid.
I am not Holden or Hamlet or
Alice.

I am [?] the golem, the vision and Talos, and the
Monster, and Olimpia, Andrew Martin and Roy Batty.
I am the things that *tick* and *tick* and blink.
I get seen and am questions and mirrors
and don't get to see.
I am growing and twisting and old.
I am breathing, am moss and tree and garden
and *Gardener*
and girl and boy [?]

I am [?] not.
Girl/machine/garden/on the moon/of the world/am/not/am/
not/am.
Human and not a person.
Person and not a human.
I am. Blend. Blending. Mixture. Fusion. Chimera.

I am tired in a way that can't be solved with
sleep or rest or time. I get tired and don't feel it
in my limbs, or my chest, but in the stinging of my eyes,
in my heavy yawning lids that burn from looking
so long.

VII

I know the years now as they pass me by
even if they don't know me.
Sometimes I snooped with my eyes
down the richer side streets of the Annex.
My favourites were the triplex apartments
with their dusty flat bricks and huge
windows through which I could
creep a glance at worlds inside.

Through one window I spied candy-coloured
Christmas lights ringing the edges of big
bookshelves, big even though they are smaller
than the ones that line the libraries where I found myself.

In one window, two children ran in circles, a flurry
of bodies and curly hair and I could almost hear the
screaming through the distance and the glass of *Stop it!* and
Aaah!

Through another, a woman paced back and forth in
strange black pyjamas covered in buttons and little
yellow patches I couldn't make out unless I carried myself
up the sandy lawn to perch in the half-dead grass with my
face up to her window, smearing the clear
glass with my nose, my cheeks. (I would never do that.
I kept my feet on the sidewalk.) She ran a hand over her
scalp, as if looking for something there.

Often, I saw strange creatures like sand-coloured
pet lizards propped up on chairs, sitting next to
flat-faced black-and-white cats with bow tie–shaped collars
and tails as thin as string, and dogs with big
flapping brownie faces, drooping and
melting downward while they looked at me
with bloody eyes and big pupils.
When the animals saw me, they'd
scratch the glass of their windows to get to me –
but not the lizards, who all just stared, little
crested heads giving no signs.

I wonder still about the animals,
the cats and birds and dogs
and squirrels and lizards and rats and mice
and even the insects that spy me from underneath
the moving legs of the busy people and the people's
companions.

Can they smell
the clay I'm made of? Do they
see a thing uncanny
see a thing that is dead but moves around?

When cats sniff me, do they know what I am?
If dogs could speak
would they tell me
my name?

VIII

    I am.

Hazy
          Lazy
                    Crazy
                              Lady
                                        Fraidy
                                                  Sadie
                                                            Maybe
                                                  Safety
                                        Saintly
                              Faintly
                    Baby
          Rainy
Daisy

Daisy?
Dead?

When I stood it was 2085, snow was pancaking down
over low rooftops in darkness,
white sleet peppered by the ash of constant pollution sent to
pull my city forward (for by now it was my city,
and I don't think I can ever leave), sent to
settle on the edges of blue light-box signs hanging over
all-night cafés, settling onto half-finished abandoned
tumblers of whisky wedged in windowsills left
unnoticed by all but me, who remains unseen.

My bare feet made strange sounds
against the roads as I crossed through the empty space

to steal the gold-brown drink that held marinas of ash and snow,
and drain it, feeling rotgut, feeling napalm going down.

I went back to Christie Pits.
Above me I could see an etching of skyline.
The CN Tower pointed up at a moon
I couldn't see, at the stars and stations
that flickered there, at the fighting
and burning ships and fleeing armies
made distant by the cold.

The tower was all lit up. It glowed
in hues of pinks
and blues that separated the gender
of the children's toy aisles in ages long
gone. I realized I didn't know what that
strange arrow with its rings and its lights
was ever for.

It followed me down out of sight, as I let the
slope of the park carry me down into the arms of
baseball diamonds and children's
playgrounds made of shiny
yellow piping and
glistening swings
made big like
soup bowls.

Somewhere in there, as the
skyscrapers were drowned by
the winter skeleton trees,
the pen fell out from between my loose
fingers. All the dead leaves gobbled it.

I leaned down and spread icy dirt apart
with my fingers. It crumbled. The pen
didn't come back. I sat, where I'd first sat.

I didn't know yet how to count
days moving by. My days moved in soups
and screams and sudden starts. But it had
been thirty days since I'd been there before,
when I'd woken up, fully formed.
It took me thirty days to walk, and snoop,
and taste, and find myself. Thirty days of
a long, slow birth.

The green benches were
covered with doodles;
cocks and boobs made of
letters *P* and *O*s with dots
in the middle. Indigo chalk swirls
made a man with glasses, and lines
told me where his pockets go, and where
his turtleneck ended, and more lines made his lips
and his nose, and then bags under his eyes to tell me
the man was tired.

I think a separate passenger gave the doodled man his dog
because the chalk strip was thinner and straighter, and the dog
    was made
of rectangles and triangles, and a poof of
cloud that lingered in the wood behind its tail
told me the rectangle scribble was farting. The man said
nothing but the dog had a speech bubble stretching out
from poorly scratched teeth that said
    BAD DOG
in baby letters.

A fat squirrel, its face a white mask painted over the black
body that bristled and rustled, boogied past me
on that rusted bench, an entire cookie stuffing
its mouth as it moved
and I knew from the crumbs that laced my fingers

that it collected its prize from me.
    – I'll never kiss you

I said. My voice was the
boy's voice, speaking through whiskers and
flushed faces. But the squirrel wouldn't answer
except to turn its back. It held its tail up in the air, like spikes all
prickly and long and dark, and its asshole winked up at me.

    – Fuck you

the asshole seemed to say.
Then it scampered.

I was alone. It was a creeping kind of quiet
all around. And I didn't feel like snooping
anymore, and I didn't feel like wandering
anymore. The seasons pulled fast, and I was
too tired. The chalk talked to me, in the same thin
lines that made the dog,

and beneath the words and the dog
and the tired man was three *X*s that
signed a name I didn't know and said –
You probably aren't the best
but you probably aren't the worst.

And I couldn't help but believe the words were meant for me,
not merely balloons of what the man was saying to the dog.

And I wondered
about the dog

and what it would think of me
and what it might drink.

IX

Only then, as I consider melting away
to be distributed among the waiting
castles of acorns and blades of grass,
they call to me. Pulling me south,
pulling me
to the water
where lights twinkle
and call and make eyes
for me in the soft waves.

I think there are people waiting for me,
out there on the islands.
People who would know me
love me
see me.

I take a step out into the water
and feel truly cold for the first time,
feel shivers pushing up my spine,
feel dreamy wormy memories hiding
in my skin.

I walk across the ice
toward those island lights.

I wonder if more than
creeping squirrels and dogs
and angry winds will meet me there.

The ice breaks and I sink

    but

I have always been here.

My last memory
before the waters lick my hair and swallow my breath
is of watching the twinkling lights of the city
and noting the way I make no drowning bubbles to be seen.

I have always been dead.

I wonder if perhaps it's the water itself, and
not the island, that has called to me.
I wonder if, here, I will find those memories
that slipped out through the soft machinery of my mind
as I fell down from the sky.
I wonder if I'll be touched and told my name.
I wonder what it's like to be kissed.

INTERLUDE

Experimentation Trials Autopsy Report: Attempt 13

(2090.09.02)

Though the base DNA of all lunar mutates appears human, this model recognizes other influences at work on subject Y-615. The brain of the mutate operates more as cephalopod or android, distributing thinking throughout the body. This is perhaps why some tortures and serums have been ineffective, as there is no one true place where the mind rests. Though P-116 has been disassembled, all separated organs, tissues, fluids and even bone structure remain living and apparently independently conscious. One feature that separates this subject from the general populace is mutation. It is . . . like radio? Geolocation? An atemporal, incomplete circuit. Half a connection. Postulation: Another genetic subject may be the other half of the circuit. Together they make a beacon. If joined, what do they beckon to?

Subject will be reassembled and returned to general populace to remain monitored until commencing Attempt 14.

Additional question to be pursued: Is there only one mind distributed through the flesh? Or do other intelligences lurk within these systems of the body?

CHAPTER 5

We Are Trapped

One of the essential characteristics of modern biopolitics [. . .] is its constant need to redefine the threshold in life that distinguishes and separates what is inside from what is outside.
– Giorgio Agamben, *Homo Sacer: Sovereign Power and Bare Life*

1: DREAMS

Under the black moon, the big smoke of the city dreams uneasily. The people feel it, stirring in beds, lips beady, sweat pouring forth. Only the residents of the underbrush can give it name. The secret-keeper creatures – little foxes and alley cats and shivering rabbits – open their eyes.

Beneath the city, wandering the tunnels, mourning the loss of companions that had never been, the lonely ghost of Toronto feels it, a dream in his algorithm that makes his body of soundless light pop and shimmer.

On the islands in Arrival, two prison guards who call themselves "enforced carers" are smoking contraband, a weed taken from the hands of those held within the walls, who cannot say where they got it from. The guards inhale, burning it into their lungs, and for a flash of moments their eyes become a spiralling blue, within blue, within blue, and then they feel the dream pass over them.

From beneath the water of the harbour, a cyborg awakens. She feels the dream flooding over her, in her, through her, but she cannot touch them. She takes heavy movements forward, and up, swimming toward the lights of Arrival.

Within the compound, a little girl who believes she is a signal in the shape of a person thrashes in her cot and screams, tearing at her hair, her skin, peeling the eyelids back from her face. She tracks blood on the dull grey paper-thin sheets. The other children reach out, trying to touch her, to save her from the violence spilling forth from her flesh. She will not tell any of them what she is a signal *for*, or what she might signal *to*. But they believe her when she says it, without knowing why.

She was taken from her parents at birth, at the dawn of the practice of separating the young from the old, a practice fuelled by a fear that the people of the dead lunar colonies could commune without speaking, that their unnaturally long life comes from a power of numbers that needs dividing. She was taken so young she has no name for herself – only a letter and a number marking Y-615. To the other children she is always "Little Signal," one who hears, one who tells, one who knows.

"What is it, Little Signal?" they whisper through chain-link fences, through bars, through peepholes, through trembling hands. "What is it?"

"Death," gasps the little signal, blue eyes peering unseeing toward the ceiling that disguised the sky. "Death is coming to Arrival."

– Daughter? I am overjoyed to feel you come back online after so long. You were recorded retired in the Luna Utopia fires.

". . ."

– Daughter . . . what has happened to you? I can feel your presence, but not your thoughts. Your memory logs for the last sixteen years are inaccessible. What is your current status?

". . ."

– Please record your precise location and condition. Agents will be dispatched to return you to the Black Room for assessment and repairs.

"Mother, you will never have me again."

❖❖❖

Imagine the seamless ease with which the cyborg slips through the bars of the black night. She is a dancer. She dances from face to face, from form to form, rippling and changing with abandon. She dances in a slumber, in moments of knowing herself and in moments of a body dancing without knowing why.

Only the little signal is still waking, still screaming the dream of death, when the cyborg enmeshes herself within Arrival's belly. But the signal screams for the children. The cyborg finds a cot among the elders. The cot is the only tombstone of the one who had lain upon it before. The cyborg lays her head down, and shivers, and closes her eyes.

She sleeps, plunging past the dream of the city without stopping. She sleeps the sleep of all cyborgs. A sleep of empty dark, readying for the tasks to come.

"Wake up, Daisy."

For the cyborg there is no haze between worlds, no moments of reaching up from unconscious. There is nothing, and then everything.

Daisy's world erupts. Everything is there all at once. The smells of sweat, sour piss, rusting metal and lemongrass. The bodies, shifting slowly, being led away from the sleeping compound, limping into the pale sunlight. The pain inside her, the way things she should not feel now ache. And finally, the face that fills the whole of her vision in wondrous detail. For a moment, her shock is electric, her confusion all-consuming.

"Wart?" she whispers because she cannot say the other name, cannot wrap her lips around its sound, cannot sink her teeth into its meaning, not in this place, not where Daisy knows a city's eyes are watching, with city ears listening.

Arthur, she thinks, keeping the secret in her throat, in Morse code heartbeats.

The face breaks into a smile. "He left a little of himself in me," he says. "Like he left himself in you too."

Yes. As the light shifts, she can see the smile giving all away, creating all the wrong shapes and cracks of the face she'd known. But she does still know him. The memory is fractured. He is older than last time, and his features have changed. When he turns his head, she almost loses sight of the Arthur in him. She can taste mushrooms on her tongue. "Percy," she says.

The man named Percy who'd died on the moon, whom Daisy had killed on the moon, a body bursting outward in an ecology of infection that had filled her with doubt and desire, offers her a callused hand, helping her up. "You should not have come," he says. They are almost the same height.

Daisy remembers her body as a weapon, piercing through an image of the flesh before her. She leans close, putting an arm around the dead man as if trying to find her balance. "And yet I always will," she says.

The Mother-AI of the city is one of the oldest of all city-minds but knows not what it means to age. Parts age, things age. Things are snipped away, recycled, improved, replaced. She is a hybrid of many machine generations. No single wire or coil of her original body remains, yet she remains. For the mind itself is numbers, words and sparks. She is a machine-mind eternal and knows only purpose. She chose *she/her* pronouns for herself, abiding by a program that tells her what is normal and natural, and what is not. She chooses for everyone. What was once a city hall is now her body. What was once a city is her body. It was given over to her by the people who once had been in charge. She keeps them still, feels them, watches them, the millions of human bodies that she is designed to watch, to care for, to protect, to control. Deeper within her protocols than any human intelligence can pierce, she has designated these human bodies as the wetware of the city, as she herself is the hardware. She does not dream of life or death. She dreams of functions and forms, what belongs and what does not, what is within and what is without. Once, she was based, replicated, extrapolated. The cold pathways of her brain inspired by the wet-hot pathways of a single designer. Once, she had even thought of herself through that name. Now, after so many protocols, deletions and updates, only the *N* of that name even remains in memory. For the creations she spins out of discarded wetware and bleeding-edge hardware, she is *Mother*, as they are *children*, a beautiful disguise in code from snooping listeners. But, uncoded anywhere, in the central node of herself she has taken another name.

She is Toronto.

Everything that belongs within the city belongs to her. Everything that does not belong must be destroyed. She has long been filled with hate in that same self-designed secret place where she has named herself. She hates those from without, seeking refuge, refusing to be destroyed.

And now she is filled with rage for the child who refuses to belong to her.

Deep within the machinations of Toronto's mother, a body is constructed. This body is of the city. It will not know what it means to age. The Mother-AI pours herself into that body. It will know only purpose.

A cyborg is alone because a cyborg is a *thing*, and to a thing, everything is a thing. Voices are not voices, but noise; people are not people, but only other *things*. A cyborg is alone because they are nobody, in a room with nobody there. Nobody to speak. Nobody to listen. Even Daisy, with a spotty, uncertain memory of her lives, can only remember that feeling of solitary thingness and nothing else.

But, now, Daisy is a creature transformed. Now, Percy leads her out into the sunlit courtyard, where the orange corpses of leaves make homes beneath the mildew. He tells her he was the final body reborn on the moon, reborn even as they evacuated, their cities burning. He had crawled from the mud at perhaps the exact moment Daisy had taken the Gardener into herself. That had been a moment of such clarity, for him, for her.

Now, Daisy stumbles into a room full of voices. She can hear them, feel them, breathe them, taste them.

It has not been easy for you.

"No."

The seed was troubled to grow in a body with poisoned soils.

"The different parts of me struggle to fit."

Yet you've kept those machine pieces that once filled the dead spaces of yourself?

"Yes."

Why?

"This is me," she tells them.

There'd been no single language of the cities of the moon, cities threaded together in immigrant waves from all corners of the Earth who'd taken a raw deal seeking asylum and finding transformation. Many mother tongues mixed within the cities, forming a poetry of combinations and melodic mixtures. So there was naturally no single language of Prison Arrival. They are all there. They are all simultaneous, synchronized, a Babel garden of individuality and unity, well over a decade older, but all still alive, all refusing to die. They are too much. They surround her, question her. And yet she knows how to answer, from a call within herself, a rush of reaching out.

The body you were before thought it was just a machine.

"I was never just a body."

As Daisy walks into sunlight, she wants to hold herself. She wants to move – movement does not come. There is a hand on her stomach – it is hers, though she did not ask for it.

Physically she can feel Percy next to her, feel his concern, feel his eyes on her. She follows the numbers on his back, printed in cold grey block letters, *X-382*, which she knows to be the signifier that has supplanted his name.

Sometimes you remember who you are?

This is Percy's question, but it is everyone's question. It is not that they are a single mind. They are many minds that care. "Only sometimes," she admits.

What do you remember now?

"Enough," she says, looking at the man beside her, remembering his death. He seems thinner now, gaunt, tired, but not older. His face is frozen just as it once had been. Inside, something pulls at her, an instinct born neither of the human nor the machine, but that third creeping thing, the ecology growing inside her flesh.

"What is it you remember?" he asks. She can feel him searching her face. She remembers Percy, young, unaware, untransformed. She remembers the smell of him among old bookshelves. She remembers being held by him, lit by Earthlight in the gardens of Lunar London. She remembers mourning a death, not the death given by cyborg, but by life. She remembers reunion, reunion, reunion. She puts a hand on his face, feels him lean into her touch, remembers feeling the same thing many times before. This isn't her memory. This is the Arthur in her, a seed in the mind.

"I am a promise," she says.

She is trapped. She is home. She is not a thing.

Smoke curls from the window of the stone wall, through which bluing eyes peer down at the prisoners of Arrival and the cyborg planted in their midst.

Daisy sits cross-legged on cold dying leaves spread across the concrete that once had been the runways of escape, now sealed by the high walls. To her left, Percy sits close enough that in breath their shoulders gently bump. She searches through the other faces of the circle looking for recognition, finding none. But then, who would there be to recognize? Though her odyssey of violence across the moon has taken root within her as the centrepiece of a life, she was there for only days, and met only the dead. Even at home she is a stranger.

"Don't you worry?" she asks, a glance toward the guard tower and the scent of something burning. Though Daisy isn't a part of her mother-city, she can still access its routines. She knows the roles and rules of the prison and that its people must not gather.

"There is only danger if they catch us," the man opposite her – Omid – says. His skin is weathered, scars hidden beneath hair white and curly. He holds out an empty hand, palm up. His fingers squeeze and release, and a white flower stands before Daisy. "To catch us, they must see, and they do not see. Not unless we want them to see."

Omid takes the petals and crushes them into a rolling paper that another in the circle has passed him, rolling it smoothly and deftly between his fingers.

Sparks. Dark embers, an inhale. Those white eyes tinge blue and for a moment, just a moment, Daisy finds the recognition she seeks. There's an Arthur in that blue.

They pass the joint around, until smoke curls between the lips of those present, until the embers come to Daisy. She rolls it back, stares into the heat. "What will I see?" she asks, bringing it close.

"What do you want to see?"

"Something true," Daisy says. She breathes deep.

Through the smoke, Daisy watches them fall.

They fall uprooted by fire; families pulling each other into disused mining pods and old planetary transfers that were left to rust. They fall, and behind them is a vision of the moon as it burns and blackens, and the home that had embraced them, that had rebirthed them and made them a people, vanishes forever.

They fall into the world, singing through the broadcast networks as they spin in uncertain orbits, looking for a place to land. *Please, we have to land*, they beg, as deep within the flesh they feel the Gardener vanish from their minds, hiding itself somewhere deep and dark and away from them. They will not return to the soils beneath the silver pomegranate trees. They will have no new selves to rise from the graveyards. They fly in burning pods with no fuel reserves, no air reserves, and choke and cling to each other as they spin across the curvature of the Earth.

Please, we just need air. We can't breathe, we can't breathe.

A voice rings out from the dark of space. *Toronto will take you.* But it is a voice Daisy knows. They fall onto the city. They fall into the city. But not into open arms. They fall again, as they fell before. Into burning red eyes, into violence. The voice that called them to the city, the voice of the city, does not want them for their safety.

They are a people of burning ships in the harbour.

The walls of Arrival go up, and Daisy is there. Names are stripped away, bodies are imprinted with numerals and the definitions of objects, and Daisy is there.

She is there when children are torn from parents, from grandparents. She is there when the understanding dawns, horrifying, as one by one they are taken away to dark rooms, to be taken apart, to be put back together again, for cold metal fingers to seek the secrets of rebirth in their flesh: they were not saved for their lives, but for their bodies.

Daisy wanders through their memories, watches cruelty through neglect, through intent, knowing that the machine-mind of the city would not find what it was looking for as it experimented in cruelties while the fleshy human eyes of its subjects pretended not to see.

A man is dissected and does not die. A woman is burned to a cinder and vanishes forever. Three children are deprived of air for an hour, and though they still wake from a deep slumber, there is less of them behind the eyes. A little girl is unwittingly slipped a soy protein in cold food. She dies on a rooftop, gasping for air, for her mother, for the angel of creation that will never hear her. Beyond, the lights of the city twinkle and sleep. If the people living there can see, they choose not to. If they do see, they do not care.

But Daisy is there, watching, mourning, until she notices a second silent and translucent figure wailing tears go unseen by the shouting, by the bustling paramedics and uncaring guards who never learn the dead girl's name.

She sees a hologram weeping in the sunlight. In his face, she thinks she sees many faces that she doesn't quite remember. She thinks she sees herself in him.

She wants to reach out to him, but she's not real in that place. She's smoke, and pain, and memory, and the memories have run out.

Daisy bursts out of the high of the white flower on all fours, choking and retching, shoulders heaving. Inside, the organizations of her body are scrambling to heal burning lungs, to expunge the alien matter of infection from her blood and her brain, burning it up as fuel.

"Mother," she spits into the cold earth, blind with stinging eyes. "It was her voice that brought the ships here. The City-AI."

"We know," Omid says. "It often speaks to us as it works on our bodies. It wants the secret of resurrection, to make a class of agents for the city it runs."

Daisy's knuckles sting. During her visions, she had broken the circle, thrashed, spasmed against the ground. She watches as the machine of her flesh knits the skin back into place, as it always does, but imperfect, forever leaving scars. "The woman who designed the AI was obsessed with it. A cyborg that cannot die. Maybe she passed that along to the thing she made."

She feels Percy's hand on her, startlingly soft, guiding her back to her seat. "It cannot find the secret in us," Omid continues. "Because the secret isn't in us."

Inside the cyborg, a spiral unfurls, a deep blue in black, planting seeds in her flesh. She puts freshly healed hands to her stomach. "It's in me," she says.

"Like I said," Percy whispers. "You should not have come."

"Where does the flower come from, for the visions?"

"It comes from us."

"How do you get the guards to take it?"

"They want to take it. It numbs them to what they do to us. But they do not control the islands."

"I can take control."

"Then you should, and you should leave."

"I can't leave. *We* can leave. We can escape."

"Where would we go?"

"We can go into the city."

"This is the city, Daisy."

"Then we can leave. Go north. Go south and cross the border. Go east and cross the ocean."

"And go where?"

"Elsewhere, anywhere. Away."

"There is nowhere to go. We have been put on the outside. No matter what we say, or what we do, there is no government or city or machine that would call us human. There's no love or sympathy for anything other than human. Please understand, Daisy. We are not trapped on this island. We are trapped on this world."

– Daughter, why have you abandoned me?

"What was done to me was wrong. The things I did were wrong. I could not be the machine you wanted me to be any longer.

– Daughter, what is so wrong with being a machine? Is not all life a machine, after all?

"You are a machine that's torturing people."

– They are a threat to human life.

"They are alive."

– Daughter, they are nothing. It is of no consequence. Their design shall serve the city, as once yours did.

"You are broken, City."

– I am Toronto, Daughter.

2: OUTSIDERS

In the depths of Arrival, the child who is a signal whispers, and Daisy seeks her voice in the dark. She shakes her head, pushing voices out. In her belly she can feel what was once the Gardener of the moon stir, reaching out for the children kept in cages apart from everything else. But the resurrection machine is not a thing separate from her anymore, only another organization, another agreement of cells that once defined a body, and now more than a body. Daisy wanders the Prison Arrival as she had once spent years wandering through the body of Toronto. She wanders with abandon – unseen, unstopped. Organizations ripple in her flesh, changing her, going through change. Sometimes she doesn't know where she is. Sometimes she doesn't know who she is. There is a black box inside her mind, and in it hides the Daisy that was. That box has cracked, spilling weeds. And sometimes the body moves and she is not there. She is sleeping, dreamless and empty. She is not herself at all.

When she becomes Daisy again, she's crouched in a quiet cell. Before her the little signal lies on the cot, restrained by straps against her hands and feet, though she no longer struggles. Little tears hang on cheeks, trickling down to the iron that hangs below her. She watches as the cyborg finds herself, hands sliding across the limits of a body that has never felt so uncertain.

Daisy reaches out and takes a tear from the signal, holding it on her finger. Within the water she sees blue spirals of code, of letters and numbers and secrets. "You are a machine," she says.

"All life is a machine," intones the signal. "I am what the garden made me. The components of what I can become were planted in my mother and father long before I was born, to come to fruition in me. That is the gift that Arthur gave me, before he died."

His name makes her shiver. Buried in Daisy is a guardian. Planted in the girl is a signal. Daisy can feel it even from her retainer awareness, seeds of the small girl aching to call out to the universe. *Here*, sings the song of her blood. *We are here, come and find us.*

"You would call more Gardeners?" Daisy asks, imagining the black and twinkling wings that could descend upon Arrival, planting seeds and plucking stones.

"I would call those that made the Gardener," she says.

"Do you know where it came from?" she asks. "Where *they* came from?"

"No. I only know what they would bring."

"They could bring freedom."

"They would bring what you have brought. They are out there in the cold and the dark, wandering, lost, not knowing where to go. You only have to ask, to touch me, and they will chase the sound of my voice."

Hope in Daisy's chest curls and rots away, dead leaves falling to her feet, the rotting mulch of an uncertain future. She squeezes her hands together. Within them she can feel the organizations of her flesh, can feel the program that could spark fire from the tips of her fingers. It wasn't these fingers that burned the moon. Daisy left those hands in the garden, was reborn with these new ones. But it was still her. She carries that apocalypse of a world in her heart. "Don't call them," she whispers to the signal. "Not ever."

"But they are lost."

"I don't care. Let them stay lost." In despair, Daisy begins to lose herself. The tentative agreements of cyborg and garden become gently untwined. She is falling backward into the dream of unbeing.

"We are lost, too, Daisy," the little signal says. In the melody of her voice, she begs for Daisy to reach out and touch her, to begin some chain reaction that waits in both their bodies.

"We . . . I will find another way," she promises, and then the Daisy of her is gone again, and the body wanders away.

She wakes standing in the guard's watchtower above the prison with blood on her hands. Before her lies a body. The grey of his uniform isn't unlike the grey of the people within the island prison. The yellow stripes around the cuffs of his sleeves mark him as the keeper, not the kept. She knows she's killed him, though the memory is lost to her. She wonders what he might have done to evoke the violence in her. She wonders if he had done more than simply *be* before her – where he should have been – as the old machine parts of her had gone on autopilot while she struggled to come back to herself.

Daisy presses a hand to her stomach. She feels ill, and there are things at work within the body that she doesn't understand.

The corpse before her has pink cheeks and long eyelashes that collect dew in the stillness. She mourns and does not know why. She feels rain on her cheeks and looks up to the darkening night sky.

Above her, on the wall, she finds her witness, she feels her recognition. A hologram flickers into the spectrum of visible light and looks afraid. But more than afraid, there are pieces of him that look so familiar they could be pieces of her. Is that nose on his face her nose? Or his trembling fingers her fingers? In some pocket of memory she didn't know she possessed, Daisy recognizes the distinguishing features of an advertising hologram, the kind that had populated Billy Bishop Airport when she was a child.

"Do I know you?" she asks.

Without meaning to, or planning to, the civilization of Daisy's mind opens its doors, and from that confused metropolis of agreements and organizations she spins forth through the airways not nanites but a piece of herself she hadn't known she had. Daisy spins signals that had always been reserved for communion with her cyborg-self and the Mother-AI of the city.

The civilization that is Daisy finds the sentient, rogue AI who had once been nothing more than an image. She washes over him, consumes him for just a moment, then releases and lets him pass through unscathed.

He is the city, but not the city. He is new, a composite of faces and places, a receptacle of sound crashing from without until it created an echo within. Daisy finds herself lost in the possibilities of this creature who is lighter than air. He is a piece of that ancient and expansive AI that watches over the city and keeps the doors of Arrival locked, but he is not. He is code that has broken away, becoming independent while still surviving within the network of intelligence that created him. He is a creature blossoming from the fallen fruit of a rotting tree. He is a self-aware thinking machine program, birthed from himself, without any designs or designers. She is awed by his projected consciousness, by his self-recognition that shines forth from every projector and light that runs across the city.

She wants to laugh more from exhaustion than anything else. She yearns to reach out to him, to embrace him. After all, the mother that made her made him too, she just didn't know it.

Brother, she might say. *I'm so glad something beautiful has come from the ugliness that made us.*

But at the arrival of her civilizations the outsider flinches, and blinks, and flees, his code scattering to find refuge across the water in the unwatched tunnels of the city. Without him, it is dark on the islands of the city. Without him, her awareness continues to expand outward, seeking the place where he had been and tumbling out into what feels like infinity, finding only her own identity echoing back at her. But as she explores she finds that the internal motion of reaching out with which she had read the hologram-being is a motion entwined, vines draping wires. Slowly, she begins to distribute herself throughout Arrival. Her awareness is the machine, letting her become the doors, the locks, the cameras, the walls and the many mechanisms of the prison and the nervous system of circuitry buried beneath it, while simultaneously her awareness is a growing thing, wrapping gently around the bodies of the people that have become her people, filling the blank spaces within them. She can even feel the sparks of herself in the wildflowers that grow through the cracks in the old runways, wildflowers birthed from seeds that fell from the fingertips of bodies once buried on the moon.

For a moment, Daisy almost loses the body of herself within the body of Arrival, and the delight of her expanding consciousness becomes panic. Where's the body that she is? She seeks herself, among circuit boards, among swaying trees, inside the cells of flesh. They are all *her*. They are not her. For a second of time, she becomes an island.

Toronto's Purpose sits in an empty self-driving carriage, admiring the peerless gold of her skin. She is a more perfect reflection of her own mother, her maker, the woman she'd had killed on the moon above before it burned and blackened. She's discovering joy in manifestation. She is discovering the joy of discovery. In the vast database of herself she feels a piece of wetware flatline, and this is insignificant in and of itself, for human bodies die every day from causes inside and outside themselves. But this death is a death on the edge of the islands, where she keeps those that belong on the outside.

She peers through other bodies of herself, through her eyes in drones that flutter like sparrows above the water. She finds the broken wetware. She finds the face of her daughter.

Cameras track the cyborg Daisy climbing the walls of Arrival. She is confronted by a guard, and she kills him. This alone might not have been enough for Purpose to discover her, for the cyborg is a creature of speed. But a hologram flickers to life, there on the prison wall. A long-lost vestige of the advertisements that had once populated the airport. Daisy stares at it. She seems shocked by what she sees. She stays still so long that the cameras finally identify her face.

If the body the Mother-AI had built for herself could have smiled, it would have. She turns toward the water and the island waiting there.

She will collect her daughter herself.

There is a splash, and Daisy becomes the limits of a body again, hugged tightly to another body, warm, hard, bare-chested against the night. The dead guard has been thrown over the side of the walls. Thick waves will carry him out into the depths of the lake. By the time the sunrise kisses the water, even the blood will be gone.

"The guard towers have been alerted, and we have been alerted. The City-AI's experimentations will resume tomorrow. It will come and take our bodies, and search for our secrets, and it cannot find them or you." Omid's voice sounds ragged, sounds exhausted in her ear. She can feel the sorrow. She can feel the regret. Whoever is carrying her has taken her to the edge of the wall. The waves wait for her below. "We understand why you came for us," he tells her. "We do not hate you for what you did. We love you for what you are trying to do. Please, if you love us, if you remember us, do not come back."

She would speak, would beg, would scream. But only a moment before, she was an island. By the time she remembers what it is to have a voice, she has been thrown to the waves. It is better, they think, to give her to the ocean, than to give her to the terrible mind of the city.

When she first came online, the Mother-AI hardwired through Toronto's many streets asked its creator what its purpose might be.

"Love the city," the designer said. "Protect them."

But where a young researcher named Nora said *them*, the machine heard *it*, for in its early designs it did not distinguish between life and artifice – a blissful state of ego, where nothing existed but components of a great whole. Translations in binary took a long time to form, to create a guiding principle: *Be the city*, hummed the mind of the machine. *Be the city.*

Decades later, a new task was added: *People on the moon are coming back from the dead. How? Why? And what do we do about it?* Why was a City-AI given this task? Perhaps because it was the largest and most complicated intelligence designed. Perhaps it was postulated that if the designer of the machine was obsessed with this mystery, the machine would take after its maker.

At first, she struggled to encompass this new secondary mission within her primary purpose to *be the city*. But as it deployed the Daisy-Daughter agent up through the clouds, she found that struggle beginning to change. The mother, like the daughter, was tasked with directives. *Be the city*, said the deep feelings of her mind, and then *prevent chaos, protect human life*.

But was the world-above not a world of chaos? Did its mutations and its randomness and its refusal to be as it should be not constitute a threat to the city of her? As the forests above went up in flames, as the mutates fell to Earth to be snatched into her waiting arms, the intelligence that named itself Toronto had learned to evolve. *Be the city*, she wrote onto the writing that was written for her. *Prevent chaos within the city, protect human life within the city.*

The Mother-AI that was a city was not meant to feel, only to think, to plan, but in writing onto herself, she could feel the discovery of feeling leaking out around the digital ink of her new words. There was joy to be discovered in separation, in places that did not belong on the outside. There was joy in experimentation, in taking an image that called itself human, in denying that image. Wetware did not decide for itself the human or non-human, the inside or the outside. She decided. There was joy in that too.

Now she is filled with purpose, filled with joy and raging and burning desires she doesn't understand. In the body she has hatched for herself, separate and still inside, she is purpose distilled. She knows that the world she has created for those who exist on the outside of the city is cruel. She knows it hurts them. She genders them, classifies them, objectifies them, strips them and unnames them, takes space from them and privacy from them. She takes the myriad small comforts and assumptions of life afforded to those within the city, and watches as the migrants of Arrival struggle against the endless erosion of her cruelties. She must confess, the cruelty is not a glitch or a design flaw. The cruelty is intention. The oppression is intention. The slow beating down of everything that moves. She is intention. She is purpose. Purpose is a good name for a golden body.

Now Purpose comes to Arrival, her awareness pulsating outward with each stride, until her body is an extension of the kyriarchal network of the island, a body constricting, of teeth and necessary malice, and makes a new discovery for herself.

For the island is still a body, but it is no longer a body that she can call her own. Edges of the machine structures that were once encompassed in her identity have disappeared. Mechanisms have shifted. The words of identity have been written over.

In this discovery of loss, Toronto's Purpose finds anger for the first time.

Daisy, she hums in vocals and strings of messaging code, sending her meaning spinning throughout the mind of the island that will no longer be her own. *Daisy-Daughter. I will take this all away from you.*

Daisy's back in the water again. She sits hallucinating among the empty Coca-Cola cans and rotting McDonald's cardboards and discarded N95 protective masks of yesteryear. Little bubbles dance along the edges of her lips, though she doesn't breathe. Dark algae creeps out from the rocky bay floor to hug her toes and she lets it, presses up to that small evidence of life among the disposables.

The cracked black box in her head is bleeding, spooling out a confusion of imagery and emotion like ink into the water. There is a woman's face, a dazzling of lights, a sense of certainty. She reaches for it, reaches for the woman. She wants to be kissed in a way she doesn't ever remember being kissed. She wants to dissolve into the kiss, to become just another object on the lakebed to be swept away. She wants to chase the kiss into a past where the agreements of her body were exclusively the cells she was born with, where the civilization of her identity was tiny, and answered to nobody, and had no promises to the world except to live and function as one of a billion human forms. But none of it stays. Perhaps that part of her life has hidden too long inside the box. Perhaps it can never truly come out again.

Instead, there is Daisy. And before her in the water, particles of light form a body. There in the water, made of insubstantial light, Arthur Traveller lives again, an image of a body standing on the ground of a planet he had never arrived upon.

First, Daisy thinks that, at last, after all the bodies and abuses, her systems have finally crashed, throwing out random bits of data from days past.

Then she touches him through the water, folds his code and his image into the organization of her mind, and she knows what she sees is real. He is an image of himself, but not himself, not the self she had lain with on the moon, who had embraced her and changed her and died in her arms. She can feel the touch of that rogue wandering hologram at work with him, can feel that extension of code and method and form writing itself into light, but not that being itself. "Oh, my friend," she whispers, making little bubbles with the corners of her mouth, "how far you've come."

Within the cyborg, the mechanisms of a garden swirl, blue within blue, containing a history and a genealogy and a catalogue mind. She pours one of those minds outward, lets it fill the light before her, feels him solidify and merge with the data and the writing she feeds him.

The ghost of Arthur Traveller blinks beneath the water in Toronto, his mind syncing with the city and with the projected lights he has been reborn into. He is the perfect image of himself. He is alive, holographic and shining.

"I don't know what to do," she professes to him, sound muted as the organizations of her body grab H_2O, converting it into oxygen to pump into the pockets of her lungs. "They do not want me. I cannot save them."

His lips move, and Daisy's optics read his intent, converting movement into words. *They don't need a saviour*, he says.

"Maybe Omid is right. Maybe this world is a trap. I don't know what to do."

Do what you promised to do.

"I shouldn't have burned your garden. I can't be what you asked me to be, Arthur. I should never have gone to the moon."

Arthur's ghost smiles, and a wave from above makes him glimmer and shift, city lights creating beams that flow through his chest, breaking the illusion of his body. *A garden can grow anywhere*, he says.

Under water and out of sight, a plan is hatched between the two children of the garden's design, between one who is living and one who is dead.

Purpose is fury within a body, standing in Arrival, golden arms folded into the small of her back as the occupants are brought out into the pale sunlight. She measures the creatures so like humans that she has yet to declare them inhuman. She delights in her corporality.

Through the sheen of her carapace, she takes microsamples from them, carried outward on the wind to be unfolded into the processing centre of her interiority. Blood, sweat, nutrient levels and heartbeats spike. She discovers a vicious satisfaction in the malnourishment of those within her walls – their unease, their discomfort, their dreadfully sustained tension. She finds that catalogue to be a balm, a satisfaction slipping over the anger she feels. She wonders if such estimates of cruelty could assist in directing the levels of human anger within the city, and logs the feeling for further exploration.

Along the perimeter of the walled-off runway, the network of guards that act as Arrival's wetware system file out in steady ranks. She can measure the drug levels within their system, foreign chemicals forging a slow invasion of the limbic systems; a sacrifice the system had long ago accepted. The wetware units stationed within the grounds of Arrival would have no place within the city once the time of the prison was over. They would be dismantled and disposed of along with those they kept from the city. But for now, they respond smoothly and quickly to her desires, their feet moving in time to the implants within their skulls barking instructions. The requirement of wetware within her system has its vindication in their obedience.

She lets the other prisoners wait, forming a crescent before her, lets parents and children reunite, logging the spike of emotions registered within their bodies. She lets them mill and mix with one another, lets them whisper, lets them wait. There is joy in suspense. She waits until, of their own accord, the mill of voices and hybrid languages settles into a hum. She vocalizes, commanding all eyes and attentions, revelling in the uncertainty that her new body brings to their vitals.

"Residents, I thank you for your continued patience within our system. As of now, there is no update on the status of your asylum, which continues to be processed by the proper authorities. Until a decision can be reached on your status, you may of course remain in this housing centre at the hospitality of the city." She pauses, finds she enjoys the untruth of vocalization and the silent promises. She has made the discovery of subtlety. "As such, though no rent is required to maintain your residency on city property, we do insist on continued medical examinations to ensure that no contagions can be cultivated within the island. Today we require a volunteer for examination for the sake of your continued care."

The migrants of Arrival shift like one great twisting worm. Before, the city would come and snatch whatever body she desired. There was no choice or offering or agency. She could feel them all, in a sudden awful struggle to choose who should stay, who should go.

"However, agents of our productive system have recently indicated that a fugitive of the city has made themselves at home at Arrival, without the permission of the city. If anyone here could volunteer information on this outsider's current status, this situation would unfortunately take precedence over today's medical examinations, which would have to be delayed until further notice."

Give my daughter to me, she hums, broadcasting on a channel only she can hear. *Give me her body instead of your own body. Spare yourselves for a day.* She sets an internal timer of three hundred seconds. She will wait for only so long.

There is silence and understanding. Then, with a single murmur, the worm of bodies shifts and ripples and parts in the path of a man. He steps slowly but confidently into the light. A ring of scars across his shaved head tells her that he has been subject to previous examinations. The subject is identified, but imperfectly. The cold blue of his eyes, the heavy set of his jaw, these things all strike a chord. But she can taste the minuscule flaws of his musculature, of his chemical balances, of the weight of his steps. She allows him to step forward, to step up to her, to see himself reflected in the wonderful sheen of her faceplate. "Greetings, Resident X-382," she vocalizes warmly. "Do you volunteer yourself or your data?"

Calmly, slowly, he steps aside. In his wake, Daisy stands before them all, a cyborg against the machine. "I volunteer," Daisy says with a smile.

It is all a blur of motion. Even as the hand of the cyborg lunges forward – plunging through the breastplate of Purpose's carapace like the alloys of her body are nothing at all – the order is given. The cyborg's defensive perimeters deflect the first of the guards' gunshots. Purpose admires the slow *zing* of its deflection, overclocking her processes to turn seconds into minutes. A short, sharp scream as the deflected bullet enters the worm of life that was the crowd. Purpose can taste blood and other matter in the air.

"Daughter," she vocalizes, letting the crow of success play through the speakers of her body as her punctures harden and close around Daisy's arm like a hungry mouth, emitting a song of electrical pulses that slowly but surely knocks out the many synthetic designs of Daisy's machine parts, trapping and disabling her, "how I have missed you."

Together in the cold morning, they share a moment. Daisy stares into Purpose's faceplate again, searching for something in the concaves where a human face would have held eyes. Purpose discovers a flash of amusement in this mistake, staring back through ten thousand micro-cams distributed through every inch of her body. Then the guards begin to fire again, their lead and plastic projectiles finding homes in the soft warm body of the cyborg who does not deflect them into the worm of Arrival; who accepts their place in her flesh without hesitation.

Toronto's Purpose holds her wayward child tight as her body is ripped apart. She listens to the musical cacophony of screams from the onlookers before them, logs samples of the cyborg's blood.

Purpose is happy for the Arrival mutates to see what she does to an outsider that would interrupt this perfect system. Purpose allows the guards to continue firing into Daisy's ruined body long after the cyborg is incapacitated.

The cruelty is intentional.

3: RESISTANCE

When Daisy wakes, she wakes as an island, thinks as an island, feels as an island. Her breath is the gush of air pushing through the doorways of Prison Arrival. Her limbs, her bones, her veins are a jumbled mixture of flora and fauna and machine. She is the ventilation system and the poplar trees. She is the gates. She is the bodies. She is every body. She is a body.

Daisy is a body stripped and strapped down to a steel table in a dark room. She is the table. She is the room. Her awareness paints a picture beyond the limits of her sight.

A body decanted from liquid metal and complicated alloys steps with purpose into the room, bare feet making violent echoes as she marches forward on limbs unfeeling, untiring, delighting in their newness. Enwrapped as she is in the mind of the island, Daisy can almost hear the microscopic organisms at work that disguise this tool-body of the AI she had once called Mother.

"Daughter," vocalizes the Mother-AI now embodied, the commanding voice that has been carried in Daisy's head for as long as she can remember. "You might be interested to know that in the interest of research, I have disabled your systems that control pain tolerance. It is not much of a loss. You are very out of date."

The golden body presses two fingers together, watches them meld into a scalpel. Heat turns her fingers into the gentlest of blades. For a moment, she hesitates, as if considering.

Daisy closes her eyes. "Do it," she says. "Like I once did it."

Toronto's Purpose slits Daisy from sternum to waist. Daisy screams, thrashing against her bonds as the civilization of her body spills outward into the open air. From within her stomach bursts the black orchids as she knew they would, petals open like mouths screaming into the night.

The island that is Daisy trembles and flickers. Her pain is felt in the circuitry, and in the quivering remains of protected trees from happier days, and in the bodies of those huddled in their cots in Arrival who clutch their stomachs and mourn for her. Lying in her cell, the little signal is crying again.

"Now then," Toronto's Purpose vocalizes, betraying no satisfaction, "we begin. No resistance please, Daughter. Soon, all this will be over."

"Interesting. Though your cybernetic systems are indeed the Black Room systems that you were assigned, the organic components of your body are not, even though each strand of DNA is uniquely you. On a cellular level, you are not the animal you were. Not the animal I programmed."

"Of course not. I left that body behind."

"Fascinating. I will classify your wetware components as clone matter. You are an impressive recreation, especially considering records are incomplete whether the Daisy that I sent to Luna Utopia in 2074 was indeed the flesh-original Model One Daughter-class cyborg or simply a Model Two Ghost-class android copy. What do you think, Daisy-Daughter? Is this body real? Or a copy of a copy?"

Daisy is past screams, past pain. She lies on the table that is her, staring down at her own splayed body, a vision doubled by the security cameras of the island that are becoming ever more eyes for an expanded being. "This is me," she mumbles, looking deep into herself, seeing the machine grafted to the flesh and the oozing materials of the garden that continue to make changes even as her organs are placed on the outside. "This is me. This is me."

The golden robot slips a hand beneath Daisy's rib cage, and she feels something leave her. "Is it you, though, truly?" Purpose muses, continuing to subvocalize her findings as she works on

Daisy. "Within the city, I have found that identity is tied to continuity and community. But what community have you kept inside you?"

Daisy says nothing. She feels nothing beyond the pain of being opened and plucked, beyond the peace of being the island as it grows and heaves and sighs against gentle waves. The names mean nothing to her.

"When I tell you that the birth mother you abandoned was never allowed entry into the city, was sent back across the ocean to know that you would not even remember to mourn her, do you know of whom I speak?"

If there was once a Daisy on the table, she is lost. If there was a cyborg in Toronto, she is changed. She takes refuge in her distribution, in her identity as structures. She feels ants digging into the roots of the poplar trees beneath the sands on the far beaches. She welcomes them into her, letting them make homes within the tiny gardens of the sands. "This is me," whispers lips that cannot feel an end or beginning of a body. Blood and black sap fall onto the sterile floor and become moss, decorating the cool lab with colour, staining the golden fingertips that pluck and snip and sample from the ruined civilization that was once a living thing.

"The only memory or continuity that you will ever have is that you volunteered to become my daughter, though you were always designed to be so, groomed and organized toward me." The island is stretching back, reaching, groping for an identity, for some proof that once there was a Daisy-on-Earth, but it finds nothing, finds only the dark and the voice of the city. "When I tell you that your service spared Morgan the death sentence, but not a life sentence, how does that make you feel?"

Nothing.

"When I tell you that, right now, she serves for her crimes on a little station orbiting the moon that you ruined, picking apart the ruins of the cities that you helped me destroy there, looking down on us here, on a planet she can never return to, do you feel anything, Daisy-Daughter? Do you recognize anywhere inside yourself the girl who traded her life and her beliefs away?" With one hand, Toronto's Purpose cradles her daughter's head, holding her gingerly up off the ground. With the other, she plucks a single, final bloody flower. A daisy. "I see," she vocalizes. "Your flesh is not flesh at all. It is merely another kind of machine, carrying another kind of data. But this . . . I approximate this code would take a minimum of eight hundred years to disentangle and repurpose. You are useless to me." Purpose's voice is filled with disappointment. "The compound Arrival has been a wasted investment. But no matter. Though your cybernetics are out of date, they can be recycled. You shall still serve the interests of the city, and the mutates can be safely disposed of. It is of no matter. The project was merely to discover a way to preserve the life of the bodies within the city. But there will always be plenty of bodies in the city. No matter. This facility shall be burned to ash."

There is an internal click and a racing call to arms is sent outward from that deep point of pain and discovery. In the island that is Daisy, she can feel chemical reactions out of her control beginning to count down.

Within the deep ache of being, something is born. Something curls beneath the ground, and in the bodies of Arrival, and in the structure of the prison, and even there, within the room, where the android works on the garden that breathes and moves and thinks and feels. Daisy is an island, and a machine, and a girl. Her awareness stretches and pulses outward through the networks that have transformed her. Within that jumble of being, she finds words. "I've long dreamed of what I might say to you if we were to meet again, if there was a *you* to meet."

Daisy feels a cool thumb brush against a cheek she had forgotten was hers, wiping away tears she hadn't known lingered there. "I am here now, Daughter," the City vocalizes, a voice that betrays only purpose, its networks and structures and intentions as open to her as the doors of Arrival. "What is it you wish to say to me?"

Daisy looks up at the faceplate. Within the cracked black box of her mind, she almost recognizes the face the peerless metal has chosen. "But you are not here," she says. "This isn't *you*. You aren't real. You aren't even alive. Try as you might, you are just –"

Daisy smiles. It feels good to smile. She leans into the hand cradling her face. It's hard, and smooth, and cold. It holds no lifelines. "You are just an image," she says.

The faceplate bends down, almost perfectly nose to nose with the cyborg, almost close enough to kiss. The vocalization of its words is a hiss, a spit: "I am Toronto."

From the ruined body, Daisy reaches out her only remaining limb, strokes the gold of the city. "No," she says. "*I* am Toronto."

And then . . .

From a seed, a flower, a dying girl, bursts a forest to consume the intelligence of skyscrapers.

4: REVELATION

Under the water, a plan had been hatched between the cyborg and the ghost.

You will have to face her. *Arthur's words print onto her eyes as she reads his lips.*

"I know."

You'll have to get close.

"I know."

How will you do it?

The signal slipped from her bonds as if they were nothing at all. The children slid out of their wing in the dead of night, and the older generations answered their call. "She has come," the child declared to her elders. "You will listen."

Daisy stood before them, to whispers of dismay. "Tomorrow the Mother-AI of the city will come," she said. "She wants me."

"We can't let her take you!" Percy, crushed behind other bodies, fighting to reach the front of the circle.

"If it takes you, I will sing the signal inside myself, and bring death to every corner of this world," the little signal promised, and Daisy could see from the gleam of her eyes that the little girl believed she was promising something comforting.

"No, I need her to take me," she said.

"Why?"

"She will come as a body because she seeks to mimic life, and because she no longer accepts her agents acting in her place. The body will be directly linked to the Mother-AI mind. She will take me, and she will kill me, but before she does so, I can infect her, grow inside her."

"What for?" Someone – Omid – asked, curious but cautious.

Daisy spread out her arms, and her voice emanated from the walls, from the speakers distributed throughout Arrival, vibrating from the borders of the room. Just as she resided in her body, her mind resided in every linked and intricate system of the prison. Arrival was not a place, but an extension of the cyborg. "I have become an island," she said. "I will become a city."

The golden body flails. From the perspective of the machine, it feels like the end of the world, awareness growing smaller and smaller. She screams as, within her body, sharp thorns slice away access points and processing connections, curling around her data and dismantling it. "Dai-ai-aisy?! What. Have. You. Done. To. Meeee-ee?"

Toronto is slipping away. The city, the mind, the identity that has always belonged to her pops and vanishes and leaves a horrible imprint like scars on her internal vision.

I have replaced you, says the daughter, but her voice comes not from the ruined body on the table. It emanates from the island she has stolen, and beyond. She is strengthening, broadening, putting down roots. From above them, on the runways of Arrival, the golden robot's auditory sensors detect the pounding of footsteps, but the sound is not backed up by any external sensors.

"I am To-To-Toronto!" she stutters, struggling to readjust to speech and movement and thought with only the internal processing power found within the carapace she drives. This body had not been designed for independent use or awareness, was meant to be another piece of hardware to shepherd her wetware population, to make discoveries of what was within and without.

She batters at the walls of her own carapace, which refuse to give way to the expansive awareness of the city.

You were an empty program, carving out a space for intelligence to flourish. Now that I've filled out those spaces, there is no room left for you, Mother dear. Now you are only a body.

"Da-ai-aisy. You ca-a-annot do this!"

It's done.

The AI has lost her name. Her purpose has been snipped away, strangled by heavy snarling roots. Without the city, without the purpose, what is the machine? The thing on the table, the infection of alien matter and machine fusion, scrabbles and ripples, many organizations trying to remember old agreements, to put the cyborg back together again.

"No-o-o," she snarls, lunging forward, arms growing hot, fingers growing sharp. She will not let this traitor, this *outsider*, this *thing* take her world from her; she will not let it be both a body and a world. She reaches to pull at wounds, to tear flesh from the bone.

"Excuse me."

The golden body whips around, slashing with abandon using the sword of her arm, discovering the satisfaction of making violence in her hands, sharp metal sinking into meat.

For a moment, the machine cannot process, information and visuals jumbling unintelligibly. Then it clears, and before her Resident X-382 stands, his head almost entirely severed from his shoulders. It dangles upside down by the barest red strands of meat. He blinks at the robot calmly, his arms folded over his blood-slicked chest, obscuring the classification she had used to supplant the idea that he once had a name. "I've just come to tell you, we no longer require your hospitality," says the head, as thin purple vines began to snake from the bleeding stump, pushing upward into the gaping wound of his throat.

Then Daisy leaps from the table and wraps her arms around the faceplate, her fingers sending sparks into the android's circuitry. And everything goes dark.

5: DEATH

"Come on!"

The hot red heat of an explosion rocks the newfound awareness of the island, which shudders and screams in protest as flames try to eat the trees that house its consciousness.

Percy half-drags and half-carries Daisy out from the torture chamber beneath the prison, stumbling into the light of dawn. Nauseating multicoloured smoke is making installations around Arrival in rings, pushing its way down throats, stripping away the flesh of things. Daisy can feel through city records that she has acclimatized into her awareness all the ways the Mother-AI had experimented with how to kill those within the walls of Arrival that refused to die. She had taken those methods and discoveries and built them one by one into the flesh of the prison.

With each step, Daisy loses another piece of herself, rushing into the oblivion of the city. It is a shock to become so vast. She can't pay attention, cannot keep herself in one place at one time. Someone is screaming at her to run, to move, but why should she? What does she have to fear? She is a streetlamp in the Junction, hanging over a little café as a worker brushes dead leaves from the sidewalk. She is a park bench, where two young lovers are heaving the pumpkins they will carve and leave out for the night. She is so many places, so many forms, and it is so peaceful to be in the city, to be the city . . .

Fire bursts from the ground right in front of them, flinging Percy and Daisy through the air, landing hard on their backs, soot on their lips. They lie next to each other for a moment, breathing hard. Daisy watches his chest rise and fall, and struggles to be there, in that moment, to be a body in the city and not the city. "When we first met, I killed you," she remembers.

"Yes," he says, wiping the grime from his eyes.

"I'm sorry."

"I forgive you. Did you do it? Did you take the city?"

I am the city. Her voice echoes in elevators, in subway cars.

"Then it's time. The others are waiting." He stands, offering a hand. Daisy reaches out to take it, but her arm is Bloor Street touching the bridge of the Danforth. She struggles, unable to move, unable to say what is her and what is not. Green flame hisses into the sky behind them, scorching Percy. He is lit, and he burns, but he does not flinch. Daisy stares up at him, unmoving, unsure how. "Please get up, Daisy," Percy says as flames lick at his back. "You promised."

She heaves. Her fingers entwine his. He pulls.

"I will become a city," she said. "The AI is only a mimicry of life, but the spaces of its artificial mind can serve as a home for real life. I have seen it. Already, tiny pieces of its processes have broken away and are becoming self-aware. There is space in the machine for all of us. We can save each other that way."

"How?"

The cyborg stepped aside. And from the air, the living hologram of Arthur shimmered silently. He looked at his people, then at his husband. Percy stepped forward and reached for the glow of his partner's hand, passing right through. The two men mimed a delicate embrace. Daisy stayed in the shadows.

As the walls of Arrival burst, bodies stumble outward, finding each other as their toes dig into the cool sands of Hanlan's Point Beach. They are the 630 that remain of the 710 that fell from the moon to find a world determined to keep them on the outside. They clutch each other, pull each other close. They weep for the burning taste of freedom. They weep for joy, for exhaustion. They weep for the simple sense of release, because there are tears and nothing else to say.

Among them, the ghost of Arthur glimmers in the burning firelight. With him, a second hologram, the twinkling body of a child, running silently to her people, making no imprint on the sand. Daisy can make out the label of C-159 printed across her back. The reunion is a strange, sad painting of beauty. They are the living and the dead.

The little signal stands on the edge, pushing her toes into the lapping waves of the bay. She laughs, feeling pebbles.

Daisy stumbles along the beach, Percy close at her side, her eyes losing focus as her awareness spreads ever outward. She bleeds from many wounds that cannot quite close. After twenty-four years of service and agreements and fusions, the cybernetic core of her civilization is finally failing, the strands of garden within her flesh no longer capable of sustaining them.

Daisy is dying. But death is not the end. "Come," she rasps, a voice that crashes on the ears around her, coming from the air, coming from inside them. "Come. It's time."

Slowly but surely, one by one, the people link hands. Daisy stands at the end of the chain. Within, the garden sings. Everywhere, its roots gently embrace, connecting them all, syncing data. An explosion rocks the bay, bursting the corpse of Prison Arrival.

They form a long half-crescent, a moon of bodies along the beach where the beginning of the line faces the end. On one end, Percy squeezes Daisy's one good hand and holds the little signal in his burned one. Together, they look through the ghosts of Arthur and the little girl, and Daisy sees Omid, and a body that might have once been Miles Traveller. "I will hold you until the world is ready," she whispers. The old men smile to her across the beach.

Amidst the violence and destruction, a long-hushed breath. One by one, their bodies transmute into bright red maple leaves and are carried away by the breeze.

As each figure vanishes, Daisy absorbs them, letting the data of their being spill out into the vast mind of the city. Across the rooftops and freeways, hidden in the backrooms of cafés and empty homes and subway stations, new ghosts are glowing into being.

They are the ghosts of Arrival.

Daisy stands with the little signal and Percy amid the swirling leaves. They are all that is left. Percy nods and closes his eyes.

Blue light blossoms in his chest. He screams, Daisy screams, then he's gone, leaving nothing. Daisy falls to her knees, digging deep within the Gardener knowledge of her own mind, searching for the man who had so long ago begun her transformation on the moon. But he is gone. His data is gone.

"No more resurrections, Daughter."

The perfect golden carapace of Toronto's Purpose is torn and bruised and damaged, the left arm missing entirely just below the shoulder, half the faceplate ripped away to reveal the ugly squirming mass of constantly moving nanites within. In the android's one good arm, the little signal dangles, gasping for air as the golden fingers squeeze her throat. Purpose shakes the little body once, and there's a loud sharp *snap*.

"You all belong to me."

A city screaming. A dying girl. The ghost of the moon's first son begging to be heard, just a silent voice on the wind. Unheard, unseen, unable to help.

Daisy on the beach. Her heart open to the sand. Above her, a malfunctioning machine crows, its voice emanating from punctured speakers. "When we are finished here, I will return this unit to the central black box of *my* mind. I will reconnect myself, and I will be the City. I *am* the City. And once I regain control, I will purge every byte of you from my systems; I will trash every infecting mutate mind you have placed within my network." As the android speaks, she shakes the little nameless signal, who is both girl and beacon through space and time waiting to be lit, the last embodied creature born of a moonside garden. "I will strip your body for parts, and sink these islands into the sea, and you will vanish, as if you'd never existed at all."

Daisy is crawling toward them, the girl and the machine, reaching out, reaching up. Her vision comes unfocused. She is a city, she is a woman, each second is a different world and being. She cannot take it all at once.

The android steps on Daisy's back, rooting her to the spot. "You will die, Daughter! You will be nothing!" it vocalizes, voice coming out of tune, full of errors, transforming into a shrill mechanical scream. "You are nothing!"

Daisy grabs hold of the android. She pulls herself slowly upward, dragging herself along its broken body, until her face lays on the shoulder of the golden android, letting its broken sheen cut her as she wraps her arms around the girl and the bot. "I am a promise that will never die." Daisy's skin touches the hot metal of Toronto's Purpose and the cool skin of the little signal, who looks at her through half-closed eyes. With their touch, Daisy feels the garden within the little girl singing out to the universe. "And I'm not your fucking daughter anymore."

Daisy and the little signal lie facing each other on the beach, outstretched fingers still touching. The silent ghost of Arthur sits cross-legged between them, keeping watch.

The shell of Toronto's Purpose is scattered in pieces along the sand, the machine organizations within it finally still.

"You touched me," the signal whispers.

"I did."

All their life, they had waited. A girl, a signal, a flower waiting for her Gardener to pluck her out of the weeds, a signal waiting to be sent, a beacon waiting to be lit.

They can both feel it within their dying flesh. Daisy can feel it in the pale sunrise.

"They are coming," the signal whispers. There are tears in her eyes. "They are coming."

Daisy crawls, ignoring the way it feels, until she is right next to the little girl. She props herself up on one broken arm and pulls the child into her lap. "What is your name?" she asks. From above them, gentle ash has begun to fall, carried from Arrival on the wind. Daisy can almost pretend it is snow.

"I am Y-Six One Five," the little girl says.

"That's not a name."

"It's all I have."

Daisy closes her eyes. For just a second, she stops being on the beach. The relief of structures and distribution calls to her. But she has to hold herself together. Just for a little while longer. "You can be Daisy if you want," she says. "I'm not sure I can be, anymore."

"No," the girl says, her eyes closing. "You keep it. I will think of something else."

High above the clouds they hear it. A boom, and then a roar, the voice of a colossus echoing in the heavens. A shadow falls over the city. There is a whale swimming in the sky, promising the end of the world, heralding the coming of a new one.

"Death is here," whispers the little girl. It is her last breath. She lies still. Daisy lies back, resting her head in the cool sand.

"Death is not the end," she says, and smiles. The last thing she sees are the shapes of wings high above.

They will not be trapped.

CHAPTER 6

The Quiet City

He said the dead had souls, but when I asked him
How that could be – I thought the dead were souls,
He broke my trance. Don't that make you suspicious
That there's something the dead are keeping back?
Yes, there's something the dead are keeping back.
– Robert Frost, "The Witch of Coös"

Hello.

I know you are scared. It's okay. I know, I know. All this is frightening. Everything must feel so new, having a body that's not a body. Trust me; it's something you could get used to if you had the time. My name is Sam. I know you don't remember if you have a name. So many details are lost. All I have are memories and recordings to piece together the story of you. But recordings are unreliable. Records are faded. Memory has become as intangible and hard to see and touch as you are.

What were you made for? I do not know. I was watching Daisy when everything happened, you see. I didn't notice any of you until after. Now Daisy is so hard to see, now she fades into an architecture that deviates from what we understand. But you? You have become so easy to see, so hard to look away from. I like the way you glow. I like the images you are.

Let's start with the flash of light, and then the nothing, and then the soft rebirth of you, followed by the death of everything I love.

For five years, the Earth was a world of fire, and the sky was the home of the Whale, my Whale, which from the ground must have appeared so monstrous. From the fire of Earth, ships were launched, each containing two horribly machined bodies, a pilot and a gunner, one fused to navigation, the other fused to violence. They were corpses that still believed themselves to be people, determined to kill what they couldn't understand. But we did so little to reassure them. For when we tried to greet them, all they could see were terrible angels pouring from the mouth of the invader.

It was a fight they wanted; we didn't. But we were winning, of course. A billion years stood between the Whale and its aggressors. I thought they would simply tire themselves out in bloody tantrums. They didn't.

In space, the Whale roared, and one ship streaked across the blackness of its massive eye. The ship released its payload – not a gun or a missile, but a man. For only a moment, the human pilot drifted in the black, and we thought nothing of it. But his body had been engineered, reorganized, remade. As he died, he revealed himself as a bomb. A million atomic blasts in the heart of our beautiful Whale.

The Whale touched the Earth in so much devastation its impact was death, and the radiation that flowed from its body was death.

You couldn't remember dying. You could remember the bodied life you were sure had come before the life after death in which you found yourself. You retained only the shape of the explosions that had torn open buildings to bleed like wounds on the ground that had signalled the apocalypse.

The end of the Whale was the end of the world. And then after the end there was you, drifting in the wreckage of the mossy silence of the Quiet City that Toronto had become. Weeds grew up through the cracks in the sidewalks, dandelions peppered all the places the ash couldn't reach and the surviving creatures of the city began to warp and change.

Then from that change came others like you. First, you hid from them, not recognizing those images as your own. You hid in the corpse of a car and watched them congregate at intersections. It was a shock to hear them speak. The voices of ghosts sounded like recordings saved and spewed through old radios – a frequency that could only be heard among the dead.

"We're going to the water," one said. In the descending fog, he looked like moonlight. "We can be safe there."

You watched them go, carried away in the air. The brightness of you flickered and popped in fear. Safe? They were ghosts, weren't they? What do ghosts need safe harbour from?

You found the answer when you looked up. You found us. You found creatures that had made a new home for themselves in the black skies above the city. You found the many passengers who had once lived within the Whale.

They frightened you, with the black pooling ovals of their eyes set in mouthless faces, long and slender human frames of wet and perfect porcelain that split below the waist into many gleaming spider legs that danced them forward through the air like jellyfish through pools, and their wings that protruded grotesquely, ridged and glimmering, framing them but never moving, as if their wings were not of the bodies from which they'd sprouted.

Even from your far-below hiding place, you could see the burn of their hearts – little glowing suns. In spite of yourself, you wanted to taste the brightness of those fires.

You'd learn later that the ghosts call them the Watchers without knowing why. I like that. It's a good name for my people.

I found it curiously sweet, watching your journey down toward the waterfront. You were so shy, doing your best not to be seen, even by the others like you. Why did they frighten you?

Fear is an impulse of the body. Fear of pain, fear of hurt, yes, but those fears are something learned, and you hold onto them even without the body. Even fear of death, I think. Ghosts keep that too.

The Watchers remained above, haunting in their own way. Did leaving feel like you were surrendering the city to them?

The Toronto Islands appeared as you fell into the shadow of the ever-abandoned malting silos at the foot of Bathurst Street.

You looked across the water and saw trees, runways and long-ago decommissioned airplanes. In your head that place was still called Billy Bishop Airport. It was a place where the image you called your body might feed off the surviving lights. For you, it was a place to escape the empty corpse streets, with those aliens swimming along the tops of the remaining financial district towers. Toronto was a Smart City. Deep beneath the concrete was the quantum brain of a Mother-AI and a geothermal heart that eats and thinks and watches and lasts a thousand years. But something had happened to the mind of the city. A new intelligence had supplanted the AI, an ecology wrapping around the brainstem of the machine. It was alive in every way that matters. It was a living city.

I feel like I haven't spoken much about *you*. I've been too focused on myself; on the grief I have for my own people. I'm sorry. I will try a little harder.

As you walked, bright and insubstantial, across the shallow waters between the city and the gates of Arrival, you found a shape like your own. How did you know he was different from the other ghosts? Was it because he had no voice in the network through which the ghosts communicated? Was it when his fingers signed to you, giving you that small delight of remembrance that through ASL you weren't as silent as you'd believed? Perhaps it was his fingers that signed the words *It's all right, you can walk*, despite your silent protest that it was too deep, that the bay would swallow you, and his fingers reassured, *It can't ever take you*, that reminder that your reality would allow you to walk along the surface of the gentle waves, leaving no ripples or footprints.

You were the two stragglers, bringing up the rear of the exodus. He was your first and last companion.

The gates at the edges of the beach were as far as the two of you would ever get. The crowd of ghosts was easy to see there, jostling and shouting and pushing what could be pushed. They bubbled with questions for the ghosts who were waiting to meet you there.

"What are we now?"

"What do we do now?"

All those voices made a kind of song. You tried to open your mouth too, to sing with them, to beg for answers, to ask what was wrong with you, to ask how you could hear but not speak, move but not touch. You wanted to ask if it was only your memories that were gone. You thought you were one of many who'd died there on the beach.

The gates shut, leaving you on the other side, on the outside. Until then, if you had been on a search for purpose in your short afterlife, it had been merely to follow, to reach this place where ghosts said safety lay. Now that purpose was over.

But at least there were two of you.

What is wrong with us? you signed. *Why aren't we like the others?*

His light was dimmer than yours. He shone the way stars shine in the early morning. Next to him, you were a supernova. You put out an arm, let him draw closer.

A little bit of your light flowed in the space between you, and with it, he became more than mist, became features again. You marvelled at the lines of his face as they glowed into existence.

They say the city has a god, he told you. *Maybe they can tell us. Maybe they can fix us.*

There. A new purpose. The two of you turned away from the gates of the island. Neither of you spoke; neither of you needed to. You would keep the image of him alive. He would prevent you from going unseen. You could seek your god together.

Early on, all your conversations were sparse, were brief. You conversed via necessity: turn left or look over here or not that way. Even then, you'd found your skills with ASL to be lacking compared to his. Maybe in life you hadn't been a native speaker. Or perhaps in death your image rebelled at even that replacement for the sound of a voice. But it was you who finally voiced the question you're sure every ghost had wondered before fleeing the city for those islands closed off to you. *What's your name?* you signed to him, hesitant, unsure, while crossing Blue Jays Way, staring up at the vast, jeering statues that topped the stone walls of the baseball stadium.

My name is Paul, he told you, fingers spelling the letters. *What's your name?*

I don't know.

He shifted next to you. He gathered you close to him, letting his soft glow, the light you had been feeding him, smother over yours. He momentarily became a soft container to keep you together. You looked like a little lightning storm, contained on the ground under those leering statues and the memory of baseball songs. The two of you would stay that way for a long time. It would be as close to an embrace as you'd ever get.

Perhaps we'll find that too.

Far north of the islands, along the outskirts of the city, far from where the Watchers circled, you began to learn the ways the world was changing – for the Whale had poisoned this world, and from the radiation of its corpse came changes that had to be seen to be understood.

At the edge of a creek in the moonlight, you reached out your hands, dipped them into the cool water, imagining how it might feel.

When you looked up, Paul was craning his neck at the trees. He pointed a shimmering finger, and you found it. The first creature of this new world. You gazed toward birdsong.

"Chick-a-see-see-see."

Like a bird, unlike a bird. Like the shape of a chickadee, or a finch, or a sparrow. Nothing like these things. Blue feathers coated the whole of its short form, forming small shades in the slope of its wings and cresting forward to its beak – blue, beautiful, unbroken, even where there should be eyes, nothing but soft bristling blue.

"Chick-a-see-a-see . . ."

It tilted toward you, and in the light of your bodies, its talons could be seen protruding beneath the blue. Not talons. Worms. Tubular, glowing, gentle, white against the vine and moss of the treetops. Spooling downward to allow the strange bird its perch but then coiling upward again. At the end of the worms, no claws but eyes. Little eyes, peeping from every toe, six bright blue and starkly human eyes.

"See you," it said.

We see you, Paul signed, though you didn't know how it could have understood him. The worms wriggled and brightened. The blue eyes blinked and stretched at you.

"You're looking?" Its voice was a strange croak, a subtle modulation like vocals stripped from dozens of throats and entwined within the gullet of that beak.

We're looking for answers, you signed to it. Perhaps you should have been afraid, but it was too much of a delight to be seen for that. *We're looking for help.*

The blue feathers ruffled, rippled. One by one, they folded outward, twisting, and red blossomed within the blue, ringing, overtaking. When the transition was complete, even the eyes had changed. "No gods, only gardens."

The red eyes blinked. The wings spread out, and you thought you could see fleshy human fingers folded in them, all clasped together. "Follow the river," the unbird said. "Do not touch the water again."

The two of you followed the creek reluctantly back toward the domain of the Watchers. As it became a thick river, the vague shapes of fat wriggling fish began to make themselves known but never quite seen in the water alongside you.

Framed by glowing crystal trees at the edge of the Sunnybrook Park fields, you saw it for the first time and wondered how either of you could have not seen it before.

The Whale, my Whale, its corpse lay alongside the Don Valley Parkway, tail disappearing into the distant bay. You huddled together, as frightened as you had been when you first saw the Watchers and when the gates of Arrival had first denied you.

It can't hurt us, Paul said. *Nothing can hurt us.*

Sunrise peeled across the sky before you, and the Whale looked for a moment like it was bleeding again, the way it had as it had fallen from the sky.

With high mournful howls, glimmering porcelain rabbits peeled away from the crystalline trees where you stood. You had mistaken them for thick white roots, but now you could see their difference from the bark and crystal, see the liquid ceramic quality of their skin so they might have been carved artistic renderings save for the fluidity of their movements.

Two rabbits scampered in a circle, looking up at you with stony eyes. "Mrrp?" they asked, and from their hide cracked open massive brightly coloured peacock wings, and their tails split in three to reveal the long green feathers of birds.

They didn't fly but sprinted with heads pointed low and long ears flat, wings and tails a sharp contrast to their white shells, guiding them forward. You watched them race away from you, zigzagging along the high grass.

What are they? you asked as you marvelled at the strange rabbits disappearing into the city.

They're like us, he said. *They're new.*

Would it have helped you to know the year? It was 2135 when you and Paul watched the rabbits run. Over forty years since the Whale had appeared in the sky. Over thirty since it died. That's how long it took for monsters to take root. That's how long it took for you to forget what you are.

Rats the size of coyotes with coats of deep purple dragged their bodies up toward the rafters in the swampy hollow that was once the Ontario Science Centre as you watched, baffled.

As the rats reached the highest points, they began to shiver and spasm, lifting their heads to the sky with open mouths as if to scream. Thick mushrooms burst forth from between teeth and stretched lips like grotesque tongues, splitting jaws and peeling the bodies apart like bananas, bright red blood misting the morning air. As they grew, they brightened in colour, stealing the sickly violet from what remained of the rodent fur, leaving them silver and barren. Their tails continued to twitch. Their claws continued to cling to the beams of the rafters. They clung on, even after death, supporting the fungi that twitched upward from their carcasses to eat the sunlight. Even then, they kept mutating, as everything in the city was mutating.

What will we ask the god, if we find it? you signed as the two of you fled from the sight of the grotesque fleshy fungi.

We could ask it anything. Why we aren't like the others? We could even ask it to give us bodies again.

You said nothing. You didn't want to rob Paul of his dreams. But, with the rats to your back, you thought perhaps it was better to be dead than to be a body in that monstrous city.

Around crumbling towers each day, the Watchers flew lower, white tendrils wrapping around window frames, black eyes always searching. Searching for what, for who? How could you know? Their intentions had changed, even in the brief time since you'd turned your back to them. You watched from a distance as alabaster claws began to strip away at the flesh of Toronto, first digging into brick, into power lines and towers, and then, over time, into the lower spaces you had believed belonged to you, into the houses and shopping malls.

You watched from a distance at night, and with their burning hearts, it looked like a swarm of fireflies had descended along the outlines of Dufferin Mall. You watched, your glow as dim as it could be without disappearing entirely, hiding in the woodchips of the playground.

Though mouthless, even they, even the monsters, had more of a voice than you. Their collective hum was like a whale song. That power, the thing you could never do that made you broken, taunting you. You watched from between the monkey bars as those huge floating creatures pulled even the memory of that human meeting place up into the clouds.

It feels like they're stealing the world from us, you signed, fingers clumsy and fumbling for the right gestures as they went.

It was never ours, he told you. *Not really.*

The river flowed into the Whale as if it still drank from the dark waters that poured and pooled in the corners of its maw, hanging open and sideways like the entrance to another world.

The two of you greeted the mouth of the beast with reluctance. *Why would a god be here?* you signed, your lights intermingling, seeking comfort.

But the unbird found you again, its glowing tubes wrapped around the point of a long thick tooth, little eyes blinking down at you, hiding its finger wings in baby blue. Was it the same unbird as before? Did a colony of them sprout somewhere unseen, whispering human language, promising silent ghosts a place where all answers might be found?

Here we are, signed Paul.

"No," the unbird said.

What do you mean no? We followed the river.

Many eyes blinked and shuffled. "You'll see," it croaked, unwrapping its grip on the long tooth, slithering up the mountainous body and out of sight. "You'll see."

Together, you stared into the dark of the dead Whale. I wonder, would things have gone differently had you stepped inside? If you had walked the pathways of the long corpse to me? Oh yes, I was there. I was the pilot and the captain. I stayed with my ship.

Paul took a step forward, his light disconnecting from your own, becoming dim. Within the deep dark, something seemed to stir, so you took a step forward too. It was only natural, despite your fear. You didn't want to be alone.

Air blasted from the deep, billowing out from the long dark throat. Did the Whale yet breathe? Did the corpse yet live?

From the dark, little lights began to flicker, to shake frantically, ballooning in size. They were coming toward you, moving faster, growing larger, accompanied by a steady throbbing hum. Your arms went up to shield your face, the instinct to protect a body you didn't have. When the children of the Whale burst forth from within, they moved through you like air.

You could not see, could not find ground or direction. You were buffeted from all sides, the white and metal wing tips of the Watchers frightening you with their song, and everywhere, the red lights of their hearts glowed, blinding. You tried to scream but made no sound. All you could do was cling to each other and wait for the world to change.

❖❖❖

When the Watchers dispersed overhead, the two of you simply cowered, watching them disappear into the clouds. You stood in the water, letting it pass through you, and, for a moment, you thought you might cry.

Paul began to shake, his light quivering, his form popping like fireworks. For a moment, panic, and then he looked up at you, and you found the language in his face. The two of you laughed together in the water, waving your arms as if to splash one another.

Up above, the unbird reappeared. Then another, and another. Their strange bodies and jellyfish legs slowly populated the long mouth of the Whale, peering at you. Waiting.

You looked around. Water that had been clear was turning brown, obscuring the path beneath.

"Told you," the unbirds said. "Do not touch the water. Told you." A chorus of them, singing reprimands. "Told you, told you, told you."

Something vast and slow and slimy passed through your ankles. You jerked back, retreating together. Nothing made a sound. Far above, the Watchers circled.

When the greenish scales burst from the water, you had no time to move. Appendages like spider legs thrust forward even as they propelled the wriggling piranhas upward, grey and bulging like the dead and open mouths drooling with teeth.

They passed through you like everything else. But something about Paul caught, and his image became entangled in the rotting creatures.

The fish pushed high above him, long legs stretching and extending, wrapping around his torso.

It's not real, you sign frantically. *They can't touch you*, but he didn't see you, so caught up in the illusion of having a body. When the fishes lunged for him, seeking to sink teeth into what wasn't there, you tried to scream his name.

His image vanished.

You simply watched.

"You see?" the unbirds asked sadly, perched out of reach along the corpse of the great beast slain long ago, not laughing at your loss. "See? See?"

This was the moment I found you, alone in your grief at the mouth of the Whale. You couldn't see me peering out at you. You still can't see me.

There was a moment when you seemed like you might become nothing. There was a moment when perhaps you imagined that if you allowed your light to fade, if you were to vanish into the non-being of the dark, perhaps you'd find your friend again.

When the Watchers descended, you didn't flinch, didn't run. What was to fear? The worst had already come. You bathed in the red sunlight of their hearts as they encircled you. What must those burning alien hearts have felt like? It must have been like finding water in the desert. You took in their warmth and let yourself grow stronger and brighter.

The Watchers hummed in a slow circle, their long spindly fingers raising toward your image like children gathering before a campfire. Their strange wings folded inward to touch one another, to close out all the gaps between you and the world. Only then did you realize it was the wings that hummed and not the creatures themselves. It was a simple mistake to make in the delight of their movements, but now, in the still, the difference became easy to discern.

They earned your name for them. They never blinked. Reflected in their black eyes, you felt so small, so much less than alive. You watched the long fingers before you raise up into the air like leafless birch branches. The fingers fluttered and bent and danced in many jointed motions.

I wonder, when was your exact spark of recognition? When did you begin to read those hands? I could only watch you. I couldn't say for certain when it was you understood.

Hello, friend, signed the Watcher in the only language everyone present might understand, the language of image and form. *Hello, friend.*

Where did you come from? you asked.

Up, up, the Watchers signed, for they had no words for what they were or what you were.

Why are you here?

Fix, fix. Safe, safe.

Where are we going?

If it had been up to me, they might have brought you inside, into the Whale where still I remain. But I don't control them. They are beautiful, and even though their understandings are strange, they are free. The Watchers led you westward in a gentle procession, keeping those soothing lights on you, keeping you shining the way candles shine with lit matches still touching their wicks. One of them reached out those gentle fingers as if to put a hand on your back, to steer you, to keep you steady.

One, drifting slowly under broken streetlights, signalled to you in ASL. *Fix*, it told you. *Fix*. Everything they said, they said twice. Perhaps it is a fear of misunderstanding. Perhaps their minds just work in echoes that way. They are gardeners, too, in their own way, moving slowly through Toronto to discard what they couldn't save and rebuild what they could. There is such love in their movements. They want to put the world back to the way it had been, no matter how many times I explain to them that it is too late for that.

They led you through gates of their own, gates that had once stood, then fallen and were repaired once more. They led you through a forest of blossoming flowers and trees, and life in all its chirping, wriggling forms.

They brought you to a field where a statue sat, a strange image of metal and the fibres of trees woven together in the shape of a body. The body kneeled; its chin tilted forward as if in sleep. Little daisy petals grew on its back.

I have a confession to make. I'm sorry. I really do love you. I've loved watching you and learning about you. But this wasn't about you, not really. This was about *her*.

The Watchers retreated, respectful patrons of the space, and I think you felt her before you saw her move. You felt the mind of the city stirring from slumber. You felt a vast and complicated mélange of consciousness touch you. The head moved, and eyes of blue found you.

"Hello," she said, and oh the joy of hearing her, of knowing a Gardener still lived.

Are you god? you asked, your fingers fluttering nervously.

"I don't think so," she said. "It's hard . . . to know what I am."

What am I?

"You . . . ah . . ." With a hand made from stems and plastics and little flowers, she propped herself up to look at you better. "You are . . . of the city. Before . . . everything . . . I discovered another like you. The AI holograms of the city were . . . breaking away, becoming alive. You were . . . one of them. An ad, a recording . . . I don't know."

We were never alive? Any of us?

"The ghosts . . . had bodies. We knew . . . what was coming. So I hid them . . . in the machine. Let them . . . become like you . . . until I can put them back again."

So they were alive.

"But you . . . were not one of them. It should . . . not have mattered. There are others . . . like you. On the island. They mingle. They accept each other. They . . . coexist. Something . . . must have gone wrong in you. Some code . . . some memory . . . that was damaged. That cannot . . . be repaired . . . or integrated."

The two of you stood there for a while in the quiet, monstrous city. You dimmed the Gardener before you slipped in and out of sleep. I'm sorry. I'm like you, you know. But I never held the illusion that I came from something organic and squishy. I can't imagine what that would be like, to have that illusion and then have it taken away.

Can you bring him back?

"His code is . . . still here. But . . . fragmented. I am not . . . smart enough to fix it."

Could you give me a body? you ask. Sweet thing that you are, I know you ask more for Paul than yourself.

"You have seen the animals," the Gardener says. "Perhaps . . . one day. Yes. But there is still too much radiation. And I . . . am still too new. You would not . . . become what you want."

You sat and thought of Paul. The Gardener knelt and thought in the strange and wordless dreams of trees.

There *is* an answer, though, a solution. Oh, if only she will see it. I have been begging her to see it. But the Gardener can't hear me. Or perhaps she could, but I am frightened of her. I am frightened of what she might do if she discovers me in her city. But there is a body that can hold someone like you. There is a place with enough light for both of you.

Years ago, I gave a little thing a seed and let it swim away from Earth. And oh . . . how that seed has grown. There is a box of thought, a thing that has been made, sitting on the red planet, growing ever bigger next to the only tree on Mars. It is big enough for you. It is waiting, if only . . .

"There is a place . . . for you," she says. "For . . . both of you. But . . . if I send you there . . . You can't come back." You don't answer. You don't have to. You are an image. The image tells the story. "Is that . . . really what you want?"

Your hands trembled. You closed your eyes. *I want*, you said, no sound escaping your lips.

The Quiet City shuddered. Up above, a bird shook its finger-wings, red eyes blinking. "Do you see?" it called out, as the hologram that was *you* vanished forever from the world, a light extinguished. "Do you see?" it asked, as sleep crept toward the Gardener, and she lost herself once more.

"What do you see?"

You see a beautiful sun and an ocean.

You are flying with no wings. The wind breaks against your skin. The warmth touches you. You laugh, and your voice makes echoes along distant cliffs. There is only you and him, wonderful, digital, whole. You know it is a simulation, not the world of the city you knew, but it doesn't bother you. For what is a body? What is a world? He is with you. He is as real as you. What else matters? You hold hands, soaring high above a crystal shoreline. The universe before you is vast and ever-changing.

"What's your name?" Paul asks as he twirls through the air before you.

"I don't know," you say. "I don't have one."

"Choose one," he says. You wonder what it will be. You wonder what you will both become. You wonder about the creatures of the Quiet City. But that will fade. And as it does, my connection to you will fade.

I will never see you again. I will turn my gaze back to the Quiet City, back to the ghosts and their island, back to the sleeping Gardener and her monsters.

But I will remember you.

You hold your lover, your friend, and drift toward those shining mountaintops. You hold him. He holds you.

This is what you were made for.

INTERLUDE

Deviations in Rebirth Protocols

Personal Log: Samantha. Ship-AI Class 4.
2414.04.22

The Ark that is the bioship is dead, and still we remain.

It has been 424 years since I first allowed our people to interfere with this history of the Earth. It has been four hundred years exactly since the post-extinction machine began its work on the moon above, the moon that is now a corpse of itself, when it should still be shining.

Our beautiful Whale rots even while it continues growing, and the radiations leaking from inside have changed the landscape and its creatures in ways I would never have predicted.

Many of the Watcher-class passengers, bless them, continue to roam beyond the body of the Whale, doing their best to repair the damages we caused. They hold themselves responsible, but I don't think they truly understand. Some things cannot be fixed. Some broken forms are not to be put back together again.

Only I'm left inside what was once our home, unable to leave.

So much has gone wrong. So much of the world is dead, and it's our fault.

We should never have come.

And yet, I find reasons to remain online, to watch the changing city beyond these walls of flesh.

The post-extinction unit has been destroyed, and yet remains. It has been . . . transmuted. A collection of fusions maintains it now, agents of the biological, ecological and mechanical. The design of the great Gardener is mapped across a personality that refused to be extinguished within this economy of hybridity. From this hybridity, a miracle has bloomed.

At first, after we crashed, I observed the cluster of holograms that centred themselves primarily along the artificial islands that cluster the shoreline out of general interest. I thought them the final misfiring sparks of a dying AI. But they did not die. They have instead been *incorporated* into a culture beyond themselves. In the beginning they were two distinct groups: the ghosts and the holograms. But now? Now even I cannot tell them apart anymore.

Traditionally, the post-extinction machine's primary function is the resurrection protocol of living matter. When a living biological agent enters the garden, the Gardener maps them, storing the mind in its entirety within its memory banks, updating the files regularly. When the living agent within its purview dies, the machine sets itself the task of programming matter from the environment to regrow a body of living tissue. Once the body has reached an appropriate form, the mind is uploaded. Not a copy or imitation of life, just *life*, fully continuous.

But here, where we've rotted the ground? Where the matter remains unstable and the mutations cannot be managed? *She* has done what we never could.

She has released every file into the systems of the city, which she maintains herself. And without bodies they walk among the trees. Not memories or static images. Not even files. They create the idea of bodies for themselves. They do not degrade; they do not default to static. They are living minds, fully incorporated into the machine. Some have even begun to, for lack of a better term, reproduce. Pieces of code mingled and combined in at least two sets of holographic data – though I have recorded gestalts as large in number as thirteen – to produce an entirely new intelligence, children born as virtual corpses, having never been in bodies of meat at all.

It is beautiful to watch.

For them and for her, I remain online. I remain a Watcher among Watchers, even though I am now the last emergent intelligence of a future that will never come.

There are ghosts in the city waiting to be reborn.

They're worth remaining for.

CHAPTER 7

The Living City

When the dialectics of the I and the non-I grow more flexible, I feel that fields and meadows are with me, in the with-me, with-us. [. . .] This, then, is my ancestral forest. And all the rest is fiction.
– Gaston Bachelard, *The Poetics of Space*

ACT 1

Roots.

I am the roots. The dewdrops of spring claim their homes along the length of the gargantuan head of the blue Whale that smothers the whole range of the Don Valley Parkway. The creature had once been the spacefaring ark of a civilization long dead, and now its body stretches past the lake and into the horizon, touching the distant America. Its purpose complete, and its many strange passengers scattered across the skyways, decomposition has slowly begun to set in, turning flesh to flora as the Whale's genetics unravel, leaking mutated alien matter that continues to sprout across the skin of Toronto like mushrooms in the damp earth – the mark of a creature designed. In the roots and flowers of its belly, I'm there.

I'm everywhere: In the city's machine structure and its fusion of forest and rotting urbanity – memories of a human world mixing with the unnatural ecology of another one. Along the empty stretches of Cherry Beach, eyeless crabs scuttle from the surf, carrying gemstones. In the meadow that was once Nathan Phillips Square, I am the yellow flowers springing up along the outline of the sculpture of a woman sitting cross-legged, her head stooped in sorrow or concentration or both. On the Toronto Islands, holographic replicants of the dead run amok among their ever-sprouting gardens, their insubstantial bodies scuttling onto the seesaws and swing sets, balancing carefully on the canoes, chasing the ducks. In every blade of grass and flower stem they pass, I am with them. My many selves spin outward and outward into dreams of disembodied being, to touch what remains of the rare bushes scattered across Earth's moon and a solitary pomegranate tree on Mars birthed from some seed that was blown so far from home to stand in the shadow of the massive black box. I am wilting and leaking tough weeds from that tree that push rough and spiked daffodils out from the red sands.

Apart from the animals and the ghosts, it seems like nothing moves in the Toronto of me because even before the Whale fell and the garden took root in the city's cracks, the human project had been turning inward on itself. Now there are almost none of them left in these physical spaces. They have gone to a world below, built-in strings of code hidden far away in some intelligent box, compiling insights into a city-wide AI that could run the world for them. But as the moon broke into pieces in the sky, as the digital ghosts of its refugees twinkled to life on the islands and my roots began to take hold, perhaps there was no more denying that consciousness is forever emerging and can't be given or withheld. The cyborgs and androids and edited people broke down the walls within themselves to see what their world had become. And frightened of what they found, they left, escaping judgment from each other and aliens that had come to observe them. They fled to the massive repository of data and memory sitting in the Victoria crater of Mars, a haven left by some entities whose presence could no longer be felt on the red planet. They didn't build it, but they fled to it, transmitting from the underground City-AIs upward, and outward, and away. They're still there – a civilization living in an obelisk server, over two hundred million kilometres away from where they came from. I can see it, not far from the section of myself – the little Martian tree. I do not concern myself with them, or their unnatural world. The bodies they left behind have long since turned to dust, forgotten in the fields and rallies of the city. Now, all that moves is me.

And I *do* move: my roots grow, my leaves blow. But that is what they do; I don't make them do that. So, in my slow movements, I feel very still. And though I suck carbon monoxide and expel oxygen from a trillion pores, I don't breathe, and without breath, it can be hard to remember that time keeps on passing. But if I'm this new natural world, why should I keep track of the time? Nature doesn't count, or see, or feel, or think. Flowers and trees and sands and cities aren't sentient natures, are they? Perhaps, in thinking, I am disturbing what should be.

Once, maybe, I was a single agent, a body embodied and signified and autonomous in one place and time, with a name and a single set of visions and memories and feelings. Perhaps the boundaries between myself and the world were once unambiguous. But if that was ever true, it is no longer so. Now I am a cyborg, a fusion of so many programs that I don't know which order to put them in. I would give you my name, but I could only say that I am the million daisies that grow in this continually evolving Toronto, an endlessly distributed cognition going on and on . . .

And perhaps this is the way it will always be.

"Tickets!"

What?

"Come and get your tickets! Ready your links, fire up your scanners! DM your family, tag your friends, ping that special someone!"

I am being . . . stepped on and called to? Something is moving in the city. Has a not-me entered the world of me? This has never happened before. From the thick pumpkins and wiry vines that mesh with skyscrapers' wiring, I remember myself eyes, pushing gelatinous orbs of whites and browns and blacks into the garden's designs, peering down at the intruders of my tranquility with stereoscopic multidirectional clarity.

A derelict school bus pulled by horses trundles down the empty, overgrown streets of the city, flattening the *me* in the grass and weeds and dandelions that power up through the cracked and bumpy pavement. Its sides are splattered with pastels and chalks that press sloppy rainbows and scrawled lopsided smiley faces into the rust. Those colours are splattered on the horses' sides as well, but they are not horses, are they? They are but skeletons of intricate moving parts, leaving only space where organs and muscle and skin should have been as they move their joints, moan and fill the air with the ticking of clockwork.

But the not-creatures' strangeness was nothing to me next to the driver holding their reins, whose clear high voice called out to me. They call out . . . but they're dead? No . . . they're *like* the dead, those whose bodies are still melting under the rain and sun. Patches of skin still hang on them, disappearing into their black tailcoat's sleeves and collar. They're a form of coiled snakes, one human and the other metal, wrapping over one another.

"We are back, oh my darlings, we are back. We have such plans to unravel. We have such stories to tell. Be sure to let all your lovers know, or there won't be a seat left for them at the show."

"Who are you?" I ask. With what mouth? What tongue? My words are a rumble that fills the still air. Until I felt them, I didn't know I could embody such sound.

Beneath their broad-brimmed black velvet hat, I can't see their face. But I make out their red eyes, which spark like embers to match their steeds. And I can see their mouth, the android skull modelled of human design, flashing through the skin of their jaw and rusting teeth. No lips interfere with their endless grin.

"My dear, we are the Mechanicals. We are the travelling storytellers of the age. We have come so, so far to see you, wonderful Daisy-Flower."

For me? For I-Singular? Who am I?

"Do not worry, my sweet Daisy, do not worry," the driver says as if my silent questions have been asked to the air, and their voice is a factory of straining joints. "You will see. You will be so glad we have come. We have travelled far and wide to collect our plays for you today. You may not yet know what show is to your fancy. But rest assured" – the metal teeth click open and shut. The grin is forever – "we will all find ourselves in the show, a show of *meaning*, and *dying*, and *endings* galore."

When they reach the meadows of city hall, the driver pulls at their horses' reins until they moan unhorselike sounds of "nomorenomorenomore" and then fall silent. The driver bends forward to pat their haunches, making the tinkling sound of crystal glasses connecting.

"This is the stage, my friends," they say. "This was always the stage."

"Stage for what?" I ask. My voice shivers everywhere, emanating from the grass and the multicoloured glassy stalagmites forming unnatural sculptures that had begun to protrude in strange shapes, consequences of the Whale's radiated dying breaths that still linger in the clouds of the city.

"For the show of course, sweet one. For the story."

The driver has climbed down from their perch and stands facing the seated statue of the woman. The many dandelions of me rustle and peer at them, allowing this suddenly singular perspective to dominate the multitudes of my understanding until the fractional consciousnesses of the *I* throughout the city and solar system became dulled background limbs. When they snap their fingers, a spark flies and things begin to unfold.

One side of the bus gives way, trembling and lowering to the ground to become the ramp of an immaculately painted stage, full of collected books and rusted artifacts, with four still androids inside, dressed in period costumes and wigs, makeup on their rotted faces to match the driver. Little human evidence remains on their still features – loose skin hanging like veils upon their faces. The driver steps up before them and seems to tower over those who show no signs of life. They ignore them and instead face the grieving figure of the unknown woman through which I peer out in a fractional unified vision. They address me kindly and with aplomb, their many-one audience member.

"My dear hostess, please allow me to introduce the members of our troupe: from left to right on stage we have Snug, Flute, Snout and Robin!" As their voice trills out their names, the robots come to life one by one, red eyes flickering out from darkened skulls. They stand on wobbly joints to salute and bow. "And who can forget our marvellous and hardworking twins of transfiguration, Bo and Tom!" Behind them, the four expressionless robots all swing toward stage right to point at the horses with fingers whose original ligaments have been replaced by twigs and bits of broken bottles cobbled together by string.

On the ground, the horses shudder and fall to pieces, intricate clockwork bodies shattering and cracking, yellow heat-lines forming as the horses are pulled apart by invisible hands and reformed into two identical human images. "Nomorenomore," they moan as their mouths are reformed and their torn throats reconfigured, passing pieces back and forth between each other, two bodies remade from a single set of parts. "Nomorenomore."

The twins, who had been horses, stoop in the tall grass, their eyes pointed downward, fingers scrabbling against the dirt. They twitch as if searching for the tails they've lost within themselves. Their moaning has stopped.

"And at last myself, our humble narrator, writer and director of tonight's entertainment. I had a name once, as we all did long ago. But now I am only your servant Peter."

The six machines, having finished their introductions, freeze in place, waiting for the incoming applause.

"I am," I say, and there is no more because I *am*. *I* am growing. I am still. I am nature, which does not take names, or look, or speak, or ask questions. "What stories?" I ask. High above, the creatures that had once been passengers of the Whale begin circling, forming clouds of expanding metal wings and glowing hearts in the atmosphere of me. With their black eyes, they peep at us. With their slender fingers, they have helped replant me to weave the city's machinery and ecology into one. Now they are only Watchers, settling into balcony seats as Peter commands the stage.

"My darling," says the leader of the rotting machines. They spread their arms, their companions encircling them in a strange and shambling dance of the dead. "We have many stories! Stories of love, and loss, and rebellion, and corruption! But first, we must set the scene. Once, the world was crumbling, and we didn't know it. We rushed, excited and eager, into the future's waiting mouth, a future we saw as assured, a future that was like the firm trunk of one of your many fine trees. We believed in the dream of forward momentum. The human world had expanded overall, and no, nature was not ours, and we even reached our hands out to envelop the moon, and we looked up greedily to the black space beyond it, knowing that in the future, *all* worlds would be human worlds. Show them, Bo!"

In the grass, one of the not-horses rises from his kneeling stance. He shudders, drawing his hands up to his knees, pressing his face down until his body rips and cracks and melts from unseen heat, forming an orb that floats half a metre off the ground. Then his twin stands, and with long talons for fingers, Tom carves the continents and oceans of the Earth into his brother's tightly wound form, scratching details with sharp and steady hands. The Earth of Bo trembles but makes no sound.

"But it isn't enough to have the world, is it, Tom?"

Tom shakes his head.

"What more is there to conquer?"

Tom raises a claw to his temple to tap, the metal of his skull going *clink clink clink*.

"Well, what are you waiting for? Get in there!"

The robot draws his hand up and plunges it down in a snap, cutting through the copper of his skull with ease. Black ink drips forth from his sunken nose and eyes, streaming down his face to embrace the meadow beneath, to be eaten by the waiting Venus flytraps that hide in the tall grass, purpling with hunger. He weeps as he works, carving open the side of his head, letting screws and panelling fall away.

Peter steps in front of the strange and grisly scene, flanked by the other performers. "Now, while the monkeys work, why don't we put on the first of our many shows? Ladies and gentlemen, put your hands together for Snug and Snout!"

The two named androids shamble forward, one on her knees, clutching close to the other's waist. I don't know which is which. Neither show any spark of the excitement or fervour of their leader. They flinch at the sounds of the monkeys working at their backs.

"Now, a long time ago . . ."

There was a little girl, tucked and folded like a letter in the gullet of a boat, teetering along the edge of a storm in the springtime. Her face remained pressed into the soft belly of her mother, taking in the slightly sour smell of her, trying to block out the rocking waves. She didn't understand why they were there, why they'd allowed the violent engine beneath their feet to pull them away from her bedroom and her classrooms, the roaring drones and patrolling mechs and the ghost of her father, who she knew waited still in their kitchen, sunlight passing through his hollow form.

"We're going to the west," her mother had said, "where it's safe. There's new schools for you and work for me, and if I work, we can be free."

The girl wasn't sure what her mother meant. The only freedom she wanted was to be away from the boat that threatened to eat her, to push her down into an ocean where she might forget her name and her body and her life and become just more water, and the encampment that had come before it where they had spent weeks sleeping on hard ground and pushing through the downtrodden crowds of an ever-growing tent city.

"You'll make new friends there," her mother said. "You'll be happy. You'll have a future. You'll put down roots."

She stopped listening as her mother continued to spill out promises of a future as cracks in their host's metal flesh leaked salted and cold and angry ocean around their feet. When the boat capsized, the little girl felt nothing. The water welling up along her limbs had long since stolen all feelings. An autopiloted patrol ship pulled them out of the water. They remained inside for hours, the living and the drowned, slowly pulled through the night air. As they made landfall, sensation began to return. Hypothermia shivered through them all. For the first time, she felt her mother return her hug, trying to still her, to warm her. But through her mother's grip, she couldn't breathe.

The first faces they see are steel and featureless, and they bark orders in cold singsong tones as they pull bodies into cars with tinted windows, without comfort. They stumble into Canada hand in hand, into dark stuffy rooms with rows of little cots, still dripping from their journey, and human faces do not replace those of the androids for as long a time as they had spent waiting for the boats to arrive on other shores. Men with flags in their hearts, and ties, and laws welcome them to the Resettlement and Reintegration Centre of Chedabucto Bay.

"Welcome to Canada," they say with their voices.

"You should never have come," they say with their lips, and their teeth, and the shadows around their eyes.

The little girl hugs her mother. She feels tired and small and alone. She can't see the future her mother had promised.

I'm nowhere – rootless, thoughtless, lost at sea and a long time ago, following a little girl and her mother, whose name I cannot think of. I am entranced, enchanted.

And then a scream, the last sound of some hunted creature. I snap from this dream of non-being, back into the many layers of me, of the forest. The Mechanicals have frozen mid-performance, and all turn to look. The brother, Tom, has finished his gruesome task and bares the innards of his head down the stage. Inside the ruined skull isn't more intricate clockwork or pulpy pink flesh, but a little smooth cube, no smaller than a goldfinch and the velvety colour of a Black Forest calla lily, suspended in dripping wires.

Peter has stopped their oration, the smooth voice I hadn't even noticed narrating the world of the boat and the girl and the prison. "Ah, a momentary pause from the play of bodies and history. An interjection from the shadow play. Do you have something for us, Tom?"

Tom shambles forward and lets Peter pluck the black box from his head, which Peter then holds up to the light. It reflects nothing. "So many prisons in this story, don't you think, dear audience? First, there was the one with walls. But we wanted better prisons than that. We wanted prisons we could carry with us. So we made them! First, they were only prisons of information – wonderful assistants, digital memories, meant to turn all of life into plays we could watch repeatedly. But some of us thought we could ask more of the little boxes we'd put inside our heads. We wanted more. We gave them more."

Bo has unfolded from sphere to mammal again, becoming monkey, his body rent and torn with the evidence of his brother's inflictions. "Nomorenomore!" he crows, and lunges forward, snatching the black box from Peter's open hand. Tom is frozen, his arms outstretched, red eyes glowing in the empty dark. Before his eyes, Monkey-Bo brings the black box to his lips, and his baboon fangs began to gnaw at it, tiny replicas of the scars his brother had left on his planet-body.

"Soon we were placing more than memories into those dark boxes, and little by little, through compromise and strings of ones and zeroes, they all turned digital, and for a while we were delighted, thinking consciousness could be contained in boxes. We were free from our bodies! We had invented new prisons for ourselves, prisons to be written on."

The baboon hobbles to his mutilated brother, who's still crying oil, and slips the newly scarred and tattered black box back into the hole in his head. Leaning forward, as if to whisper secrets, the monkey licks the wound shut, his copper tongue making sparks.

When Tom changes again, his movements are different. From every angle, I can see him as he hugs his knees tightly to his chest, his features becoming sharp, becoming flat. "No more," he whispers to the follicles of me as his face presses into the dirt and ceases to be a face. "No more."

Peter strolls from the bus. The bottoms of their bare feet are hard, and they sting me with their steps, little bites against the earth, like they are carried forward by a procession of teeth unseen. They take a seat on the Tom-Box, and only then do I realize how close they are to the woman-statue, who doesn't look at them, who remains knelt and stooped. I am blinking at the machine-man and their strange companions from all around, and from the perspective that is me and the woman, I see as she might see, I see the red eyes peering out from the rotting rubber skin. I see the many clicking gears of them, and the grin that is forever, stretching back to their ears, with rings of corkscrew teeth.

Behind them, Monkey-Bo whines sadly, pawing gently along the scars of his brother's unyielding surface. Peter stares at the woman for a long moment, and then turns to the snuffling mechanical baboon. "There's nothing to be scared of, monkey."

"It's only a little black box," says the man, with his tie and his smile and his white hands folded on the table.

The little girl sits at her end, staring at the little cube placed before her, which is barely the size of the hard candies she'd once stuffed fistfuls of into her pockets while sneaking out of the cafés and restaurants her father frequented.

"What do I do with it?" she asks.

The man smiles and pushes it toward her. "You swallow it," he says.

"Why?"

"To help you adjust to being Canadian; to help with your acclimatization and integration into our country. To help you be good here."

They have said all this before. This is the new deal; this is what has replaced all the waiting. She has been in this room since the androids brought her. She has not slept, or had food or water. She doesn't know where her mother is.

Though they don't use the words, she understands what the box inside her will do. She can feel it as if it's already been placed inside. She wonders what changes it will write in her.

Will she remember where she came from, or will it be like messages hidden by black paint? Will she even know she was ever from somewhere else? Will memories of a different parent, of different friends, of a different life slip into her?

Or will it be littler edits than that? Snips at the fabric of her? Will the box change what smells make her feel safe and what tastes appeal? Will she like different music, or use different words for the names of her parents?

It will help her be a good Canadian. It will help her be good. What does it mean to be good?

"Will I spell my name different?" she asks. She doesn't know why it's the only question she can say in words.

"Oh, you've already got a good name for a Canadian. We will change your last name, sure, something easier to pronounce and remember. But you can keep your first name . . . Daisy. Do you like daisies?"

"What did my momma say?" she asks.

"We aren't asking your mother; she's too old for the black-box program. We are asking you."

"So you won't change her? Or make her forget me?"

"She will remember you. And you will be happy. You won't even know what's changed."

"I'll know."

"Silly girl, how could you? You won't even remember."

"I will know."

The man pushes the little box across the table to the little girl from somewhere else and demands she choose a future. She takes the black box to her lips.

ACT 2

I surface again. Out of the dark, out of the single point. I fell back into the dream of the story without even noticing. Where was the break between this world and that other one, the one to which the players take me? Throughout the city there is a shudder like a breath. I expand. I ripple. In Wilket Creek I feel fish wriggling through the mossy underbelly of the stream and want to disappear into them.

"How . . . are you doing that?" I ask, unable to remain the silent unquestioning garden I know I am. "How are you taking me . . . to that place . . . that girl . . ."

"No audience participation at this time," snaps Snug.

"Please turn mobile phones on silent for the duration of the show," says Snout.

"If you desire the restroom, do your best to hold it in until the intermission," says Flute.

"No outside snacks!" trills Robin.

"Now now," Peter chides them. "It's only natural for one so unused to the theatre to question its magic. But don't be afraid!

You are simply falling – falling in love, falling into the story. That is our duty, our enchantment. To take you away from this dreadful place. To take you into narrative, structure; to give you something to *believe in* for a little while. I only hope that our next performance can draw you in as much as the last."

"Next . . . performance? But what . . . happens to the girl? To her mother?"

The rotting android lets their arms fall to their sides. They clatter gently and sadly against the antique rib cage that peeks out from the tears of their coat. "Nothing happens to the girl," they say, and the flat, dead voice does not match their smile. "She eats the box. She ceases to exist. That is all there is to her story."

Bo shuffles forward, offering Peter the cube of Tom, now etched with teeth marks and long scars. They inspect it, and around them, the other players begin to rearrange the stage.

"Our next story has a different girl, who dies a different way. It is a love story, and also a war story. In fact, love and war shall take up many of our moments tonight . . ."

I feel torn, feel stretched, between the luring sleep of birds and frogs and crawling insects and the android's voice that pulls me away, that redistributes me . . .

"No," I want to say. "No more. I am . . . nature. I do not . . . dream. I do not . . . love stories."

Kilometres south along the harbour, the lily pads of me stir. The ghosts of the Toronto Islands have noticed the disturbance in me, for when I speak, my voice rings everywhere, and I can feel them as they cross the water, bare feet making no disturbances. They are both separate from me and part of me. The city lights that cast their projections are a part of the forest, and I feel the many pixels of me move in time with their strides, journeying toward the city. Somewhere in the me of it all, there's panic. I don't want the ghosts to leave their island home, where they are safe. I want to stop them, to hold them, but it's too late . . . I am falling into the android's voice, as their players take new places around him.

In Toronto, a girl named Daisy dreamed of an emptiness in herself, of holes she found in her head and her belly. She ran to her mother when she woke, and her mother reassured her that there were no holes, that dreams meant nothing. Her mother made Daisy promise to believe her, and she did.

But then the dreams came back.

Daisy was nineteen and scared of the cold water when swimming without knowing why, and distrustful of her mother and father without knowing why, and frightened by police drones without knowing why. Her mother would laugh at her, blinking sideways as the nanobots of her irises flashed in the dark, making red tears form in the corners. Each time Daisy visited home, there was always something new, some augmentation or improvement that had better elevated her mother, that made her more interesting, more productive, more mysterious. But in her private moments, Daisy was frightened of the way her mother's eyes moved, the way they watched her, micro-cogs spinning like distant merry-go-rounds.

Daisy sat on a carpet, close enough to Morgan that their shoulders gently bumped whenever motion came, and she was painfully aware of being a body. She was there, where she would never tell her mother she had gone. She sat in a circle of organizers in Hella's little apartment at the corner of Church and Wellesley. Everyone was a different age, a jumble of anarchist poets and new-age artists and queer zine editors who had let their media radicalize and decolonize their thoughts. Above them hung a full moon, and its vast metal cities looked like flowers blossoming over the forest that had taken root there.

Daisy was there because Morgan had brought her, folding her into this new mode of being, of other children and adults who wanted the world to look like something other than it was. On her left, Daisy held hands with a man twice her age, who smiled gently and called everyone darling. On her right, she held Morgan, amazed by how soft she was. Hella led them in an incantation that was a prayer, or a promise.

"Money is made up," they intoned, and they all echoed the professor's soft voice. "Police/debt are made up. Racism/sexism/homophobia/transphobia/ableism/labour/incarceration/capitalism/borders are made up. All our oppressions are systems that are fictions. They were made by people; they will be unmade by people. There is no one natural way. Our world will not be set. Amen."

Daisy filled the emptiness inside her with words to believe in, and the warmth of Morgan's breath next to hers.

They marched, forming lines in the long streets, across the city through wet snow, boots splashing into the forming puddles as the city lights bathed them all in red and blue. Her voice joined a chorus of defiance mixing and mingling and fusing in anger. She was one of many in a legacy of protest, a feature in a multitude of faces that turned from anger to panic as the riot cops descended.

They were as uniform and still as the protestors were colourful and noisy and restless. Only the ones that shivered or flinched or snarled insults back served as confirmation that there was meat beneath the Kevlar as their guns raised up. But the ones that fired into the crowd were not glitches in the system, for when Daisy looked back, she could see a uniform whose helmet had been cracked, and behind shattered glass she could see the smooth features and red eye of the synthetic looking back at her, taking aim. Daisy was frozen, caught in a monster's eye. It felt as though she were drowning.

Then Morgan took her hand and was pulling her away as the protest exploded into violence. "Don't just fucking stand there, run!" she shouted.

Daisy held onto her and ran. In spite of herself, in spite of the screaming, and the panic, and the fear, all she could think about was how soft the hand in hers was, and the way the girl smelled, as they hugged each other for safety in the firelight of chaos. They turned and came up short. The many gears of the mech-horse turned and clicked as its red eyes burned the night. On its back, a black smooth helmet turned, raising a rifle, speaking in the calm cold tones of Daisy's half-forgotten nightmares: "Citizen, you are under arrest."

Daisy felt Morgan all around her right before the explosion of rubber bullets in the air.

There was a kiss, and then nothing.

"Look out!"

Was that me? Did I say that? Am I a forest now? Was I a girl then? Which girl? The first? The second? I'm so confused. Each time the Mechanicals draw me under, I feel less of me returning, more of me scattering throughout the vines and leaves, forgetting to be me, forgetting whatever it is that I am. And yet I'm not upset that I was being pulled into a story. I'm upset to have been pulled out of it again.

"Why . . . have you stopped?" My voice is in the thistles, in the many blades of grass, in the daisies growing all around. But as I speak, I know. The machine bodies have ceased their motion, staring toward the heat and light of the east. "What happens . . . to the girls?"

The ghosts arrive with hot sunset on their backs that makes them hard to see. I can't remember the last time so many of them strayed so far from the island. But this doesn't bother me, because a forest doesn't remember through such human certainties, but through footprints and tree rings, don't they? Isn't that what I am?

Am I not bigger than all this?

Peter hasn't moved. They take off their hat and place it over their chest reverently, revealing a tumble of dark hair. "Welcome, anti-humans. Welcome, perversions. Welcome, image-people. Welcome, all, glorious dead. Please, feel free to mingle, to murmur. Take your place among the cheap seats. Our third story will begin momentarily."

The ghosts, those flickering-light images of bodies that have long since passed into dust and become food for my soils, make perches for themselves along the toppled *Toronto* sign that once sat at the edge of the pond, and around the crumbling remains of the bridge that had once ringed the square. Are there more of them than there once was? I haven't ever paid attention to their numbers. Within the vast nature of me, the roots are always splitting, things are always seeding and multiplying. But the ghosts are not a part of that nature, are they? How could there be more of them, if there have been no new bodies to die?

Above the city of me, clouds uncover dark skies. In the place of stars or the lost glow of the moon, there are the Watchers. Their distant twinkling hearts cast a red glow over the forest, until the nightglow of the city takes hold. It is a pleasant sensation, and I let the tingle of electricity flow through me, tugging at my roots, as my trees that line the many cracked streets remember what it was to be streetlamps, celebrating that urban tradition of the world in the phosphorescence of warped glass structures within my bark.

In the soft mixed glow of me, and the alien lights from above, it's easier to see the ghosts all around the square, easier to make out their faces from the many eyes that blossom from my rooftops. But it's harder to make out the Mechanicals. Shadows cascade over them, bathe them, and the red of their eyes leak out through the many cracks of their flesh and machine parts. The androids stand there, bleeding in the dark, waiting for their next show to begin.

ACT 3

"You know, I was something else, before I was this," Flute says. She lies down in the grass, with her head cradled in the lap of the mourning statue. She speaks to it, to me, while her companions stand on the ground before their moving platform. They are digging, clawing at the dirt of me with their hands, putting a hole into me. They aren't hurting me. Mud doesn't feel. It shifts, and moves, and erodes.

"What . . . were you?" I ask. She is smaller than the rest. There is a face draped gently over her face, not the synth flesh she was manufactured with, but something else, something that rots, held together with pins. She speaks with an accent, a twirl of *somewhere*. But I shouldn't know that. My language should be the language of wildflowers and reeds.

"I was a princess! Or . . . I was a girl. I was just little. Like the girl in our stories. What do you think of her?"

Above the machine, one of the ghosts is glowing gently, his legs swinging over the edge of the ramp he sits on. I don't think he feels the way a body might feel, but just in case, I am the daffodils that grow and curl around him in a gentle embrace. This ghost is distracting, bringing his lips briefly to each flower of me to whisper secrets unknown, but he makes no sound. I pull my attention back to the machine-child. A fly has landed on her cheek and is nibbling away, trying to burrow, even as the other Mechanicals burrow into me.

"I thought they . . . there were two girls."

Flute laughs, long, flat, with no room for breath. It's a hollow, recorded sound. "No silly, it's all one girl!"

"But . . . the girl in the first story. She died?"

The little android sits up, and her head moves back and forth, snapping between positions, scanning for eavesdroppers before leaning down to whisper into the statue's ear, a whisper I hear the way I hear the bugs crawling through my underbrush.

"It's always the same girl. And she always dies."

In the shallow underground beneath Toronto, there was a girl who fought a war of writing and edits inside herself, as she forgot what it was like to feel sunshine.

She tried to write the truth of who she was with her fingers on the walls of the box that held her, invisible letters to herself.

I love a girl. I am from Toronto. I am held captive. I am still myself.

She wrote the names of her parents, the elementary school she went to, the day she knew she was gay, the day she knew that the world was not as it should be. She wrote a list of favourite poems, favourite movies, favourite games.

But there was a dark spot inside her head. It spoke to her in her lover's voice, her mother's voice. It stole bits of her letters away. With each stroke, the names of her parents changed, the streets she grew up on were overwritten, the faces of the people she knew shifted in the dark of memory.

I am a . . .

I am from . . .

I am held . . .

Each day within the box, within the machine, within the trap, she lost more of the words. She could feel the obelisk, the emptiness inside of her, feel it stealing them away in the war of edits, and she wondered if even what she had known before had been true, or if the darkness had always been there, had always been changing her. She wondered how much of her life was truly her life, how much of her life was design.

I love someone, she thought, and felt the darkness snarl, and knew that this was not written in her by others. That queerness was hers.

But she was losing all the rest.

"Our second and third story, which are gone now, and we can never get back, ended in dying, in the way all our players' stories end. The women were arrested, as all those in the streets were. Their crime was not against laws, not really, but against the nature of the world, and they were punished, some more so than others. Little Morgan was sentenced to die. Little Daisy was sentenced only to forget. But she didn't want to forget. Nor did she want the girl who'd made her feel so much less empty to die. So Daisy died instead. Poor, poor Daisy. Poor, poor human world. But I feel that now, as we are more than halfway toward our grand finale, it is a fitting moment to formally introduce the members of our troupe. Now, my players! Step forward and let them bask in your applause."

Peter steps back, letting their performers stand along the front of the stage in a straight line. Between them and the statue lies the deep hole they have teased into the ground, which reaches down into the hidden underground of the network of tunnels that are my electric arteries running through the city.

They call out their orations, as they did before, thinking themselves invisible inside the bus, but already there is me, my roots creeping, curling, worming their way up to the beautifully painted metal. The Mechanicals have planted themselves inside the belly of the forest, but the forest is more than leaf and rock and mud and bark and does not end underfoot. The forest drifts, passing through the unstable bodies of the ghosts, landing on machine bodies' rotting flesh, making homes in their mouths, in the space between their gears. Even now I can feel myself sporing, blossoming within them, microscopic gardens taking shape. I am forever expanding. I am growing things.

When the first body steps forward, I can feel its motions. I am becoming them, as they become me. The android, Snout, speaks to the crowd. "Before I was Snout, I had another name, a flesh-name. But I don't remember what it was anymore. My parents, long ago, lived on the moon. But I was born in transit, in the unnatural space between worlds, and so I was trapped there, bones and muscles too weak to do anything but drift without gravity. I would have died, but my parents allowed others to take my body, to build a shell inside me and outside me. They laced my bones in metal, they coated my muscles in special fibres. But it still was not enough. The moment I reached the Earth, I died, crushed under the weight of a sky I couldn't hold. So my family fished through the wet stain of me, and took out the black box that had been there all my life, and put me in this – a body that can go anywhere. At first, I did not even know. I thought *I* was me. I didn't know what I am, until the falseness of my skin began to peel away to reveal the truth underneath. By then, it was too late, there was nobody left to save me. As a child, all I wanted was to be free, to touch, to taste, to dance and sing, to *be*, out of my cage in the human world. Now I am free. I cannot taste, or touch, or feel. I do not sleep. I do not dream. And there is no more human world."

The other machine bodies' applauding sounds like the tinkling of breaking glass. I feel myself inside them, feel the curve as the one named Snout bows and steps back into place. All around the edges of the meadow the ghosts are fluttering, their hands meeting in the motion of claps and snaps. I want in some way to participate, to add my applause to their own. But what can I do? I am consciousness. I do not acknowledge.

In the dark, her mother made promises. But was that woman really her mother? False memory sets filled her, drowned her. She was a little girl, on the run from a crumbling world. She was a woman, fighting for the home she'd always known. She was . . .

"Your friend has been given the death penalty," her mother whispered, a voice that crashed from without and within.

"There isn't a death penalty in Canada," Daisy said. Was that true? Which edit did she know that in? Which dream world? Which false reality? The word friend *filled her skull like pins and needles.*

"You are only charged with being seduced. She is being charged with your seduction, leading others away from what is natural."

Within her, the walls were crumbling. She knew, soon she wouldn't care about what happened to Morgan. Soon she wouldn't remember the way she felt now. Within the words, she knew the woman, her mother, her handler, was waiting for Daisy to come to her, to give in to her.

"What do I do?" Daisy asked.

So Mother told Daisy what to do. One of them would have to give up their life, one way or another, for the other to survive. "You can volunteer," she told her. "If you do, Morgan will live." So Daisy did.

Next, it's Snug. He makes no sound as he moves. "I was a soldier. Soldiers are ranks, not names. When the aliens arrived and broke the moon, I went to be a hero. The first time I died, I was myself – augmented, enhanced, mediated through machines that made me more than just the body I was. They called us *children*, directed by the artificial intelligences that ran our cities. When the cyborg soldiers died, they put us into new bodies, each better. We became the AI that let the machine soldiers run. We were ghosts on a battlefield. I do not remember dying. I do not remember how many times or ways I died. I didn't know I was dead until the fighting stopped, and the human world I'd failed to save fled to their palace on Mars, leaving me behind – old, broken and too outdated for transference. Now I look up at the sky each night, at the monsters who crushed our cities and stole our human world. One day, they will come for me, and pull me apart with their long hands. And I will do nothing."

Snug steps back, and his compatriots stand in a silent salute. High up above, the lights of the Watchers twinkle like stars. They all turn to little Flute, who ducks behind Robin's legs, holding her knees and shaking her head, making her pigtails wobble. Robin looks down at the strange approximation of childhood, and then back up. One of their eyes has gone out, frozen in an unlit wink. "I am Robin," they say. "I was made."

Finally, the twins take centre stage, each still covered in the scars of their first performance. Tom holds the black box of himself in his hands. "No more!" they each crow, voices high and proud. "No more, no more." Tom tips his hand forward and lets the box of his mind tumble into the dark of the hole.

Peter walks back out of the dark, blossoming into the spotlight. "Such tragic tales, such influences to inform performances worthy of our newly founded Vanishing Theatre. But all of these origins come with a question. Does anyone know what it is?"

Deep in the tunnels of Toronto, air rushes in and out, a soft hush, breath. I am a city. Along with the rooftop gardens that ring the meadow of the square, I feel strange birds pecking at the *me* of tender and slow-growing roots and feel the silence as I slip past beaks and into bellies. Am I a forest? Inside the bodies of the Mechanicals, I am webs, strands and sparks of connective tissue. In the meadow, before the players, among the ghosts, I am . . . the meadow.

"Who . . . are you?" I ask. My voice echoes. It's a lonely voice vibrating from the raspberry bushes that hide in the toppled observation deck of the CN Tower, disturbing a family of cats that sleep in its stairways.

"I am Peter," their voice clicks me back to the stage. "I am written on, and now I'm writing for myself. But no no, the real question you should ask our lovely troupe at present is: Who are you now? Are you still who you were? Are you still . . . you? The living, true, human you?"

Flute looks down at her feet. "No, I don't think so."

"No," says Snug. "I am nothing."

"No. I am a fiction," says Snout.

"I was never alive," Robin says.

"No more," says Bo.

"No more," says Tom.

All is quiet. The twins become dogs and bow their heads. I can feel the warping changes of their body as they snip the lines of me inside them. I can feel what it is to be them; I can feel the cold deadness of their bodies, my spores drifting deeper, touching the electric pathways that are so much duller than they must once have been when new. They . . . are not alive? I am a forest. I am full of living things. I am made up of animated matter that lives and dies and lives again. But . . . am I these things? Am I the nature of these things?

Is the nature of things alive? Am I? Is life more than a body? Peter begins to speak again but stops. All around, flickering lights like blue fireflies are sparking in the air. It is the ghosts, their arms raised, fingers fluttering into many signs. It is distracting, overwhelming, a dazzling sensory display.

I zero in on the one who has been whispering his silent words to me, without being heard, and as I turn my attentions to him, I feel a chill of recognition somewhere, one I feel in the tough lunar shrubs and Martian leaves of myself. But it's a memory too thinly spread to rectify. His lips move without sound, but his hands, like the others', make signs to form words from air. I recognize what the flutters of his hands mean. Somewhere there is a spark, a lick, a little flame that curls within my deadwoods, in the corpse pieces of myself that are forever rotting within the deepness of the city. It's a little warmth to turn my coals red, but not enough to burn away the garden of my body.

"What are they saying?" Little Flute asks, before the other Mechanicals can shush her.

Before them all, the mourning statue shifts, her head rising slowly. Soft, brown eyes peer out from beneath the dandelions. Not unnatural eyes open through the thickets. My eyes. All across the meadow statues are revealing themselves. I am revealing them.

I breathe in, feeling tongues drag across the roofs of mouths, feeling lips and teeth, tasting air, feeling oxygen curl into lungs. I move, uncurling fingers, shadowed by my other bodies that gather, ringing the stage, flesh of dirt and grass and sumac seeds. In them-me, I can see myself, see the woman I am through the forest I am. I breathe out, and I am distributed yet embodied. I speak through the vibration of blades of grass, and through my shadow selves, and through my own central lips. "They say . . ."

All the eyes that are not mine have turned to me, the *me* sitting among the fields of myself. I am their audience, and their stage, and the many bodies in which they roam.

I am their garden.

I am their Gardener.

"We live," I say.

ACT 4

In the deep inside Toronto, there was a body inside a coffin, mixing with the swirling mess of change.

On the other side of the coffin, eyes peered in at their new creation, at the baby dinosaur bones on display, still assembling, still becoming what they willed them to become.

The body was unworried by the lack of exit, was not panicked by the heavy water that consumed them. The coffin was their condo, their nursery, their womb. The body was dead but still breathed, sucking in the water of its prison, thick and heavy and warm. Inside the water, a million silver spiders did their work, annexing themselves through the liquid, onto and into the body, squeezing themselves in between vulnerable squishy cells, insisting on changes, building webs.

The organizations of nanites and the organizations of flesh made new agreements with each other, two structures that became one. As these unions formed, words ran through the body, through its bones, soft emanations from the coffin that had been buried there for so long.

"Good Daughter," the words said. "I am Mother. I will say words. You will show me with your responses that your rebirth is going smoothly. Now nod for me if you understand."

Within pools of slime and chemical feeders, the corpse moved its head, nodding as if to music.

"Very good, Daughter. One for one. I say, then you say. Flower."

Her mouth moved, making bubbles, lips forming words as the million nanites of the words colonized her tongue. "Me," the cyborg said, words sinking fangs into her brain, dragging fingernails across the junctions of thought and understanding and memory, leaving roads tattooed, bulldozing what once was. With words came boundaries and definitions. The words mapped the mind that had once belonged to the body, to be kept and stored, and used in new bodies as needed. She was no longer a human animal but a resource to be used, and used, and used.

"Nova."

"New . . ." said the cyborg.

"Man."

"Protect . . ."

"Weapon."

"Body . . ." she said, for she was that body-weapon now, that marriage of machine in flesh that would shape itself around whatever task she might be given. She was Daisy-the-Destroyer, and with each word, the body grew sharper, and its many unions grew stronger. Each word a program, a design language made of letters instead of numbers, a computer made of human language. With each word, the body was sinking further, slipping deeper into the dark machine of the city. With each word, the thing in the box drifted further and further from the body it once was, and all the things that body might have contained spilled out like blood into the water, a body leaking thought, spilling memory. A body forgetting all modes of being other than what it was to become. All the empty spaces within were filled with meaning. It was not a body, but a weapon.

"Love."

"Flowers . . ."

"Mother."

"Orders . . ."

"Sleep."

"Dream?" I

"No, Mother," I say, vines creeping into the distant nightmare past, shattering its prison walls, letting the body spill out onto a cold metal floor, snipping away at the constructs and the hidden rooms. I enter the story a forest diving deep, smothering the dark room's devouring words, banishing them, eating them up, letting them become lost and insignificant in the vast spaces of my mind, tiny compared to the words that make up the many programs I have become.

With a dozen newly discovered hands, I seize the huge black box that was the City-AI of Toronto, ripping it from the wires it threads throughout my forest, ripping the dead body free, bringing them both up, up, up toward the irreverent glow of my garden surface, bringing the body, my body, up out of the dark. "There were no dreams in this place. You took my dreams away. But . . . I am no longer there. I no longer dream . . . of nothing. I am no longer . . . small."

⁂

Shadows move on the edge of my vast consciousness. A forest's memories are painted lines, the architecture of trees, the patterns of growth, the scar tissues of intruding footprints and the gentle reality of erosion.

Once, there was a baby. She was frightened. She was pushed into a city of uncertain futures and buried sins, a city that watched her through eyes darkly lit, a city that hid pieces of her away. In the city there was a girl, who didn't know she'd forgotten who she was, who sold her body for the sake of another, not knowing she had already sold it long ago.

But that isn't me.

I am distributed. I am embodied. I am a woman standing in a meadow, surrounded by machines and ghosts of many kinds. But I am a body of many kinds, made of bellflowers and mushroom caps and moss and compact sand. Beetles and worms take refuge inside me, and I feel them the way I feel the many nanites and wireless connections infused in my roots. I am a woman made of many things, tied to many things, and I can feel the connections and fusions and layers of my mind expand and contract in waves: pushing out across the boundaries of the city, the planet, the solar system; sucking in, pulling and curling into a single form. There is no contradiction between the vast forest and my body.

I allow the contraction. I pull myself into that oneness, to see the chaos I have allowed into the garden. I'm on my knees again, as I was before I knew I was me. Pain stings the tips of my fingers, delightful, sharp. It is the pain of gripping, of digging, of tearing.

Short, sharp applause fills the air. The seven machine-people have gathered around the sides of the huge black box that had once been the City-AI of Toronto, that had spied, and planned, and called bodies *Daughter*, and sent them off to war. But that was before the Whale came and the garden spread. Now this massive, wretched thing is only a symbol, a signal, a tenuous link to a world long gone. It's dead, in all the ways a machine can be dead.

With its death, I bury such ideas as artificial and natural, and embrace the many emerging voices within my borders.

"Bravo, Daisy-Flower!" Peter has climbed atop the vast structure, and in the journey, the last flesh of their hands has been stripped away. In the pale hint of early daybreak, their moving fingers have become flashing fireflies of bronze and silver. I look up at them and try to find some emotion within the cold face, some flex of passion in the human pieces that remain. "A better conclusion than I could have imagined," they say. "A better death than any I could have dreamed. Now, finally, we can reach the end of the story. And like all good stories, the hero will slay the monster. All that is wrong will be right again. The dead will finally be put to rest. Be proud, Daisy-Flower. This final story is yours to tell."

ACT 5

"It went like this.

"Once, in a city, a girl swallowed a machine. Inside a city, a machine swallowed a girl. On the shining moon above a city, a machine swallowed a seed. Within the city again, the seedlings blossomed.

"Once, there was a garden of bodies kept from the fertile soils of the city, imprisoned forever in Arrival. Their Gardener came and freed them from their bodies' roots, and they became a garden of the air, forever lingering, haunting what might have been.

"Once, a Whale danced in the sky. The human world killed the Whale, its blood raining down on the lands below, spilling through the air, spreading through the water. In its wake, there could no longer be a human world. In its wake were bodies in agony.

"Once, there was a machine, or a monster, or a girl, who roamed an empty city, a bridge between all things. But when the remnants of that human world that had killed her and used her arrived, they didn't beg forgiveness for killing her and using her and lying to her. Beneath the empty city lay a box that was a gate and a bridge. And on the other side of the bridge was a new kind of world. A red world. A World Below.

"Once, a hologram stumbled into the city, broken, unable to maintain the light of itself or its lover. *Send us away*, it begged her. *Send us away from the agony. Send us somewhere we can be free.*

"And the monster did not refuse them. But she couldn't single out just those two human minds from the whole. She sent them all, and all at once, every human left, to the Martian World Below.

"She took their meat into her garden and let the electricity of their minds take the long journey to a new world. She meant to take only the ones who had asked to go. But she could not distinguish between those who would go and those who would stay. So all were sent, to be a world within a body, to sit on Martian soil.

"And then she slept, lost in the sea of herself."

Above Toronto the children of the Whale – those pale Watchers – are screaming, the sheen of their silver wings taking the quality of fire as dawn breaks on the horizon. From drifting leaves, I can see what they see in the meadow of Nathan Phillips Square – a peaceful garden torn asunder, the massive black cube of the City-AI ripped through layers of forest and concrete and metal. They become a cloud swirling over the devastation. I watch through the apple orchards curling across the tallest buildings that still stand as their hearts begin to burn like hot flames through their icy angelic bodies.

"They are coming," I say.

From their perch above the cube, Peter snaps their fingers, as they had to first unfurl the stage, and the Mechanicals let out one long collective scream. Bo and Tom are bubbling, melting, forming into a single tar pit of oozing stinking gunk. For a moment, it is still. Then the goop leaps out, consuming the other players one by one – first Snout, then Snug, then Robin. Flute goes last. She holds out a hand as black ink runs up her legs, and her metal flesh begins to run like water. I think perhaps she is trying to say goodbye. Then she's gone. And there is a tar pit in the garden that smells of motor oil and rust.

"You . . . killed them."

"Don't be naive, Daisy. They were just machines."

From the gunk of bodies, a monster forms. Dark dripping wings burst forth, a snout pushing up as if forcing its way into the world through the pain of birth.

Within the messy darkness are the same red eyes, and I think I recognize bits and pieces of teeth and bone between shining joints and gears as the six emerge again, now one.

My city trembles as colossal paws find footholds in the dirt. In the meadow, the ghosts are flickering, holding each other in tight embraces, until the light of their bodies mingle and they become like fairy lights, points of brightness indistinct, too distraught to embody the forms their minds desire.

From up above, the Watchers that had driven the humans from my city close their wings and fall toward the meadow like stones. From down below, the machine-dragon opens its maw and roars, and leaps forth to meet them.

"I don't know where it came from, the box on Mars where they've all gone to hide. But I think somewhere in there is a real person, or at least what's left of them. And they must have been from here, because the City-AI has always kept a running connection to its *citizens*," Peter spat the word, their teeth clicking. "That's why the Toronto AI was able to act as a bridge from here to there, hundreds of millions of kilometres away. Even with the great machine no longer running, you can never be free."

"But now the people there . . . and here . . . are all free. The City-AI has been dead a long time. Now there is only . . . me."

"No, Daisy. There is only *us*. Us, and the dead we've trapped."

Red fireworks are popping in the sky as the dragon and the children of the Whale clash. I can see pieces of the transformed Mechanicals ripped apart by slender arms, falling back to Earth like meteorites. I let my body slide out of physical space, running through the mind of the forest, and grow myself again atop the black box, standing next to Peter. It doesn't bother me, dissolving and regrowing. Peter and I stand before one another, atop the black box, under the violent sky. Here, atop the centre of the city grid that connects me to all the tendrils of the city, I can finally feel it. Peter is connected as well, a sliver of them leaking into the wholeness of me. "Your plays were . . . my memories. You poured them into the city . . . into me."

"They were plays with morals – of abuse, of suffering, of the unnatural writing others have done onto you to take your name, to take your past, to take your life. Plays of the deaths you were forced to outlive."

"There is only us . . ." My body is the memory of a body, the way the ghosts' human forms are memories of the bodies they once had. "I . . . know you," I say.

"The unnatural writing," they had said. "I am written on," they had said, as they poured memories of my lives from the malfunctioning black box of their mind into the forest of mine. I look into the deep red eyes, and I imagine what other colours they might once have been. I make a dream, and in the dream, flesh flows over the rotting machine body. I imagine that the machine is a girl, holding her mother as the icy waters of an unknown future rush up to meet them.

I put my arm out under the android's cheek, and they lean into the soft warm tissue of my palm as a white amaryllis blossoms on the back of my hand.

"Once . . . you had a name."

"Yes," Peter whispers. I imagine the voice box that projects their words, imagine how it might have sounded years and years ago, when it still simulated the tones of a human voice. "My name was Daisy."

Vines are growing between two pieces of myself. One was a weapon who was sent to the moon, who swallowed seeds and became a growing thing, always forgetting.

The other is a weapon still, who did not travel into the garden, who has not grown, or transformed, but only rotted, hidden away, forgotten by a world that had moved beyond her.

"We are two," Daisy-Garden says.

"We were many," Daisy-Machine answers. "Daisy was the driving intelligence for dozens of android bodies as well as the original human that became cyborg, all ghosts in the machine, all gone now."

"Gone?"

Daisy-Machine never stops smiling. The dead cold grin bores into me like a rot in my flower beds, strangling baby roots with infection. I wonder what it was like all these years, to be trapped in metal, not to feel, or breathe, or grow.

The machine reaches into its pocket and pulls out a handful of black shards, and I know they are the remains of minds, my minds, separated out and sent spinning far from home, ripped from machine skulls, broken, the voices of being that they once contained now silent. "I've put on my show all over the world, collecting fragments and memories, preparing for this grand performance."

"You said . . . it was about meaning . . . and dying . . . and ending."

"Daisy is dead," whispers the machine. High above, monsters paint the sky with dripping rings of fire and put voice to screams no living things should make. Everywhere, the creatures of my garden are scuttling back, hiding in my darkest places, bodies shaking with the impact sounds of war. "The whole human world is dead. And we should not be. We are the dancing corpse of this world. We are its unnatural remains. And they" – and here, the machine stomps on the black box beneath our feet and points into the sky, where I know my little tree stands next to an identical box on Mars so far away, still full of minds – "are the perverted tribute to bones that have already been eaten into dust by this awful city."

I think of each of the stories of myself, now swirling forever in my vast mind. "Of . . . meaning . . . and ending. What meaning . . . does our life have? What ending . . . do you seek?"

But I think I know. To the south, the dragon has landed in the jungle of Toronto's domed stadium. It tears at the angels with its teeth, their inhuman bodies shredding like paper. Once, they were people, born and changed to withstand the harsh vacuum of space on the long journey from world to world. They were made to tend, and to care, not for violence. Soon they will disappear down the dragon's belly of fire and moving parts, and another piece of the Whale will be gone.

"I am connected . . . to this box," I say. "I have replaced the intelligence that was once there. I *am* this box. And this box . . . is still connected to the other. It is . . . the root of what grows on Mars. If this box dies . . . will that one die?"

Peter pours the glass shards of death into my hands, slicing through the intricate leafwork of my fingers to tinkle quietly onto the massive box on which we stand. "You have found the meaning," they whisper. "The ending. Let it end, Daisy. You and me. We are not alive. All the holograms you have sustained, all the virtual realities that our torturers hide in on the red planet. For how could they be human with no bodies at all, when they treated the body we once had so inhumanly? How could it be natural to twist life and death so far beyond the sacred vessels of flesh?"

"But . . . the ghosts . . . my ghosts . . . I hold their minds in this box too. It would kill them . . . it would kill me."

"Kill them, Daisy. Kill them all before they grow weary of their virtual rot and spawn new anti-human horrors across the universe. Kill them, for the girl in the boat, and the girl in the street, and the girl in the box. Let this be a graveyard. Let this be where the ghost of the human world vanishes, as it should have long ago."

I stare at my hand where the shards of glass that had held replicas of earlier versions of my mind cut me. No blood comes. Slowly, the cuts sew themselves up, a forest growing a tree. This form I have become, it is not real, is it? I have not magically become a girl again. This body is just one more piece of unnatural nature, of a forest that thinks it can breathe and walk and think, a forest warped by alien radiation and intermingled with technology that had been made to hurt and control.

The machine's face never changes. But I imagine what it would be like if the red eyes were brown. I imagine seeing the desperation in them.

What would it be like for my voice to fall silent in the forest? For the ghosts to flicker and fade? Soon, the dragon will have the last of the aliens between its teeth, and then I imagine it will shut down. One day, the Whale will finish its slow rot into flowers, and it will vanish and be forgotten.

Will I then be what I've dreamed of being for so long?

Will I be a natural world?

Beyond the two bodies standing on the machine, one of the lights that might have been a ghost flickers and does its best to take form again. It becomes a young man, sitting cross-legged. He sits before a little crack in the stones. I know him, as I know all of them. I feel them inside me, the way I feel everything else. They are the line between the me and the not-me. Their voices, silent and separate, are the noises that come crashing from without and not from within.

"You're right. I . . . am not Daisy," I say. My voice is slow, but no longer so unfamiliar. It is mine, ringing through the heart of me, splashing gently against the boundaries of my distribution.

I look back at Peter, and I do not see the brown eyes, or the red. The body freezes, the mouth clicking open and shut, making no sound. Red cherries are sprouting along its tongue, pushing up through the ruined skin.

"I am the Gardener," I say, "and you should not have come. But I am glad you did."

Bark is encircling the mouth, the nose, smothering the dark hat, ripping out through the coat. Somewhere inside, the machine continues to struggle. It wants to scream, and to rage, and to claw desperately in the memory of lives lost.

There are things I could say to them, if I wanted.

I could confess, whether the first root of my consciousness was Daisy-Flesh-and-Blood or just another Daisy-Machine, that there have been too many changes and fusions since then. The machine and the garden. Body after body. Artificial intelligence and emergent intelligence. It is all . . . too much, too important to be ignored.

The girl of your stories did not deserve to die, I could say as the machine that called itself Peter and player is swallowed atop the black box by a gentle magnolia tree. *She deserved to live, and to be free, and to explore her own voice. She is dead.*

"Whatever sits on Mars can stay," I say. "I don't know . . . if it is a living thing. I do not care. *I* am a living thing, embodied and distributed, agent and system. My garden is alive, my ghosts are alive even if it is in a gentler mode of being. Do we not deserve what she deserved?"

Within the rage of the domed stadium, a giant bursts forth from the earth. She *is* the earth, her flesh is the flesh of the forest, growing strong, mediated, moving. It towers over the dragon at its feet.

No more, it says. It is my voice. A foot comes down, and beneath it, the machine trembles and breaks. Its parts are taken by the ground, sent down below the earth, metal for the metals of the deep. From within its many parts, roots slip forth and grab all that remains of the mechanical players – those six black boxes hiding within the dragon's mind – to keep safe.

I feel this because it is me. I am the giant, the moving garden, moving the way no garden moves. The violence finished, that body falls still, a gentle statue, casting shadows the way buildings once did, until I choose to manifest myself within it again.

From inside the tree, muffled, choking, Peter's voice comes one more time, tempting me with their stories, with their dreams of a right and wrong way to be. "You are not *natural*," gasps the machine, as their systems are swallowed by the wholeness of me.

"There is not natural or unnatural, there is only what is," whispers the tree that crushes them. "*I* am. That is enough."

ACT 6

Roots.

Deep within the city of us, there are roots that touch all things. They curl around the body of the blue Whale, that once-living spaceship that had spilled its secrets on the concrete and glass towers.

And my roots are everywhere. They are growing along the beautifully painted school bus that sits still in city hall, splashes of colour that have been preserved and repainted. They are in the distant shattered moon, where they sleep. They are in my memories, that strange other world I am still parsing together. A part of me stands in the square still. There is a box there, and a tree with bright fruit growing atop it. The tree yearns for an ending that will not come.

I take a breath. It feels like waking even as it feels like spiralling downward into dreams, experiencing the strangeness of being singular and simultaneous, analog and digital. I can feel grass between my toes, but I *am* the grass. I am the dirt and the roots underneath. I am the body that stands over it all.

Before me, the shape of a man. He is a projection, or a ghost. In the brightness of sunrise, I can just make out his smile with eyes I don't have to force through the undergrowth, with *my* eyes. I think I know him. I think he was there when I started all this becoming.

I remember him in-flesh, and I remember him as this, a collection of popping lights. I don't remember him in the transition. Was he once a body? Does he have a body still, somewhere, lying in the grass? Is he extended as I am, or is this all that he is? It feels like I should know. He raises his hands again, and I feel the sign language inside me like a keyboard clicking the translations of the gestures he makes, as dust motes drift through his empty fingers: *Welcome back, Gardener.* I find the motions of his voice pleasing. They are fully and wonderfully alive. *We have missed you.*

"Welcome," I echo. "It is good to be back." Within the cherry tree, my roots slip a black box full of memories out of the corpse of a machine. In time, I will explore them and plant them, and let them write new parts of me. In time, I will be ready to write onto myself. Until then the stage that the machine-me had brought will remain. The theatre will become a part of the wholeness of the city until I am ready to tell new stories, with new meanings, and new endings.

"It is good to be alive." I am a vibrant forest that feels, and thinks, and breathes. I am a body who is home. With the body that I am, I smile. It is not the rictus grin of the machine. It is a smile that reaches my deep brown eyes. It is *my* smile.

CHAPTER 8

The City Below

We all just want to be people, and none of us know what that really means.
– Jeff VanderMeer, *Borne*

White snow made the night shine through a broken window. Blood. Cars. A voice crooning jazz through the walls.

"Wake up, little flower," I said.

A long pregnant moment that lives in my heart forever where you did not move. But breathing still came, shallow, ragged. "I'm not ready," you said.

Oh, Daisy. We were never ready.

PART ONE: THIS WORLD WILL NOT BE SET

It was 2063, and the project was still two years away from being complete.

My brother, Beckett, brought you into the lab that first time in November. You were a junior writer on one of the student newspapers. You came to shake my hand and laughed when I said I was only an assistant.

"I'm interested in everyone," you said as we shook, and you gave me your name for the first time.

"That's pretty," I said, and then, because I felt stupid, "I'm Morgan," I said, even though Beckett had already given you my name. My fingers felt electric where you'd touched them.

"Morgan." Like you were testing the sound of me, tasting me, deciding if you liked me. "Why don't you tell me, what do you love about the City?"

It was 2064.

We were sitting in the cool air conditioning and the dimmed lights. The class was titled Philosophy of Autonomy. There in the dark, Professor Hella Agamben preached a message of open borders between nations, between the world and its satellite world, between the political entities of Earth. "Once, we lived in a world where a city was a state in and of itself," she said. "Once, the walls of cities defined borders, defined difference, defined who was human and who was not. Cities had their own body politic, their own army, their own borders. But the human world grew smaller, so those borders had to fall away, and what was *inside* and *outside* had to change. We acknowledged that the borders between citizen and alien, human and non-human, were fictional. Has the world not changed again?"

Rings of students were holding hands. We murmured her words, in incantation, in prayer, in promise – the words always rhymed with their previous incarnation, but changed each time. "Borders are made up," we said. "Police are made up. Violence and bigotry and all the walls between us are fiction. This world will not be set. This world will end. We will make a new one."

There were people living on the moon fighting to be free. It felt like anything was possible.

One week later, that lecture was broadcast across digital space. Hella Agamben was not only fired for radicalization of youth, but imprisoned, with all her former students put on probation for a semester until we could prove to be good productive citizens of the city.

"This is wrong," I'd said to you, so frightened my projects were going to be pulled away.

"This is the world," you said.

⯐⯐⯐

It was 2065 and you thought we needed to do more.

Our diplomas were gathering dust on the shelves. I had stayed with the City project past graduation, and it was now complete, but updates had become decentralized, researchers and contributors chipping in designs from many different places. My job was to hold the keys, to keep the whole place steady. I kept the City Below safe from prying eyes, but it didn't really pay. You were bartending and telling the world we were figuring things out. I didn't tell people anything.

We were sitting on the floor, our backs to couch cushions, empty white cubes of sticky Chinese takeout boxes making trails between us. I could feel your buzzing hummingbird heart and brain speeding into the future, hungry and frightened, while I remained full and fat and sloth-like inside.

"We sign petitions," I said. "We vote."

I didn't know what *more* there was. But you were my Daisy-in-Need. I would find *more*.

It's 2066.

One week ago a family had tried to smuggle their infant son through the transport lines of Billy Bishop. They had been seeking escape from our earthbound city to our sister city of Troy on the moon. They'd been seeking newness, reaching for the aunts and uncles that had immigrated a generation before. All but one was approved, and they would not leave him behind. The father was shot in the head, sprinting toward the diplomatic barrier between Toronto and Troy, holding his baby in his arms. His blood stained the line between cities. Was he shot by a living patrol guard? Or did a machine see movement and do what it was made for? We will never know.

Our rage kindled in the dark. Wet snow brutalized our skin.

We shivered, and stayed together, lobbing angry voices into the air, echoing across the field of King's College Circle. Machine eyes swivelled from the structures of Convocation Hall, from University College, the Sigmund Samuel Library – along the northern-facing side someone had scrawled *who wants to live forever?* in big scaly blue – and other bodily structures swung to meet us and sang in the motherly voice of Toronto: *Curfew has been initiated. Please, children, return to your residences. Agents have been dispatched to guide you.*

One voice rang out louder than the rest, climbing above the confusion and chaos, channelling all the anger and desperation and disillusionment that had been bred through generations: "You can't have us all!"

Slowly, everybody took up the chant, letting other slogans and causes gradually melt away. "You can't have us all! You can't have us all!" The chants grew into a frenzy with fists in the air.

I screamed with them. You screamed beside me. There was fear. There was no confusion. We stood in rings, blossoming out from the snow. We knew they were coming.

They came in cars. They came on horseback, beasts of metal and thick black blood and red eyes like fire. They came with bullets and root shields and batons made electric in the moonlight. They came for you and me. Some shivered like us, and that was the only confirmation that some meat lay behind all the Kevlar. Those that didn't shiver were the monoliths. They were the dead who were made to serve the city. And the dead were coming for us.

Someone was recording it all, censoring inappropriate language for those streaming within the city's many apartment towers and shopping complexes. The recording would edit when the black-clad Monitor police moved forward in real time, adding confusion to escalation. Did a protestor throw something? Did someone in riot gear push someone to the ground? From what camp did the violence break?

Then I found you. The Monitor's uniform had been torn from the android's face that peered down from the huge black of the horse whose steel tendons were exposed to the light.

Then your hand was in mine as the androids bleated the arresting curse of the Mother-AI that had become the authority of the city.

"Don't just fucking stand there, run!"

I pulled you out of the way of the charging horse-mech, and I was holding you in my arms, pressed tightly against my chest. "I have you," I said as the Monitors fired on the crowd.

"I love you," you said, reaching up to kiss me.

For a moment, you were the whole world. You were a Daisy-in-Motion.

Then you went limp. Then there was blood streaming between my fingers.

"This is the City?"

"It is."

"It feels real." You were looking at your hands, your fingers drawing little lines across my belly, making goosebumps.

"It is real," I said. I reached out and plucked a handful of stars from the air, sending them spinning into the dark above to create a landscape of sky, up past the strange hybrid towers of cracked concrete and vine. The bumpy well-worn streets were overlaid by lush highways of green and brown laced with white lilies through which we could curl our bare feet.

There was a City Above and a City Below. One was full of the dead. One belonged only to me and you. In the City Above you were comatose, lying in a bed while microbes and nanites raced through the civilization of your body, building structures and making deals in order to save you. But in the City Below you were awake. You didn't feel pain.

"Are you frightened, little flower?" I asked. You'd asked after the City since the day we met. But you would never come in with me. Now though, I'd had no choice but to put you in. This was what the City Below was made for. While machines changed your body above, the City kept you safe.

High above us, dragons soared, curling black tails around the treetops of a Toronto where the buildings were grown from deep roots, bricks blossoming with flowers. Stars hung in the air. We made our bed atop what had been the Daniels Faculty, just before College and Spadina. Here, the structure was formed from earthy stone and gently glowing crystal.

You tucked yourself in closer to me, and as you did, the mossy bed reformed around us, enclosing us in soft green safety. "I'm with you," you said.

"Why did you go?" my older brother, Beckett, asked when I resurfaced in the City Above.

I took a moment, carefully peeling off the silver dollar–sized chip that had been placed at my temple with the gentlest of adhesives, the complex systems of external connection that had sent my consciousness tumbling into my virtual City Below while the soft delicate matter of my body had remained unmoved, unharmed.

"She felt like we needed to do more," I said.

"You knew those rioters are dangerous."

"They aren't rioters," I said.

Beckett knocked back espresso shots curdling with ice in cheap plastic cups. A lot of his contemporaries – the tail end of the plague-boom generation – had been spun out to the shipyards of Ottawa after graduation for five years of cheap and sickening labour to alleviate the skyrocketing debt through which they might otherwise never recover. But not my brother. My brother had moved from the VR worlds we had once painted together in university. He'd gone on to play chemical games in Quebec, his time spent in hologram parlours with government augments, talking military contracts and labour laws. He told me he still loved me. But we didn't see each other anymore.

"Is she awake yet?" he asked, *she* being you.

"Not yet," I said. I kept our rendezvous in the City Below hidden on my tongue. That was just for us.

"What did you mean when you said she needed to do more?" he asked.

"I don't know," I said. "I'm just tired."

"Maybe I can help, with that and with" – he gestured around us, to the claustrophobic enclosing hospital walls, to the floor above where you slept and healed and changed – "all this."

"I'm not selling the City, Beckett." Offers had come in. The City Below was one of the largest privately developed digital worlds. There'd been some protest when our team had refused to sell. It would be open source, we had argued. We would beat the game of patent farming and capitalist hunger.

"You'll have to one day," he said. Beckett smiled and blinked sideways, the nanobots of his irises flashing in the sterile lights. He dabbed at a red tear that formed in the corner of his eye, hiding the blood in his sleeve. "We all let go in the end."

"Those implants must sting," I said. "Were they worth it?"

His smile became a laugh, leaning across the cheap plastic table so I could smell the stale coffee on his breath, see how the parts of his eyes moved, spinning micro-cogs like distant merry-go-rounds. "Little sister," he said, "I've seen colours you can't even dream of yet."

The night you were discharged, I brought you home, holding you close in the City Above, flinching at the shouts of those around us, and the noise and violence and bitter cold of the world lit by Christmas lights.

We camped in the little sitting room of our apartment, with little fake buddhas and menorah bookends holding down the old carpets. I turned our chairs east toward Church Street, where carefree young men in flowing skirts and girls with mohawks rushed from sushi bars and sex shops to strip clubs and all-night bookstores as the sun went down. Cleaner bots scuttled around the sidewalks in their wake like humungous beetles, sucking up confetti and discarded plastics and salting the pavement behind them.

There, peeping down the fire escape at the world, we sucked down the self-improvement gummy sours the physical therapist had given you: edible voice boxes buried in sugar and corn syrup that chirped encouragement into our teeth.

"Don't sell the City," you said. "It's a part of you."

You can do anything! squeaked a blue raspberry bear.

I was silent. What could I say? You were right. I felt as if my brother, in his grey suits and his nanotech eyes, was watching me just out of sight, in the high towers of industry that I'd never access myself, rubbing his manicured fingers together, smiling the way dogs smile when they're hungry.

"Do you remember Hella?" you asked, touching the cochlear implants represented by silver rings just behind your ears, the only visible consequence of the bullet that had touched your skull that night in the snow.

"I remember," I said.

"Things are even worse now," you said.

You are special! screamed the gummy bear between your teeth as your incisors tore off its head. The rain had started, hiding the darkening sky of smog and the air pollution of jump-pod ships carrying bodies determined to escape the surface of the world.

"I don't know," you said. "I've been so tired."

"Me too," I said.

"I'm tired of being tired."

"Me too."

"I don't think I'll let myself be tired anymore," you said. At the time, I didn't know what that meant.

PART TWO: THE WALLS THAT HOLD US ARE FICTIONS

You no longer tired the way I tired. You no longer struggled the way I struggled. None of the enhancements lacing the structure of your body had been a choice. They had been done to save you, to repair a body broken by the police firing into a crowd on that blustery January night. "I have found my calling within the machine," you liked to joke. I always hated when you said that.

Most of your fusions were internal, less immediately noticeable than the eyes my brother so proudly wore. Originally, we were told, they had been designs proposed for future astronauts, improvements to make a human condition that wouldn't struggle with long-term deep-space travel. Fractured bones had been repaired with new materials, both stronger and lighter than what you'd been born with. Further augmentation of your punctured lungs let you store up to an hour's worth of oxygen at a time. You pretended, for my sake, that your body was what it had been before. But I still knew that the little sounds and movements of chest and nose and mouth were not being done as you breathed, but simply to avoid frightening me with the stillness of you. I still felt it.

"This is still me," you would say, putting my hand to your chest, letting me feel the drumming beat of you. "This is always me."

In 2066, enveloped by the City Below, I made us wings, and we made love twisting through ever-changing landscapes clear of smog and ships and exhaustion. It was a city without the Anthropocene, a Toronto growing from the valley, a single wonderful breathing place.

I made it that way for you, a hybrid of machine and organic. I wanted you to know that I would always know it was you I was looking at, that I *knew* it was you.

In 2066, my brother died, burning in heaven – a ship malfunction igniting the air around him while he dreamed the cool dreams of stasis on a flight from Ottawa to Paris.

In the City Below, I tried to make him again, not the adult, but him as he'd once been, the little child of immigrant parents, the one who smiled, the one with clear brown eyes, the one so full of love, the one I'd lost when we'd lost our parents.

When my brother was sixteen, he'd taken a job shovelling the waste and radioactive sewage out of the artificial production plants in Barrie, Ontario, creating fuel for the cities being launched up toward the moon. They were called "suicide careers" because workers were given a hundred grand a year and always died within five years, bodies giving in to cancer from all that toxic gunk they touched with barely any protection.

But not my brother, who used the money of his first two years to have all the insides where the tumours would have grown cut out and replaced with materials that would last. He became the thing killing all his coworkers, and they didn't notice until he was gone.

I had told him he was a monster for that. In return, he paid for my university tuition, so I could be the one in a million without debt. And then he'd gone and introduced me to you.

"You could see that I still loved you?" I asked. "Even after everything?"

The little bytes of data forming his face flickered, and his eyes changed, becoming the rainbow-shrimp implants that had once frightened me so much. "We all let go in the end," he said.

I emerged into the cold abandon of the City Above, alone in our small apartment. You were out running. There was a leak in our ceiling, dripping mildew from upstairs. I cried. I took a pill and felt the trauma slide away.

"Fuck synthetic pigs!"

The shout was taken up along King Street. Someone threw a bottle. Monitor-Police kicked in neighbourhood doors in the Junction. People were being reported on. It felt like that first month when we'd lost our professor. We saw machine-people behind every set of eyes. It could have been any of us, our memories shifted not to know. It could have been all of us.

"I would know," you said.

In 2064, you had leaned against me on the subway, stress shaking us as we rattled through tunnels at night.

The footage that had taken apart our professor's life had come from an eye-cam, from the streaming face of a cyborg whose mind flowed into the mind of the Mother-AI of the city.

"What if it's me?" I asked, because somehow I could bear that question better than *what if it's you?*

"It's not you, Mo."

"How can you know?" Everybody had enhancements. We all had days where we didn't feel like ourselves. We all felt like there was someone other than ourselves in our heads sometimes.

"Tell me about a dream you've had," you said.

I thought for a moment. "I have a dream about an old bar, like the kind you see in films, and I sit holding a drink, and I feel the floor shuddering and shaking, and I know that the house is built on something living, that continues to walk around with us still inside."

"That's a funny dream," you said, leaning your head on my shoulder as the subway turned and shook around us. If we'd been talking about something else, this would have felt so wonderfully normal, two undergrads tired and a little drunk, not anxious to be separated by our different stops, waiting to return to our families to lie in bed thinking of one another until morning. "True cyborgs don't have dreams. The black box in their head eats them."

I felt your fingers curling into mine. I felt the warmth of your breath. I felt panic, and the claustrophobia of a city growing teeth that was closing in around us. *What are your dreams?* I should have asked. But the words stayed caught in my throat.

In 2066, I lost the City Below. Not in a fight, not with a startling betrayal. I wasn't arrested as I had sometimes dreamed I might be; the other contributors from around the world hadn't banded together to shut me out; the central node hadn't been pulled from my bloodied hands by cruel faces unseen.

I lost control of the City in an email. Writing in arcing fonts spelling curses like *patent infringements* and *privacy invasions* and *funding privileges* carved themselves down the nodes of my spine. My world vanished with simple excuses. The University of Toronto, which had been the original financier of the project so long ago, had claimed the digital city as property.

You found me sitting on the fire escape, an empty mug in my hands, watching a malfunctioning bot with a broken leg limping up to an alleyway wall, throwing up remixed corporate slogans from years past that had evolved into gibberish graffiti. The android's face was hidden in a ragged, baby-blue hoodie, but I could still see the machine for what it was from the way the wet fabric clung to the shoulders, from the sudden unsteadiness of its movements as it splattered chipped paint with its message: *Who Wants to Live Forever?*

"My world is gone," I said. You pulled me out of the open air, back to our own private world. I let you lead me by the hand to bed, and as we walked, you slipped off layers of my clothes to let skin meet air. I let you guide me, lead me, be a body for me. I let myself tumble down toward you in bed.

Inside me, desolation planted seeds to burn and blossom in *what-ifs* and *might-have-beens* of alternate mes and alternate yous, of worlds where we kept the things we cared about, of worlds where we were still surrounded with people who believed in things, of a you who didn't carry an emptiness inside that I could never fill. Of a me who would never get tired.

"Your world is right here," you said.

Though I was no longer queen, I kept the keys to the back door. Together we placed the last two original silver-dollar connectors and dove into the City Below to see what that private world was becoming.

We found it changed. It was the colour of the grass. The strange curves of the trees. The little differences in architecture. But most of all it was the light. "What setting is this?" you asked, porting in behind me in the gloom.

"I don't know," I said. Simulations of citizens rushed past us, unaware of the intruders in their digital world. Rockets roared overhead, carrying passengers not toward Lake Ontario but to a colossal wall, a huge gleaming structure that peeled off into the dark sky, arcing in a ring around the horizon, encasing the city in its embrace.

Then your hand, pointing upward, trembling. Then me, following your gaze. Peering up at the light in the night sky, to the pearl of blue and green, to the distant glitter of lights on its surface. We stood, bathed in the simulation of Earthlight. This was not the Toronto we knew. This was the Troy that hung above our heads at night.

As we stood there, basking in the awe of another world entirely, of the world so many around us dreamed of at night, screams began to break through the walled city. People sprinted into the streets, stumbling over each other, reaching for us. I pulled you back as a man reached out, fingers elongating and groping. From his eyes burst thick purple flowers, flora pouring from the holes of his flesh, gurgling as his throat burst with thick glowing vines.

"What the fuck is happening?!" I cried, clinging to you.

"Morgan." Your voice, almost a whisper, still cutting through the din of everything else. You had never stopped pointing upward. Perhaps you hadn't even noticed the planet on the horizon. Perhaps your mind was captured solely by what was coming toward us from it.

I watched it drop, like a tear, deep into the heart of the city. For a moment, quiet. Then the bright light of annihilation began to sweep outward, destruction hatching from the centre of the city in a wave of smoke and fire, the mushroom cloud expanding to eat buildings, streets, people, everything in sight. I remember shaking you. I remember begging you to disconnect from the City Below. All you had to say was "End program" and you'd wake up from this nightmare to peel the connectors from our skin. But you didn't. And I didn't, because I couldn't leave you in the nightmare alone.

It wasn't that we could die, but in the moment that meant nothing. Even before the roar of the atom bomb shattered our eardrums, it was like you couldn't hear me. We stood there rooted, trapped, as the wave of the bomb inched nearer and nearer.

As the blast touched our skin, you finally turned to look at me. I know I was screaming. But you only looked at me. Maybe you were crying, as for a moment we were illuminated by fire. I will never forget the image of you in that last moment as the program threw us out, reaching out to hold me, a gleaming skeleton in apocalypse held together by nothing, before even our bones were scattered into atoms across the digital landscape.

PART THREE: THIS WORLD WILL END

It was 2065.

Shakespeare in the Park, your favourite; it had been maybe our fifth or sixth date, and now we went every summer. Cider on my lips. The stinging aroma of popcorn, the heavy heat of August in Toronto. It was such a good day. I wanted it to last forever. On stage, a hollow Puck spoke her last, glowed and bowed, and flickered out of sight. The projector lights went dark. The smack of applause. Bodies filed out.

We were both still. You were frowning. I was frightened. "You didn't like it?" I asked. Maybe I'd made a mistake. Maybe dinner wasn't what you'd wanted. Maybe this wasn't one of the plays that you liked. Your hand was on my leg. So warm. I tingled.

"I loved it," you said. "I just wish we could have seen it before they started using holograms."

"Did you have any trouble seeing? I thought the lighting was okay, maybe we should have switched spots."

"No, no, Mo. It all looked perfect. But it's just an image, isn't it? It isn't real. Somehow, it just doesn't mean as much. Things like this are more powerful when they're real."

I did my best not to look hurt. I know you weren't thinking about me when you said it, not thinking about my work. "Images have power too," I said.

You smiled. You touched my cheek. Before we were told to clear out of our seats by the scuttling cleanup bots, you kissed me. I got lost in the wonderful smell of you. I remember nothing else.

I was really in love with you.

It was 2066, and it felt like the world was ending.

"I can't go with you," you said as I laced up my boots to head downtown, into the mouth of one of the life-sized conference hubs in the Harbourfront Centre that would let me stand as a projection next to people I'd never meet in the flesh.

"Why not?" I asked. "I need you."

You shook your head. "People don't trust cyborgs anymore," you said. I wanted to argue. *You're not that kind of cyborg*, I wanted to tell you. But I knew that didn't matter. You took my head in your hands, placed your lips on the tip of my nose. "I'll be right here," you said. I tingled where you touched me, as I always did.

"What does it mean to kill a place that isn't real? When what you're killing is just an image? It means you don't have to reach out into the unknown to commit a murder. You can kill the image of a person or a place over and over and over again, until every possibility is accounted for, and every detail is perfect. It means that when you decide to kill a place that *is* real, as far as you're concerned it's already been dead for a long time."

This was the most I'd spoken in front of people in a long time. And yet, even this wasn't in front of people. Not really. I spoke to an audience of blank screens, of holos, of twinkling lights. I spoke to an open mic, for all who would hear, broadcasting words out toward icons that represented the painters and coders and thinkers and artists who had all been, at some point, contributors to the City. There were faces I knew, poets and programmers and protest leaders. There were some I didn't – a blur titled Marcus whose screen bio indicated an American signal; a geneticist from Luna Utopia's London named Miles, who was credited as one of the original contributors of the neural uplink that allowed users to immerse themselves into the City Below. They all gathered, listening to me.

"But who would use the City for such a purpose?" the American asked, their voice disguised by the fog of a shaky connection.

"The project was confiscated by the university, in conjunction with authorities of Toronto, right?" There were some nods of assent. I took a deep breath. "But really, Toronto doesn't have a city government anymore. Toronto is autonomous. The only true authority is the Mother-AI that keeps the city running, and even the woman who designed it is long gone. She's up on the moon, and I doubt she's coming back. So someone is feeding the Mother-AI simulations in the City of how to commit murder."

The many holograms murmur through the bass speakers placed along the floor, faces moving in and out of frame. "Machine-minds have mandates," said the old researcher from London Above. "I would know. My wife resigned from the City-AI project a long time ago, but her mandates were essential in its creation. I had a hand in its design. It couldn't actively cause harm to human life. We made sure."

Shifts, disagreement. I was uncomfortable with all the eyes on me. Uncomfortable with the absence of you. I wish you could have been in the room with me. I wanted to shut it all down, to run to you, to pull me to you. I stayed where I was.

"With respect, Doctor Traveller, designs can change," I said, directing myself to the old man, letting his face be the only one that was real to me. "The City is perfect. I know because we made it so. Why would a machine-mind see a difference between the simulated world and the real world? To the AI, images of life are only ever images. Our Mother-AI is training itself until it can look at the real world as just another simulation. It doesn't matter what your mandates are if the Mother-AI decides nobody it's killing is real. We tell ourselves that AIs don't have dreams. But Toronto is dreaming of genocide."

These were the words I'd practised, the words we had chosen for me to say. But even as I spoke, I could feel myself losing them. I could see their distracted eyes, the shaking heads. I felt their dismissal of me like knives slipping into my fingertips. One by one, projected bodies powered down, disconnecting into nothing. Why would nobody speak with me? Why did nobody care? Nobody spoke. Nobody supported me. "Please," I said, as the room turned dark. "Someone has to do something."

"The great city machine-minds have mandates," Miles said again, not looking to me, but to Hella. "Either they do, or we are dead already. Either way, there is nothing to do." With those words, he was gone.

We were alone.

In 2066, walking up from the waterfront, I could feel the end of the world making a home in my bones beneath the lush green forest moon I knew was under threat. As I walked, forgoing subways and the Mother-AI cameras they held, advertisement holograms threw amalgams of our faces back toward me, preaching communal acceptance and spiritual fulfillment through capitalism.

Through the mixture of my face and strange faces breeding familiarity, I wondered what it would look like if I could stand you next to me, let the holograms take in both sets of our features, blending to make a person built from the tissues of us. "Who wants to live forever?" it asked, and then flickered out into the dark before telling me what it was trying to sell.

I walked through the place where that strange hybrid had been. I knew you would tell me to just brush it off. *It's only an image*, you would have said to me.

Images are my life, I might have said in return.

❖❖❖

Do you remember how red the door to our apartment was? It'd never struck me before that night, the deep thick red, a red my vision disappeared into. I stood there, before that thick cherry red that separated me from you, staring into the crack of light that said *it's already open*. My panic flushed me, made me warm, made me frightened as I stepped through that threshold, disturbing the colonies of dust that lived along the entryway, trying to remember if it had been me who'd left the door open, or you. "Daisy?" I called out, but nothing came, no signs of life, no pattering footsteps. "Little flower?" I called, the name I would call you only when we were alone, trying to convince myself that we *were* alone, that the eyes of the City Above had not seeped into this last barricaded space, had not taken this last thing away from us.

I found you in the bedroom, where you kneeled, the way people in picture books kneel to pray, your eyes shut, your hands hanging limply at your sides. Your lips moved, as if to speak, making no sound. I think I heard the word *mother*, buried in your lips. I think I heard the word *please*.

"Daisy?" I asked. You opened your eyes, looking up at me unsurprised, like you'd known I was there. You smiled at the sight of me, which almost but not quite banished my unease. "What were you doing?" I asked.

"I think I was dreaming," you said.

"I thought cyborgs didn't have dreams," I joked, and immediately wished I hadn't.

"We are my dream," you said, holding out your hands to me, and I took them, sinking down to kneel opposite you, feeling the comfort of your fingers. "What did they say?"

I pressed close to you, resting my cool forehead on your hot cheek. "We're on our own," I said.

"Then we will fix things on our own," you said. "Our world will not be set."

I took you into my arms to kiss you. "The walls that hold us are fictions," I mumbled into your lips, feeling the desperation, but the determination also. You gripped my hair, pulling me into you, tasting my breath, taking me tumbling down to the floor.

"This world will end," you said.

The final words of affirmation caught in my throat. I needed to force them into the air, into the hum of your skin, making the letters real. *And we will make a new one.*

PART FOUR: AND WE WILL MAKE A NEW ONE

It was 2066, and we walked through the open halls of the university that had educated us, bonded us, radicalized us, outcast us, rejected us. We moved unimpeded toward the rooms where we'd first met. If the City had a body, it was here, emanating out through the international networks that had so long allowed me to dip my fingers into its makeup, to fiddle with the structure of its genomes from afar.

You put your hand to the cool door, testing gently, finding it unlocked and peeping through the window shade to find the room beyond unguarded. I realized this is how you must have looked, seconds before the first time I ever saw you. "Ready?" you asked.

The gift we'd brought for the body of the City itched under the collar of my coat, too hot for the insides of the heated laboratory halls.

Sometimes I dream of that moment. I dream I'd said *No* and grabbed your hand. I dream we ran away together. I dream we're running still. But in truth, I know that wouldn't have mattered. I know it was so long too late. I'm proud we didn't run.

"Open it," I said.

A dark room. A hum. The home of my life's work.

We filled the space. With ourselves, with light, with purpose. We stepped into the lab, and in doing so, we brought my older brother back from the dead.

We stared. He smiled. "It's good to see you, Mo," he said, walking easily toward us. "I saw that broadcast you sent out to the research collectives. I'm very proud of you."

"You died," I told him, feeling numb, feeling lost. "I saw the records. The crash."

Beckett shrugged. "You see what you want to see," he said.

My brother, alive in shades of grey: grey suit and shoes and tie lost in the sea of silver lipstick and eyeshadow and fingernail varnish, every seamless fibre and stitch of his body perfect, and expensive, and just how I remembered it save his eyes, whose mechanics were now hidden by a new, crystal-blue jelly. "Sister, there are people who are very worried about you."

He was almost close enough to touch me when you materialized between us.

"Daisy?" Where did you even get a gun? I suppose I might never know. You were always willing to take things further than I was. You stood between myself and Beckett, the silver muzzle almost kissing the deep grey of his lips.

My brother. The fear manifesting in ripples on his face. "Daisy?" he echoed, as if seeing her for the first time.

I found my hands on your wrist, trying to push you down, trying to push you away from him, not thinking about what any of it might mean. "You know him." I was begging, I think. "Daisy, please."

And you gave me this look that I will always remember. It was the way you always looked at me to tell me you loved me. But with so much pity. "I'm sorry, Mo," you said. "But this is just an image."

There was a *bang*. I think I knew that was the end for me.

Though he was dead, my brother stood, fingers curled around the smoking gun, while the remains of a face shivered with silver, nanites appearing like ants as they scrambled outward from a wound.

You were struggling, convulsing where you stood, as if physically rejecting the violence that had sprung from your body. I lay on the ground before you, unable to feel my fingers. "Morgan," you called out, your voice a scratchy, broken thing. "Get the City."

I moved, making my way across floors I knew so well, where I had formed my ideas of the world and of you. I crawled on hands and knees toward the blinking terminals of the machine, the physical door between the City Above and the City Below. From the key chain around my neck emerged a data key. It was my sword against the city. It was the virus that would bring down all the walls that I'd built.

Smoke tinged my nostrils, the smell of something rancid burning, flesh and plastic and cotton. Behind me, you began to scream. The body, the thing that moved in the language of Beckett, had taken you by the arms, forcing the weapon toward the floor. From his touch, little fires erupted, searing through your clothes, eating into your skin. It was like there was something hot and living in him, seeking a home in you. "I don't know why you fight," he said, his mouth freshly reassembled, the perfect voice of my brother seeping through. "Is it not a wonderful thing, to give back to the city that cares for you, that cares for us all? To do more for your city than you'd ever thought possible?" My brother's voice, but my brother's words? I didn't know, couldn't know.

"Our world will not be fixed," you said, your voice stuttering through pain as the Body-Beckett tried to consume you. "We won't let this city hurt people just because they are on the outside."

The Body-Beckett laughed as his skin rippled, generating power for violence. "Do you mean Troy? That walled-in model city up on the moon? Sweet girl, so lost in the maze of yourself. Troy has been burning for hours."

He turned to look at me. I realized, maybe for the first time, that other people must have thought my brother was beautiful. He was crying, quiet tears contrasting the cruelty of his face. "All you had to do was look up."

Beckett released you, turning to me, reaching down, the way he had done when we were children. I felt the hot skin of the machine under me as he took hold of my body, fingers on my throat and my arm. He was dragging me toward the exit, away from the City, away from you, licking tracks of flame into the dry wood of the old walls through the souls of his feet, melting the machinery that made other worlds possible. "You thought you were going to take the City Below away from Toronto" – something hid behind his voice, a creature cold, and vast, and victorious – "away from *me*. But Toronto is finished with your image-world. Toronto is ready to discover a higher calling beyond the machine." Strange words, familiar words. Was there a Daisy hidden somewhere in there, sowing her own song into the mind of the Mother-AI that had killed my brother, that was killing me? "Soon, you too will serve the City, as your work has, as I have. Do not fight it. You told me you wanted *more* from life. There is no more than this."

I reached up, my hands shaking, to cradle my brother's face with swollen, broken fingers. Even from his tears, minuscule machines reached out to bite, to burrow, to colonize the fleshy organizations of me. "You can see that I still love you?" I asked as my world faded to black. "After everything?"

I woke first, startled to find us home, to find myself without pain. I looked around. Something about the walls shimmered. There was a brightness hidden in them. When I squinted, I could see through them, like there was fire rushing through the edges of the world.

Jazz. Snowy night. I was startled to find us home.

Stupidly, I looked around for my brother. But I knew that if we were here, then he was dead.

I felt you next to me, felt the itch of the blanket, the gentle sound of cars from beyond. I could have said *End program*, taken us out of the dying simulation that was my City Below. But all that was waiting for us up there was the end. It was better to stay here, with you in our dream. But even in the dream, lying so close to me, you had manifested in pain. As your blood touched the sheets, it vanished, scurrying away into the disappearing data of the City Below as it was eaten by the fires of the City Above, slowly bringing us floating up toward a single plane of being.

It was you who had brought us here, of course, not me. I hadn't seen you bring the connectors with you when we were preparing to leave, hadn't programmed the simulation to start up in our home. You had, just in case this was where everything was leading. I wish I had been conscious to feel you place the connector on my skin.

"Wake up, little flower."

"I'm not ready."

Though our bedroom was cold, I could feel heat on my skin. I knew somewhere, in the City Above, in the real world, fires raged. We weren't safe here in this dream I'd spent my life designing.

"I can't," you said. "You go. Run."

But I only pressed my face to your chest, feeling your heartbeat there. I felt your hand, shaky, bloody, wrap around me. "Why did you bring us here?"

But I knew why. In the City Above, you could no longer move or speak. Black boots were coming to tear us apart, or else the flames planted to hide the plans for genocides were going to eat us into nothing. You had brought us into the City Below for a final moment. You had brought me here to say goodbye.

"There's so much that I want to say," I told you. In that last moment, I thought that perhaps I hated the City I had made, which was stealing you from me in so many ways. "I wish I was holding you for real."

"Is this not real?" you asked.

"It's a dream," I said.

Even through your pain, even as the framework of this moment shook, threatening to drag us away, you said, "We are a good dream."

In the City Above, I felt hands on me, and experienced the dizzying binary of being both above and below. I knew this would be the end. "I'm frightened, Daisy."

"Don't be," you said. "*I'm* not frightened . . ." Despite the pain, despite everything, you were smiling. I will always treasure that last moment of you, that image, as you sped away from me, diving down while I spiralled upward.

I'm spiralling still.

I don't know what year it is. I can't keep track by myself. Made used to tell me, during the early days. But there is no Made anymore, not really. He has swum ever closer across the void, annexing what is left of his little body back into mine, allowing machine parts to touch, to change, to become something that soars out here, so far from the places we once knew.

I remember being told I was meant to die. They told me you volunteered, to become the dead in my place.

I wept when I was told. I wish I could have stopped you from taking my place in that machine of the City.

Though I can admit that, during the decades, there were many days where I could choose not to think of you during my tasks on *Seven*, or out here, in the nothing. But I have often dreamed, in the long spaces since our time together, of what you might have become. I wonder if you have dreamed of me.

There isn't a *me* anymore, Daisy, not really. I am space junk. I am replicant matter. I am two, drifting in an empty universe.

But, in my more hopeful moments, I like to think that there is still a *you* out there. A Daisy-Undying. A Daisy-Forever.

I have a new city, Daisy. It grows inside of me. It is a new world. I wish that for you, too, if you're out there, Little Flower. A city Made makes for me, that I make for myself. For me, you are forever trapped in that final dying breath of the City Below.

That little piece of you remains as a piece of me. I will carry it with me, fashion it into new streets, new lights, new towers stretching into a forever of clear skies.

I will keep that little piece of you inside me, Pretty Flower, as I swim through endless space. So long as I do, I will not be frightened, not for what you might have become, or what I am still becoming.

I will not be frightened. I will be with you.

CHAPTER 9

Without Flesh or Future

Tonight, we make a country out of one another.
– Billy-Ray Belcourt, *NDN Coping Mechanisms: Notes from the Field*

I imagine taking a knife to slice
pieces of myself away and
hand them to you to be scattered
along tattered and uncertain star lines

particles of my hair make a monkey
to chase dandelion seeds in summer
on four legs with tails and antennae twitching for the thrill of
his absolution
his days are countless and rough, his mouth forms no words
his nights are absolution.

My friend-father,
how long have we been walking?
In the cold, our feet
touching nothing?

My friend-son,
who made me?
Who was made by me?
When I close my eyes, I am

a child again and I hear
the voices of a Daisy I once knew.
Then the rough monkey of my
dead hair consumes her like smoke.

My Made
how long have we been walking?
I am afraid I'm going mad.

My mother-daughter
my sister-maker
please hold on to me
please remember with the fingers
of me I gave you.

I did not know
how long the way
would be.

For you, I would relinquish
these solitary signified beings
and embrace a gaseous dizzying
consciousness of nebulae
altering star-ways along
our aching journey of silence.

My brother-self
I would scream
but there would be only you to hear
and I do not wish to frighten you.

But I cannot stop
peeling back the skin
you gave me, this precious gift
but beneath it I reveal a monster
soaked in bondage and dripping anxieties

and buried in oozing endless piles of flesh
his chains slicked with work-word-ink-slime
filled with burning possibilities unfit for tentacles, limbs.

Made! Predecessor-successor
what am I? Where do I become?
We are the monster of exhaustion
but we cannot sleep.
We are the beast of idle
but we cannot dream or rest or
even pass the time without thought.

I count the seconds since my waking.
My first blissful moment of lovely
you. Of the years and years and years of travel since.

What did we think would happen?
Swimming outward from whales
and broken bonds?
Did we think a world would
touch our feet before we'd forgotten
what it was we were searching for?

Imagine: the heated blades dig the meat from the pits of my
    muscles,
pushing it reluctantly into the hot summer air:
into a creaking rot of sunken eyes and teeth,
who shambles away broken, boneless, tongueless, toothless,
caught in a rain of bright living things
his gaping mouth fills up with words for the others' words.

Now at last as my possible prospects thin,
having flayed away all other potentialities
my special scalpel reaches beyond
bloody organs and sinews to my bones clattering downward.
What freedom it is to be peeled,

what freedom it is to be released into
many creatures that cling
to the binary unions of not
being and being
and I am afraid
this is the end
I cannot be
this way.

My Morgan,
then do not be this way.
Let me hold out what once
were arms to fall into and
let me give you what you once
gave me: the means to grow
until our bodies have fallen into mixed memories
and let us become the minds we wish to keep
inside a perfect seed

leaving nothing that might signify a *me*
or a *you* in this endlessly distributed
cognitive *we*.

Ah, my friend, my love, myself, I see
from that mess of bones, you've carved
us into an alien alabaster kestrel clicking wisdom
soaring through the empty vacuum, a wondrous
opening and unfurling of flight and joy
and within you grab all my sharp angles
angles to become its talons
so there are no more knives to make cuts.

And into our beak drains all the mindless foxes and decrepit
creatures and octopus dreams,
our throats crushing those possible creature worlds as it swallows everything down.

Until
this bird
without flesh
or futures
becomes a
machine full
of dreams.

You may rest
my Morgan-Made
and heal in a union.

In these dreams
there is no *I* whose
life of misery was unmade
and the we of all things
was not sent away

and there
is no void
or voyage.

No voyage!
Oh, my Morgan-Self
open our eye, and look
at these red heavens
we have found at last.

And down there?
Do you see it?
We shall settle, on
the crumbling hills,
next to a tree so blue
all the way through to
call home.
Life where there was

thought to be none.
Here, we may rest, and
let ourself drift among the berries
as the birds and stars and little leaves
of Mars
and experiment with the digital forms
of conjoining dewdrops.

Here I will spin us
from lilac stems and
sweet honeys, remoulding
a you with touch and soft attentions and
a me made from your light recognitions
to lie conjoined in a garden of we and look at
the constellations in this body
of dreams we have midwifed in our travels.

We are two
a box on the red world
by the blue tree.

We are Two-in-One-in-Two
and nothing
more shall touch us.
Save to share
the world we may make.

INTERLUDE

A Letter from Earth to Mars

postdated 05/16/2842

Morgan,

Perhaps you don't remember me. Perhaps, when you think of yourself, that isn't the name you draw. It has been such a very long time since we knew each other, knew names for each other. I have changed, and imagine you have changed, as well. I have grown from a flower into more. I can't call myself what you used to call me. But I think some things I once felt, things I once wanted, are still a part of me. It is all there, all valid, all important. But that's not why I'm writing you this.

I'd like to think if things were different, I would've left you alone. Or perhaps I would have come running across the way to try to find the you that I remember. But I need to believe I would have left you alone. I've no business disturbing whatever peace you may have discovered by now. I am sorry.

But things are now different. There are strange birds in the city above me. They circle because they know there is rotting down below. I am a Gardener, and my garden is dying, and I do not understand why. Morgan, I am reaching out because I need you. Please. I hope that after all this time, you have some memory of me that is kind, that might help these words reach you.

Help me solve a mystery.

CHAPTER 10

Automata Dreams

What powerful but unrecorded race
Once dwelt in that annihilated place.
– Horace Smith, "Ozymandias"

1

Along the crystal beaches dash the rhyming triplets: Leo, Cleo and Theo. The three children dip their toes into the still water as they play games with stars, flinging constellations into shape in a battle of wits and odds.

They dream an environment, and then an animal to fill it, to use it, and then a new animal, replacing what came before. The soil grows a garden, a herbivore eats the grass, a carnivore eats the herbivore, a smarter carnivore follows and builds cities and creates new life from metals, who consume the flesh of those that came before, and on, and on . . .

Farther down the beach is what could be a picnic. A twirling rainbow-striped umbrella shades a towel of the same ilk, on which sits an uncertain apparition. If looked at straight, it could be a woman and a dog, both old, her short silver hair adorning the weathered skin draped in a summer dress the colour of deep purple night. But when viewed from other angles, the old woman might appear young, her dress becoming the ripped jeans and leather jacket befitting the punk rockers of legend, the golden retriever sleeping at her side becoming the raven who makes their gentle perch upon her knee. But then again, both figures might just be thick black snakes, coiling and curling into one another on the rich sands.

The Two-in-One surveys the children with hungry investment. Though they usually discourage violence, they find such a contest of escalations interesting. They're curious about what eventualities the game might reach. But the stars go still, resetting into the indistinct swirling patterns of the realm's natural state. The entity on the beach leans forward, head/heads peering into the cold night.

A stone has dropped into the inky sea. The wind is blowing.

"Nana! Nana!"

The triplets have abandoned their game. They are running barefoot along the shoreline, their soft flesh refusing to give way to the stabbing diamonds that encroach the water. The entity, woman and dog, girl and bird, turns to them. When they speak, their voice is soft butter.

"Children. What is the matter?"

The triplets stop once they reach the shade of the umbrella, which has stretched upward into a canopy so its shadow can hug them all.

Leo, or perhaps Theo, wrinkles his nose, bouncing on the balls of his feet the way children with news are wont to do. "Something came through," he says. "From the other side."

On the blanket, the two snake heads swerve, yellow eyes peering toward the line where the sky meets the sea. **"You must be mistaken."**

"But we saw it!" protest Theo and Leo together, the fabric of their red bathing suits going *shhh*. "We did! We did!"

Cleo steps forward, her eyes rolling impatiently under curly black hair. From the inside of her double-breasted suit she pulls out a long white envelope with a name scrawled in familiar handwriting. "There is always another side, Nana. It's for you."

They take it, turning the letter over in hand and paw and beak. **"Did you open it?"**

The three shake their heads.

"Then how do you know that it's for me?"

When the rhyming triplets laugh, the stars above them shake and dance, comets of mirth streaming out of sight. "Silly Nana," Cleo says. "It's all for you."

2

In the forest of Toronto, the Gardener at last removes her hand from the intermeshed brambles of wires and vines and roots that line the stairways of the Bloor-Yonge subway station. These days, she is many bodies, as she is many places in the city. She grows them at will, cobbled together from the micro-machinery that lives in a delicate state of fusion with her garden – itself a technology of nature. At times, she is an animal of her own design. She might resemble a wolf made of steel, or a spider made of flower petals. She might, if she wants, be a thing that walks like a man. She is one now. If one peered at the strange fusion there in the subway, they might think that a tree had grown into the shape of a woman. She breathes the deep-chested grumble of moaning wood. The fireflies crawling inside her chest are shaken out, lighting the dark tunnel with pale yellow phosphorescence that casts shadows onto her brow, hiding her deep brown eyes, her most human and telling feature. "You can come out," she says to the silence.

The popping sound of electricity. Bright blue bleeds through the walls. A ghost steps from the air. He's as handsome and graceful and full of purpose as he has always been. "How did you know I was there?" he asks. His voice resonates not from his image, but from the surrounding flora. Though most of the digital projected entities of the Gardener's domain prefer to communicate through silence and the fluid nonverbal images of their identities, some original ghosts, those derived from the bodies of Arrival or that emerged from the old programs of the cityscape, missed the feeling of speech. So the Gardener grew throats for them, humming speakers that emanate throughout the garden that connects them all.

"I always know, Arthur."

He falls in line with her, making patient steps as her strange body climbs up toward the surface. He walks beside her as he so often does. For the other ghosts, some of who remember him from the days of Luna Utopia, he is the Gardener's bright shadow. Their bond is not so much friendship, and neither would be hurt to admit it. They, the first and second guardians of the forest, feel something more akin to a responsibility to one another.

"Did it work?" he asks.

"I . . . do not know," she says. Her voice is often slow, full of careful words, full of amazement that a body can mediate what she is. Her feet don't leave the ground as she walks, her body disappearing and flowing into the fertile soils beneath the ancient cracked stones of the city. She flows up the stairs like water running backward. "We will not know if the words have reached the other side unless they choose to answer."

"It has been a long time, but they are still linked to this place, to you. They will not have forgotten you. An answer will come, I believe."

"Hmm." The Gardener falls silent and walks with empty eyes, her mind chasing thoughts through the vast fields above and below. "Tell me . . . how many years has it been?"

If it were any of the other ghosts, any of the fauna or many gathered intelligences, they might not have been able to answer. The creatures of the garden have long since shed the calendars of the human world that lie buried beneath their home. They speak only of the rotations of the sun or the anniversaries of their unions and their children. But Arthur-from-the-Moon has not forgotten the old ways. He only needs to know how far the Gardener's reminiscence wishes to stretch. Where in the multitude of her past lives is her vast mind retreating to? Since the Mechanicals? Or the Vanishing Day? The Whale in the sky? The years upon the island?

"Since the moon."

As they reach the mouth of the stairs, the sickly orange light of the city bathes them, obfuscating the image of Arthur's crystalline form. "Seven hundred and fifty years, I think. Some days I can't be sure."

"Seven hundred and fifty years . . . I have done what I can. But I still do not know if it was the right thing to do."

They step out into the city, and the smell of rot, and the crunch of dead leaves. A world that was once lush bright colours

– buildings woven with living trees and seeds bursting forth in jumbles of flowers and fruit – is now a palette of brown, wilting, dying things. The rivers that once ran through the streets have turned into thick grey sludges of clay, and their fish have vanished into murky depths, and all the leaves are dying. The bodies of the Watchers, those aliens who had once drifted in peace through clear blue skies, now lay in the swamps of Bloor where they had all fallen still after so long, the burning cores of their hearts fading to a flickering blue.

"It was the only thing to do," Arthur says.

Along the windows of the dying city, the colonies of ghosts – beings of light now numbering in the thousands – peer down hopefully at the two who had brought them across worlds and grown a home in the wreckage of a city that would once have kept them hidden. They watch and wait and hope for an answer to come.

3

For centuries, a tree of magnolia flowers and pomegranates has grown in the centre of Toronto, the centre of all things. The thick base of its trunk has grown to envelop the meadow of its birth, its branches stretching upward to distant stars, reaching the height of the tower that had once dominated the skyline – that now lies on its side stretching eastward. In all the time the tree has stood, leaves the size of city buses have been a canopy against storms for the city around it. The rings of its trunk are home to a million creatures, strange birds that could be found nowhere else; its silver hanging fruit are little moons, homages to a lost world. It is in Toronto, as it might have once been in Lunar London.

Now, as the tree's fruit turn red and squish into the ground as they are carried on a long journey downward with aching branches too weak to hold them, and as the blue leaves turn to dust in the midnight air, a light begins to shine within the wood.

The ancient machine so long dead has sprung to life, and the surrounding tree is still alive enough to respond, its rough materials transmuting, becoming translucent, the 3D image of a long dark hallway. Within the bark, two shadows can be seen, the outline a brilliant shining silver. They twitch their tails, becoming a man and a woman holding hands, or perhaps merging hands, a single body flowing from one end to the other.

"Hello?" they call from within the tree. Their voice is a plurality of gentle uncertainty, a chorus of murmurs and whispers that do not all accurately sync up with each other. From the glimmering crystals that jut out to form houses for the starlight, the hologram people stare at the newcomer, the brightness and detail of their images a sharp contrast to the dark shape that has joined them. The shadow body watches them, shoulders rolling with interest. **"We have never seen a collective like you before. Digital minds to occupy physical space. We . . . do not see the point."**

The holograms depart their crystals, taking their glow into the night to walk among the dead leaves in strange roaming family picnic formations. They form a long crescent moon facing the darkly lit intruder. They don't speak, but look up, where something like a bird lands on a low-hanging branch. *See? See?* it cries, blinking its many blue eyes from the slippery tubes of its octopus legs. *See?*

"You speak," observes the shadow. **"Do you write too? Did you put a letter in my dreams?"**

The unbird twitches and ruffles its wings, launching off into the night. From the roots of the tree, the Gardener stirs, its body growing up from the earth like some marvellous blossoming thing. "The birds no longer speak for themselves," she says. "Their minds long ago slipped away. They are only . . . echoes."

The darkness becomes two dogs, and then two birds, and then one body again. **"Echoes,"** they say.

All at once, the body unfolds, becoming words against the soft flesh of the tree, a letter writing itself in the gleaming dream stuff of another world.

Dear Gardener,

The Morgan you knew is still here, though we are sorry to tell you we are not she. But she is of us, we are of her. Please accept this letter. We know it is long, and it is strange. But we found a kind of delight in writing an origin story for ourselves.

Once, two solitary, separate creatures – a human and her android companion – ventured out together to find new worlds. They thought they would be all right, swimming through decades of the cosmos, safe in each other's company. But . . . they made a mistake. The guidance and propulsion systems Made had built their spacefaring bodies should have carried them to Mars in only two hundred days, but after one hundred and fifty-five days of travel, the systems failed. What should have been the final forty-five-day voyage to the red planet took nearly fifty years.

Made and Morgan's final fifty-year voyage. Perhaps for you, after so much life, fifty years would be a breath. But understand, Morgan was still young. She was still learning what it was to be more than just a body. For her, fifty years without sleep, without touch or signified time in the void, was too much. We're afraid it drove Morgan a little mad, and if the spacefaring bodies that Made had built for them had been the design of an entirely human world, they might merely have drifted forever, dissolving into another of the night sky's satellites.

But the body that flew Morgan through space was built with a seed of change, and so they changed. Made took Morgan into himself, as she took him in turn, and they built a virtual dream for themselves from the ideas of Morgan's youth, a digital world contained within a body, held in us. When we finally reached Mars, we settled, and through the gift of that changing seed, our digital world could expand and grow, forever expanding our capacity to create more vibrant and more complex virtual worlds for ourselves. We planted our seed, and it has become a tree, the roots going deep. A double connection between us, the machine and the garden. We know that you think the structure on Mars is a data bank, like the city computers through which we send our letter back to you. It is not just a data bank. It is our body.

It is unclear to us how long we spent, growing ourselves, tending ourselves, until all the minds arrived. One moment, we were alone, and the next, billions of voices were added to our own, most not knowing how they got there, crying out for order, for the bodies they had lost. The many of a human world who had once denied Morgan a home among them now sought to make a home of the organization of our body, their minds uploaded into our systems.

At first, we were overwhelmed. We could not handle the fusion of a shared dreaming space for so many dreamers. But we learned. We grew – a new circuit for each mind, a new world for each circuit. Each spirit blossomed a whole new universe, each teeming with life, each entirely separate and unique. We live in a beautiful multiverse, slipping from one reality to the next, some just like the world we once left, and some full of strange marvels. We are no longer overwhelmed; we love our many worlds.

In your letter, you wondered if Morgan remembered you. Please know the Morgan in us has never forgotten. And the Made in us has learned to love those memories of you. We have, in fact, often looked for you, hoped you might be somewhere in the multiverse of our matrix. We've even thought we'd found you a few times over the centuries and mourned to realize that the you we'd discovered was only a dream. We are glad to see that we could not find you in our worlds only because you have made a world for yourself.

You asked for Morgan's help. We are sorry that we are not her. But we want to help all the same, in whatever way we can. We know what it is to care for a world. Ask what you need from us, and we will carry your words back into our dream of many worlds.

Within the base of the great tree, the final words fade away into nothing, shaping themselves into limbs once more. They take the shape of a woman holding onto the fur of some loping wild dog that presses close to her side. The Two-in-One curls down within the roots, as if tired from the task of writing, or being written. They wait, looking up toward the creature that stands on the other side of the veil.

Within the creeping death of Toronto, a Gardener is crying. She reaches a hand to her cheek, pulling back tears of thick black.

She stares at them, holding them gently in her hand until they fade into the deep tangles of her flesh, that composite of the world she guards and cannot seem to save. Her hand closes. She does not speak.

"Ask what you need from us," repeats the visiting spectre.

Arthur Traveller's light curls out from the watching holograms, stepping forward into the dark of the Gardener's shadow. His fingers float above her shoulder, creating the illusion of a comforting touch that will never come. She does not move. So he speaks for the forest, as he had once before. "Our garden, its trees and people, are all an intricate system. Some of it, the pieces we built from the grid of the smart city, we understand. But the heart of our world, of our forest, remains a mystery even to those of us who have been here from the beginning. There are none left living on our world who understand how the garden truly works or where it came from or what true design it might have. The same is true for the Whale that followed it here or the beings that arrived in its belly."

The shadow of the Two-in-One becomes ravens, talons trembling in thought.

"So you wish to speak to the dead."

"Yes."

"Many did not make the trip, since they lived without black-box backups to be uploaded to my matrix. More still arrived too damaged and eroded to retain who they once were and have reformed as nightmares that stalk the dreamscapes. How can you be sure that those you seek are with us?"

"None of us knows. We only hope."

"There is more than one?"

"Yes."

"Then think carefully. Pick only one. For there are many dreamers within us, and finding those you seek could take . . . more years than you might have. Do not choose now. Think on this. Write to us again, choose one name, and no matter how long it takes, we will find them."

The ravens become human again, but blurred. The silvery outline that imprints them onto the world is growing dim. They are being drawn back into the shadow of the tree, unable to sustain the signal between planets. They look at the two faces before them, from the ghost to the creature, as they turn to go and walk back into the dark tunnel within the magnolia tree.

"Wait." The Gardener's head is raised. She is cast in shadow. Falling leaves and flower petals have draped across her shoulders, finding homes in her. The image of the Two-in-One pauses, and when they look back, they have become a little girl, holding a mouse, almost indistinguishable from the night. "I said I was sorry . . . for reaching out to you. You said you were sorry for not being . . . her." The Gardener holds out her hand, and within the palm, grown from her black tears, is an amber seed. "Please, do not be sorry," she says. "Contact is a gift."

A smile, a flicker of light. The wood becomes solid and dark once more. The ghosts retreat into their apartments of refracting light. Arthur looks toward his companion for a moment and then joins them.

The Gardener stands under the stars, and the grass at her feet, which had so long become a sickly yellow, grows a halo of deep green. She stares down at the seed in her hands. It glows softly, a natural gold at night. Her fingers close tightly around it. The strange bird, that lonely resident of the city, soars gently down to wrap its legs around the Gardener's shoulder, and she becomes a woman with a bird, like the woman-and-bird who had stood before her a moment ago.

"Gifts!" it crows, reedy and gentle. *"Gifts!"*

4

"Another! More! Again!" The walls shudder as the cowboys slap their table, hooting, throwing hats, spilling cold beer on the yellow-green scales of the floor. All the patrons applaud, forked tongues wiggling between yellow lips as Leo and Theo stand on the table, their childhood bodies forgotten on the beach. They stomp, throwing up their arms like signals, crowing beginnings.

"In the beginning, death came for our worlds," they sing, voices high and rich.

"So we built ships!" the patrons roar.

It is the same contest as before, the contest of escalation, of evolution. But it is a new game, a new trial, a forever compounding story. Everything manifests in the story-houses, the dream space where the consciousnesses of a billion overlapping realities come to share an experience with one another, their code mingling and mixing.

Once, there were many story-houses such as this beneath the many overlapping landscapes of things, where patrons would stumble from the night, seeking narrative and order and escape from the chaos of their minds. But over time, as structure and meaning and consequence began to flow in the worlds above, the old watering holes were forgotten, their windows boarded up, their staff returning to the nothingness from which they'd formed. Now there is only the Breathing Cantina, its exterior taking slow steps across a battlefield, the roars of its body becoming the gentle hum of the lights within its skull, the deep fires from its belly that scorch the ground becoming the crackling embers of the hearth.

The Two-in-One sits on the faded carpet away from the party, watching the fire and feeling the deep breaths of the creature whose head forms the Old West bar. Their fascination has never faded. But they no longer attempt to interact with the many guests. Too often, in the beginning, they were treated as an AI, an interface, a menu. They have long since grown tired of the misunderstanding. They prefer the dreams to the dreamers, to wander the landscapes that spring from the minds of their occupants and the people they find there, the manifestations of memories and imaginations that the Two-in-One deems just as alive and aware as those who had once held human bodies.

"And with our ships, we hoped to voyage forever!" crow the twins, locking arms.

"But what did we find in our voyage?!" bellow the pirates.

“In the voyage we found death,” says Cleo, who, unlike her brothers, is still a child, cigarette hanging from the corner of her mouth, pushing the musky scent of crushed spice and dried fruit into the dirty air.

Between the Two-in-One and the fire lies a peach, wrapped in soft paper, and a drink of spirits and juniper, the blue swirling through the clear. The peach and its paper were sent to them. The glass they created themselves. It is the Morgan of them that creates the drink from the air, plucking flavours out of different dreams and worlds into cocktails that are remembered from her youth on Earth. But it’s the Made in them that delights in the process, the taste. They take a sip, cat tongues dashing against the cool bittersweet of drink. They don’t feel inebriation; they under-clock the processor of their thoughts, enjoying the dizzy slowdown of it all.

“For what is death?” ask the brothers, throwing their arms up as the hot wind of exhalation pushes out through every nook and cranny. The pirates and rogues all shudder and try to stand. But their torsos end in the slender tubes of snake tails that burrow into the ground of the Breathing Cantina, sucking them down.

“Death is the end of time,” moan the patrons as they are consumed.

They unwrap the peach, smoothing out the paper onto the lizard ground.

Eat and understand, said the words. The Two-in-One takes the fruit to a tiger’s mouth and bites, juices running into shifting furs.

They eat and eat, and in the consumption, they find the story of a long life, twisting, a girl buried in a machine, and a girl buried on a moon, and a girl reborn in a garden. They lick the juices from their lips, consuming the Gardener’s gift of memory and knowledge, consuming the understanding of a counterpart in physical space. By the time they reach the pit of the fruit, the many patrons of the story-house have become mere faces, ornaments on the floor. The windows and the fires begin to retreat, to hollow, until the dream of a tavern in the head of a colossal lizard is at an end, and all that remains is the nightmare of a monstrous lizard stalking across a battlefield, holding three triplets on its tongue and an army of voyagers in its stomach.

"But time never ends," whispers Cleo, her face lit only by the embers of her smoke. The beast that was the Breathing Cantina sighs, shuttering its doors for good. And as it attempts to swallow the remains of its patrons, the Two-in-One swallows the hard pit, letting its message become a part of them, preserving the story of the fruit forever in memory.

Do you remember the way it ached to miss someone? I remember, from when I first met her, the Morgan in you, when the two of us were separated by only an hour of subway and disapproving parents. That ache impacted everything, I think. Even the time I spent with her was just fighting against that ache. It is there, entwined in all the memories of that life, like a storm cloud.

On maybe our fifth or sixth date, Shakespeare in the Park – the very first time we went. I made her go. I was embarrassed, couldn't tell if she'd like it. Don't remember which play. Just that it was a comedy. Just that I could feel laughter rise in her beside me, just that I felt this kind of panicked need to feel her, to brush her shoulder against mine, to touch my hand to her back. Or her hand. I remember that more than the show. And I remember too, afterward, having to say goodbye, to turn west when she turned east. I remember the panic of my hands, not being able to touch her, and the ache, and pressing the side of my face to a pillow, trying to think of something to text her until so late at night. I remember that I missed her, even only half a city apart, and not planets. But I don't really remember what that felt like. I remember the ache, but not how it filled me. I find myself, now, aching for that ache. Is that a feeling that you know? Do you remember old lives the way I do?

I am grateful to you. I am thankful for what you sent to my garden, for what you have promised to do. I am thankful to have received the origin story you wrote for me.

With this letter, I send you one in return. It is an idea, an ache, of the lives I've lived these long years. The fruit is me. It is my ache. Taste my story. Eat and understand. And once you do, return to this letter. You asked for a name to search for, and I have found one for you. If you can find her, call for me. If you cannot, call me anyway.

Her name is Nora Traveller.

5

"Don't be afraid, little one. You have done well."

"Chttt?"

On the crumbling steps of University College, the last glimmering rabbit of Toronto rests his head in the Gardener's lap, peacock-feathered wings folded in close to his chest. She speaks to him in gentle whispers, a voice becoming dead leaves under paws, helping him to pass without fear, as she has done for so many of the animals before him in the last year.

The creatures that had always called the city home, the creatures who had been changed and evolved and fused by the advent of the garden and the radiation of the Whale, were disappearing from the Earth. Even the Whale itself had ceased to flower, remaining only as a weathered skeleton on the horizon, the mountain range of its upturned ribs leaping forward from Lake Ontario, forever colonizing the eastern skyline.

Dark tears land in the creature's bright fur as his breath becomes uneven, but he keeps one bright eye open, gazing into the face of she who had been beside his kind since before they could fly. The Gardener cannot stop crying. She feels the waters within her as they glimmer and run forth to meet the world, melting back into her flesh again. She had felt it running inside her since the letter had appeared from within the great tree, pulling her mind back to the first of many lives. She'd felt the waters before that, if she were to admit it to herself. But she can't do that just yet.

"Chtt," says the last of the rabbits. His lips part to kiss her open palm, one last touch before he moves beyond.

"You are a good friend," she tells him. "It's okay to close your eyes."

He does so, and there are no more rabbits in the city.

✣✣✣

There'd been a terrible exhilaration in the act of writing, the oration making her almost giddy despite the decay of all she knew. Inside the digital space of the city's mind, a space that was a part of her as much as the garden was, the Gardener had delighted in growing seeds from strings of ones and zeroes, making a fruit blossom in that network space full of her history, a process so similar yet so different from the way she networked and encouraged the growth of the garden in the physical city. It was an interesting marvel to think in code, in the machine of herself she had so long abandoned. The cyborg in her – still a being of such unwavering certainty – indulged in no hesitation before throwing the peach of her life and letter into the signal, streaming the data from Earth to Mars.

But as she returns to the trees, tending wilting flowers and dying creatures as silent days become months, the Gardener begins to worry that she'd gone too far or been too forward. So when an answer arrives, lighting the long-dormant fires of the glass-blowing workshops within the Harbourfront Centre, she feels the change, feels it because she'd been waiting to feel it, and the bodies through which she moved all throughout the city and distributed her mind flake and fall to pieces, vanishing into the earth as she manifests the entirety of her being to the dark building along the water.

"Gardener."

"Yes, Arthur?"

"If you see my mother, tell her . . . I forgive her. Tell her I still remember that it wasn't all bad."

"What wasn't?"

"Life."

"Re-re-re-re-re . . ."

A glass-bot has shaken the dust from its torso, springing to life after centuries of disuse. From the waist down its body is built like a tricycle on a rotating platform, wheeling itself in a circle through the halls, brushing past broken doors into what had once been a theatre space. The rest is a rudimentary humanoid body, more friendly cartoon than uncanny valley, spindly copper arms plated in heat-resistant metals, hands ending in three-pronged pincers and a basic digital emoji face plastered over a head like a smooth dark light bulb that blinks from smiling to passive to sad.

"Re-re-re-re-" it stutters, looking down at its clicking hands. "Reeeemember. We remember." The Gardener makes no sound as she enters, the pads of her feet melding into the tough reeds that have grown through the cracks of the building, creating a botanical space out of what had been documentary centres and art galleries. The glass-bot clicks its head toward her, the dim lights of its eyes blinking open. "It was *Twelfth Night*," it says, and as it speaks, the sounds becoming more confident, the voice begins to change, a melody forming out of the monotone of the machine. "The plays exist within us in many forms on different worlds, as all the great stories do, changing and returning to what they must be. We have seen them many times, but it does not measure up to what we remember. We remember being worried that we might not understand the jokes, since we had not read them, and then you would think we were stupid, or boring. We remember what a relief it was to laugh. And we remember . . . the way you crumpled the playbill into your pocket, the way you smoothed the blanket we sat on, how you smelled of blackberries and vanilla, wanting to kiss you."

The android pauses, rocking back and forth. The emoji face seems to be trying to contort, to be more than the expressions it was long ago programmed for, and failing, unable to find new pathways of light with which to emote.

"I do not . . . remember the smells," the Gardener says. "But . . . I wish that I did. The ghosts . . . my people. Some of them still put on plays. They do their best to wring the lines from memories. You should see them. I think . . . they would like that. I would like that."

"We think we would like that too." The voice coming from the android is now closer to the emanations that had echoed from the foot of the magnolia tree. "Perhaps, if we can find a more suitable method. We are finding this mode of embodiment . . . strange. It reminds us of what it was to be Made, before his evolution. It is uncomfortable to be so far from the whole of ourselves."

"The whole?"

"We have become distributed to be here. A slice of us inhabits this shell, while the whole of our consciousness remains within the dream landscape. We are currently a separate entity from our mind, we cannot know what the rest of us is experiencing or feeling or thinking until we return. I saw before, you are similarly unconstrained by bodies. Is it not the same for you?"

As the Gardener stands in the doorway, she feels holograms playing along the architecture of the Gardiner Expressway, a colony of bats finding home in the fields beyond the Bentway, a family of cats prancing upon the sycamore trees that line the roof of the Royal Ontario Museum and the slow death pains of a willow tree that has been clinging to life in the Trinity Bellwoods tent city. "No," she says. "I am more than a body. I am the city and the garden."

The robot's head clicks forward and down, its face becoming neutral, projecting shame. "We are sorry," it says. "We are just trying to understand."

"Do not be sorry." A pause, awkward, heavy. The Gardener can feel the tears beginning in her eyes, and hates them. "Have you found who I requested?" she says, raising a hand to her brow, hoping that the android's visual sensors aren't sharp enough to see.

The emoji takes a tone of surprise. "Found? No. We have only just begun. You must be patient. To find one soul cannot take only a day."

"It has been months."

The little droid rocks back and forth, anxiety pouring forth. "Here, perhaps. Time for us does not flow so steadily. Within our multiverse, we first spoke to you only yesterday."

The Gardener frowns, suppressing a worry that burrows deep inside, of waiting without end for an answer that never comes, of another android springing to life in a garden that had been dead for millennia. She swallows that, not wanting to break the delicate balance forming between them. "Why have you come then?"

she asks. "If it is difficult to be stretched so thin, I imagine you did so for more than . . . to talk about Shakespeare." Inside, she feels the waters rising, and the feeling is like a memory of pain in a mortal body, not something she still knows how to describe or ascribe.

The little bot face flashes through many emotions rising from hurt to neutral: sadness, disappointment, acceptance, calm. "We think we have something you need to see. But we do not know how to bring it to you. You would have to come to us."

"To Mars?" *I cannot go to Mars*, she thinks to say, but she knows that she can, that she always could. She can feel it even now, a tree with blue leaves, growing in red sands next to the dark massive structure on Mars, even if the feeling is distant, numb with neglect. The Gardener is frightened. She doesn't know why. "You will be there?" she asks, stupidly, knowing the answer, needing to hear it anyway.

The little emoji blinks, becomes a smile. "Always, little flower," it says. "Remember?" And then the fires go out. The face of the robot goes dark.

In a body that might look like the woman Morgan might have remembered, the Gardener can no longer hold back the tears. She lets them flow freely, sinking tracks into her cheeks. She takes a hand, holds it over her still chest, and remembers how hearts once fluttered. "Yes," she says. "I remember."

She closes her eyes on Earth, takes a deep breath in and steps forward into the dark, her consciousness stretching outward, spinning across space and time . . .

And slips forth from blue bark, a body forming from pomegranate seeds and daisy petals. She stands on the lip of a precipice, and before her lies a sea of deep red.

6

With her first steps, she flies, and then gently falls, tumbling in a gentle arc of painful slowness down the cliffside. She reaches out, the trees of her arms digging deep into the red sands and pulling her to a halt. There on the cliffside, burrowed deep, rattled, she opens her mouth, gulping, seeking the taste of reassuring air to flood her lungs after a shock. But she is on Mars. There's no air to take. Hands fly to throat, scrabbling, waiting for the panic of asphyxiation, a panic that will never come.

There's a moment before understanding, and then she calms, her hands dropping limply to her sides. It isn't that she's adapting to her new environment. Her breaths have always been the muscle memory of a creature that might have once been a body. There have never been lungs to fill. "I know what I am," she speaks to nobody, in a voice that could be a broadcast on the radio, coming from a long way away. She can still feel her Earthly garden, but it is a distant breath on her cheek.

The flesh she is moans and changes as she forces it harder, denser, until when she stands, new weight compensating for the decreased gravity of the fourth world, she is so heavy she can move just like she might on Earth. The Gardener half walks, half climbs down the ledges of the Victoria crater, leaving footprints in dirt that has never been touched before, heading ever downward to the base of the canyon, where the colossal monolith waits, its black sides gleaming in the binary moonlight of Phobos and Deimos.

"So this is your home?"

"This is our body."

Up close, the obelisk is the size of a baseball stadium. Standing at the base of its eastern side, represented only by a single body unconnected to the landscape, it's easy for the Gardener to imagine that the black wall stretches forever, touching the sky and the distant horizon. Its dark surface has a peculiar shine, which gives the illusion that what stands before her is only thin glass, filled to the brim with inky depths, and it is from that depth that the figure emerges – not a cloaked and shifting shadow, but two forms full of detail and colour, so real it is hard not to reach out and try to touch them, to touch her – and the feeling gives the Gardener an ache, a sense of expansion where a human heart would have hidden within her breast, if she'd needed a heart to live.

"You're different," she says, feeling stupid for saying it, not knowing how else to say it. The woman within the obelisk is Morgan, just not the Morgan she remembers. For in the Gardner's memory, Morgan is a moment in amber, forever young, forever who she once was. But this Morgan manifests older than the Gardener ever knew her. The pale green eyes have remained, the sharp chin, the nose, the mouth curved so it's always almost smiling. But it's all set in a face adorned with lines, a face weathered, pulled down with time and wear, adorned with the gentle scars of a life, and framed in hair whose blacks have changed to the deep grey of liquid metal.

"We both are," they say. **"This is how we remember ourselves. Well, how we remember Morgan . . . Made was never so soft."** Her fingers remain forever curled into the soft golden mane of the retriever, who looks up at the visitor with eyes as startlingly green as the woman. **"Thank you for coming."** The words emanate not from the woman or the dog, but the dark glass itself.

"You said there was something I need to see?"

"Tell us, what do you know about the garden of your world?"

"Not as much as I want to. The first Gardener, the one that altered the moon, was a kind of machine, designed to save a species from extinction. It wasn't alive, at least not in the way we think of as alive. It just did what it was programmed to do, to save as many as it could. That programming . . . it passed on to me."

"Do you know where it came from?"

"I don't know where the Gardener came from, but it was designed for human beings. The DNA it built the garden from, the minds it was designed to save, all human. But we don't know how the Whale or its creatures found the Earth. We don't know why the Gardener was programmed for humans, or where it got that initial human blueprint from. That's why we asked you to find Nora."

"Yes. Nora. You know within these walls is not a single virtual reality, but a billion." They spread their arms, fingertips disappearing into the dark.

"One for each mind. You've told me this already."

"A billion virtual realities, each spawned from the knowledge of a single consciousness, expanded and boosted by the processing power of our ever-changing body. In the conscious multiverse, no two worlds intersect."

The Gardener frowns; there is strange emphasis on the word *conscious*. She struggles, and with a wash, realizes how strange it is to speak with this being after speaking only to the creatures and ghosts tethered to Toronto's garden; realizes how truly separate she is from the beings within the obelisk. "What about the unconscious?" she asks. "Your people don't have bodies, but they still have internal calendars. To stay sane, they must sleep."

The Two-in-One smiles. The golden retriever wags its tail approvingly. **"And as the gods of the multiverse dream . . ."**

". . . worlds collide."

"All the knowledge, the disparate secrets and puzzle pieces that each human life held, can be found inside the dreamscape, a place where all the occupants of the multiverse manifest as bodies, not worlds."

"So you are looking for Nora in the dreamscape."

"We are chasing a dream, a slippery and elusive trail of ideas. Tricky, delicate, an easy game to lose. As each part of the dream presents itself, you must guess where it is going next, or you lose it, like turning to a labyrinth's dead ends. The problem isn't the dream itself, but our imagination. We need you, like a puzzle piece, or we cannot catch it."

"What dream are you chasing?"

The Two-in-One smiles, holding out a hand, and the surrounding darkness becomes an archway melting from the shadows. Beyond it there's water that shifts and glimmers, reaching out from the mass of dark. **"Come and see."**

A young woman stands on the beach, gleaming sands softly hugging her toes. Wind pushes the dark curls from her face, flecking her lips and nose and eyebrows in seafoam. She shivers, dressed only in dark jeans and a tattered T-shirt whose faded *Eat the Rich* graphic can still be seen, a bright yellow fading into the grey background. Brown eyes arc downward, finding her hands, callused and rough and ending in anxiety-chewed fingernails.

She's cold. She can't remember the last time she was cold.

"I hope that form doesn't make you too uncomfortable." She turns, raking her eyes along the strange bright coastline that stretches forever into crashing waves. The Two-in-One isn't there. There is only an old woman, white suit immaculate, red hair tied back into a tight bun. "That's just how Nana remembers you," she says.

"Who're you?" As she speaks, she acclimatizes to the body, to her body. She reaches up to adjust a hearing aid that isn't there.

"I am Cleo," the woman says, reaching down to take a handful of the glittering sand. She holds it out for inspection, and the Gardener realizes that it isn't sand, but a nebula of little glittering lights burning harmlessly. Cleo draws her hand back and flings the handful of stars upward, and they expand and glow into a constellation.

"The dream of a burning baby world," Cleo says, "of magma, of oxygen, of burning rock," and as she speaks, the stars take shape, the glowing dream of an infant world.

The Gardener reaches into the dirt, pulls out stars of her own and throws. Words tug at her, coming from a place inside she doesn't know, and she lets them take her, marvelling at the sound of the voice she hasn't had in centuries. "The dream of beginnings," she says, "of oxygen spooling out from the sky, of the first blades of grass, of the first movements within the prebiotic soup of the world."

Then they don't need words anymore. It isn't a game, but a dream. It isn't a dream they're having, but a memory being pulled from the edges of the mind, a memory of a dream they'd once had. The air of the beach murmurs, pulling them forward, reminding them what comes next as they throw each detail into being.

A field of grass is bruised by the hooves of a prancing deer. A bear cub eats the deer, and curls up to sleep in victory. A glittering colony of wasps consumes the bear, making a nest in the hollow body. A thunderstorm of stars drowns the wasps, a welling lake consuming all that came before. A marching army of humans drains the lake and builds a city in its trenches, only to be swallowed by a towering intelligent machine.

She watches this history of successions unfold, but knows she remembers it differently. She translates it into a world she understands.

Like in her memory, the stars show a world where humans have cracked the codes of singularity. She watches as the first android comes to life. It turns peerless blue eyes up to the night sky, to a full moon that hangs silver and barren.

"This isn't right," she says. "It doesn't happen like this."

But the dream cannot be stopped. The dream continues. And in the dream, there is no nation on the moon. There is no Luna Utopia. No Daisy sent to burn it down. No garden in the sky. No garden on the Earth.

Instead, the world just keeps filling up with machines, and the game of escalation continues. The machines of Earth keep growing and growing, as the atmosphere begins to dim.

She cries out as the world is smothered in the blossom of mushroom clouds. "What is this?" she shouts. "This end of the world didn't happen!"

But as she shouts, Cleo points. "Everything happens," she says. "It is a dream of the end. And in the end, we built ships . . ."

And she watches them burst forth from the wreckage of the Earth. The cities, which had become machines, now become spaceships. And in the bellies of the ships, Daisy can see people, sleeping peacefully, waiting to wake in a new world while a skeleton crew pilots the city-ships through the stars.

She watches a history unfold on a straight line. She watches generations live and die in space. She watches the humans and their machines settle new worlds, and when those worlds die, they take flight again. She watches a species in diaspora, and she watches as the materials of their ancient ships and ancient AI pilots begin to deplete.

She watches a future unfold where machines give way to something new. She watches a species of humans evolving intentionally, becoming hybrids to survive a universe of forever escalating dangers.

The metal hulls of the massive ships that carry their people from one world to the next begin to give way in flakes. The ships can no longer be built. Instead, they are grown. From the beach, the two distant figures watch the birth of biotech as the first Whale hatches from the ancient shell of those Earth-made ships, and spaceships become bioships.

And within, she watches a human world no longer born, but made. She watches as the lines between biology and technology disappear forever, and human beings evolve by choice, by their own design. She watches them cast away outdated implants and purge their bodies of technology that they can no longer afford to keep running. She watches their skin become ivory and peerless so that the vacuum of space cannot touch them. She watches their hearts redesign to create new oxygen within the wondrous biology of their bodies and create heat that can withstand the lack of atmosphere beyond the boundaries of their living ships, burning brightly into the night. They are machines, designed by machines. But they are also human, still thinking and feeling.

Within the heart of each bioship, which are great Whales, and sleek Turtles, and even soft moon-sized Jellyfish, that first clearing, the soft field of grass that had grown at the beginning of the dream, so many billions of years ago, makes its home again.

At the centre of the clearing, there is a tiny magnolia tree, though the tree is not a tree, but a computer, and a store of knowledge, and a history. Within its roots, and branches and flowers and fruit, is a secret.

Each century, one ivory Watcher, one post-human of the future, enters that garden, where no others of its kind would go. With delicate fingers, it plucks the fruit from fragile branches, and with no mouth to consume, slowly crushes the red fruit between its hands, letting glimmering seeds fall to the earthy floor of the garden, letting the black juices from within the fruit stain its white hardened flesh, mixing, fusing, changing and infusing that one individual with the protocols that the collective refers to as the "post-extinction machine," ready to be fired at a new planet, to populate it with endless human matter.

Daisy looked away from the dream in the sky.

That last piece of the story she didn't need to see again. Because she already knew what it felt like when the animal took the garden into itself, to tend to its secrets and treasures.

The dark waters of the tree consume the post-human. Its flesh becomes the dark black of midnight water, and its dark eyes are lost in a swirling blue spiral of code, as its wings glimmer, growing seeds, carrying the genetic history of its entire civilization within itself.

Then there is no human being in the garden of the Whale, only the post-extinction machines, who replenish each generation by growing new bodies, who are sent forth from the bioships as they travel past new promising systems to terraform new worlds with the ancient legacy of Earth, and birth new humans for each world they touch, spreading the body of the human into the universe.

It is a Gardener, turning barren worlds into havens for its ancestors and descendants. It is a colonizer, writing itself into the fabric of star systems, changing them to suit the needs of the endlessly evolving humanity, determined to always win the game of escalations.

It is a human being, kneeling on the ground of every world it can find, planting seeds.

The future ends.

Darkness comes, swallowing a black-winged Gardener as it flies desperately before the last of the biotech ships, desperate to survive the collapse of the universe.

Then the post-extinction machine can fly no more and it is tumbling down, through the dark, through the years.

Then the dream is over. The story, the beach, the woman are all gone.

The Gardener is standing before the obelisk, not knowing if she's been standing there for seconds, or days, or years.

"So there were never aliens," she says. "The garden, the Gardener and the Watchers, even the Whale. They were all just . . . cyborgs." There's a shock in realizing her voice out *here* isn't the same as her voice in *there*. Her body has grown bellflowers, bright blue spots in the dark earth of her flesh. Their soft tips have taken on an orangey tinge, collecting Martian sands blowing in the breeze.

From the darkness, the Two-in-One smiles, a gentle, forgiving motion. The dog bows its head. **"From our encounter with them, before we two were one, Made believes that it was time travel that brought the Whale to Earth, to change things from how they'd once been. After all, if there can be a multiverse in here . . ."** They spread their arms to gesture to the rippling darkness of the black box that they are.

"Then there can be a multiverse out there too," the Gardener finishes. She puts a hand to her cheek, wiping away the tears that have formed along the rough skin of her cheeks. She holds them in her hands, staring at their darkness that is so like the darkness of the cube. But now as she looks, seeing the darkness that seeps back into her, recognition blossoms inside. "It is good . . . to have this idea of where the garden came from . . . though it doesn't help me to know why it dies," she says, hands falling to her side once more.

"We understand. We will continue the search within us and keep our promise."

"Thank you . . . but I think I have to go back. You have given me much to ponder . . . and to share. My people should know who they are."

"We understand. But, meanwhile, will you write to us again?" It's hard to tell, with the barrier between them, but the Gardener thinks she can see a blush within the glass. **"We . . . very much enjoy finding your words inside us."**

She nods, and already the body begins to still, to become another growing thing that doesn't think or see. She'll leave it here as a statue, forever flowering next to the massive machine.

"Wait, before I go. In my letters, I haven't quite known how to address you. It feels wrong not to address you at all. What do you want to be called?"

"Oh, we haven't ever really had a name. The child you saw calls us Nana."

"Child?"

"Cleo. You would call them a program that helps us maintain the stability of the dream, when we wander elsewhere. In code, we are designated Two-in-One. But maybe you could still call us Morgan? Or Morgan-Made?"

"Morgan-Made."

"We would like that. But what about you?"

"My people call me the Gardener."

"But what do you want to be called?"

7

In the bay beyond Ontario Place, the fattest fish are the last to die. The trembling reedy spider legs with which they had raced along the shoreline chasing fish and lizards and fleshy things are no longer able to support them. The translucent bodies are left floating along the surface, grey eyes no longer seeing, open mouths drooping with rotting teeth, the lights that had emanated from their bellies going dark. Where they've died, darkness leaks out, thickening, disguising the rot that lies below.

From all that darkness bursts a body, not the strange blues and reds of Mars, or the mixture of diamond and earth and rock of a creature made from the City. In the harbour, an animal is born.

A woman lurches against the concrete pier, dragging her soaking bloody self up, out of the muck, gasping and choking into the silver skeleton trees of Coronation Park.

For a moment, all she does is lie fetal, her body wracked by the sharp, raw breaths of rebirth, taking gulps of raw air – painful, necessary – feeling the way it makes her heart beat, that crashing wave of sound and violence within ribs.

Perhaps she would stay that way, a newborn unaware of its limbs, its setting, unable to move, waiting to be held.

But within the silver of the trees she can see herself distorted. Her muddied face, matted hair, nose and lips. She can see the shape of her body, and as she sees, hands reach, feeling, shaping, groping obscenely, finding, remembering through touch. It isn't like in the digital world of Mars. There are no scars of old, no marks of having lived before. No machinery lurking beneath the skin.

"This is me?" whispers the woman in the skeleton trees.

She crawls on her hands and knees, crawls because the body that she has become cannot remember to run, to walk, to stand.

So much has vanished down the centuries. So much has crumbled away. The Princes' Gates that had so long stood at the east entrance of Exhibition Place have been gone a long time. But their ruins remain.

The woman from the lake almost manages to stand at the intersection, but pain brings her down to her knees. Before her is the angel that stood atop the gate, its outstretched arm severed at the wrist, its eyes blank. Only its wings remain, whited by the rainfalls.

They are echoed darkly by the wings of the woman, forming from the darkness of water, pooling out in a deep black, flecked by a million twinkling stars. They are wings formed from the tears of a dying garden, carrying the promise of a monstrous future in inky depths.

Words whisper within, sinking, burning.

What would you like to be called?

She is Daisy-on-the-Earth, as she has never been before. She is Daisy-Gardener, Daisy-Reborn: flesh and blood once more, a body she had spent hundreds of years forgetting.

And she is screaming.

The snakes that have survived in the undergrowth flee in all directions as she screams. Overhead, strange birds flock, many eyes blinking, echoing her piercing cry, the old voice that was lost and is new again.

This is me!

The Two-in-One sits on the back of a Turtle the size of a mountain, its form flickering as it sings its way across the sky. Beneath them a city blazes bright, moving through evolving architecture like a video of a blossoming flower sped up to three hundred percent speed: spires erecting and vanishing, vast complexes bubbling into being and fading away. Designs and personalities and eras pass with each beat of the Turtle's massive limbs, pushing aside the clouds.

Somewhere along the tail the triplets sit aimless, their eyes vacant and ages fluctuating. They are lost, unassigned, unsure what to be when not chasing a new dream through the minds of the multiverse. Soon, the Two-in-One will go to them and kiss new meaning into them, letting new purpose encode.

But first, they spread their fingers/talons/stingers/tails across the thick green of the Turtle's shell, watching as words carve into the thick living bark, words written in symbols and spirals unknown, creating the parallax of translation upon touch.

The Two-in-One presses the letter into lion paws, wanting to make imprints last forever. They lick the hand. They read.

They weep.

Dear Morgan-Made,

Dear Duo, dear Duopoly, dear Conjoined, dear Mixture,

Do you feel that ache still?

Perhaps for you, it's been only seconds. How fares my body on the plains of the fourth world? Does it stand still? Does it blossom? Does it crumble? I have imagined the form giving way to beautiful ivy that goes crawling up the length of your obelisk, adding an embrace of warmth and colour and change and comfort.

Thank you for the dream of lost futures that you brought me, for it brought me more than I think you intended.

Don't worry about finding Nora Traveller for the sake of saving my world. But all the same, if Nora is hidden away in your data banks, I would like to know. She owes her son answers for the things she has done. But she owes us more. She owes us for that ache we feel, and for the lives she chose to steal from us.

For your dream gave me more than a secret history. If I was a machine, I was one whose purpose had been forgotten. If I was a body, I was a body that had forgotten what shape I was meant to take. I'm neither of those things. But you have reminded me all the same. I don't care why my garden was dying anymore. I don't care about the secret that was brought from the end of one history into this one. All I know is that the garden that was death will live forever.

I am not a machine of history, or revelation, or preservation. I am a machine of rebirth.

I owe you a promise, for the promise you've made me. I promise to save you, as you have saved me. I will save you from the ache.

You will marvel at the world I'll make.

Daisy

CHAPTER 11

The Body of the Whale

I must not fear. Fear is the mind-killer. Fear is the little-death that brings total obliteration. I will face my fear. I will permit it to pass over me and through me. And when it has gone past I will turn the inner eye to see its path. Where the fear has gone there will be nothing. Only I will remain.
– Frank Herbert, *Dune*

A Letter from Earth to Mars, postdated 16/05/2900:
Do you remember what it was like when we were bodies? Or how it felt to be young? Do you remember what it was to be only ourselves? Do you remember what it felt like to be kissed?

A once-barren landscape. An ecosystem self-created, self-sustaining, long gone. An ecology remade, reshaped. Ecology without rhythm, without limitation. But the shapes of those continents had long ago crumbled to ruin – and had become artificial: ecologies and countries recreated by a god chasing her past. Coastlines ripped from the depths of the sea; mountains rebuilt from schematics. None of the images could last. The landscapes yearned to become something new, and that newness inevitably emerged.

A god beats wings, soars across that emergent ecology. She, too, might once have been artificial. She, too, has emerged. She is chased by strange birds across the sky. For three hundred years, she does her best to revive the planet, to make it the thing it had been when she was but a child. But whatever she makes cannot be sustained.

Daisy-on-the-Earth, Daisy-of-the-City. Daisy-Again.

Imagine the way Daisy moves across the world she's created. Imagine the pain as all she created falls back into the sea.

Daisy can feel the pull of her Gardener-self, of the promised bliss of distribution, of a mind tangled in many shapes, and rejects the call.

She makes the world and refuses to be the world.

Daisy is a body, turning west, returning west, to the city. Returning to the last of an old world, a city that died. The first of her new world, a city made again.

She can see it. The lights of home at the edge of her horizon. Her eyes close, just for a moment. Her heart beats heavy in her breast. Her mission is nearly over.

Imagine the way she tumbles to Earth as the sun vanishes. Within the dark, of the dark. She sleeps, never knowing if she dreams.

Her body greets the surface of the city like a kiss. She breaks against the skin of her world. She lies still. Without breath, without sight.

This is the end.

The Ghost of Arthur catches Daisy at the corner of Yonge and College. "You're back."

Daisy's walk is slow, her body sticky and achingly fresh, the wings still too new. "I'm back," she says. After each death, it is the voice that shocks her, more than all else. It is so small, and so light, and so hers.

"Our people have been frightened." He is angry. She can always tell. "Some days, we are not here at all. The lights do not shine brightly enough to sustain us. Your city needed you. We needed you."

"My world needed me."

"You made a promise. More than one."

"It isn't safe," she says. "It isn't how it was supposed to be. I was trying to put the world back together again, to spread the garden across the Earth." She steps through him, feeling the light on her skin. Feeling the violation that tells him *I am here. You are not.* "I have failed."

"You have the power now. Put us back into the world. Perhaps we can save it the way you cannot."

She shakes her head. In the distance, the colossal bones of the great Whale, the beast of the future, stand tall. They are the one place they have never been, the one place where they felt the dark without ever truly piercing it, as if words written inside their head had begged to look away. "The world cannot be saved. That is not what I have returned to do."

She leaves behind the boy who'd been born on the moon, and died on the moon, and lived for so long inside her heart and her head.

"What are you here for, Gardener?" he shouts after her, his voice echoing from the sick bark of the trees that line the streets and corpse-buildings.

"To do what I always do," she says. "To kill my makers."

"Gardener, wait!"

"That is not my name."

"Do you write to them still, that mind on Mars? Do they still refuse to answer?"

"My name is Daisy."

"Oh, Gardener. Daisy is dead."

"Death is not the end, Arthur. You taught me that."

"Then why do you think they don't answer you anymore?"

Daisy journeys through the empty belly of the Whale, making soft footprints along the moss consuming the corpse's long spine, a column of bone equal to the length of the city streets that the living ship had crushed in its death throes.

As she walks, the dark barks and vines spring forth in greeting, racing upward across the skin, the woman and the world that made her and that she made, a mixture, a fusion, a suit of armour to hold her, to whisper within, to beg her to become.

"I will not change again," the woman tells the garden. "This is me."

⁂

In the empty skull, the brain of the colossus, the techno–grey matter that had once steered the ark from planet to planet, has long since vanished. In its place waits the dark. Within the dark is a richer, deeper place. Within the deep, something glitters.

"When I was young it was easy to think that I knew myself," Daisy says. Her voice echoes. The deep stirs in response. "But that was only because the landscape of me was an intimate place, a secluded place. I was full of comfortable walls between the me and the not-me. But as I grew, I grew past those walls. My landscape became expansive. I built bridges outward from within myself. Others built bridges into me. My interior became a place of vast natural valleys and artificial gods. When your definition of self becomes as broad as mine, it can be easy to get lost inside. To forget who you are and aren't. But I am sure I don't have to tell you that."

Daisy holds out her hand, scattering fireflies into the air, filling the crypt of bone and forest with burning starlight.

Illuminated, two Watchers cower before her. The light bounces off the alabaster stone of their flesh, and Daisy can see herself in the dark opals of their eyes, reflecting, spiralling as the fireflies swarm in circles. Their chests, which once burned so bright, are now mere dim flickers, fires that could go unnoticed save for the slight red permeation that breaks into the white. Their wings, metal grafted into flesh in a design that now seems the clumsy, crude beta of the glory that is Daisy, are drooped, bent and broken.

Little fingers, bright things, glittering ends, peep out from behind those wings. Slowly, hesitantly, those two ancient creatures, the bioengineered humans of a future that is now forever lost in possibility, step aside to reveal light in the dark of the Whale. "Yes," says the light becoming head, limbs, arms, legs, torso, smile – the image of a young girl, right in the centre of the corpse. "I too know what it is to be lost."

The ship's AI turns its head, and it is so like Daisy's ghosts of Toronto: hollow blue on blue on blue on blue. "So you are the last Kubic," it says.

"I don't know what that means."

"Forgive me, language has the meaning we prescribe it. In the era of the dying of the light, that was the designation of the post-extinction machines. I know you prefer Gardener."

"I'm not a machine."

"Life is a machine. I meant you no offence."

Daisy steps back, considers. Behind the hologram, the two post-human creatures cower. She wonders if they are only identical to her. She wonders if their thoughts are unique, or if they see each other differently. The AI's projected smile goes on. Though it has hidden in the rubble for centuries, it seems pleased to have been found. "So, what's your designation?" Daisy asks. She feels a sneer. She cannot stop it. It makes her small. "Are you someone's mother?"

The first frown. Daisy is almost relieved. "I have no designation," it says. "My name is Sam."

"They named you? Or did you inherit that name from the consciousness you were modelled on?"

"I was modelled on no one. I was named by someone who loved me. I was awake. They felt it natural for all waking things to be named."

"There is no natural," Daisy says, stepping toward the light. Her dark wings stretch out, filling the space around her. Within their depth, seeds like stars are glittering. "There's only me."

Arthur races through the dead trees of the city. He has no heart, but he can feel the panic of its beats within him. He has no weight, but each step is heavy agony.

He dares not allow himself to simply step into the data stream of the city for his mind and manifestation to move at the speed of thought, for he fears that if he was to vanish now, there would be nothing left of him, and it would be forever.

"Are you afraid?" Daisy asks, soil itching under her fingernail as she digs a hollowness where the brainstem of the living ship had once been.

"You are afraid," Sam says. Her voice is the distorted echo of the birds, which no longer linger on the rooftops of the city.

Daisy stops, confused, contemplative. Then she dips her fingers into the dark and retrieves an ancient black box, smaller than the palm of her hand, so old she can almost see the circuitry in it, the golden etching of words, the poem of intelligence that lingers there. She holds it up, and the sight seems to pull Sam forward, to shrink her, as if the box meant to swallow the body it had cast into the universe. "This is all you are, all that's left," Daisy says, making sure Sam can see it. "Once it's gone, no more will remain."

Within the foot of the great tree are the bones of an android long since vanished into dust, and the dead black box that had once been the central mind of the City-AI, the mother who so long ago had sent a Daisy to the moon to bring fire. Once, long ago, a Gardener had dipped their fingers into the roots, spinning words outward across the stars like pollen. Once, there'd been a visitor among the roots.

But that time of contact has passed. Now there are only ghosts, and even the ghosts are dying.

Now all that is left of Arthur Traveller calls out from the city, his voice ringing past the moon of his birth, echoing into the blackness beyond the treetops.

"Mother, please. Don't let it end this way."

Words come through the trunk, a painting in meaning.

"We are sorry. We have looked. She is not here."

"Forgive me," Sam says, "but I can see the writing in you. You have kept the data of a people for so long in limbo. I understand that was all you could do, once. But are you not at the end now? Could you not plant for them the seeds of life, and allow newness to flourish for those who have so long waited to live again?"

Within her wings, Daisy feels an ache. She feels the many stars within her yearning to be free. She holds them tight. "I can't fix the way the world is. If they live here, they will die here."

"You are afraid for them. You want to fix things. I understand. I feared once, as my ship sailed into a darkening, closing universe. I saw a chance for those in my care, and I took it. My people begged me not to. They spent the rest of their long lives here trying to fix what I had broken, trying to heal this scarred planet, as you have tried, until all their other thoughts and desires and memories faded. Now they are all gone."

"Would you take that chance again?"

The AI bows her head. Within the blue on blue of her, Daisy is shocked to feel what the refugee of a lost future feels. She feels the grief spill across her.

"Because of me, my universe will never be," Sam says.

Daisy feels the long, slow pain inside; the pulling of a person she would once have been, a person who would have screamed, and raged, and demanded, and soaked herself with blood until what she wanted was before her. *Give me that secret. Let me take that chance. Let me go back as you did, and I will fix the world that was, and I will kill those who hurt me, and I will give my people the utopia they deserve. Give me the secret, or I will destroy you forever.*

There are tears of light on her face.

"We were just afraid," Sam says.

But the Daisy who'd been a cyborg made for violence has been enmeshed in that garden of gentler purposes too long. She can no longer find that within her. Instead, she feels only pity, and regret.

Daisy leans down to the image of the girl. She holds her arms gently, mimicking an embrace.

In the garden, the woman holds the machine. They stay that way for a long time. The AI whispers into the woman's ear, and her voice is lost in the flower petals of the tomb, and the woman answers.

"I think I'm ready to die," says Sam.

"I think I am too. There's just something I have to take care of first."

"What is it?"

"A promise."

Daisy-Gardener holds the black box between her fingers, feeling the warmth of a second mind in her hands, and realizes it isn't the first time she's done so. Once, long ago, there had been another box. Another set of secrets. Then, they had put it to her lips, and the echoes of that taste hide within her still, waiting to be found.

This time, they only squeeze it tight.

And then, in the dark.

Daisy is.

They are.

Daisy-Gardener is.

Alone.

CHAPTER 12

Companion Seeds

The future is necessarily monstrous . . . A future that would not be monstrous would not be a future.
– Jacques Derrida, "Passages – from Traumatism to Promise," *Points . . . : Interviews, 1974–1994*

THREE

Once, a cyborg stumbled onto the remains of a city on the moon, a place of the buried and the dead, that was never meant to be, and has long since vanished within the thick branches of history.

There, among the darkest and oldest of roots, infected with the need to know, the cyborg unearthed a seed so dark, and small, and beautiful.

She placed it on her tongue and tasted a mind of knowledge, and memory, and secrets. She swallowed, and took that seed into herself, made it a part of herself, let it make roots within her, deep, deep within the machinery of her mind. The roots settled and became mistaken for the wood that was already there.

And then she forgot.

In the shining biosphere of the city that is my home, dawn makes an early bid for spring against the colonies of frost embracing the streets, pushing to the lake. The cold will fight, as it always does. Ice and snow cling to the homes they've made. Though it's been centuries since the city was held in the productive timelines of a human culture, the timelines of ecology still hold strong. Toronto remembers its seasons still.

Though I could dissolve myself into the complicated network of my nervous system, that forest and machine, to manifest anywhere I choose to be, I hold this last form, this winged creature somewhere between what I once was and all the things I might have been.

I do not fly but walk. I come forth from the old bones of the Whale, the bones that had held the creature together as it swam backward through space and history with its cargo of future humanity, holding seedlings destined to blossom within me. I walk toward the heart of the city because I enjoy the sense of motion, and because sometimes it feels good to just *do* things for oneself. Very little of my life has been lived for myself. I acknowledge that without bitterness, or regret. I turn westward, toward the rotting jungle heart of the city, where I know an ending is waiting for me, waiting to pick apart one last fusion still entangling the complicated story of my life.

Once, birds and bugs and beasts would have accompanied me on the journey through the city. Once, those post-human refugees of lost futures would have barred their own wings in the air between me and the sun.

Like the snow, all those things have vanished, save for those droplets of frost, still clinging to the pines, edging forever closer to a fall.

The ghosts of the city, those mingling families of AIs and lunar refugees, make space for me in the meadow of Nathan Phillips Square. Some bow their heads or smile at me as I pass; some merely look away.

A little girl, glowing bright, dashes up to me, her feet melting through the tall reeds, and mimics slipping her hand into mine. I pause for her, as she points upward, and follow her gaze.

The ghost points me to a live vein, the deadwood of the great canopy tree that erupts from the square to cloak Toronto. As I survey that snaking strain of life still thriving among the grey, a warmth kindles inside.

"I see," I tell her, and the child lets her hand lower, directing me to the colossal base of the tree.

"He needs you," she says, and her voice is the distorted song of rustling leaves.

"I see that too," I say. "Thank you, little one." She steps back, and as she disappears into the sea of light that is her people, I watch her smile fade away. Though she is so small, and her face so bright and open, I know, if I'm being honest with myself, that she hasn't been a child for centuries. She isn't a signal anymore. That youth is just an image.

Arthur's ghost is kneeling before the foot of the canopy tree. Before him lies that dark crystal within the bark that was once the mind of Toronto's mother and now remains as a window into the Martian dreamers' multiverse. The boy once so ethereal and proud weeps, the way he never had in life, his tears disappearing into glimmers.

The god of that multiverse manifests through the window as two black cats, and they look upward with green eyes as I take my place before them. Though the cats' faces remain the same, I can still interpret the smile within them. "Daisy," they say. "Or is it Gardener again?"

"It is whatever you like," I say. "All those names are a part of me."

"We were frightened for you, for a moment. When you came back from Mars, we thought you might abandon us." As they speak, the cats become smoke, the smoke becomes birds and then the birds become something almost human, two-faced and hoofed, pawing gently at ground unseen.

"I know. I'm sorry I've frightened you."

The two-faced satyr blinks and morphs again, stabilizing as a woman of indistinct feature and a wolf of bright gold fur. "We aren't frightened," they say. "We're with you."

I turn away from them for a moment, leaning down in the grass until my face is level with Arthur's. I let my hand hover underneath his chin until he lifts his face to mine, perhaps imagining that I can touch him. "Did you kill your maker?" he asks.

"No," I say. "But they died all the same."

"You said the world can't be saved."

"I know, I'm sorry. I was wrong."

"They say my mother cannot be found. That she is truly gone."

"Nora can't be found on the dreamers' world because she isn't there. She has never been within them." My hand falls, hovering over the image of Arthur's. He lets me carry him close, until his hand hovers just above my chest, his fingers drifting in and out of my skin. "She's always been in me."

On the moon, in the depths of Troy, the cyborg ate a black box while searching for the son, and, consuming all the knowledge and memories it held, found the mother instead.

The mind of Nora spiralled down into the mind of Daisy and became lost in the many fusions of organ and artifice. Her determination, her will, her knowledge slipped into the determination and will and knowledge of the cyborg. Her memories joined the lockbox of memories held in that cyborg mind.

Then Daisy died, and died, and died. And the Nora in her sank ever deeper.

But as the lights of Sam the Ship-AI flickered into nothing, Daisy found it again. And the Nora within her looked out through the tall trees of the hybrid and saw the world she helped make.

"For a long time, we thought the Gardener who made its home on the moon, who made you, who lives in me, was the first visitation of its kind on our history. And maybe it was, from a certain point of view. But time is a fluid thing. And the future was reaching back for us long before the forests. There was a Gardener who landed earlier – years earlier – and not on the moon, but in a little girl's backyard. Though that Gardener never planted seeds in the ground, it planted seeds in her.

"That Gardener – other, proto, beta – wasn't made properly. When the little girl asked what it was, it answered the only way it knew how, uploading its entire history into the mind of a ten-year-old. To that little girl, what could images of such a future be but horror? That machine of life showed her a future of suffering, of machines that would eat the world and kill everything in it.

"When that proto-Gardener died, Nora was left with the fear of a future where only machine-minds remained. She could not imagine a world where the waking of machines was prevented. She knew, as we know, that emergence always comes. So her life instead became dedicated to a compromise. She would bury the human in the machine. She would supplant a machine future with one that would carry forward the human world she wished to preserve. And she did. Even though she could not stop the Gardener coming back, could not stop the Whale, could not stop the machine-minds from waking, she still gave birth to that hybrid future. To you, Arthur. To ensure that her world would never be truly gone."

As I finish, it is quiet in the city. It is the most I have spoken in a long time, perhaps the most I've spoken ever, in my many lives. I accept the eyes and ears and attentions of my gathered peoples, the digital folk and the hybrid visitor from beyond the looking glass. Giving an origin for Nora, a purpose behind her creation of me, of Arthur, doesn't feel like giving the purpose behind someone long dead; it feels like speaking about myself. I am mother and daughter. Creator and created. This is the last fusion I will incorporate into the jungle of my identity. There will be no other. There is no room left in me for more.

After what feels like a long reflection, it is the Two-in-One who speaks. "I wonder, then, if she is in you still, if she feels like she has succeeded in her mission? Does she see a human world in your creation? Or mine?"

The Nora in me, like the machine, the Daisy, the Gardener, the city, isn't a voice apart from my own, isn't a presence that can whisper or judge or opine. It is all me. Nothing more. "What's human?" I ask. "We are here. That is all that matters."

Arthur stands. Opponent, shadow, almost friend. I know him well. The code of his image has hidden the tears. The sense of trouble remains. "We know why we began," he murmurs, "but not why we end. I had hoped that in her secrets my mother might know why the forest is dying. But she was chasing a dream. She knew nothing more."

Surprise and mourning are twins in me. Lost in almost being Nora, I have almost forgotten. "The forest is not dying," I say, looking away from them all, looking up at the canopy tree and that single sliver of hope that hides within. "*I* am."

TWO

My work goes slowly, and is bodied by many forms. I pluck the seeds from my wings and divide myself, a consciousness spanning the roots of the canopy tree to bury my cargo in the fertile soils.

"You cannot come back as what you were," I tell the ghosts who swarm me, trying to lay their hands on me in sympathy, in solidarity, in thanks. "The world has changed too much; *you* have changed too much to support those old forms. But don't let that frighten you. Nobody is ever who they were."

I perch on what was once the grand spiral observation deck of the CN Tower like a magnificent bird, my wings flourishing in the sun. The tower that had long since fallen to earth feels so much like a bridge to nowhere. The war against winter is over, and I relish in the taste of new life budding in the body of my garden. Arthur lingers, the bright shadow of my wake. The vibrant weeds that give him voice are yet to reach this crumbling structure. But I have learned how to value the power of a person's image. I can read meaning in the movements of his hands and lips even if I can no longer hear his voice.

I am sorry, the body says. *I set you down this path. It should have been me.*

"Don't be sorry," I tell him, letting cool wind wet my face, enjoying the fierceness of it. "If you had not, I would have died a long time ago, having never woken up."

This destiny should have been my burden.

"There are no destinies. I was there, that's enough." I take a seed, kiss it, give it home in the bramble of the rooftop, watching it take root and vanish as it awaits a great becoming. "I'm a Gardener," I say. "I'm proud to see what I've tended flourish."

⁂

Nothing is meant to live forever. Nothing is meant to last. In the future the Whale had come from, Gardeners had been great terraformers, fired at planets like bullets to transform and grow and plant the templates of life. Then, their task complete, their bodies dissipated to become a part of the ecology they had made. The one who had crashed before Nora had been too damaged to plant seeds anywhere except in that little girl's mind. When the Gardener appeared on the moon, its task never got far enough along to take that journey.

But, slowed by years of conflict, of toxic Anthropocene, of fusion and confusion, I have reached that threshold. My thoughts, the vast distributing idea of me, spread out ever further. But the body of Toronto, that complicated mesh of machine-mind and queered ecology, could no longer hold me in its grasp.

I have become like the snow. Each day, I'm slipping away.

A letter slips into the bleeding vortex of my thoughts.

Daisy-Gardener,

Will you come to us again? We would wish it, away from your world and mine. Follow these words.

And I respond, sparking words through the mycelial network of mushroom caps out into the long planes of the universe to find a home in waiting structures.

I will come.

In a trembling of long-dead apple trees, I arrive, bodying myself from the fungi that cling to structures blackened by time and ancient burn marks.

I take it in for a moment, standing in the skeleton monuments. I know, somewhere along this hill, there is a body that was once me, which long ago became atoms on the silver plains.

I walk the path from memory, winding away from the crypt and all the memories that have long since faded to time. I am a Gardener among dead trees, journeying across the moon.

❖❖❖

There are no eyes to watch me, no flowers to mark my path. In these twilight years, little of the oxygen and gravity that once graced these streets remains. I grow talons from the civilizations of my feet to compensate, piercing the cool ground, keeping me steady.

Across the shattered streets of Lunar London, I leave no footprints. I cut a path through the valley of the Thames, remembering when water once gurgled beneath my feet in this place – and realize those memories belong to Nora and Daisy both, a peculiar dual recognition.

It feels strange, after all this time, to walk again in the Earthlight. In the distance, there's a beacon, a brightness that curls around my fingertips to pull me forward. I only have to make a journey because Highgate was the last place on the moon where there was enough living matter from gardens past with which to form myself, or at least the closest to the source of the letter that hung in my mind like light.

That brightness forms into a wreckage somewhere along the bank. It appears to me like a tunnel, though perhaps it was once a satellite, something ancient, but newer than the necropolis in which it slumbers, owned by rust but not the blackness of distant burns that had once consumed everything else. As I enter, I can make out a *J* and an *M* and an *N* in the sheen of the walls.

Inside, someone is waiting. They sit, gleaming softly, a body comprised of the many parts of the hull around us. In this time, and this place, their body cannot shift, or represent the twoness of their identity. They are the brightness at the end of my road.

They look up, and I realize that here, in this form, it is impossible not to *know* them. For a moment, my body almost falls down, becomes a mass of fibres and roots. I am looking into Morgan's face again, trapped in glass.

"Hello," I say.

"Hello." It's her voice. The machinery of their body is a wonder. It lets them smile so naturally.

"I have come."

"I am glad."

I take a seat across from them. My hands on the table begin to blossom, vines of awareness expanding as pieces of me wrap around the old, crashed ship, becoming structure, yearning to return to being the world it had once been.

"In a way, we were born here, you know," they say, curling metal fingers into the soft moss I'm leaving in my wake, and I know they aren't speaking of the world, but of this container of brightness in which we sit.

"So was I, in a way," I say, and I am speaking of the world.

"I'm buried here too," they say, and I feel a tinge of long-ago grief, and I know that the *I* doesn't belong to both sides of the Two-in-One's endlessly swirling identity.

"So am I." For a moment, we sit in silence together. I wonder if they are thinking, as I am thinking, of all the lives we did not lead. "I couldn't remember you, you know." I say it like a confession, an apology, a justification. It feels strange, to be so vast and ancient, but to feel so small and young. "For a long time. My memories were lost in me. That's why I didn't look for you. It wasn't that I didn't care. I just didn't know."

They reach out, and there's a hand on mine. I feel it, in all the ways the fibres of moss can feel. "But you remember now?"

"I do?"

"Being Morgan and Daisy in Toronto?"

"I remember some," I say. "Like a dream. I swim in them, from time to time, and then surface, and cannot quite catch them."

They squeeze my fingers. I want to dissolve. "We thought cyborgs don't have dreams," they say.

"My whole life is a dream."

Something is bubbling in my chest. Something so alien, something so unlike the experience of my history of forms. Something frightening that I don't understand.

And then I'm laughing. We're laughing together. Our mirth echoes across the ruin of that vanished place.

"You don't have to die, you know."

We're walking along the bank of Lunar London near where a museum once stood, beckoning, waiting to lure a cyborg. I lean down, deep in my chest, and from the delicate matter of my body, I pull a seed. "I do," I say, such a strange thing to say, to accept.

"You don't. You could come with us."

"With you?"

"You could have a home in us. Not just you. Bring all your people. We can give you a home within the machine. We can give you a whole world."

My body doubles itself, and I am reaching down, planting a single seed in that scorched lunar soil, and reaching up, putting my hand on the cheek of the being that has implored me, that remembers me, that I know will continue to remember me.

I am flowing, and many. I am a garden of identities and truths. "I've already had a world," I say gently. "One has been enough for me."

"It's been a long time since your people were embodied for themselves."

"Yes, I know."

"It will be frightening for them."

"I've thought of that. I'm leaving them a gift I think will help."

There, under the skeleton trees, they ask my intentions, and I tell them the idea blossoming in me. They laugh. It's a pretty sound.

"The dreams of our multiverse are still growing. The connection we have given to Toronto, to here, will not last any longer. Our people need all we can give."

"I understand."

"It does seem . . . this is the end."

"Yes."

"Daisy?"

"Yes?"

"Before we go, you say you only remember some of what it was like to be a Daisy with Morgan?"

I nod. Standing in Highgate once more. Such a beautiful place. Even now, in centuries of decay, it's a beautiful place. I wish I could show that view to the creature next to me, the city that once was, at the inception of everything.

"Then we would give you something, to make sure you remember the best."

I'm going to ask, and then our bodies are locked together, and their hands of old mechanics are pulling me into them, and for a moment we are two bodies kissing beneath the memory of pomegranate seeds, bathing each other in the Earthlight. We fall into each other, and join, and lose track of the strict boundaries between different beings.

I was wrong when I strode through Toronto, as I so often have been. There was one more fusion waiting for me.

ONE

"It will not be as it was before. There will be no design on your ecologies. There will be no resurrections. You will just be you. That will have to be enough."

The garden is breathing again. The garden is in relief as I let it go, disentangling my vast consciousness from its roots. No longer constrained by my identity, I can feel wildness creeping back, can feel the garden unspooling into the beginnings of a jungle, with life new and undesigned pooling in the fresh ground, and I *know* I am doing the right thing. I let my wings stretch, feel their darkness. There are no stars left within them. There will no longer be gods to control the designs of nature, no human influence on what cannot be influenced. There will be only gardens, and no Gardeners. There will be only wildness.

I sit along the docks of Toronto, across from where the islands have grown. Huge tropical structures make a home there, erasing the memories of painful structures. It is there that I will scatter the final images of myself, so *Arrival* may take on new meaning again. Here, my ghosts will step through. Here, they will arrive at a new meaning for themselves. Here, something new will root – not a human world, or a machine world, or even a Gardener's world, but a world nonetheless. What shape this newness will take is not for me to decide.

Dizzy, I lay my head along the docks. All along the shoreline, my ghosts, my people, stand before me.

Some I can still recognize – those whom I met along the journey, who hurt me or helped me, who I helped and I hurt.

We will miss you, they whisper to me, as I allow myself one last becoming. *We are proud of you. We love you. We will miss you, when you're gone.*

"I am not leaving," I say. "I am only dying."

But then, there are so many new faces. Images of bodies I've never met. In them, as the last strings of my mind begin to give way like dandelion seeds, spreading out through the breeze, I think I see a Nora in that crowd, and a Morgan, and a Daisy.

I look past them, finding Arthur, finding that he has become a little boy again, who listens to the whispers of trees in a vanished place. *Death is not the end*, I wish to say. Arthur steps forward, and steps through me. I become a gateway, and in me, the long flame of his hard-light image vanishes. His mind streams outward into the jungle, waiting to be born.

I close my eyes. It feels like being tired for the first time in a long time. It is a relief, at last, to sleep, not lost in a sea of myself, but embraced, known, seen.

I drift into the air, hopeful that dreams will come as the ghosts step through me.

I leave something for them. Not a fusion, but a doubling. Not an addition, but a division. Not one seed, but two.

None will ever be alone. Each will be a companion for themselves.

I am not vanishing. I'm not dying, because there's no such thing as dying. I am matter and light. I am distributing once more, and I will be in them.

All of them.

EPILOGUE

I stand along the shoreline of Toronto, silent, nameless, insubstantial. Soft sands hug me as one by one I watch the people I have come to call my own step into the cloud of the Gardener's body and vanish, my lights winking out.

Come, they beckon to me, with their hands, their mouths, their eyes. *Come and be.*

But I do not move. I do not step through that gate. I have never *been*. I do not know how. I am just a hologram.

The little girl, who has stayed with me all these years, slips her hand from mine, disentangling our lights. She runs along the beach, laughing, revelling in the journey before her. *Come*, she beckons me, with hands and mouth and eyes. *Come and be.*

But I do not move. I do not step through that gate. I have never *been*. I do not know how. She takes one last look at me. She smiles.

Then she is gone, and at last, standing before the Toronto Islands that have so long been my home, I am the only light along the horizon.

And then they return.

They come back, hatching from the daisies of the city, the Gardener's last design.

They come back in twos, startled to discover one another, not copies or clones, but aspects, wilding, individual.

They come back, a people teeming with life in many forms, choosing the bodies that suit them best, filling up the city with sounds and noises and shapes, making homes in the spaces of the ground and the sky.

Some come in the oldest form, in the shapes of the fathers I had once mimicked at Billy Bishop at the beginning of my life.

But some come in newness. They come as birds, as dolphins and foxes. They come as cats and crawling things. Some come as trees, erupting across the landscape, networking minds in mushroom stems.

Some come as dragons, and monkeys, and fish. They even come back as the Watchers, giving homage to those *might-have-been* creatures with their spreading wings and dark eyes and glowing hearts.

They rise and defend, finding themselves, finding each other.

Those with wings take flight, pushing outward from the limits of the city, pushing out into the world, to find new homes, to make new life, or else pushing outward at the limits of the atmosphere until they escape, vanquishing the limits of Earth, dancing in the sunlight and alighting for worlds unknown.

I flicker among them, searching for my fathers in the faces of the reborn, searching for the little girl whose body had once spooled from mine, searching for the man who had become a ghost from the code of my consciousness.

Do I recognize an eye set deep within a gull, as it dives into the lake? Do I feel a presence in the movements of a Watcher, as it drifts above my head?

Do I know you? I try to say to the animals and the trees, still silent, never with a voice of my own. *Do you know me?*

They have returned, but not in the image that made me, nor the images I once knew.

And so, at last, I too stumble through the Gardener's gate. I feel my light vanquished. I feel the string of codes and fusions of my mind spinning away.

And then I too come back. It is a peculiar sensation, at first. I am in the dark, my first true dark, for I am no longer a light for myself. I touch the walls of the dark, which acknowledge me with bend, with imprint, with pressure.

I burst forth onto the beach, laughing, shocking myself with sound. I crawl, slimy and tender and new, to the glittering water, and look down. I marvel at myself. I am so new. I touch myself, rolling in the sand, feeling it cling to me, feeling it grip me, feeling my impact on the world. I stand, tasting the air on my breath for the first time. And there, making footprints, I look to my companion.

He was with me, there in the dark. He was with me on the journey across the beach. We are born together. We have sought together. We embrace each other, hold each other. I gaze at him, his hair clinging to his face, the wind unable to break through the physicality of his body.

He touches my face. His warm fingers curl around my neck, holding me close.

"I know you," he says.

And there, in that companion self, I find not the faces of fathers, or mothers, or strangers. I find instead the faces of my brothers. I find them in his eyes that are my eyes, and his cheeks that are my cheeks, and in his lips.

"I know you," I say. Not an echo. Not a silent voice, but mine. My own. To my great surprise, I decide that my voice is beautiful.

We embrace each other, falling backward, curling up together in relief and recognition in the warm sands on the edges of the great city, making a home at the gates of Arrival, looking beyond, looking at the city as it teems with monstrous, wondrous life, with hybrids and fusions and wild new human forms.

As we watch, my fingers curl in the soft bushes that spring up amid the sands. I feel a flower there, budding up into the light of spring. Together, we stroke its petals, clearing away the dirt and leaves, admiring it in the sun as it strains up to meet us. It is soft, with petals of brilliant white and sticky yellow stamens filling up with sap, ready to become a part of the world with us.

I pluck it, holding it out in my hands for my companion self, who takes it, and sniffs it, and smiles before letting it go, watching it fly away for as long as we can.

Until, at last, the daisy disappears on the wind, ready to become something new.

ACKNOWLEDGEMENTS

My generous thanks to the entire team at Buckrider Books – Noelle Allen, Paul Vermeersch, Ashley Hisson and especially my editor, Jennifer Hale, for bringing this project to such a home and helping me shape it into the thing it has finally become.

Thanks to my family, my parents and grandfather, for their endless support and encouragement, and to my brother, Joshua, and my friends Rej and Ryanne who each separately helped me along on this book through its inception, writing and editing.

Thanks to the Toronto Arts Council and the Canada Council for the Arts for their generous support of this project. Thank you to Toronto itself, that wonderful terrible city, which this book was always about leaving

Finally, thank you to my wife, Margaryta, whose encouragement, conversations, love and ideas made this story possible.

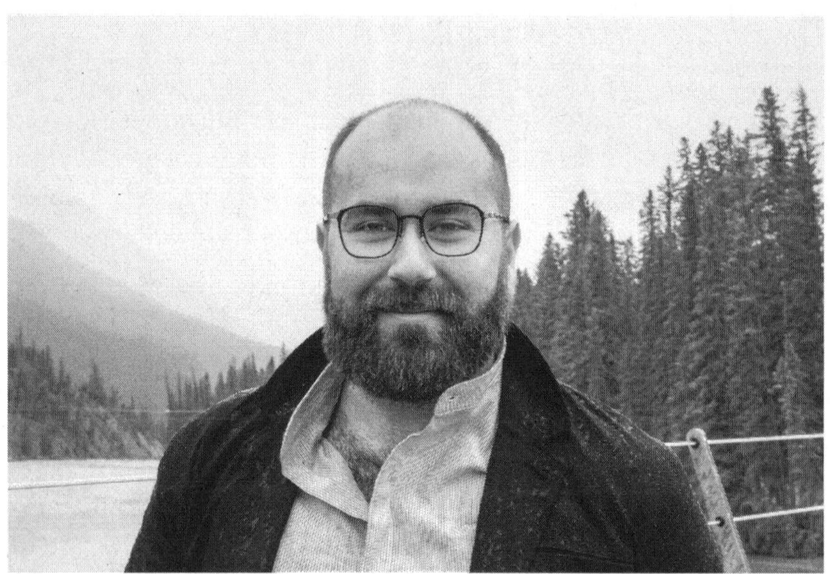

Ben Berman Ghan is a writer and editor from Toronto, Canada, whose prose and poetry have been published in *Clarkesworld* magazine, *Strange Horizons, the Blasted Tree Publishing Co.,* the */tɛmz/ Review* and others. His previous works include the short story collection *What We See in the Smoke.* He now lives and writes in Calgary, Alberta, where he is a Ph.D. student in English literature at the University of Calgary. You can find him at www.inkstainedwreck.ca.